FOR ALL TIME

PART 1

ABOVE

THE

CLOUDS

Janelle Clawson

Fablespinner
Books

U.S.A.

Fablespinner Books

For information visit
Fablespinnerbooks.blogspot.com
or email Fablespinnerbooks@gmail.com

Printed by CreateSpace in the U.S.A.

Acknowledgements

In reaching my goal to publish *Above the Clouds,* the first book in the trilogy, *For All Time,* I have had the help and encouragement of many people. My heartfelt thanks go out to the following: Cherri Williams—my first proofreader and sounding board; the Precision Editing Group for an education in an editor's point of view; and to Jessica Miller and Janis Carter for doing the final proof reading.

I am also deeply grateful to: Patricia Engelbrecht, for her musical talents in helping with the song "Only You"—included in this book; to Natalie Langford and Blake Bischoss for their wonderful singing voices; and to Rick and Laurie Vander Does of *Music to the Maxx* who allowed Natalie and Blake to record "Only You" in their studio.

Lastly, my thanks to Byron Gotberg for putting the song together with the pictures of the one I want to be with—*For All Time.*

I have been blessed by all of you!

The song "Only You", included in this book, was written for Michael—my eternal love.

ABOVE

THE

CLOUDS

Prologue

Utah, July 1924

Ryder Garrison rounded the west end of the weather-beaten barn and came to a gasping halt. He leaned against the barn's side sucking in breaths of white-hot air, waiting for his heart to slow down. *I don't have time for this.* Sweat streamed down his pain-pinched face, and stung his eyes. Impatiently, he brushed the sweat from his brow with his forearm, pushed off the barn wall, and limped to the pump behind the house.

He stripped off his shirt, dropped it in the dry mud puddle under the mouth of the pump, and furiously worked its handle, sending sharp shooting pains along his shoulder blades and down his back. Heat blistering seconds passed before the icy well water burst from the faucet. He dropped to his knees and thrust his throbbing back under the pump. Letting the freezing water run over his head, neck, shoulders, and torso, he pumped hard with one hand and then the other.

Five minutes later, he let go of the pump handle and hauled himself to his feet, shivering under the hot July sun. *I never thought I'd feel grateful to be numb with cold—but it won't last.* Shaking himself off, he banged through the screen door at back of the house, leaving it swinging. Pain shot up his legs as he trudged up the stairs and into his attic bedroom.

The suffocating heat in the top of the house made his head reel, immediately diminishing the numbing cold that held his pain at bay. Disgusted with so short a reprieve from his suffering, he yanked the handles on the middle drawer of the dresser so hard that the whole drawer came out, crashing to the floor. Grabbing a shirt, he pulled it over his wet back, and slammed out the door.

The last thing I need is to be late getting back to the torture of tossing hay bales. Still, his feet lagged as he came to the open door of the barn. Uncle Jared's brand new 1924 Model T touring car sat just inside. Running his hand over the car's hood, he gave the shiny black car an admiring look, then a menacing smile. *What sabotage can I do—without being blamed?*

He glanced into the car, and stiffened, struck by an unexpected realization. The barn was between the lane, and the field his aunt and uncle were sitting in. *They can't see me.* Warily, he took hold of the door handle and hesitated. His heart accelerated, thudding in his ears. He jerked the door open and slid behind the wheel. Pain flared across his back, and ran down his legs as he settled himself in the driver's seat, inhaling the aroma of new leather and fresh hay, mingled with the heat of the day.

Everything his dad taught him about driving a car, poured into his mind. Pulling the handbrake back, he put the transmission into neutral, turned the ignition switch on the coil box to battery and stepped on the starter. The engine purred to life. Adjusting the throttle, he set the spark advance and pushed on the pedal. The car moved slowly forward.

Elation put a grin on his face as he drove down to the end of the lane and came to a stop. Tapping his fingers on the steering wheel, again he hesitated. An agonizing minute of indecision passed before he pulled out onto the road.

He pushed the hand brake forward, lifted his foot from the pedal and opened the throttle. The car shot forward in high speed, down the deserted country road.

"Freedom!" The wind whipping through his wet hair carried his jubilant shout out the window.

He sped past several buildings on the outskirts of Provo, Utah, before the sign on Derk's Soda Fountain leaped out at him. The taste of cold chocolate ice cream beckoned. Pushing the clutch halfway down, he put the car into neutral, pumped the brakes hard, and screeched around the corner, nearly lifting the two outside wheels off the ground.

A young girl with a bouncing platinum ponytail, danced into the road. Her eyes widened as the car barreled around the corner and sped toward her. She froze, dropping a bag that erupted in a rainbow fountain of gumdrops.

A woman, with the same Nordic hair, dropped her purse, and a sack of groceries: eggs, tomatoes, beans, and white butcher paper splattered against the ground. She launched herself into the road, and with a tremendous shove, sent the frozen girl flying through the air, out of the path of the oncoming car.

Before the girl hit the ground, the woman's terrified face swiveled toward Ryder. He stood on the brake with all his strength, his hand desperately fumbling for the emergency one.

The impact threw the woman onto the car's hood. Wide eyed, her face crashed against the windshield. Raindrops of blood splattered it.

The car finally screeched to a stop, throwing the woman off the hood, and slamming Ryder's head into the steering wheel.

Dazed by the blow to his head, he gripped the steering wheel, blinking to clear his vision. From the corner of his eye, he saw the girl struggle to her feet, stumble over to the car, and disappear in front of it. Dizzy, he opened the car door and fell out. Every instinct he possessed urged him to run.

"Mama, Mama." He heard the girl sob.

Against his will, his shaking legs took him to the front of the car.

The girl's scraped hands brushed the woman's disheveled hair back from her face.

Ryder recoiled, his stomach convulsing. The woman's face was smashed and bloody. Her wide hazel eyes were open, staring blankly up at the girl. He fell to his knees opposite the child. *I have to take her away from this awful sight.*

Disbelieving, silver-blue eyes—far too large for the girl's delicate face—locked on to his. Her body shook violently. She whispered in trembling disbelief, "You . . . *killed* her."

He took hold of her hand, intent on taking her away. She snatched it back; then raked it across his face.

He jerked upright, holding his hand over the bloody tracks on his cheek, unable to escape the shock, horror and pain in the girl's magnificent eyes.

"You killed her," the girl's voice increased in strength and volume as her eyes demolished him.

Then she was screaming it.

Breaking away from her condemning eyes, he turned, took a couple of fast retreating steps, doubled over and retched until nothing was left in his stomach.

Several pairs of rough hands grabbed his arms, and dragged him into the soda fountain. The door swung shut behind him, but he could still hear the three terrible words the girl wouldn't stop screaming.

One

Ten years later—

The Incan's black eyes squinted against the glare of the sun. His finger traced the backbone of the southern Peruvian Andes, and came to an abrupt stop along that shark-toothed panorama. "There it is—the demon that guards an ancient evil."

The wind keened the Incan's words like the wail of a banshee into Ryder's Irish ears. An eerie sensation shivered down his spine. He shook it off, pushing back against the squall that threatened to knock him from his precarious vantage point on the peak's precipice. *It's taken a week of hard mountaineering just to get within visual range of my goal, and I intend to savor this moment—not be spooked by it.*

Directing his binoculars along the path of the Incan's finger, he found the mountain shaped like the head of a dragon. Scanning the cliffs of the dragon's towering neck, and reptilian head, he muttered, "It's uncanny." Then moving the binoculars slowly, he examined the twisted horns on the beast's ferocious skull, and the spiked teeth in its gaping jaws.

The hair rose on the back of his neck, *well . . . spooked it is.* The dragon surpassed all his expectations. Not only would the climb be monstrously challenging—he grinned—but there was something decidedly sinister about the beast too. A locomotive of anticipation built up a head of steam that swelled his chest. He blew it out through his lips in a long breath.

"I will take you to the place I camped long ago with my father, but I will not go any farther," the Incan said, flatly.

"How long will it take us to reach the campsite, Pucara?" Ryder asked, lowering his binoculars.

"We should be there by evening."

"How far is it from there to the dragon?"

"I was told as a boy, by my great grandfather, that his grandfather went two days journey toward the dragon—from where we will camp—before fear of its countenance turned him back."

Ryder raised the binoculars again, ignoring the foreboding in Pucara's voice, considering the peaks between himself and his goal. "Is there a trail?"

"No, a trail isn't necessary, the dragon will draw you."

Ryder chuckled. "Will it use black magic to pull me in?"

Pucara's hand gripped his arm.

He lowered the binoculars.

"Hear me, and understand. The old Incans consider the dragon a supernatural guardian. What he guards is a forbidden place, overshadowed by evil."

"That's what Tupac told me." Ryder searched Pucara's black eyes. "Is that what you believe?"

"I only know, no one drawn by him—whose hand has touched his scales—has ever returned."

"Then I'll be the first." He patted the Incan's shoulder. "You don't need to worry about me. I'm a topnotch technical climber."

He'd proven that on the east face of Long's Peak in Colorado, climbing the perilous Stettners Ledge route with a few of his own dangerous deviations, and again in the Black Canyon of the Gunnison. He recounted those adventures during the afternoon's strenuous trek to their campsite, trying to reassure Pucara of his technical prowess.

"I don't doubt your climbing skills"—Pucara huffed out a breath—"and the dragon may even allow you to make your climb, before claiming you as an offering for your trespass."

A rumble of thunder reverberated along the tops of the jagged peaks, and the smell of rain hung with certainty in the air by the time the climbers reached their campsite. Ryder hastily put up their tent in the overhanging shelter of an arching cliff. The first heavy raindrops began falling as they settled into their blankets. Curled up in the cramped confines of the tent, Ryder leaned on his elbow, and listened to Pucara relate the legend of the mountain he now thought of as Dragon's Head.

"The oldest stories date back over four hundred years, to the days of the Spanish Conquistadors. It was said—by my ancestors—when the Spanish began conquering the land, a group of Incan outlaws fled into this remote region of the Andes. Years of robbery and murder had made them immensely rich. They sought an impregnable fortress to protect their treasure and hide from their enemies. The powerful god they worshiped—a creature of the night—led them to the place the dragon guards. He protects them and their treasure, warding off everyone by the fierceness of his countenance."

"I can appreciate that part of the story." Ryder squirmed, trying to find a more comfortable position in the limited space. The tent wasn't big enough for him, let alone another man—even one as compact as Pucara. "The mountain's strange resemblance to a dragon is remarkable. I can see why he strikes fear into the hearts of the superstitious. Thankfully, I am a man of faith, not superstition."

"Do not discount the value of superstition. It saved my third great grandfather, and many others from the dragon's jaws. The old Incans believed the dragon came to life, roaring fire, devouring all who threatened the people and place it protects. Those stories, combined with earthquakes, and the eruption of volcanoes in this region, fed the superstitious, and fear of the mountain grew."

Pucara's ominous tone made Ryder smile, and only added to his enjoyment of the tale. His dominate Irish heritage, mixed with a potent dose of rare—Nahtow—Native American blood, made him susceptible to banshees, fairy stories, and dark tribal folklore. He enjoyed those kinds of tales, but truthfully, old superstitions didn't have the power to frighten or dissuade him. He was a man of faith and confident of his skills, he remained undaunted. Still, he relished the legend the dragon inspired and the ghoulish chill he'd felt when he first saw it.

"Did anyone in your family succumb to the lure of the dragon's treasure?"

"My great grandfather's brother and his friends sought it—never to return. Even the Spanish lost expeditions there. Over time, people avoided the area, and the dragon was forgotten by all—but a few."

"It's certainly an interesting story, and one I've heard parallels to in the Book of Mormon," Ryder said, having told Pucara a great deal about his religion. "It also tells of robbers who fled deep into mountain fortresses to hide from their enemies."

"Indeed."

Again, Ryder adjusted the position of his long legs, regretting the rain made it necessary to sleep in the tent. He recounted a few stories of the Gaddianton robbers and shrugged. "The similarity between your story, and those of the Gaddianton robbers makes my quest to climb Dragon's Head even more intriguing, and who knows, perhaps I will even learn the truth of your story."

Pucara sat up, his normally stoic face, deeply creased. "How can I make you hear me, and see the danger?"

Ryder silently shaded his eyes against the dim glow of Pucara's flashlight. He'd come to trust that stoic face, and the life experience it held. In the short time they'd spent together, their bond of friendship had grown strong. Their love of the mountains made them kindred spirits, but he wasn't willing to give up his quest. Nor did he want to continue arguing the matter—something they'd been doing since the day they met. He couldn't tell Pucara the real reason he needed to climb the dragon, it was just too complicated—too personal.

Shaking his shaggy head, Pucara snapped off the flashlight, plunging the tent into darkness. Ryder was grateful when the older man maintained the silence. He closed his eyes, listening to the gentle rhythmic sound of the rain against the canvas of the tent, and slept.

Pucara laced his fingers behind his graying head, listening to the grumble of distant thunder and the steady sound of Ryder's breathing, unable to sleep. This young American had intrigued him from the moment they met. He could speak Quechua, the language of the Incan's. That in itself was remarkable, but it wouldn't have convinced him to lead Ryder to the dragon. Only the use of Tupac's name—Pucara's uncle, and head of the family—convinced him to take Ryder to his goal. Still, he couldn't grasp Tupac's reasons for telling Ryder about the dragon. The ancient sacred places were never spoken of to outsiders.

He frowned into the darkness. *Tupac, what did you see in Ryder that caused you to break that taboo?* His grimace deepened on a more disturbing question. *Did you knowingly tell him about the dragon, hoping he would seek it?* Tupac's recent death, made these gnawing questions unanswerable.

Pucara had never believed all the old stories surrounding the dragon, but this volcanic region of the Andes was dangerous. It was understandable that people disappeared here. He knew Ryder could easily fall victim to an earthquake while climbing.

What more can I do, or say? He searched his mind for another Incan site to distract Ryder, and sighed. There was nothing close enough. Besides, a month spent tramping through the Andes, showing Ryder the glory of Cuzco, Machu Picchu, and many hidden wonders—forgotten even by his own people—hadn't accomplished what he'd hoped. It hadn't swayed Ryder from his purpose. *There must be a way to persuade him not to challenge the dragon—if only I can find it.*

A minor predawn earthquake woke the pair, and sent them scrabbling from the tent. Yet even that stern warning, accompanied by Pucara final forebodings, proved to be insufficient deterrents. The looming outline of the dragon's twisted horns, visible against a pink cloudy dawn, teased, and enticed the young mountaineer, holding him spellbound.

"You were right, the mountain does have a very powerful draw, and I've needed this mountain for a long time. Don't worry"—Ryder clapped the older man's shoulder—"when I come back, I'll look you up. Then you'll see it's only an old superstition."

"I wish you wouldn't do this, but since I can't convince you, I will shake your hand and pray for your safety." Pucara extended his hand, holding Ryder's remarkable gold eyes.

Ryder's hand engulfed the Incan's as he tried one last time to chase away Pucara's concern. "I've done a lot of solo climbing. I'll be alright, thanks for bringing me this far."

Pucara drew back. "No one will come to look for you—when you don't return. They are too afraid, and I can't wait for you. Already I have been gone too long. I must return to my family. You can find me in Callao—if by some miracle, you do return. I will be there until the end of the year; then return to Cuzco."

With a prickle of disquiet, Ryder watched the Incan until he dropped below a ridge, and was lost from sight. Turning toward the dragon, he consulted his compass, and began the trek to the peak he hoped would bring the answer his soul yearned to find.

A strenuous pace brought him to the base of the dragon's neck on the afternoon of the fifth day. He spent the remaining daylight hours looking for the most challenging route up his formidable opponent. *It has to cost me everything I've got. Only that will do for this quest.* Finally, in the fading red-gold light of early evening, his approach was mapped. Satisfied, he eagerly awaited the coming dawn.

Warming himself by a sparse campfire, his thoughts turned to the Rocky Mountains his dad taught him to love and climb. He again felt the blisters on his fingers and the nausea of altitude sickness. Too often, he'd wanted to quit, but his dad wouldn't let him. "Climbing builds character," his dad always said. "When you summit you know you have accomplished something you thought you couldn't do."

You were right Dad, he mused staring into the flames of his campfire, and for him, there was one more thing scaling mountains accomplished. He'd found that when he combined climbing with pondering and prayer, it helped him solve tough problems, make critical decisions or overcome obstacles in his life. That process had worked every time—except once. He'd scaled too many mountains over the past few years hoping to resolve the one lingering torment from the most terrible day of his life.

He peered hopefully up at the dragon's ferocious head. Somewhere over the years he'd come to think of the persistent torment as a dragon that lurked in his soul. He believed meeting Tupac in the Argentine Andes, and what he told him about the mysterious dragon peak, was a long sought for answer to his prayers. He shook his head over the insistence of the irrational feeling. Still, his heart kept telling him if he could climb this dragon, he would find the answer to slaying the one that had tormented him for ten long years.

"Please, show me the way"—he prayed—"I've paid the price of justice for what I did. I deserved every day of my prison sentence, and more. My repentance was long and hard, just as it should have been. I know thou hast forgiven me—and yet—her eyes won't give me any rest. What do I need to do to free myself from her eyes? They have become a dragon I have to slay if I'm ever going to have complete peace."

The gray light of morning was just caressing the sky when Ryder found his first handhold. He gripped the basalt scales of his adversary with a grim kind of joy tugging at his mouth, and commenced the battle, free climbing up the front of the dragon's pitted throat.

He climbed over three hundred feet before he met a sheer face, and pounded his first piton into the dragon's volcanic hide. He was proud of the custom-made pitons that were one of his first college engineering projects, but he only used them when absolutely necessary. They provided a level of safety that robbed him of the challenge, exhilaration, and danger free climbing held.

As the hours passed, his body worked to conquer the physical dragon while his mind focused on finding a solution to the spiritual and emotional one that tormented him. His Indian style headband and shirt became saturated with the briny sweat of his labor. He breathed out a prayer of gratitude for the chilly wind that continually cooled him as his hands and feet found cracks, cervices, and precarious holds.

By late afternoon, he reached the extensive overhang that was the dragon's jutting jaw. This was the crux of the climb. A rush of adrenaline surged through his veins as his feet swung free thousands of feet above the ground. The angle of the monster's jaw was too severe to allow him to keep continuous contact with his rubber-soled boots, though he did so whenever possible.

Moving with an easy grace, the finely honed muscles of his upper body took the burden of his weight. His hardened fingers played over the face of the rock with the skill of a concert pianist. Unerringly, he found the next crack to jam his fingers into, or jutting ridge to cling to as he moved up the overhang and out toward the bearded chin of the monster.

Releasing one hand, he reached out from under the dragon's jaw and grappled blindly for a hold on its bearded chin. His fingers discovered a deep crevice. He jammed them into it, latched on, crimped his fingers, and released his other hand from beneath the dragon's jaw.

A powerful impression struck him, paralyzing him.

He dangled by one hand, his heart the only part of him that seemed able to function. It thundered in his chest with such force his whole body swayed—its runaway acceleration caused by the impression that took shape in his mind, one he had never been willing to consider.

Please don't ask that of me, he pleaded. *I can't face those eyes again, and what good would it do anyway—after all these years?*

The serrated rock his fingers clung to finally pierced his paralysis. It reminded him of his precarious position. Hanging thousands of feet in the air by his fingertips wasn't the place to continue contemplating such a terrifying course of action. He swung his other arm up, grappled for another handhold on the chin of the beast and secured his position, while the impression grew in his reluctant heart.

Flexing his powerful arms, he lifted his body, inching slowly upward to the top of the dragon's lower lip. He crawled between the teeth of his adversary with an unsteady laugh. *Acting on that impression will undoubtedly put me in the jaws of a dragon.* He shivered with the thought, wiping the sweat from his face with his sleeve.

The serpent's dark mouth proved to be a yawning, shallow cave. He took a few minutes to explore its depths, but didn't linger. Standing on the beasts lower lip, he reached for a hold on one of its upper fangs. Scaling the tooth, he pulled himself over the monster's upper lip, and then slowly worked his way up the front of the dragon's nose.

When he topped out on the dragon's snout, he sat with his feet hanging over the edge. Looking down from his perch at the deck so far below him, he would need his binoculars to make out individual objects; he tried to envision any other solution.

"Please, there must be another way." He gazed heavenward, his face a grim reflection of his inner struggle. Long minutes passed as evening began to color the sky—nothing came. With a sigh, he trudged down the beast's long muzzle, free-climbed up between his eyes, and over his forehead.

In the light of early evening, he pulled himself onto the summit of the dragon's head. His resounding yell of victory echoed through the surrounding peaks. The climb had been everything he'd hoped for, testing all his climbing skills, and challenging his vast strength.

Walking between the dragon's twisted horns, out across the scaly head of his conquest, he raised both fists to the sky, and announced to heaven, "I have slain this dragon."

The words failed to ring true in his heart.

Dropping to his knees, he prayed, and waited. The impression, he wanted to reject, echoed through his mind louder than his victory shout. He knew it was the answer. The dread it generated shook him as no other fear ever had.

He prayed again, hoping for a different impression. "Isn't there another way, one that won't force me to look into her eyes again? They will trigger the memory of that terrible day . . . force me to relive it, when I've worked for years to leave it behind me—let it fade away. After all I've been through to repent and receive thy forgiveness, can't this final burden just be taken from me?"

His plead was of no avail, the answer remained the same. He took a shuddering breath, held it, and slowly released it. Submissively, he bowed his head and lifted his voice to heaven, accepting the path the Lord had shown him. "I don't understand how it can possibly help, but if facing her will—somehow—finally free me from her eyes, and slay my dragon then . . . *I'll do it.*"

He rose to his feet like a beaten man, lifted his head, squared his shoulders, and inadvertently shivered. Inhaling, he filled his lungs with the biting air, drawing it in like needed courage. Deliberately turning his back on what he had to face, he strode over to the eastern side of the peak determined to enjoy the triumph of his climb.

With the toes of his custom made climbing boots on the eastern edge of the dragon's head, he reveled in the majesty of the scene spread out before him, lit by the dying rays of the sun. The dragon was the western peak in a ring of peaks. It stood higher than its neighbors, but they were just as rugged. Each saw-toothed peak was a climber's dream.

He whistled softly, scanning their sheer faces, and craggy edges. It looked like a meat cleaver had sheared off the inside face of each peak. The shattered remains of each peak's severed face formed a common boulder field, ringing vertical cookie cutter cliffs, enclosing a huge oblong bowl.

His eyes caught a glimmer of water. Grabbing his binoculars from his knapsack, he focused on a sapphire lake, resting in the middle of a jungle like forest. Moving the binoculars south around the western edge of the lake, he tracked a river, intermittently, through the dense tangle of trees and out onto a grassy plain.

An astonished shout exploded from his lips. Pulling the binoculars from his eyes, he looked over the top of them, then immediately raised them again.

The lower part of the south and southeastern cliff faces were covered in stone buildings. They seemed to be built either into the cliff or up against it. Far above the buildings, falling down into a churning pool that became the river, a powerful waterfall burst out of the vertical face of the cliff. Its cascading splendor captured him for several minutes in a hypnotic rhythm.

Tearing the binoculars away from the waterfall, he examined the buildings. Two massive, dominating structures sat on either side of the falls. They were flanked by dense clusters of lesser buildings spreading from the cliff face out across the valley floor. A stone wall enclosed most of the buildings, but a few stood outside the walls.

The scene felt mythical, shrouded in the obscurity of evening shadows. His heart throbbed through his fingers as they held the binoculars. *Is that the outlaw's fortress? If it is—what a story I'll have to tell Pucara.*

Tramping over the rocky head of his conquest, he worked his way in the dwindling light toward the southern end of the dragon's head, hoping to get a better look at the waterfall and the buildings before darkness obscured the valley. His progress was abruptly cut off by a plunging crevasse that ran almost the full width of the peak from east to west.

The crevasse was completely submerged in evening shadows. He dropped to his belly examining the interior of it through his binoculars, hoping those mechanical eyes could cut through the dense shadows. Fifty feet below him, he spotted what appeared to be rough stairs running down into the deepening gloom of the chasm.

His pulse quickened.

Uncoiling his rope, he secured it to a boulder, tested its hold, wrapped it once around his leg, and hand over hand lowered himself into the abyss. Landing on the first step, he stooped to examine the stairs' irregular shapes and sharp edges. They dropped in a steep, erratic pattern, curved, and disappeared into the murky blackness of the chasm, making it impossible to tell how far down they ran. He switched on his flashlight, directed the insufficient beam down the steps—and grinned.

Two

The pilot checked the fuel gauge of the Douglas O-38P, and groaned. *I've got to head back.* Finished with weeks of cargo runs between Lima and the sight of a new Incan dig, the pilot reflected, *having a few days off—and bright clear days too—has been terrific.* After flying the larger cargo planes, this little bird was a welcome change. *It's light, fast, and easy to maneuver.* The chance to fly over some of the most spectacular parts of the Andes Mountains, view Machu Picchu, and spend the first night exploring Cuzco had fulfilled a long-standing ambition.

Skimming the surface of Puno Bay on Lake Titicaca, the pilot marveled at the floating islands and villages, regretting the plane's floats had been replaced with tires. People came out of their totora reed homes to wave as the plane flew by. The scene touched the pilot like a living relic. Even the night in La Paz felt like stepping into the distant past. Wandering its streets, listening to the native music, eating exotic food, brought a longed for understanding into the pilot's heart. *David Willard, you are one terrific boss to have arranged this birthday gift for me.*

After dipping the plane's wings to the waving natives, the pilot executed a slow turn to the west, heading for a refueling stop in Arequipa, Peru; brought the plane up off the lake and into a steep climb, ready to glide over the tops of the towering peaks.

At least I'll get to see the Nasca Lines before my trip ends. The pilot had heard a great deal about them since coming to

Peru. They were said to be spectacular, and a mystery. So large they could only be seen from the air, or mountains. How they had been drawn was a hot topic of debate, along with their significance. *They are definitely a sight worth seeing.*

Turning the long flight into a challenge, the pilot played a game of dip and climb, skimming over the tops of the towering mountains then dipping down into the long depressions that ran between the ranges of the Andes.

Pulling up hard out of a deep valley, the pilot sent the plane climbing sharply skyward, clearing the top of a saw-toothed peak by less than fifty feet. Intent on the maneuver and transfixed by the monstrous shape of the mountain that loomed dead ahead, the pilot was taken off guard by two enormous black birds that shot up from somewhere below.

Before there was time to react, the birds flew straight into the plane's propeller, as though attacking it. Feathers flew everywhere, blocking out the sky. Blood sprayed the clear canopy that enclosed the pilot. Dismembered body parts hurdled through the wing struts and cables, crashing into the canopy with the force of a baseball bat—cracking it. The impact shook the little plane, reverberating in shockwaves of panic that stormed the pilot.

The mangled bodies of the birds fell away from the plane. The propeller sputtered, faltered, and stopped turning. The ensuing silence gripped the pilot in stunned disbelief. Squinting through the red streaked canopy at the splintered remnants of the propeller, the pilot's stomach twisted.

Hours of training rushed to the pilot's rescue, taking command of every thought, dictating every action, as the forward motion of the plane moved it beyond the top of the peak. It careened downward toward a massive boulder field ringing a deep emerald valley. Blessing the boss for insisting on the parachute, the pilot checked the buckles, and the ripcord, hauled back the plane's canopy with a mighty tug, and bailed out.

His Royal Majesty, King Ateron—sovereign over the sacred valley of Injanae spent the morning hunting. Each man in the royal hunting party rode a llama, bred for size, and strength, and trained for riding. Everyone, but the king, was armed with sword, bow, and spear. Despite the king's somber mood, and minimal participation, the morning's hunt for the wily pigs that inhabited the forest of Lanka had been successful.

After bagging two impressive specimens, King Ateron halted the hunt, and the party rode out of the densely shadowed forest into the sunlight on the eastern road that surrounded Lake Quset. They turned north toward the royal hunting lodge. As they rode, Ateron's brooding mood increased, infecting the hunting party. Conversation died away, replaced by a menagerie of forest voices.

The party's dismal silence was suddenly shattered by an angry crack of thunder. It rumbled through the valley, drowning out the subtle sounds of the forest, reverberating in concussion after concussion for nearly a full minute. The hunting party struggled to calm their startled mounts that danced nervously and tried to bolt. With puzzled expressions, they searched the pristine sky.

"There." Chancellor Cartu pointed to the eastern cliffs.

A thick dust cloud billowed over the edge of the cliff and fell toward the valley floor. Just beyond it, a small white cloud born on by a gusty breeze, drifted over the forest in a northwesterly direction, growing larger as it descended.

"Do you see that?" The chancellor waved his hand at the indistinguishable shape floating below the cloud.

The king shaded his eyes against the sunlight. "Yes."

Gidlo, one of the king's fiercely loyal bodyguards, said, "At the rate it is moving, I believe it will pass over the forest, and fall to ground somewhere near the western cliff face." As the king's best hunter and tracker, no one disputed his assertion.

The hunting party slapped the sides of their llamas with their heels, and followed the mysterious cloud's descent. They lost sight of it as they raced north along the edge of the forest. Moving with the single mindedness of a flock of birds, they angled into the thick trees on a primitive road. It took them to a stone bridge that spanned the river on the north side of Lake Quset. Their mounts clattered over the bridge single file, and they rode hard for a few more miles before the trees thinned out, giving way to the barren field of rock that blanketed the base of the western cliffs.

They scoured the field of boulders, finally spotting the white cloud spread out over the rocks, its edges flapping in the breeze. The king's troop approached within twenty feet of the cloud, dismounted, and studied it with weapons drawn, before cautiously approaching it.

Gidlo put out his hand and hesitantly touched the cloud. His wary look faded. "It is nothing more than some kind of cloth."

"But I have never seen such cloth." Ateron, stepped forward, and touched the material that was light and soft, very densely woven, and amazingly strong. "Where did it come from, and what gives it the power to fly through the sky?"

Cartu fingered the strange fabric too. "Who can say, but it does possess some power we have never seen."

"Power that may be useful to me," Ateron said, and barked out orders. "Toba, Norr, gather the cloth up, and cover it with your cloaks. No one must see it."

Dutifully, Toba and Norr, two more of the king's hulking bodyguards, came forward. They took hold of opposite sides of the cloth, and began walking back together.

The king's outcry brought them to a halt.

Everyone stared at the unconscious pilot sprawled beneath the cloth in a tangle of ropes, attached to the strange fabric.

Cartu was the first to recover his wits. Rushing forward, he dropped to his knees, and felt for signs of life. "There is breath, and a heartbeat!"

His pronouncement brought the king out of his shock. He turned to Sual—his favorite among his twenty bodyguards, and the one he trusted implicitly. "Who is at the lodge?"

"Only the usual contingency of six servants, Sire."

"Go to the lodge, send them back to the city as quickly as possible. When they are gone, meet us on the road west of the bridge."

Sual saluted the king, vaulted onto his llama, and kicked it hard with his heels.

"Gidlo, go spread my rug out on the ground." Ateron turned, and gestured at the body of the pilot. "Norr, Toba."

Norr and Toba drew their swords, and cut the cords between the pilot and the cloth. They carried the pilot to the rug Gidlo had spread out and ready.

"Roll up the rug," Ateron said; then addressed Gidlo, "Go back to the palace. Bring Taya as quickly as you can. Speak of this to no one, not even Taya."

Gidlo bowed his acknowledgment, jumped on his mount, and flicked the reins, urging the animal toward the south, along the lake's western road.

The king issued instruction to his remaining guards as he and Cartu mounted their llamas. "Roll up the cloth, and keep it out of sight. Follow us as soon as you have searched the area, and everything of value is secured. Now, hand the rug up."

Toba and Norr lifted the rug, settling it securely across the saddle in front of the king. Slowly turning his llama, Ateron allowed the animal to pick its way over the rocky ground, following Cartu into the trees.

Three

Taya shifted uncomfortably on the blanketed back of the old llama she rode, her mind a cauldron of disquiet. As the queen's personal physician, she never treated anyone but her majesty, the king's two young sons, the ladies of the queen's household, or those the queen personally requested she treat. Her mouth drew taut. It was more than a little strange that she should be commanded by Gidlo, in the name of the king, to go to the king's lodge to treat an unknown patient, with unknown injuries, and be forbidden to speak of it. Even stranger, was Gidlo's stubborn refusal to answer any of her questions about the person needing her attention.

She began to wonder as they approached the Royal Hunting Lodge, in the far north region of the valley, if she was really being brought to tend a patient, or if it was just a pretext to get her there. *Does this have something to do with what Ateron told me this morning?* Her throat constricted, and her heart twisted, beating erratically.

Climbing the steep stairway to one of the lodge's spacious bedchambers, Taya fingered the slim blade concealed in the pocket of her tunic, and found comfort. She knew what she would do if Ateron's reason for bringing her to the lodge was only a deception.

Ushered into the room, her black satin eyes filled with relief and wonder. Quickly, she walked to the side of the bed, hesitated for a moment, and then laid a trembling hand gently on the forehead of the unconscious pilot.

The king and Cartu left the pilot in Doctor Taya's very proficient hands, parting at the bottom of the stairs. Cartu went to oversee the final arrangements for his sovereign's dinner. Ateron retired to the lodge's secluded courtyard with a goblet of his best wine.

The arrival of another person from beyond the boundaries of the sacred valley of Injanae, and in such a startling way, preyed on Ateron's mind. Absently he sat down on a stone bench, frowning into his wine. *The coming of outsiders into the valley hasn't happened in many generations, but now, two have come in . . . how many cycles of moon has it been?*

Ateron sipped his wine, going back over the time since the arrival of the one called Ryder. *He has been here for . . . about twelve moons.* He frowned. *No, it has been longer than that.* He started counting the number of the moons and seasons since Ryder's arrival, but his calculations were interrupted by a singularly disquieting question that intruded into his mind. *In light of the new outsider's arrival—was Ryder's coming Ansuetra's doing after all?*

When Ryder had mysteriously appeared, the majority of the people believed that to be true, but subsequent events seemed to crush that idea. *If the coming of these outsiders is Ansuetra's doing . . . to what purpose?* He puzzled over the newest outsider's arrival and the strange cloth that had the ability to carry a person through the air like a bird, deeply disturbed.

A sudden flight of boisterous birds into the night sky brought his eyes up. He followed their ascent toward the moon. Glaring at that faintly visible orb, his thoughts again shifted. He raised a defiant fist, feeling no loyalty for Ansuetra, Goddess of the Moon. She hadn't favored him when Darvoe was chosen to assume the high priest's scepter on Lontae's death.

If I don't find a way to check him . . . , he rose from the bench, facing into a stiff breeze. The wind blew his multiple black braids out behind him. Their gold clasped ends tinkled against each other as he paced out his agitation along the stone pathway that wound through the courtyard's maze of shrubs, flowers, and trees.

Hard-soled boots clattered against the walkway at his back. He turned.

"Everything is ready, Sire." Cartu inclined his head as he habitually did. What the gesture lacked in genuine reverence, Cartu made up for in staunch loyalty to his sovereign.

Ateron morosely held out his half-empty goblet and shivered. "If something isn't done soon, I may find myself being dictated to by Darvoe."

Cartu took the goblet from his hand, and helped him pull a red, vicuna cloak over his shoulders. "I am sure we can find a solution to the problem of Darvoe . . . but that can wait. Right now what you need is dinner." The chancellor swept his arm toward the door in a subservient manner, making Ateron smirk.

The king's party dined on fresh meat from the hunt along with cheese, bread, and dried fruit from the kitchen's larder, complemented by wine from the lodge's well-stocked cellar. Ateron picked at his dinner with little interest and less appetite. He waited indulgently while his men ate their fill before he pushed back his chair.

Accompanied by his chancellor, and two most loyal bodyguards, the king retired to his private parlor.

Sual and Gidlo drew up deeply cushioned chairs near the blazing warmth of a hearth fire.

Cartu opened another bottle of wine.

Secure in the knowledge Norr and Toba were standing watch; the king took up the subject that had brought him out of the luxury of his palace and into the seclusion of his hunting lodge. Here he could think and plan away from the multitude of inquisitive ears that resided in the palace.

He fixed Cartu with a sour expression. "I hoped the unrest among the nobles would die away, but the most recent quaking of the earth has allowed Darvoe to keep them inflamed with his lies. His influence has grown very strong," he said, annoyed at his lack of insight. Darvoe had seemed so spineless, so pliable, so willing to please. But behind that narrow, pitted, hawk-nosed face, there was subtlety and ambition Ateron hadn't foreseen.

Firelight gleamed in Cartu's narrowed eyes. "Yes, who could have predicted his power to manipulate the nobles?"

"Every day more of them are convinced reinstating the religious rituals the high priest espouses is the only way to appease Ansuetra, and stop the shaking of the earth," Ateron said, furious to find himself once again engaged in the age-old power struggle that always raged between the kings and high priests of Injanae.

Reluctantly, Gidlo reported, "From the rumors I have heard, Sire, I fear Darvoe's influence is growing even among the common people."

"That too is having an effect on the nobles' council," said Ateron, grimly.

Cartu leaned forward. "I didn't have time to tell you this morning, but I received word just before we left, that the council voted on Darvoe's petition to restore to him the full authority of his office. Fortunately, he did not win the vote." He held up his cup in a congratulatory salute to the king, and drank deeply.

Ateron put his untouched goblet aside. "Yes, but it is only a matter of time before the infection he is spreading among the council members with the ancient superstitions succeeds in undermining all I have accomplished."

"The trembling of the ground has grown more frequent," Cartu admitted.

"And Darvoe is successfully putting it about that it started when I persuaded that senile old fool, Lontae, to change the priest's absurd rituals, and let the nobles' council assume his powers. Darvoe is making impressive progress in convincing the nobles that I am in disfavor with Ansuetra for that, and the trembling of the earth is a sign from her that the full power of his office must be returned."

Cartu scoffed. "I believe the majority of people have no desire to return to the dark era of priestly dictates."

"Of course they don't, but Darvoe is not interested in the *people's* desires." Ateron impatiently brushed away a large moth that fluttered in front of his face. "All my work to free the people from the oppression of the priests means less and less as the quakes grow more frequent. Once Darvoe persuades a majority of the nobles it is vital to restore his power as the only one authorized to intervene with Ansuetra, and ease her wrath, the power Lontae gave up will be restored to Darvoe. And I will be forced to accept his dictates."

"Then we must keep him from winning that majority," said Cartu, his voice laced with menace.

Ateron slouched in his chair and scowled. "And just how do we accomplish that?"

Cartu caught the pesky moth with his lighting fast reflexes as it fluttered passed him. "The simplest way would be to dispose of Darvoe." He crushed the moth between his fingers, and flicked it into the fire.

Ateron could almost see the scenarios for Darvoe's demise running through his chancellor's head. Violence was always Cartu's solution to his sovereign's dilemmas. It was quick, direct, and satisfying. That quality was often evident in his face—a countenance more reflective of his character than his ancestry.

"Don't you think I have considered that? But Darvoe is too well guarded by his priests. They are as loyal to him as my guards are to me. Even your cunning couldn't breech the defenses of the temple where he hides. He is the priests' hope to return to power, and they guard him carefully."

"Perhaps, Sire, you should consult my father." Sual rose from his chair, and added more wood to the fire.

As the highly educated son of the chief historian of Injanae, he was well versed in the royal lines of ascension for both the kings, and the high priests. However, instead of following in his father's footsteps, he was enticed by the glory of contests of arms into becoming one of the king's bodyguards. The lavish life he led in the palace, and his favor with the king, had long secured his loyalty.

"Why?" asked the king in a disheartened tone.

Sual's speculated, "Maybe there is something in Darvoe's past, or lineage, you could use to discredit him."

Cartu's heavy brows met, distorting his face into that of a gargoyle. "Could we prove Darvoe is unworthy to hold the office of the high priest?"

Ateron picked up his golden goblet from the table beside his chair, and rolled it between his hands, mulling over the idea. "Possibly . . . and since it is not always the eldest member of the royal priestly line that holds the scepter, I could, perhaps, influence the election of the next high priest." He took a sip of wine, considering the idea's potential.

"If I remember correctly"—Sual sat back down, and reached for his own cup—"the first king to sit on the throne of Telquset, King Sinchi, held both the crown and the scepter of the high priest."

"If that is true, why doesn't his majesty still hold the scepter of the high priest?" Gidlo asked Sual.

"Ansuetra blessed King Sinchi with twin sons. He believed it was a sign that the powers he held should be divided. The elder twin would inherit the crown, and the younger, the high priest's scepter. Upon his death, King Sinchi's sons assumed his powers. Their struggle for dominance almost destroyed Injanae."

"And that ultimately led to the forming of the nobles' council," said Ateron, scowling.

Sual cringed, as though the forming of the council was his fault, and added, "If so many lives had not been lost in the struggle for power between the kings and high priests, the people would not have rebelled and demanded the nobles' council be established to arbitrate between them in major disputes."

Ateron downed his wine and growled, "Yes, but their right to dictate to me in any major dispute I have with Darvoe is beyond bearing."

"At least Darvoe is under the same constraint," Sual said, apologetically.

"And the council can't interfere in any but the most extreme disputes," Gidlo added.

The king snorted. "Like the dispute we are currently engaged in, you mean."

Cartu reached for the wine bottle, and refilled Ateron's glass. "It is humiliating for his majesty to be forced into courting the councils' favor when it is his right to rule Injanae."

Ateron stared into the fire as though the answers to his problems might be found there. "If only I could eliminate the nobles' council. I would crush Darvoe, and take back the power of the high priest."

"If only," Cartu echoed, setting the wine bottle aside.

Ateron jerked upright up in his chair, on a sharp intake of breath, sloshing the wine over the rim of his goblet. It splashed unnoticed down the front of his green robe.

"What is it?" asked Cartu.

A rare, unguarded expression grew on Ateron's face, revealing the subtle cunning of a politician with the ferocious feeding habits of a piranha. He habitually masked that persona non grata behind his striking features, the charisma of a revivalist preacher, and the charm of a snake oil salesman.

The politician raised his eyes to the ceiling as though he could see through it, and into the chamber above him where the injured pilot lay. "I believe Ansuetra has sent this outsider to me."

Cartu stared at the king in stark astonishment. "The arrival of our first outsider only served to deepen your conflict with Darvoe."

"Yes, that is true, and I only let him live to spite Darvoe." The king's eyes narrowed. "But now, with the coming of this new outsider, Ansuetra has shown me the reason I spared Ryder's life. He and the new outsider are going to help me resolve my problems with the high priest."

The king's bodyguards lean in expectantly.

Cartu frowned, and set aside his wine.

The piranha smiled—tasting the first drops of blood.

Four

Full darkness veiled the valley before Ateron sent for Pel, the brawny captain of his elite personal bodyguards. Pel entered the garden on the roof of the palace and saluted the king—awaiting his final orders.

The dancing torch light played across Ateron's face as he tonelessly issued his directive. "I have decided you will remain in Telquset. Sual, Gidlo, and Po can handle my business at the quarry. Instead, I want you to deliver a message to Darvoe, and one to the nobles' council."

Pel's brows contracted with this sudden change in his orders. Respectfully he said, "Sire, your business at the quarry could prove to be volatile. Wouldn't it be better if I were there?"

"No," Ateron said curtly.

Pel took the king's rebuke with a dip of his head, pressed his lips together, took the message scrolls the king wanted him to deliver, and left his sovereign with a crisp bow.

Irritation narrowed Ateron's almond eyes, watching his stalwart captain retreat through the door of the rooftop garden. *You have questioned my directives too many times in the past few weeks, Pel. No doubt, Lowanta is breathing his sedition into your ears. If you continue to listen to your father, a change in the guard's leadership will become necessary. I will not tolerate even a shadow of doubt or disloyalty. I must be able to trust you completely—especially now.*

Ateron pressed his lips together, and put the problem aside. *It can wait. Not long perhaps, but it can wait. Right now, I must move forward with my plans. Bringing them to fruition will take all my ingenuity.* He smiled broadly, with absolute confidence in his ingenuity and cunning.

After less than an hour's sleep, Ryder was roughly prodded back into consciousness. Rolling over, his eyes focused on three of the king's burliest bodyguards.

"You are to come with us," Sual, the biggest of three, said.

Ryder squinted up at the guards against the glaring light of a torch. "At this hour?"

"Get up. We are taking you to the king."

"What could the king possibly want with me at this hour?"

"You will know when we arrive in Telquset. Now move."

Ryder sat up in the pile of straw that was his bed, brushing it from him. "Is there time for a bath? I wouldn't want to offend His Majesty," he said, lips twitching.

Po, one of the king's less intelligent bodyguards, scowled as if considering the idea.

Sual prodded Ryder's shoulder with his foot. "You are trying my patience, slave."

Ryder shrugged, brushed more hay from his long dirty hair, tied it back with a leather cord, and reached for his short leather boots. He pulled them on, settled the heavy shackles on his ankles over the tops and stood, towering over the guards who instinctively took a step back.

Drawing his sword, Sual touched it to Ryder's chest, telling Gidlo to put the manacles he held onto Ryder's wrists.

Blank faced, Ryder extended his arms.

Gidlo clamped on the manacles, while Po bent down, and removed the shackles from Ryder's ankles, which were attached to an enormous block of stone.

With one sword wielding guard in front of him, and the others in back, Ryder strode out of his thatched hut. His armed escort wound through the maze of crude adobe dwellings that made up the living quarters for the stone quarry slaves to the eastern road encircling Lake Quset.

Under a waxing moon, the guards loaded Ryder into a llama driven cart. Po clamped a pair of shackles, anchored into the bed of the cart, around Ryder's ankles, and then secured the chain between his manacled hands to a lock on the cart's side. Po tugged on the chains to be sure they were secured, mounted the cart's box and took the reins, while the others mounted their llamas. With one guard riding in front of the cart, and the other behind, they began the ten-mile journey to Telquset.

The moon was well passed its zenith when Sual called out a word to the night watch on the city wall. The gates of Telquset opened, allowing them entrance. They moved briskly through the silent streets in the direction of the palace, looming like a skyscraper in comparison to the surrounding buildings. It stood five stories high and covered a quarter of a mile. Built up against, and into the sheer face of the valley wall, it was easy to see its evolution in the changing architecture of its different levels.

Ryder was familiar with limited areas of the palace—in the capacity of a repairman and a structural engineer. He was particularly proud of the manual elevator and dumb waiter he'd built and installed in the royal apartments, along with the rooftop garden he'd designed and constructed.

Something must be wrong with the elevator, or dumb waiter, and that's why I'm being hauled out in the dead of night, Ryder decided, knowing Ateron was never kept waiting when he wanted something.

The cart creaked to a stop. The guards hustled him into the palace through an obscure side door, up a flight of stairs, down a railed hallway, and into a short passageway that stopped at a set of gilded double doors. Sual went over the protocol for being in the king's presence before they were admitted into the royal judgment chamber.

It was a room Ryder remembered too well. The last time he entered it, he'd been condemned to slavery.

He lowered his eyes as they approached the six-step dais where the king sat. Dropping to his knees, he put his forehead to the stone floor. He heard the king rise and walk back and forth above him, though he didn't speak. The silence lasted so long, Ryder wondered if he was being given the silent treatment just to rattle him.

Finally the king spoke. "You may lift your head."

Ryder met the king's scrutiny with a blank expression; conscious of his long matted hair and beard, the rags his clothes had become, and the accumulated dirt of weeks without a bath.

Abruptly the king demanded, "Have you remembered how you came into Injanae."

The chains on Ryder's manacles clattered as he rubbed the small scar at the hairline of his left temple. He hesitated. A feeling, or was it a sound, had been nagging at him, but he couldn't seem to bring it into focus. "No."

"If you remember anything, you are to tell me at once. Is that clear?"

"Yes." Ryder shifted uneasily.

The king's lips curved up. "I am pleased with all the work Daelo has sent you to do for me here in the palace. I know it is your inspiration, and creative talents that have added to the comfort and beauty of my home, not that of your owner. Although he is quick to take the credit—as any master would—for the accomplishments of a slave."

Ryder maintained his vacant appearance with an effort. His experiences as a slave made him consider the practice one of humanities greatest crimes. The urge to speak his mind kept his teeth clenched.

"As I have a continuing need for your talents, I have purchased you from Daelo."

Ryder's brows shot up, robbing him of his self-imposed indifference.

"You will find I am fair and generous with my slaves, allowing them a greater degree of freedom than most masters in return for their obedience and loyalty. However, the penalties for any form of disloyalty or breach of my trust can be very severe. Do you understand?"

His cold stare held a threat Ryder immediately felt in the pit of his stomach. "Yes," he said, bowing his head.

"Good. Gidlo, take this slave to Oswan." Ateron waved his hand under his nose. "It seems Daelo never allows the quarry slaves to bathe."

The guards behind Ryder rumbled with laughter.

The king smiled thinly. "Oswan is the bath steward. When you are presentable, he will turn you over to Huld, the slave steward. Huld will instruct you on how to proceed," he said with a dismissive wave of his hand.

Ryder got to his feet. Gidlo unlocked his manacles. No feeling of elation accompanied their removal, instead he had the impression he had just become the devil's minion.

Five

Sunbeams streaked through the open doors of the terrace in Ateron's private judgment chamber, flashing off the gold crown he wore. "I understand you have been instructed in everything you need to know as one of my slaves."

"I have." Ryder dipped his head, again kneeling at the base of the king's dais, truly grateful for the change in his circumstances, and particularly his hygiene.

His long matted hair had been cut to shoulder length, washed, brushed, and was now held back by a braided leather headband. He was clean-shaven, and dressed in the coarsely woven, buff colored pants and matching mid-thigh tunic, worn by all palace slaves. A thick leather belt, rode just above his hips, and llama hide boots encased his feet.

The only thing that bothered him was the heavy gold collar encircling his throat. Yaw, Huld's eager, young assistant, who instructed him in all the proper palace protocols, took him to the medal smith's forge to be fitted for it.

"All the king's servants and slaves wear gold collars," Yaw said, displaying his own gold etched collar with a bright blue stone suspended from it. "Each collar indicates a person's rank, and standing in the king's service. Servants have stones or jewels of differing colors and sizes suspended from their collars, identifying their area of service and their favor with the king. Yours will be a simple gold band because you are a slave."

The medal smith's forge was a large outbuilding on the southwest side of the palace grounds. Idon, the smithy, was a barrel chest man with muscular arms, and a heat flushed face. They found him waiting impatiently for them when they walked through his door.

"Sit here while I weld your collar in place," Idon said.

Ryder balked. "Weld it?"

"Don't worry. I haven't burned anyone in a long time. I will put a thick leather pad under the place I weld. You will feel the heat but it won't burn you."

Idon was good at his job, and Ryder didn't sustain any burns, but it reminded him of all the times he'd branded cattle on his family's ranch near Glenwood Springs, Colorado. The wide, heavy band, sitting flat against the base of his neck, felt cool and smooth. Still, it was as much a brand as having a red-hot iron pressed into his skin. The collar proclaimed him property of the king.

"I have a number of jobs for you to do," Ateron said, bringing Ryder out of his dark reflections. "Cartu will show you your first assignment. I would like to have it done before the week is out."

Ateron's tone told Ryder that was a firm deadline. Ryder inclined his head, and Ateron dismissed him with a flick of his gold-ringed hand.

Cartu led him down the palatial hall of the king's private floor to the north, passed many closed doors and two sets of stairs. The hall dead-ended at a ceiling to floor tapestry of trees and flowers. Cartu pushed it aside, revealing an iron-reinforced door that was oddly out of place in comparison to the rest of the lavishly appointed hall.

Thus, the reason for the tapestry, Ryder decided.

Cartu unlocked the door, and they proceeded down four steps into a narrow passageway that ended at another door. Cartu opened it to a surprisingly spacious apartment.

Ryder paused on the threshold, appreciating the apartment's luxury. He imagined himself relaxing on one of the plush sofas that sat on deep alpaca fur rugs, with his tired feet resting on the gilded tables that were interspersed among the furniture. The corners of his mouth lifted. It would be equally delicious to idly recline in the mounds of large floor pillows, and admire the apartment's richly woven tapestries of Injanae's flora and fauna. *Best of all, sitting at the dining table, eating a hot meal directly from that well-equipped fire pit would be an unimaginable luxury.* Ryder leaned against the doorframe, picturing himself ending the day with a leisurely stroll along the bowed terrace, visible through an arched doorway that overlooked the city, and out across the valley.

Cartu marched across the apartment, and out onto the terrace. Ryder pulled himself out of his daydreaming and followed; wondering what was behind the two closed doors on the cliff side of the apartment, and what the heavy green curtain hung at the top of four shallow steps concealed, before turning his attention to the balcony.

A flowering vine, cascading over the low wall of the terrace, caught his eye. The twisted vine's large white blossoms were tightly shut cones, marking the fragrant flowers as nocturnal bloomers. It grew from a planter at the north end of a maze of stone benches, scattered pots of bushes, and trees that turned the terrace into a peaceful arbor.

"Your first project is to increase the height of this balcony wall," said Cartu with a sweeping gesture.

"How much higher?"

"To within two feet of the roof."

Ryder mentally measured the distance to the roof. "Why does the king want the wall to be fifteen feet high?"

Cartu hand went to the hilt of a sword strapped to his waist. He snapped, "Questioning your orders will invite punishment. Your duty is to do whatever the king requires. Now, how long will it take to complete this job? Keep in mind you are the only one who will be working on it."

The reprimand silenced Ryder. He walked the length of the terrace, judging the distance, thinking about the height, and doing rough math figures in his head. Turning to Cartu he said, "I should be able to complete the job in three or four days—if it doesn't rain."

"Good. The king's bodyguards are waiting to help you bring up the stone."

Ryder labored from dawn until dark, for the next three days. The weather cooperated, and the cement mortar set quickly. At dusk on the third day, he looked over the finished job. As an afterthought, he built a ten-foot wooden trellis, wove the flowering vine through it, directing the last six feet of the twisted creeper over the top of the newly enclosed terrace wall, before reporting to the king.

Ateron walked the length of the terrace by the light of a torch. "I am pleased, and as a reward I will give you leisure time to do as you choose, until noon tomorrow."

"Am I allowed to leave the palace grounds?" Ryder asked.

"Not tonight. In the morning if you wish to, you may. See Huld. He will give you the required token. I will expect you in my private judgment chamber tomorrow at twelve bells."

Six

Ryder escaped the palace at dawn, heading straight for the Telquset Falls. His progress through the streets of the city was met by startled stares from the early morning vendors setting up their stalls. However, the gold token clamped to his collar proclaimed his right to be outside the palace grounds. Striding along the perimeter of the northwest side of the deep falls pool, he stopped in the middle of the stone bridge over the river that flowed out of the pool—lost in thought.

The spray from the falls drifted over him, dousing him in a fine mist. He lifted his face to the cool droplets of water, drawing in their pure scent as though they could clear the fog in his mind, and help him remember.

Someone called his name above the roar of the falls.

His shoulders drooped. He blew out resignation, and turned, expecting one of the king's bodyguards. Instead, striding toward him was a strapping young man he knew very well.

"Kytan!" He charged over to the man who had been his greatest blessings during the brutal days he was a slave in Telga's copper mine.

Kytan extended his hand in the American handshake Ryder had taught him.

"That won't due," Ryder said, as his long arms encircled his friend in a bear hug.

"Look at you!" Kytan said, after Ryder released him. "I would never have recognized you, cleaned up, and dressed in the king's livery, except for your height."

Ryder preened for his friend. "A bath, a shave, and decent clothes have made me into a new man."

"Indeed, but how did it happen?"

"Actually I have only been in this rig for a few days."

"I want to hear all about it. Can you come to my shop?"

"Your shop?" Ryder's brows rose.

"Yes, much has changed since I left the mine."

Those days in the darkness of the mine, never being able to straighten up, not knowing day from night, feeling as though he'd been buried alive, shuddered through Ryder. He held Kytan's dark eyes, "I know it's just plain selfish of me, but I'm thankful the law decreed your father had to work off the gambling debts he owed Telga, and that his poor health compelled you to volunteer to take his place."

The dimples disappeared from Kytan's face. "I too am grateful Telga accepted the trade.

"I'm sure he was thrilled to have the use of a strong, young man—"

"Rather than an old, sick one," Kytan said, finishing Ryder's thought. He smiled sadly. "At least my father got to spend the last few weeks of his life in freedom."

"Yeah, and I got to keep my sanity. I would have lost my mind in that place without you."

"And I wouldn't have been able to bear my father's death so soon after I came in, and the obligation to finish his sentence, if you hadn't been there to teach me the gospel."

"Do you still want to be baptized?"

"I pray every day in English for that day to come."

Ryder grinned. Teaching Kytan English and being able to talk to one another in a language no one else understood was the only freedom they had possessed. "I'm glad to know you remember how to speak English and that you still want to be baptized. Because I think that day is getting closer."

"Do you?" Kytan searched Ryder's face.

Ryder's stomach growled.

Kytan laughed. "Doesn't the king feed you well?"

"Yes, but I escaped at dawn. The king gave me a few hours to myself, and I didn't want to wait for breakfast, and have the king decide he needed me for another job."

"Then let's go. I just came out to get something for breakfast, and if you don't mind sharing my poor fare, we can eat in my shop while we talk."

They crossed the bridge to the south, into the main part of the city. Kytan stopped at a bread vendor, a fish vendor, and a fruit stall, before leading Ryder through several narrow winding lanes into the southern outskirts of Telquset. They stopped in front of a shabby building near the southwest wall of the city.

"Welcome to my humble home and shop," said Kytan, unlocking the door. "It doesn't look like much, but at least it is mine."

Ryder ducked his head, entering the small workshop. He couldn't stand up straight, which was common for him in most places in Telquset.

"Sit down." Kytan gestured to a stool.

Sitting, Ryder studied the workshop. It was sparse, but clean and tidy. Tools hung neatly along one wall, over a table that contained projects, Kytan—a medal smith and jeweler— was working on. A stone fireplace covered most of the adjacent wall. In its open mouth sat a large anvil and refining vat. Next to the fireplace, a steep set of narrow stairs led up to a small loft bedchamber. Shelves holding a few pieces of simple jewelry, dishes and cutlery sat beneath a high window next to the door.

"How did you manage to get all of this? I thought when you left the mine you had nothing to come back to."

"So did I." Placing the food on the table, Kytan set dishes out, and explained, "When I left the mine, I learned I still owned this property, Telga didn't want it. Instead of taking it, he just worked me three moons longer."

"Without telling you, no doubt."

"Yes, but at least I came back to a roof over my head. Then all I needed was a job. Sawbo—the one I did my apprenticeship with—gave me one. I worked hard, and eventually had enough money to make a few pieces of simple jewelry. Sawbo allowed me to use his shop and tools for part of the price I received for them. It has taken six moons for me to start my own business. I have been open for less than a moon, but I have more customers every day."

"When you get rich, will you do me a favor?" Ryder clasped his hands together in a comical, pleading gesture. "Buy me from the Ateron."

"I have been working on that since the day I left the mine." Prying a stone from the fireplace, Kytan reached in, brought out a leather pouch, and tossed it to Ryder. "Every week it grows."

Ryder emptied the pouch's meager contents into his hand. His vision blurred.

"You have my word, when I have enough money, I will ask to buy you, even if your owner is the king."

Ryder gripped Kytan's shoulder, struggling to get the words passed the emotion locking his jaw. "Thank you."

Kytan shrugged. "You would do the same for me. Now tell me how you got out of the mine and came to be in the king's service."

Over breakfast, Ryder explained his escape from the mine. "It was literally by accident. Daelo, the owner of the stone quarry, came to the mine about a month after you left. Telga wanted to show him a large vein of copper we had just found. He wanted Daelo to invest money in the mine so he could buy more slaves to work the new copper vein. They were walking by me when the cavern began to shake. A large chunk of the ceiling broke loose above Daelo. I grabbed him, and yanked him out of the way. The ceiling fell in right where he was standing. He was so grateful; he told Telga he would only invest in the mine if he could buy me." Ryder threw heaven a grateful glance. "I left the mine with Daelo that afternoon."

"You always believed you would get out of the mine. I am very thankful you have."

"Amen. And Daelo was a decent master. He even let me build a hut I could stand up in."

They shared a laugh.

"But the best thing was the work. Daelo listened to my ideas, and when Ateron commissioned him to do repairs, or make improvements in the palace, he sent me."

"Is that why the king bought you, because of your building skills?" As Ryder explained how he came to wear the king's livery, a worried expression grew on Kytan's face. "Ryder, I think there is more going on here than you have been told."

"I think so too, but that doesn't concern me. Right now, I need the freedom being Ateron's slave gives me if I'm ever going to find a way out of Injanae—and *I am* going to find a way out."

"Have you remembered anything about how you got here?"

"No, and losing that memory, when I can remember everything else about my life, is driving me crazy." Ryder groaned and rubbed the scar on his temple. "But remembering was what I was trying to do just now at the falls. There's a vague feeling that hearing them triggers. Somehow it's connected to how I got here, but I can't seem to bring it into focus."

A knock at the shop door interrupted them. Kytan jumped up to open the door to the day's first customer. Ryder rose to leave, but was waved back to his seat.

Kytan greeted the middle-aged woman who entered the shop. She smiled, and carefully examined Kytan's limited inventory of jewelry, haggled over the price of a delicate copper bracelet and finally bought it.

After she left with her purchase, Ryder rose to his crouching stance. "I can't keep you from your customers, and I have an appointment with the king. It's been wonderful to see you, and I intend to spend a lot of my time here—whenever I'm allowed out." He flicked the gold token hanging from his collar. "We need to make plans. I want to leave here as soon as possible."

"I am just as anxious to leave as you are, but it is going to take some patient preparation." Kytan walked Ryder to the door. Before Ryder could open it, Kytan took his arm. "Wait." He reached for a knotted cord that Ryder recognized as an Injanaen tape measure, put it around Ryder's upper arm, and then his bicep. He whistled—something Ryder taught him to do—and jotted down the measurements.

Ryder shook his head, "What are you doing?"

"You will have to wait and see."

"Don't waste your time and resources on me. The next time I come, we will make a list of the supplies we are going to need. You can spend your money buying them. There are also a few things you will need to make for us."

Kytan's dimples jumped to life. "Whatever we need, I will take care of it." He took Ryder's hand in the American handshake. "Be careful my friend. The king is a very dangerous man," he said, concern dousing his dimples.

Seven

Ryder locked his jaw to keep his mouth from gaping open.

"You must bathe, shave, and change into clean clothes before I take you to meet my guest," Ateron said. "If you are able to communicate, you will be of great service to me, and I will reward you. If not, you will be immediately dismissed. Also, you are not to speak of this to anyone."

Feeling dazed, Ryder went to his quarters, took an extra set of clothes from a small wooden chest, and went down to the hot springs bath in the cavern under the palace. *Someone else from the outside is here. If I can communicate with him, he may be able to tell me an alternate route of escaping this place—besides climbing out.*

Absorbed in his thoughts, a cheery greeting from Oswan went unacknowledged until Ryder felt a blow to his shin. "Ow." Rubbing his shin, he apologized for his lack of attention to the potbellied barber, and sat in the barber's chair to be shaved.

He didn't hear much of the palace gossip Oswan's rosebud mouth poured into his ear, but said, "Ah" and "Oh" from time to time, which seemed to content the little barber as he shaved the stubble from Ryder's face.

An hour later, bathed and dressed, Ryder reentered the king's presence to find Ateron decked out in his finest royal regalia with Cartu beside him. The chancellor too, was dressed in the formal attire of his office.

Ateron fixed him with a steely eye, "You are to follow me, keeping your eyes on the floor—at all times. When I stop, you will kneel, and wait for my instructions. I will tell you what you are to say. If you can't understand the language spoken to you, you will tell me at once, and Cartu will take you out. The consequences for any disobedience will be . . . unpleasant."

Even with lowered eyes, Ryder knew immediately where they were headed. He'd just spent three days cutting off the apartment's view to the outside world. He felt an uneasy lurch in his gut, considering the implications as Cartu pulled back the heavy green curtain at the top of the stairs, revealing a bedchamber. Cartu held the curtain while Ateron stepped through.

Propped against pillows in a large bed, the injured pilot watched a familiar man enter the room and saunter toward the bed. Dressed in a splendid purple robe, trimmed in bright green and laden with heavy gold accessories from his head to his ankles, he moved with the haughty dignity of one born to command. Making the jeweled crown he wore unnecessary in proclaiming him a king. Every movement, gesture, and look from his finely molded features, demanded deference, expected obedience.

He's certainly a sight worth looking at. The pilot's gaze lingered on the king appreciatively, until it was abruptly claimed by the arresting presence of the next man who entered.

He was titanic in size, and Herculean in proportion. Sculptured muscles rippled his arms, and strained against his simple, colorless attire as though at any moment they might burst through the thin fabric. He strode to the bed with the easy grace and confident swagger of an athlete— never raising his eyes. The meekness of his lowered lids stood in stark contradiction to the brazen power his physical presence commanded.

Intrigued, the pilot scrutinized the titan more closely.

His skin was almost as brown as the king's, but a different tone. It wasn't dark by nature, but by many hours in the sun. Also unlike the blue-black hair of the few others the pilot had seen, the titan's hair was a rich chestnut brown. His bone structure was different too.

He's definitely not a native, and there's something else. The pilot's eyes settled on the gentle indentation in his chin. *That chiseled face is very . . . disturbing . . . somehow.*

Following the titan, the man who held the curtain came through it. The pilot was familiar with him too. His face resembled a toad's with an overly wide mouth and bug eyes. He was about the same age as the king, somewhere in his thirties, and like the giant, athletically built, but in a short, squat way. Even dressed in a floor length, yellow robe with a jeweled sword buckled around his waist, he elicited nothing from the pilot, but the briefest glance.

The odd little parade halted at the side of the bed. With eyes still lowered, the giant dropped to his knees, pressed the palms of his hands together and bowed his head to them.

The pilot's eyes widened. *What's he doing? He isn't going to pray over me, is he?*

The king addressed the humble giant. He inclined his head, and began to speak.

He's speaking Spanish—I think—too bad, I don't.

Concluding his address, the titan waited. The silence brought a faintly puzzled expression to his rugged face as though he was trying to decide something before he again began to speak.

Now, I haven't got a clue what you're jabbering. The pilot puffed out a breath of growing frustration, again letting the silence draw out at the end of his address.

The giant's puzzled expression deepened. He took a breath, and said, "It is my privilege to introduce his Royal Highness, King Ateron, sovereign over the sacred valley of Injanae, ruler over the holy city of Telquset, where the fountain of life and freedom flows forever to bless and nourish the people. This is Chancellor Cartu." He gestured at the toad-faced man. "I am King Ateron's interpreter," the titan said, momentarily touching his forehead to his praying hands.

"Thank Heaven!" The pilot broke into a smile at the astonishment that sprang into the downcast face of the titan. He obviously hadn't been expecting to hear a woman's voice. "Please tell King At-er-on," she said the king's name slowly, trying to commit it to memory, "I understand you."

As the king and his interpreter conversed, a generous smile grew on the king's lips—one the pilot willingly returned.

Bowing his head again to the tips of his fingers, the interpreter said, "The king will only allow me to raise my eyes while we converse, if I have your permission. May I?"

The sense of uneasiness pricking at the back of the pilot's mind since she'd first looked at the goliath on his knees sharpened. She pushed it firmly away. "Of course."

The titan said something to the king. The king responded and the titan's eyes came up.

Hers locked with his.

She bolted upright, sucking in a breath of spine-stiffening shock. She knew those terrible gold eyes. There couldn't be another pair like them in the whole world. Her face blanched. An old, festering wound in her heart spewed horror up her throat, it hissed out through her bloodless lips. *"You killed her!"*

Eight

The words slammed into Ryder with the ferocity of an avalanche. Her silver-blue eyes tore him from his surroundings, hurling him back into that one day he would never escape. Agony tore through him as the memory flared to life, and seared through his mind in every horrifying detail. He swallowed the overwhelming urge to cry out his anguish, while he desperately tried to escape her eyes. But they wouldn't let his go—enslaving him as nothing else ever could.

A sharp cuff to the side of his head spun Ryder's face away from the woman's eyes. Mechanically, he dropped his head to the floor. Trickles of cold sweat slid down his back, his breath came in uneven shudders. He clenched his hands together, fighting the quaking that ran through him like a whiplash, and the sickness threatening to erupt from his stomach.

"Forgive me, Sire," he heard himself say. "I was overwhelmed by her beauty . . . and . . . uh . . . unprepared for her injuries."

Despite the bruised and swollen lump peeking out from beneath a bandage encircling the upper part of her forehead, and the scrapes on her chin, arms, and hands, there was no hiding the fact she'd more than fulfilled the promise of her childhood elfin face. He'd also seen one long leg lying outside the bedcovers, her foot resting on a cushion, badly swollen and bruised.

The king spoke.

He reached through his dismay, gripping the king's voice like a lifeline pulling him back toward sanity from the depths of impending madness, forcing his mind to focus on the king's words.

"It is understandable," Ateron said in a constrained tone. "But you have frightened her, and will not raise your eyes again. Now do as I instructed you."

With lowered lids, Ryder pulled his head from the floor. Words escaped his mouth before they registered in his mind. He stammered, "H-His Majesty, with deepest respect would like the honor of knowing your name."

Her bitter laugh slapped him, hard. "You know my name, Garrison, or have you really forgotten?"

"No," he whispered on a gulping breath, so soft he wasn't sure she'd heard him. He didn't wait to find out. "King Ateron wishes me to welcome you. He sincerely regrets the injuries you have suffered in coming into his kingdom, and wishes to assure you that all the resources of his house are at your disposal. Nothing will be spared in his efforts to make you welcome, heal your injuries, and ensure your comfort. It is his greatest desire to serve you. He wishes you to tell him of any need, or want you may have." He stopped, tight jawed, clenching his hands.

She took an audible breath in through her nose, and blew it out through her mouth. "You may tell King Ateron," she said, her voice rigid, "my name, and give him my thanks for his timely rescue, and all his kind attentions." She paused, and her voice took on a gentler tone. "The young woman who has attended me is very skilled. I appreciate all she has done. I would like to know her name so I can thank her. Lastly," she said, her voice firmly controlled, "I need a message sent to the Willard Airfreight Company in Lima, telling them of my accident, and location."

Ryder touched his head to his hands when she finished, and spoke to the king. "Her name is Hadlee MacLean." In a deadpan tone, he related Hadlee's requests, struggled to stay focused on Ateron's elated voice, and listen to his next set of instructions.

His downcast eyes caught the wave of Ateron's hand as he gestured at the curtained doorway of the bedchamber. Ryder glanced from beneath his lowered lids as the girl who had taken care of Hadlee stepped into the room. She was delicately made, with a quiet dignity and confident bearing that made her petite form regal.

She walked slowly to the bedside and bowed deeply, allowing Ryder to catch an additional glimpse of her.

"This is Taya," he said. "She is a healer from a family of notable healers. No one's skills are greater than hers."

Hadlee's voice smiled as she said Taya's name, He heard a smile of equal warmth in Taya's as he told her Hadlee's, and she repeated it.

"Please express my gratitude to Taya. I am in her debt. She has not only been my doctor, but a kind and caring friend."

Ryder repeated Hadlee's praise. Taya received it with a humble, "Thank you."

"While you're here, Taya will be your companion, doctor, and servant. She has been instructed to fulfill your needs." He hesitated, swallowed, and rushed on. "Because I am the only one who can speak to you, I will visit—briefly—with you each morning and evening. The king would like you to tell me anything you need or want. If your needs are urgent, Taya will send for me. I will come immediately to interpret your wishes."

"And the message?" Hadlee prompted, when he paused.

"The king *says* he will send messengers to Lima with word of your accident and location. However, he begs you to be patient. The valley of Injanae has limited interaction with the outside world. It may take several weeks to send and receive word from Lima."

"Several weeks?" Hadlee's voice was incredulous. "Will it really take that long?"

"I don't know," he said, tonelessly. "The king doesn't wish to tire you. He will come to see you again tomorrow. If there is anything else you need right now, I am to relay it to Taya."

"There's nothing more I need for the moment, but rest and Taya's kind attention."

He relayed the information, catching the king's movement as he leaned over, took Hadlee's hand, lifted it to his lips, and gently kissed her scraped knuckles. He laid her hand carefully back on the bed with a little squeeze, tapped Ryder's shoulder, and walked to the curtained entry.

Ryder stood; his face a blank slate, his eyes riveted on the floor, his mind in chaos, his heart on fire with the burn of an old familiar adversary, and followed.

Nine

Taya arranged pillows, tucked in the colorful woven coverlet, and generally fussed over Hadlee who smiled her gratitude, lay back, and closed her eyes. She listened to the soft patter of Taya's sandals going down the stone steps of the bedchamber and across the apartment.

Her eyes flew open. With a shaking hand, she pulled the pillow from beneath her head, pressed it firmly against her face, and let out a shuddering sob. Every grain of fortitude she possessed was expended in getting through that meeting. She blessed Cartu for the slap that released her from the prison of those deadly gold eyes.

At first, she thought she'd slapped *him*, but the sting of a slap wasn't in her hand. She clenched it, remembering the feel of her fingers digging into his face, and his skin beneath her nails, when he reached for her over the body of her mother. Only watching the person she hated most in the world abase himself at the feet of the king with his humiliating and groveling gestures, steadied her enough to endure his presence.

She hadn't seen Ryder Garrison since the day he killed her mother, but there was no mistaking those predatory eyes. Looking into them made her relive that day in every excruciating detail. She tried to drag her mind away from it without success.

Hazel Barnes made gorgeous dresses. She was taking sewing lessons from her, but *that* day, her mother didn't take her for a lesson. Mrs. Barnes was going to make her a new Sunday dress. After a wonderful hour, searching through patterns, and picking out fabric, they went to Derk's Soda Fountain. Her mother said she had another surprise for her.

Ryder Garrison destroyed that wonderful surprise with one mindless, criminal act. He robbed me of everything I loved, and the life that should have been mine.

Throughout Ryder Garrison's court proceedings, she'd stayed at her aunt's home in Salt Lake City. Her father didn't want her to know anything about it, but she knew. Her cousins told her everything they overheard, and smuggled all the newspaper articles she wasn't supposed to see, into her room.

The State of Utah convicted him of manslaughter—not withstanding he was barely fourteen years old—because he was driving a stolen car. She'd been surprised by his age, his height equaled that of her father's, and inconsolable when she learned his motive. He'd stolen his uncle's car just to come into town for ice cream. Her mother had died because of an ice cream cone. It was so infinitely cruel, and unfair.

She was just ten years old when Ryder killed her mother. From that day on, she'd struggled to understand, find peace, and as so many counseled, forgive. Her overwhelming grief wouldn't let her heart do it. Then she hadn't wanted to do it, not when a court of law destroyed her belief in what was just and fair.

For some unknown reason, the judge reduced Ryder's expected sentence from fifteen years, to seven. That same justice system paroled him four years later. Hadlee felt his punishment was criminally insufficient to pay for the life he'd taken. The crippling wound that injustice inflicted in her heart, never healed. How could it when the injustices Ryder Garrison's actions imposed on her just kept piling up.

All the important events in her life—her first crush, first date, first prom gown, making the basketball team and winning the championship, and the day she graduated from high school—were tainted with grief because her mother hadn't been there to share them with her.

Each new injustice gnawed at her, deepening the wound in her heart. Over the years, self-preservation had taught her to avoid that still festering wound. Now it opened like a black hole, sucking her into a terrible abyss of hate.

Pressing the pillow harder against her face, she choked down sobs, willing herself to stop reliving what she couldn't change, and forced her mind back to the interview with the king. When he'd kissed her hand, an unexpected shiver had crawled up her arm.

Something was wrong with the smile on his face too—when he said my name . . . or did I imagine it? A queasy uneasiness gurgled in her stomach. *There's something about this place that doesn't feel right, and yet, they've taken such good care of me. I just need to be patient.*

Hateful gold eyes intruded into her mind. *No! I can't fathom why you're here, Garrison, and it doesn't matter, but the sooner I'm out of here, the better!*

Ten

The king backhanded Ryder's face. His head snapped sideways with the impact of Ateron's heavy gold ring smashing into his cheekbone. For the second time that day, he found himself feeling grateful to be slapped. Cartu's blow had brought him out of the nightmare, and the king's was keeping him from returning—*at least for the moment.*

He dropped his head to the floor. The dragon he'd climbed a mountain to slay was here, breathing fire through his soul—reducing him to cinders.

"Do you want me to send you back to the mines?"

The king's words registered in his mind without impact. He knew the threat was an empty one.

"You terrified her, staring so blatantly at her with your strange eyes, but that won't happen again. You will keep your eyes lowered at all times. Taya will take you in, and bring you out. You will keep your face on the floor, raising it only enough to speak when you are required to do so. If you look at her again, I will have you flogged."

Ryder followed Ateron's stiff angry strides as he paced back and forth in front of him, expecting at any moment to be kicked and almost hoping he would be. *At least if I'm in enough pain, I'll have something else to focus on besides—Hadlee MacLean.*

"You are confined to your quarters until I send someone for you. I must move you to my personal servant's quarters so you will be close enough to serve Hadlee whenever she needs you." Ateron waved an angry, dismissive hand and turned away.

Cartu's mouth split in a grotesque grin. Standing in front of the door, he blocked Ryder's retreat. "I am sure the king will allow me the pleasure of flogging you, when that time comes."

Ryder bowed stiffly to the chancellor. Cartu stepped aside, allowing him to walk through the door. As soon as it closed behind him, Ryder raced down the corridor, flew down the stairs, and fled to the sanctuary of his room.

The quarters, that this morning, he'd considered a spacious dwelling, now felt like a cage. He paced their small confines, staring out the large window at Dragon's Head.

Its grinning jaws mocked him.

He'd climbed that dragon hoping to learn how to slay it. Hadlee MacLean's silver-blue eyes had been that dragon for far too long, and even though he'd been forgiven, his photographic memory and perfect recall never allowed him to stop seeing the anguish in those exquisite, accusing eyes.

The despair he felt during his first year in prison pressed in on him. Those endless days gave him plenty of time to look at himself. He hated everything he saw—he felt worthless. Hadlee MacLean's eyes assured him of that, over, and over again, until he knew it was true.

His self-loathing exploded in frequent fights, which he paid for with extensive hours of solitary confinement, growing more despondent with each passing day. That course of self-destructive behavior continued until Hadlee's father, Haddon James MacLean—who went by James—rescued him, with a letter of forgiveness. That letter was one of Ryder's most precious possessions. Not only did James forgive him, but he also volunteered to help him along the hard path of repentance.

He quit fighting, and became a model of good behavior as the Book of Mormon, James sent him, opened his heart, and lit his soul. He poured over the scriptures until he became a walking set of them, discovering and nurturing a deep and abiding testimony—something his parents had tried, unsuccessfully, to help him find. Grounded in faith, his quest for forgiveness became an all-consuming desire, one that kept him on his knees for hours.

Because of his good behavior—after that first year—and with a glowing letter of recommendation from James MacLean, he was released from prison the year he turned eighteen. He left knowing the price he'd paid would never be enough, but with the absolute comfort of being forgiven, and with a burning determination to prove himself to his parents. He hoped to regain their trust, and some small measure of their respect.

His father, a former U.S Marshal, arranged for him to serve his three-year parole in his home state of Colorado, with a yearly trip to Utah for review.

That fall, because of the high school and college textbooks his parents and James MacLean sent him, he was prepared to enter college. However, without a high school diploma, the university he wanted to attend wouldn't consider allowing him entrance. His father called in a few additional favors, and the university agreed to allow him to take a college entrance examination. His scores amazed the university board. Still they wavered; unsure they wanted a student fresh out of prison, and on parole.

He went through a grueling set of interviews, which were so much like his trial, he almost lost his courage. Finally, they asked what sports he played, when he told them he played them all, they agreed to give him a chance. He excelled in his chosen field of civil engineering, and became a star athlete for the university.

During his first year of college, he had monthly interviews with his bishop. He wanted with all his heart to serve a mission, but his parole wasn't up until he turned twenty-one. He attended two more years of college, and waited.

His parents went with him to Utah for the final interview that ended his parole, and made him a free man. He submitted his mission papers that same day, grateful for the glowing recommendations both his bishop, and stake president sent. However, the most important letter that accompanied him to his interview with the First Presidency, to determine whether he would be allowed to serve a mission, came from James MacLean.

Two months later, Elder Garrison was serving in the mountains of Argentina. He possessed a natural gift for the native dialects, a great love for the people, and a tremendous testimony—he couldn't wait to share. During his mission, the dragon slept. Upon his release, he returned home, anxious to finish college, hopeful his missionary service had finally released him from the dragon. A month before he graduated, the dragon awoke with an astonishing ferocity. Desperate to slay the beast, he remembered the dragon Tupac described, hidden in the Andes.

Evening took possession of the sky before the tornado in Ryder's mind calmed, allowing him to sort through the twisted wreckage it left behind. Climbing Dragon's Head had taught him, if he was ever to be free of his dragon, he had to find and face Hadlee MacLean.

In that first stunning moment when their eyes locked, he finally understood why. Her father and the Lord had forgiven him, but she hadn't. The only way to slay the monster that tormented him, and finally be at peace, was to seek and obtain her forgiveness.

Is it my fault, you're here, Hadlee MacLean? He swallowed guilt. *Did my unknowing need to gain your forgiveness, and be free of your eyes bring you? Your coming to Injanae is just too fantastic to be a coincidence.* The implications and possibilities crashed over him like a tidal wave.

The look in her eyes when she recognized him, assaulted him. *Hadlee MacLean may never forgive me and living with that will be*—he pushed that despair away and thought about where to begin. *Gaining her forgiveness is going to be the hardest mountain I have ever climbed—if I can climb it. It is going to take a lot of patience, faith, and prayer.* He decided he better get started on the prayers.

Lul, another of the king's twenty bodyguards, came through the door without knocking to find Ryder on his knees. "Is this the new way slaves are punished? Making them stay on their knee's for hours?" His face became a grinning jack-o-lantern, accentuated by several gold teeth.

Ryder stood. "Have you come to take me to my new quarters?"

Lul sobered. "Get your things."

His new quarters were much larger, and included a small terrace with a bench. Ryder finished stowing his extra suits of clothes and boots in the finely carved chest at the end of the stone bed-shelf, just before Sual came through the door with the curt directive to follow him. Ryder fervently hoped Hadlee didn't need him, but his summons wasn't to her.

Sual took him to the rooftop garden, where Ateron strolled along the perimeter gazing down on the city and the torches glowed in the darkness. Ryder knelt on the stone floor, pressed his forehead against it—for what felt like the hundredth time that day—and waited.

When Ryder was allowed to raise his head, the king said in a razor-edged voice, "I trust you have taken the time to reflect upon your behavior and there will be no more incidences in which I find myself embarrassed by you."

The bruise growing under Ryder's eye throbbed.

Ateron pressed on, not waiting for a reply. "Tomorrow, you will begin work on several new projects that are very important to me."

With submissiveness he didn't feel, Ryder said, "You will have my best efforts."

"How very reassuring." The king lowered himself onto a cushioned bench, and leaned back. "In six cycles of the moon, I will hold Injanae's annual Lunar Celebration here"— he swept the rooftop with his arm—"for the leaders, and noble houses of my people. There are certain architectural modifications I want you to make in preparation for this special celebration."

Ryder kept his expression neutral as he listened to the king's plans for the Lunar Celebration, while his mind entertained grave doubts. When he was allowed to speak he said, "Your Majesty, if I am to do everything you require, in the space of six moons, I will need several crews, and there will have to be some modifications to your plans."

"Chancellor Cartu will assemble the crews. What do you need to modify?"

The affront in Ateron's tone gave Ryder pause, again conscience of the throbbing under his eye. "Constructing a staircase from the ground to this garden would go faster, if I build it from wood rather than stone."

The king frowned, "Faster?"

"It would also be safer," Ryder quickly added. "I can make the last twenty feet of the stairs removable, eliminating access to the garden, and your royal apartments."

Ateron met the security aspect of Ryder's proposal with a thoughtful expression, and then a decisive nod. "Alright, build it with wood. How soon can you have the plans ready?"

Ryder hesitated. "Before I start working on the stair plans, I should probably work up the plans for everything you want here in the garden, and then make a trip to the quarry to order all the stone they will require." He paused. "It will probably take a couple of days to go over the designs with Daelo."

"I will give you until tomorrow evening to work out the plans for the garden. We will discuss your designs tomorrow night at nine bells. If I approve them, you can go to the quarry the following morning. Cartu will arrange the trip, and assign guards to accompany you." The king waved a languid hand, dismissing him.

Ryder hurried down the six flights of stairs to the kitchen. Breakfast with Kytan was the last meal he'd eaten. It seemed like a week ago.

Ceeona, the well-rounded head cook took pity on him when he begged for food long after the kitchen was closed. With motherly concern, she filled a platter with bread, cheese, fish, and potatoes. He collapsed onto a bench in the slaves' dining hall and wolfed down the food, forcing his mind to concentrate on eating, and the bed that awaited him—even if it was too small.

With a full belly, he returned to his new quarters, pulled the mattress from the six-foot stone bed-shelf, set two feet off the floor, and stretched out. Resting his feet on extra pillows, he tried to sleep, but his mind wouldn't shut down.

How did you get here, Hadlee MacLean? Your answer to that must hold the key to my freedom, if only I can convince you to tell me. He groaned, the irony, or was it the justice, of her holding the keys to his spiritual, emotional, and physical freedom were just too hard to face right now. *My brain's too scrambled and exhausted to think about how to get her to tell me anything.*

He rolled onto his side, stuffed a pillow under his head, trying to empty his mind. *At least working on the king's projects will give my brain somewhere else to be besides lost in the torment of those silver-blue eyes.*

Eleven

"This is so aggravating," Hadlee said to the rough-hewn ceiling of her bedchamber.

For two days she'd smiled, nodded, or shaken her head until she didn't know if it still hurt from the lump on it, or all the gesturing. Not being able to talk to these well-meaning people was driving her nuts.

"If I could just get up." She glared at her right ankle that kept her confined to her bed. It was badly swollen, black and blue, and still excruciatingly painful. She was afraid it was broken.

Even more painful, the only person she could talk to was the one person she couldn't stand the sight of, but she hadn't seen him for the past two days. There were things she needed to have him tell Taya.

Her face grew hot. *It's so humiliating to have to discuss my personal needs with a man—and Ryder Garrison in particular—but I simply can't go on this way.* She'd made up her mind, and gathered her courage yesterday to do it, but he hadn't come. It made her want to shriek with frustration, and meant having to gather her courage all over again.

The resounding bongs from the city's belfry announced noon.

He's probably not going to come today either. Pounding her fist into her pillow, she flopped back down on it and moaned when her ankle gave her a nasty twinge. *Where are you, Garrison, why doesn't the king make you come? Did seeing me rattle you so much Ateron isn't going to make you interpret for me anymore?*

The door to her apartment opened, a deep male voice talked with Taya.

She jerked back up, arranged her pillows, folded her hands in her lap, and heart thumping, steeled herself.

Taya pushed the curtain aside, Ryder followed her in, his eyes on her back. She led him to the side of the bed. He knelt, silently putting his forehead to the floor.

Hadlee stared down at the back of his head. As gratifying as it was to see him grovel at her feet, it intensified her feeling that something was wrong with this primitive place. There were questions she wanted to ask about Injanae; she put them aside. Right now, there were things she needed.

She fingered her long dirty braid. *At least with his face glued to the floor, he won't be able to see mine when I tell him what I need.*

In a business like tone, she began, "There are several things I want you to tell Taya. I have been in Injanae for over a week now and . . . ," she hesitated, inhaling one more breath of courage before forcing the words out. "I need a bath. All Taya has done is give me sponge baths. I need a real bath. My hair needs washing, and I would like toiletries. You know, shampoo, soap, toothbrush, the usual things. And I need . . . umm . . . female things," she said firmly, feeling the hot flush, and bright stain that undoubtedly accompanied it, on her face.

Ryder touched his forehead to the floor, and raised it an inch. "I will tell Taya what you said."

Hadlee's requests brought a pensive expression to Taya's face, and a burst of chatter.

When it ended, Ryder relayed her reply. "Taya says she will give you everything you require, and she's certain she can explain the . . . uh . . . more delicate matters to you—after I leave. However, she feels it will be better to wait a few more days before you take a bath. Your ankle is still very swollen and sore. Getting you in and out of a bathtub will require more help than Taya can give you."

Hadlee drew in a relieved breath. *At least the worst is over.* Still, she was unwilling to give up on the bath. "Can't a couple of women come help Taya get me in and out of a bathtub?"

"I'm afraid Ateron doesn't want anyone else to help with you right now."

"Why? He said he it was his greatest desire to serve me and take care of my needs."

"I don't know. The king doesn't confide in me. I'll ask him for you, when he comes to visit you this evening."

"Fine." She folded her arms, and sank back on her pillows. Her forehead wrinkled with growing uneasiness.

"Is there anything else I can tell Taya for you?"

"No."

"Then I'll go." He started to rise.

She sat back up. "Wait. Ask Taya if she can at least wash my hair—somehow."

The question was put to Taya. Hadlee wasn't encouraged when Taya's brows drew together, and the conversation, on her part, became animated.

When their jabbing ended, Ryder explained Taya's idea. "If you will consent to be carried down the stairs and put on the dining table, with your head hanging a bit over the edge, Taya will use a pitcher and basin to wash your hair. Of course," he added hastily, "one of the king's bodyguards can carry you, instead of me."

Hadlee silently frowned over the idea, looking at Taya's worried face. "I have a better idea," she finally said. "I've gotten the impression there's a bathroom in the enclosure behind you." She blushed. "Is there a bathtub?"

"There is," Ryder said, having become familiar with all the apartment's amenities while heightening the terrace wall.

"Then why does Taya want me put on the dining table if there is a perfectly good bathtub up here? Tell her, if she will just help me into the bathroom, I could sit on a chair next to the tub, lean over it, and have my hair washed."

She again listened anxiously to the conversation between Ryder and Taya, pestered by the persistent question of why Ryder was in this primitive place, and acting like a toad-eating flunky.

When Taya quit talking, he said, "In answer to your question, Taya wants to keep your ankle elevated and your bed dry. Laying you on the table would accomplish both things." He paused. "As for getting you into the bathroom, Taya wants to know how she's supposed to help you get there."

"I'll hop on my good foot, and she can support me on the side with my sprained one."

"Are you sure it's just sprained? If it's broken, hopping around with it hanging in the air will only make things worse, besides being very painful. It would be better if you let me—"

"*No.*"

"Then have one of the king's bodyguards—"

"*No.*"

Her refusal sparked a lengthy debate between Ryder and Taya. Finally he said, "If you insist on doing this, at least let me take a look at your ankle. Taya isn't sure it's just sprained. Her field of medicine runs more to herbal remedies than bones. I have experience with ankle injuries. I may be able to tell if it's just a sprain, or if it's broken. In either case, I'll wrap it for you. That should make it feel better and give it some support if you insist on hopping around."

The note of censure in his voice brought on a nagging itch in her hand to smack the back of his head. *It's none of your business if I want to hop around, Garrison,* she blistered his back with contempt.

The limited satisfaction that afforded her was followed by the acute desire to know if her ankle really was broken. *If it's broken, I don't want to do any more damage, and it's undoubtedly a good idea to wrap it.* Warily, she asked, "What kind of experience do you have with ankles?"

"I've played a lot of sports. It's inevitable to end up with a sprained ankle or two. Most athletes don't let that slow them down too much. They learn how to wrap them so they can keep on playing. I've also watched doctors examine players with ankle injuries—both sprains and breaks. I asked questions, and they showed me what to look for."

The idea of letting him touch her was so repugnant it sent a shiver up her back. She struggled with it, kneading the bed covers, weighing it against the desire to know if her foot was broken and have it treated. "Alright—do it," she said, before she could chicken out.

Ryder let out a breath, and spoke to Taya. The conversation was animated on her side, while Ryder's voice was calm and firm. Hadlee assumed he'd won, when Taya reluctantly shrugged her shoulders, turned and went through the curtain.

"Where's she going?" Hadlee's fingers tightened on the bed covers, unnerved by being left alone with a man she thought of as a criminal.

"She's going to get the wrapping I asked for. I will teach her how to wrap your ankle, so she can do it—instead of me—if you would rather," he said, still huddled on the floor.

"She didn't look happy about it."

"She doesn't want me to hurt you. I told her I would be very careful, and I will, but I'm afraid it will hurt."

Taya came back with a small pungent pot of herbal ointment that wrinkled Hadlee's nose, and a long, two-inch wide strip of cloth.

Ryder rose to his knees, and turned toward Taya.

Hadlee's grip on the covers intensified, her jaws clamped together.

Ryder shuffled on his knees to the end of the bed.

Hadlee stared at his profiled expression of concern as he visually examined the swelling, and black and blue bruising on her ankle.

"Wiggle your toes," he said.

She did.

"Do you feel any numbness in your foot?"

"No."

"Good; and at least there are no obvious deformities of the bones around your ankle," he said, reaching for her foot.

She fought the convulsive shudder that wrenched her when his hard fingers made contact with her skin. He ran them over her ankle and under it, gently probing the bones, asking for her reaction on each place he touched.

"Ouch." She flinched with pain when he probed the outside of her ankle.

"Sorry. Is that the place it hurts the worst?"

"Yes."

He nodded and carefully flexed her foot back toward her ankle and then pointed it away. "How does that feel?" he asked.

"It feels stiff and sore, but not too painful."

Using even greater care, he moved her ankle side to side.

She sucked in a breath. "That *really* hurts."

He nodded. "Tell me exactly when you feel the pain," he said and repeated the motion more slowly.

"There," she said through her teeth, when he tilted her foot to the outside of her ankle.

He nodded again, put her foot down, and said, "I don't believe it's broken."

"Thank heaven!"

"Still, it's a very bad sprain, and sometimes that can be even worse. After I wrap it, Taya has agreed to help you hop to the tub, and have your hair washed."

Taya applied the smelly ointment. Then with practiced skill, Ryder wrapped her ankle, talking to Taya as he worked. Finished, he tied it off and stood, with his back to her. "I'll bring a chair up from the dining room and put it in the bathroom. Is there anything else you need me to do?"

Already her ankle felt better. Her spirits rose, then plummeted with the realization she should thank him. Staring at his broad back, she summoned all the social grace her aunt so painfully drilled into her and ejected the words, "Thank you for wrapping my ankle. I don't need anything else right now."

He nodded, went through the curtain, returning in a moment with a chair. He took the chair into the bathroom, and came back out, facing her with downcast eyes. "I will be back with Ateron this evening. If you need anything else, have Taya come for me."

"I'll do that," she said, frowning at the colorful bruise on his cheekbone.

Several times that afternoon Ryder found his mind wandering from the task of working out the last details of the stairs design, and the dimensions for the foundation. He wanted to have the crew Cartu had gathered start digging it today, but he kept loosing track of what he was doing.

The size of Hadlee's foot and her long limbs, told him what he already suspected, *she's very tall. I wondered if she's as tall as Hannah or mom, maybe she's even as tall as Jessie.*

His sister, Hannah, was an inch shy of six feet. His mother was dead on, and his baby sister, Jessie, topped it by three inches. Hadlee had to be somewhere in that range too. But, he was unlikely to find out if he couldn't get his face off the floor. *That has to change.*

He paced off the area for the foundation, pounded a stake in the ground, and turned a ninety-degree angle. *It sure felt good to be able to do something for her.* He basked for a moment in that satisfaction. *She looked so forlorn.* For someone who was forbidden to look at her, he'd found ways to do just that. *Even with a scraped chin, bruises, and dirty hair, she's a knockout. Her looks could addle a man's brain, and linger there like a dream—or an endless torment.*

The other thing he'd seen, or rather felt, was her revulsion at his touch. Even the tone of her voice conveyed her hostility. He didn't blame her for how she felt, but he desperately wanted to prove to her that he wasn't the stupid kid who killed her mother—anymore.

If I can just get her to see I've repented, and changed, become a decent man. Done some good with my life—maybe—she might begin to look at me with different eyes. That's going to take time, and at some point, I need to plead for her forgiveness.

He stopped, pounded another stake in the ground, and turned. *I'm getting ahead of myself. First, she simply needs to get used to my presence. She has to be curious about why I'm here in this remote and isolated place, and wondering why life has played such a dirty trick on her, putting her in a position where she is dependent on me—of all people.*

An idea blossomed.

The following morning, at Hadlee's request, Ryder checked and rewrapped her ankle. After conveying the required information between Taya and Hadlee, he hesitated when she indicated he could leave. Keeping his forehead on the floor, he inquired, "May I ask you what the date is?"

A scoff met his request. "Am I really supposed to believe you don't know?

"I don't."

"That's absurd," she said more to herself than to him. "It's April 11th, if I have counted the days correctly since I got here."

"Excuse me, but what year is it?"

"You don't really expect me to believe you're that ignorant?"

"I am."

"It's 1936!"

Ryder sucked in a hard breath. He knew he'd been in Injanae a long time, but he had no idea it had been that long. "Thank you," he said mechanically, rose from his knees, and walked blindly through the curtain.

Hadlee thought about Ryder's strange questions for a good part of the day. As much as it grated on her to be curious about Ryder Garrison, she decided she wanted some answers, and she was going to get them.

After the usual questions were asked and answered during Ryder's visit the following morning, she cleared her throat and took up the conversation where they had left off. "Tell me why you didn't know what year it is," she said, looking over the edge of the bed.

"I spent a long time in a copper mine when I first came to Injanae, day and night were all the same. I lost track of them. By the time I left the mine, I no longer knew what the date was."

"You're telling me you went into a mine and stayed there—for you don't know how long—without coming out? Did you come here to mine? And now that you know the date, how long have you been here?"

"I think I was in the mine for almost a year, but I didn't come here to mine, I came to climb a mountain. I've been here about a year and a half." He paused. "May I ask how you came into Injanae?"

"Unfortunately, I jumped down this rabbit hole."

"Jumped?"

"My plane was attached by a couple of gigantic, ugly birds—"

"Condors."

"Is that what they were? Well, thanks to them, I had to bail out and watch my plane crash into the rocks at the bottom of the eastern peak above Injanae's valley walls. So, here I am, stuck in Telquset, waiting to be rescued by my company, who will probably fire me for losing that borrowed plan," she said, punching her pillow.

"You're a—*pilot?*" he said in a voice she immediately took exception to.

"Yes, I'm a pilot and a good one too. It wasn't my fault those birds attacked my plane."

"No—of course not, it's just; I've never met a female pilot. I'm . . . impressed. Weren't you scared when you jumped out? I've heard parachutes aren't the most reliable things."

"I wasn't worried. I've bailed out before. Besides, the chute I used is top notch. It's a Switlik. The kind Amelia Earhart flies with, because they're the best."

"Where did you land?"

"Underneath that monstrous looking mountain."

"Farlana."

"What?"

"The mountain you landed under is called Farlana. It means dragon or serpent."

"Oh."

"Who found you?"

"I don't know. I hit the cliff face, and that's the last thing I remember before I came to and found Taya taking care of me. Ateron and Cartu showed up sometime after that."

"Were you frightened?"

Hadlee's lips tightened, remembering the vague uncomfortable feeling she'd experienced when the king kissed her hand, and her growing uneasiness. She pushed the impressions to the back of her mind, unwilling to appear weak or fearful in front of Ryder. *Besides, the king's been true to his word,* she reminded herself. *I'm being well cared for, and it won't be long until a message reaches David and he sends someone to get me.*

She relaxed back against her pillows, "Of course it was disconcerting to come to and not know where I was, but Taya and the king were so kind and considerate, I had no reason to be fearful," she said in a confident tone, but unable to stop the frown that formed between her brows.

Twelve

Hadlee vented frustration over Ryder's head. "It's been three weeks. I have been in this bed for three interminable weeks!"

The corners of Ryder's mouth quirked up. Listening to Hadlee express her pent up aggravation brought him the first flicker of hope he'd experienced in almost a week. "I'm sorry, but it's for the best," he mumbled to the floor, trying to keep the smile out of his voice.

"What did you say? I can't understand you half the time with your face always glued to the floor. Why is your face always on the floor?"

"I'm sorry, Pilot, but I'm not permitted to look at you."

"What did you call me?"

"Pilot," he said, tentatively.

"Why?"

"I have to address you in some way, and I thought you might prefer it to . . . uh . . . my use of your name—unless you would rather I call you Miss MacLean."

The ensuing silence made Ryder hold his breath. She broke it in a stiff voice. "Pilot, will do."

"Thank you."

"As for using your face to mop my floor, I can't say I'm sorry you aren't allowed to look at me, but *why* aren't you allowed to? Taya doesn't come in here and suck the dirt off the floor. Why do you?"

"I'm a slave, and Ateron is under the impression that I frightened you when I looked at you."

The sound of Hadlee smacking the bed with her fists had the ridiculous effect of lifting his spirits even further.

"I am not afraid of you, Garrison. I'm delighted you've found your proper place in life, but I am sick and profoundly tired of looking at the back of *your head*. I'm also tired of being told no word has come from my company, having Ateron make decisions for me, and you can tell Taya I am getting out of this bed—right now!"

Hugging the floor, Ryder choked down a laugh. Hadlee was showing more emotion than she had for the past week. Since he'd sided with Taya about making her stay off her foot for an additional week—against her desire to try putting some weight on it—she'd cultivated a cold, sterile politeness toward him that she had just shattered.

"If you can wait until tomorrow, I'll have a crutch made for you to lean on. Then you can try putting some weight on your foot," he said, finding it increasingly difficult to keep his face on the floor during this entertaining conversation. "You might also ask the king to allow me to quit using my face to mop your floor . . . if you think the sight of it won't offend you too much."

"Well the sight of you does offend me, but as you are the only person I can speak to, and since I can't stand talking to the back of your head anymore, I don't see I have a choice."

He was truly surprised by her agreement, and so pleased at the prospect of getting his face off the floor, and being allowed to look directly at her, he didn't quite manage to suppress the chuckle. He coughed to cover his gaff.

"What's the matter with you?"

"Dust," he gasped.

Hadlee picked tentatively at her lunch of fruit, cheese, and bread, trying to make up her mind. *There are things I've wanted to say to you, Garrison, for twelve long years, but I refuse to say them to the back of your head. When I speak my mind to you, I intend to look directly into your beastly gold eyes.* She nodded with decision, finished her lunch, and took a nap before Ateron arrived for his evening visit.

Ryder again found himself grinning at the floor, in response to the awkward silence Ateron's effusive greeting received after he passed it along to Hadlee.

The king's perplexed voice shattered the uncomfortable silence. "She is angry. I can't imagine how I have offended her, but she won't look at me. You are to ask her and tell me at once."

Wishing he could see the scene playing out above his head, Ryder relayed Ateron's request, and listened to Hadlee's reply, grateful her tone of voice needed no interpretation.

"Tell Ateron you are the only person I can speak to in this kingdom, and I'm tired of talking to the back of your head. Tell him I want you to be able to lift your head." She paused. "And your eyes."

Ryder inhaled relief. "Your Majesty, Hadlee feels it is disrespectful for me to speak to her with my face on the floor, as though I'm not paying attention to her. She would like me to look at her, and stand or sit in her presence, when she allows it. The mark of respect she desires is a bow when I enter and leave," Ryder said, liberally embellishing Hadlee's request.

Silence again reigned as Ryder waited, willing the king to capitulate to Hadlee's demands.

"Since it is Hadlee's express desire that you disregard the customs of my kingdom, I will allow you to do as she wishes," Ateron said in a disapproving, and slightly threatening, tone.

Undaunted, Ryder rose from the floor like a geyser to his full seven foot, two inch, stature. "I am very much in your debt," he said to Hadlee with a deep bow.

She lifted her chin and met his eyes. "I don't like you looking down on me any more than I liked looking at the back of your head," she said, just as the king reminded him that when he was in the royal presence he would still be required to kneel.

At war with a grin, he knelt.

Thirteen

Anticipation conjured a smile from Hadlee when Ryder delivered her crutch the following morning. Itching to try it out, she fought a brief internal struggle, deciding no matter how well or poorly she did, she didn't want Ryder as a witness. Cutting their morning interview short, she ended with her genuine thanks for the crutch.

As soon as Ryder left, Hadlee got out of bed. Aided by the crutch, she put a little weight on her bandaged foot. It was weak, and still tender, but she was so ecstatic to be walking that she smiled away all of Taya's frowns.

After a few practice steps, and over—what even she understood were—strong protests, she got Taya to help her down the four steps from her bedchamber, and out onto the terrace. Patiently, she let Taya settle her on a bench.

When she was comfortable, Taya pointed to herself; then gestured at the door of the apartment. She patted Taya's hand, and nodded. Taya smiled and left the terrace.

Hadlee listened to the apartment door open and shut.
She closed her eyes; filled her lungs with the heavenly cool air and reveled in the soft breeze that ruffled her hair. *What a strange place this is,* she lifted her face to the warmth of the sun. *It feels like a long lost piece of the Incan empire.*

The little she'd seen of Telquset, as she floated down and away from the city, reminded her of the Incans, something she'd studied in college. The notion was reinforced by all the gold and brightly colored attire wore by Ateron the day she encountered Ryder.

But it can't be—can it? The Spanish explored the Andes extensively. Could one remote pocket of people elude everyone's notice all the way into the twentieth century? Maybe Garrison knows. She grimaced. *Is he really a slave?*

The idea that Injanae practiced slavery heightened the fear that was beginning to take root in her mind. Still, she couldn't find it in her heart to feel sorry about Ryder's enslavement. *Justice has finally caught up with him,* she smiled grimly, *but how did it happen?*

Her fruitless speculation was interrupted by a foot long lizard coming up over the edge of the bench, not two feet from her. The beast had a wide bearded jaw and spindly claws. Its inky black head abruptly turned into a green spotted body that faded into a long gray tail.

She shrieked, grabbing for her crutch.

The reptile didn't seem fazed by her outcry. It opened and shut its mouth, advancing two more steps toward her.

On another shriek, she pushed off the bench, hopping unsteadily on her good foot, trying to get the crutch under her and back away at the same time. The long shift she wore caught under the crutch, throwing her off balance as she tried to take a step.

She fell backwards.

Strong arms caught her, lifting her from her feet. "What's going on here?" asked Ryder.

"That!" She pointed to the lizard.

"And I thought you were a brave pilot." He shook his head.

Her eyes went glacial at his laughing tone.

Before she could think of a stinging retort, he said, "Since you're stuck here for a while, you might as well meet some of the local citizens."

"I don't want to meet *that* local citizen. Now put me down!" Loathing, at finding herself in his arms, coursed through her more fiercely than if the lizard had crawled across her lap.

Obediently, he set her down on another bench a few feet from the reptile.

"You're going to run into this kind of citizen frequently, so you might as well meet him," he said.

She scowled at him as he turned to the nasty beast.

"The people here call them sunqaras," he said, catching the lizard with one deft motion.

She cringed when he turned back to her. "Don't you dare bring that thing any closer."

He stopped. "I'm not going to put him on you," he said in a reassuring tone. "He's actually a very useful citizen."

Opening his hand slightly, he stretched the sunqara out with his other one, so she could take a good look at the monster. It wiggled and hissed, trying to escape.

She jerked back. "Ugh!"

"I will admit they aren't too pretty, but sunqaras perform a very important service." He scanned the terrace walls. "There"—he pointed to the wall behind her—"I'll show you."

She looked over her shoulder at a large spider and shivered.

He put the sunqara on the wall near the spider. "Watch."

It didn't take the sunqara more than a couple of seconds to see the spider. It's long, sticky tongue shot out. By the time Hadlee recovered from her shudder, the sunqara had swallowed the spider.

"You see. They are very useful citizens, ones that are welcome in every house in Telquset. They keep the creepy-crawly population down, making life better for everyone."

"Why haven't I seen them before?" she asked, rubbing goose bumps from her arms.

"I expect it's due to Taya's careful housekeeping." He paused. "Now tell the truth. Wouldn't you rather have a few sunqaras around the house, instead of one full of interesting spiders? And they aren't the worst things you could have.

"Oh, how kind of you to tell me that, now I will never be able to sleep again."

"Sorry, I didn't mean to upset you," he said, with what she recognized as genuine contrition. "I'm sure Taya's housekeeping will prevent any unwanted guests from visiting you in the night."

"I can only hope. Now, why are you here?"

"I was doing some work outside your door when I heard you . . . uh . . . call for assistance. Being in the neighborhood, I thought I'd see if I could be of help."

"Well, you have. So thank you. Now, I think I'll go in."

She struggled to position her crutch and stand. His arm encircled her waist, lifting her to her feet. She returned his helpful gesture with a stony eyed rebuff.

"I'm only trying—"

"Don't." She cringed, but he kept his hold on her until she had the crutch firmly positioned. "I don't need your help." She shrugged off his arm, hoping to crush any further urge he might have to help her into the apartment.

He gave her a doubtful, apologetic look.

The apartment door opened and shut.

She turned toward the sound.

Taya strolled across the apartment and out onto the terrace.

She breathed relief and said, "If I need any more assistance, Taya can give it to me."

Fourteen

Ryder was directing the digging in the six-foot deep foundation hole for the stairs, when he lifted his face to the cool breeze and saw Taya walking purposefully in the direction of the construction site. He pulled himself out of the nearly finished foundation hole before she reached it, bowed in a gesture of respect for her, and together they moved away from the curious ears of his crew.

They stopped by the water stand. Taya handed Ryder a clay jug of water, and said quietly, "I am sure you have noticed that over the past ten days, Hadlee has gotten increasingly restless in stride with her ability to walk—and her confinement to the apartment."

"I have," Ryder said, lifting the jug to his lips.

"She is particularly restless and bored today. All she will do is walk back and forth, back and forth, from one end of the terrace to the other."

Ryder set the jug down. "At least she's walking, but you're right, I'm sure she finds her continued confinement boring, and that's the source of her restlessness."

"So what do we do?"

"Find her something to do." He frowned. "Do you have any ideas?"

"I could teach her some games, but that won't keep her occupied for very long."

"No, but it might take her mind off her confinement, at least for a little while. And there isn't much else we can do until the king decides she has recovered enough to leave her apartment and be introduced to Telquset society."

"You could ask her if she weaves or sews. Maybe she plays the flute or likes to cook. Those things would at least occupy her time."

"Good thinking." Ryder dusted the dirt from his clothes, dunked a rag into the jug of water, and ran it over his face and arms. "Let's go see what we can find out."

Pausing in the terrace doorway, he watched Hadlee pace down the terrace toward him with only the barest hint of a limp. *I was right about her height.* She stood an inch or so over six feet, in his estimation. Her lean, sleek build made him want to ask what sports she played. He bit his tongue. Asking might draw her attention to the fact he'd been looking at her too closely. He didn't want to do or say anything that would make her back away from what he hoped was starting to happen. She was beginning to tolerate his presence with a greater degree of equanimity.

In the past week, she'd even begun to say more to him than necessity dictated. He thought that was a very encouraging sign. The only mistakes he'd made so far, were holding her in his arms when the sunqara frightened her, and trying to steady her while she positioned her crutch. The look she'd given him was exactly the same one she gave the sunqara. She favored him with that look as she continued to walk in his direction.

"Getting your exercise I see," he said with a smile.

She turned her back on him, and this time, paced down the terrace without a trace of a limp. "I know Ateron doesn't want me to leave this apartment until I have fully recovered from my injuries"—she threw over her shoulder—"but I have recovered, and I'm tired of being cooped up." She turned and looked at him, gesturing at the terrace wall. "This wall is so high I can't even see the mountains. It makes me feel like a prisoner."

Ryder kept his face neutral. He'd made up his mind to tell her certain facts about Injanae, but kept putting it off. *What good will it do to frighten her at this point? Beside I don't have any credibility with her. She won't believe me, not with Ateron treating her like an honored guest.*

The king seemed determined to lavish her with attention and small gifts. Ryder looked at the heavy gold bracelet she wore—Ateron's latest gift. She hadn't wanted to accept it, but when Ateron continued to press her, she finally gave in.

"Is the king coming today?" she asked. "I haven't seen him for two days. Do you know why?"

"I've heard he is out of the city on business, and I don't know when he'll be back. If you like, Taya could help you find ways to spend your time while you wait for the king's return."

"What ways?" she asked, pacing back in his direction.

"Well do you sew or play an instrument, do you cook or like games?"

She rolled her eyes. "I'm well educated in all the domestic arts, particularly sewing, I play the piano, and games are alright . . . I suppose."

Ryder conveyed the information to Taya, who assured him she would bring cloth, so Hadlee could make something, and would teach her a few simple games.

After he told Hadlee what Taya said, he added an idea of his own. "I have a notion how you can pass some of your time—if you're interested."

She shrugged, "I'll try just about anything right now."

"Good. Just remember you said you would try anything."

She groaned, and gave the sky a longsuffering look.

He locked his jaw against a laugh and cleared his throat. "One of your biggest frustrations is your inability to communicate, right?"

"Yes!"

"Then let's play charades."

"You want me to play charades?"

"When I got here, I couldn't speak the language either. I started to learn it by playing charades, and doing pantomimes."

"Really," she said doubtfully.

"Really," he assured her.

She huffed out a breath. "Alright. How do I start?"

"With the help of your doctor." Ryder gestured to Taya who smiled encouragingly. "Why don't you tell her how you came into Injanae?"

"Couldn't I just start with simple words like eat, sleep, go away—or more to the point—let me out of here?"

"Yeah, but it wouldn't be as much fun." *Besides, what you really need is a good laugh.* He turned to explain things to Taya.

She nodded, and sat down on a stone bench behind her.

"I told her what you're going to do," he said to Hadlee.

"She won't understand." Hadlee's foot tapped frustration. "You will need to explain a few things as we go."

"Okay; so how do we play this?"

Hadlee ran a contemplative hand down her long flaxen braid, and held up a finger. She stepped into the apartment, grabbed a towel from the dining table, came back out, explained, and took her place behind Ryder.

Spreading his arms wide and holding them at shoulder height, Ryder started rumbling.

Taya put a delicate hand over her mouth.

Ryder's arms dipped and swayed as he moved slowly across the terrace with Hadlee behind him, using his ponytail to guide him. As they came around the last bench, Ryder plucked two huge leaves from the trellis vine, and headed back in Taya's direction.

Both hands were clamped over Taya's mouth now, her shoulders shaking.

When they reach the bench nearest her, Ryder moved in front of it, and Hadlee jumped on top. Ryder hit himself in the head with the leaves and began sputtering; telling Taya condors had just hit the plane. As he dropped the leaves and started to reel, Hadlee grasped the corners of the towel, threw it up over her head, and jumped lightly off the bench. The air rushed in under it, ballooning it out for a moment before she tumbled gently to the ground.

Ryder crashed into the wall and crumpled.

The dam holding back Taya's laughter cracked and burst. She let it gush out, falling onto her side. Hadlee and Ryder joined the torrent.

"That was very amusing," Ateron said, applauding as he strolled through the terrace doorway.

Taya and Ryder hastily righted themselves, their laugher dying instantly.

Hadlee took the hand Ateron offered, getting to her feet.

"It is gratifying, Ryder, to know your work is going so well that you have time to spend playing games."

"Sire, the work is on schedule, and I will go—"

"You may go after you translate for me." Ateron dismissed Taya with a word; gestured for Hadlee to be seated, waited until she was, and then talked at length to Ryder.

The king's narrative made Ryder's eyes dart to Hadlee.

Hers shot rapid-fire questions at him.

He shifted his back to Ateron before she could see his guilt. *I should have told her—whether or not she believed me—I should have told her.*

When the king stopped speaking, Ryder's eyes returned to Hadlee. "The king is very pleased you're feeling so much better," he said, and paused.

Hadlee leaned forward and pressed, "And?"

"There are some things he wants you to know about Injanae, but has put off telling you until he felt you had fully recovered from your injuries. Now that he has witnessed our charade, he feels he needn't wait any longer."

"By the look you shot me, I would say they must be very important." A wary look darkened her eyes. "So what does he want me to know?"

Ryder blew out a breath. "Over four hundred years ago when the people of a rich and prosperous community called Tel were threatened by powerful invaders—undoubtedly the Spanish—they set off in search of a new home. They eluded their enemies, pleading with their god to lead them to a place beyond the reach of those who threatened them."

"Were they Incans?"

"Incan dissenters and outlaws—I think. Anyway, the Moon Goddess, Ansuetra, heard their prayers and brought them into the valley of Injanae."

"The belief in a moon goddess does fit with the Incan's, but they called her Mama Quilla or Mama Kilya."

"Whatever her name, to this day, the people of Injanae—who were the people of Tel—worship, and believe, Ansuetra blesses and protects them."

"So they're moon worshipers."

"Yeah."

"How does she—supposedly—bless and protect them?"

"Over the centuries, travelers, like us, have found their way into the valley. That part I know is true. From what I've seen, at least some of the Conquistadors made it here."

"What things?"

"The buildings, many of them have a Spanish flavor, especially the upper stories. The lower levels don't have mortar between the stones, but the upper ones do, and many of the buildings have tiled roofs. The furniture too, shows some hints of Spanish design—just look around your apartment. Then there's the fact they read and write. Many of their words have both Incan and Spanish influences. Even their clothes have some old Spanish flare."

"So how often do they get visitors from outside the valley now?"

"According to a friend of mine, no one remembers outsiders coming here in their life time—except for me."

"No one?"

"No one," Ryder echoed, watching her fingers grip the edge of the bench. "Still, the people of Injanae consider the coming of outsiders as a blessing from Ansuetra. She decreed that anyone she brought into Injanae was to be welcomed and accepted," he said, nearly gagging on that bitter irony.

Her grip on the bench relaxed. "They have certainly treated me well."

"Yeah, except the coming of outsiders also brought the threat of the valley's exposure to enemies from the outside world. To prevent that, Ansuetra closed up the way the people of Injanae came into the valley."

Alarm disturbed Hadlee's placid expression, and she demanded, "Why is the king giving me this history lesson?"

"To help you understand that to protect the people of Injanae, Ansuetra decreed that no outsider who found their way in—would be allowed to leave."

Hadlee sprang to her feet. "Are you saying I'm not going to be allowed to leave?" She took a step toward him. "And that no message was ever sent?" Fear like shrapnel flew from her eyes. *"Is that why you're still here?"*

"Pilot—stay calm. We can discuss this after the king leaves. Please, believe me. We *are* going to get out of here." His burnished-gold eyes battled against the disbelief and fear in her silver-blue ones.

She broke the stare and sat down.

Ryder turned to the king. "As you can see she's very upset by this news. She needs time to reflect, and accept her circumstances."

"Then we will leave her to her reflections. Tomorrow you will start teaching her our language."

Given no choice, Ryder was forced to follow the king out of Hadlee's apartment. The desperate need he felt to stay with her, to soften this all too familiar blow, tore at him.

As soon as he shut the door, Ateron demanded a progress report on the stairs. He wrenched his mind from Hadlee, explained the need for nails before the stair's construction could begin, and mentally crossed his fingers. "I know an excellent metal smith, named Kytan, who can make quality nails. With your permission, I would like to hire him."

"There is no need, Idon—"Ateron stopped, tapping his pursed lips. "You may go see your metal smith tomorrow afternoon, have him make some samples and bring them for my inspection."

That's why Ateron hasn't let me out of this apartment. I'm not his guest—I'm his prisoner!

Hadlee's heart pumped fear, like an infection, through her until she could feel its sting behind her eyes, taste its fetid flavor, feel its disabling paralysis.

"We *are* going to get out of here." Ryder's words whirled endlessly in her head as the only remedy available to fight her fear. She tried to find hope in his words, but found no comfort.

It's so horribly cruel that I should find Ryder Garrison in this prison, and be compelled to seek his help to escape it. That bitter pill was almost worse than the fear. She gagged it down, knowing she had no other choice, but the noxious taste of fear returned with the question that repeated itself relentlessly. *If he knows how to leave, what is he still doing here?*

She paced out the remainder of the day and a long sleepless night on the terrace, knowing it was now her only link to the outside world. The comfort of being able to see the sky—even a small piece of it—was necessary to her sanity. The sky had always been her escape, her freedom.

As the sky above the terrace began to lighten, she stopped pacing, unlatched the gold bracelet from her wrist, and flung it over the high terrace wall. *Fool's gold—just like Ateron's promises.* That ugly reality fed the voracious fear she couldn't find the means to control.

When she finally sought her bed, the longed for amnesia of sleep eluded her.

Fifteen

Hadlee's reaction to Ateron's revelation kept Ryder awake all night. Giving up the effort to try and sleep, he rose early, made short work of his breakfast, and took the five flights of stairs up to the king's private level three at a time, anxious to see how she was doing.

Lul, who was standing guard outside Hadlee's door, told him Taya had gone out. He knocked to announce his entrance and went into the apartment. Not finding Hadlee in the living room, he poked his head out the terrace door.

Hadlee was six feet up the trellis.

He charged down the terrace. "Stop!"

She flinched like a criminal caught committing a crime, just as she firmly grabbed the vine above her head and pulled. It came away from the wall, sending her flailing backwards off the trellis.

She yelped, and he grunted when her elbow collided with his jaw as he caught her. He immediately dropped her onto her feet. "What do you think you're doing?"

The palm of her hand jerked up. She drew it back, hesitated, and dropped it, letting her eyes deliver the intended slap. "Escaping! And it's your fault I fell!"

Rubbing the welt forming on his jaw, he shot back, "The top six feet of that vine isn't trellised. If I hadn't come in when I did, you would have broken your neck."

"That would be preferable to being held prisoner here for the rest of my life! It's undoubtedly the best place for you to spend the rest of yours, but I am going to find a way out—right now!"

"Do you really think I've spent the last year and a half of my life in this place by *choice*?"

His guttural response pushed her back a step. "If you're trying to convince me Ateron is holding you against your will"—she looked him up and down—"I don't believe it."

He lifted his eyes to heaven and shook his head. *Why does everyone assume my size makes me invincible?* Life had taught him otherwise and kept humbling him with ongoing lessons.

He straddled a bench and sat, still rubbing the welt turning red on his jaw. "Do you want to know why I am still here after nearly two years?"

"Yes I do," she said, dropping guardedly on the other end of the bench.

"Mostly because I don't remember how I came into Injanae."

"You don't . . . *remember* how you got here?"

"No. What I do remember is looking through my binoculars from the top of Farlana. The next thing I remember is waking up with a terrible headache, and a gash on my head." He pointed to the small white scar near his hairline. "I was in the home of Chancellor Cartu. Like you, I was treated with great kindness."

"That little toad treated you with kindness?"

"Yeah. His wife, Renla, took care of me while I recovered from a concussion that left me without any memory of how I came into Injanae. Cartu said I was found lying in the Telquset Falls Park near the cliff face."

"Don't tell me you jumped over the falls into Telquset."

"That's not possible."

"Then, how?"

"I was told there was a mild earthquake that day. The quake probably knocked me off the cliff face while I was climbing down."

"Do you really believe you climbed into Injanae?"

He shrugged, "I can't be absolutely sure, because no one saw me climb in, but I'm almost positive I did."

"Don't you think it's odd that no one saw you? You couldn't climb into Telquset unnoticed. You would be like a giant spider on the wall getting bigger as you came down."

"True, so maybe I didn't climb down into the city, but I must have been here when the quake hit. Maybe I got clobbered by a piece of the cliff face that broke away during the quake."

"Alright, but what makes you *almost* positive you climbed into Injanae?"

He massaged his jaw. "The grand tour I went on."

"Tell me."

"After I recovered, I was introduced to the cream of Telquset society, even the king and queen. They all made it their business to entertain me, showing me all the sights of the city. I enjoyed myself for a week before asking about the way to leave. They told me—as far as they knew—there was no way out of the valley because long ago the Moon Goddess closed up the way they came in. Of course that made them very anxious to know how I got in."

Hadlee's hands bracketed her hips. "You knew Ateron had no intention of letting me leave that very first day, didn't you?"

"Pilot, I really hoped when Ateron said he would send a message that it was true. When they told me the moon goddess story, I thought it was to keep me from looking for the way out—not because there wasn't one. These people are obsessed with the idea that Injanae is a sacred place, one that protects them from the evils of the world. To keep the world from finding them they can't let anyone who finds their way in—out. But I've never been able to buy the story that there is no way out, and no one's ever left. It only makes sense that if people can get into Injanae, they can get out."

"Not if they parachute in," she said bitterly.

"No," he said, still working his jaw. "But I wasn't discouraged by all the talk of not being able to leave. I felt sure—given time—I could find the way out, and even if I couldn't find their way out, I could always climb out."

"Could you really do that?"

"Yeah—given the right equipment. I'm an expert technical climber, and with that in mind, I asked to tour the valley. Over about two weeks' time, Cartu took me on trips to see the south and west sides of Injanae. The last tour I went on was to the northwestern end of the valley. On that trip, I even stayed in the king's hunting lodge."

Hadlee's eyes lit. "I think that's where I was, until the night before I met you." She sat forward. "It's a large stone building in the woods with a river running by it—right?"

"Yeah. We stayed there overnight and did some fishing the next morning in the river. I talked Cartu into fishing the river all the way to the where it leaves the valley. I thought there might be a way out there."

"Is there?"

"No. It just disappears into the bottom of the cliff. You know, if I believed in pagan deities, I would have to say Ansuetra did a great job in protecting the inhabitants of Injanae from anyone who wants to come or go from this valley."

"So you didn't find the way out on your grand tour?"

"No."

"And that makes you believe you climbed in and that climbing is the only way out," she said, twisting the end of her long braid.

"As far as I can tell . . . it is."

That daunting pronouncement hung in the air between them as a brilliant yellow butterfly fringed in a delicate pink edging, floated over the terrace wall and landed on the trellis. Hadlee released her braid and reached a finger out to touch its bright wings. It took flight before she could, gracefully soaring into the sky. She watched its ascent with a yearning face that Ryder knew mirrored his own.

When it disappeared, she turned her attention back to him. "If climbing really is the only way out, and you have that ability, then what are you still doing here?"

He hesitated, still working his sore jaw and gathering his nerve. "When we finished the northwestern tour and got back to Cartu's house, I stayed in the stables and talked with the stable hands about the llamas. I wanted to know more about them. They're almost twice as large as any I've seen outside this valley. They're so large the men here can ride them. Anyway, I spent about thirty minutes in the stables, before I went into the house and up to my room. I . . . uh . . . opened the door . . ."

"And?"

Heat flared across the back of his neck. "Renla was lying on my bed. She was bruised and bloody, and . . . her clothes were scattered all over the floor."

Hadlee flinched backward.

The heat he felt climbing his neck, stormed his face. "At first, I was so shocked, I couldn't move, but I had to do something, so—I went to the bed, covered her, and took hold of her wrist to look for a pulse."

"Was she dead?"

"No, but just then, Cartu came in. He started yelling, 'What have you done to my wife!' I tried to explain that I'd just found her, but my language skills were still pretty basic and he wouldn't listen. He drew that sword he always wears and pressed the blade to my chest. Several of his men came running in. He told them I had beaten and raped his wife. Before I could take another breath, there were half a dozen swords pressed into my gut." Ryder jumped to his feet, and walked up and down the terrace.

"It's Joseph in Egypt," Hadlee said, hugging her knees.

"Yeah, real Old Testament, but I wasn't as smart as Joseph. I should never have gone into that room when I saw her. I should have run as far and fast as I could. Except . . . I couldn't just leave her like that—not knowing if she was alive or dead. I felt compelled to do *something* to help."

"Well of course you did." Hadlee frowned and muttered, "What Boy Scout wouldn't."

His eyes hardened, and he nodded agreement. "Yeah, and I was dumbfounded by Cartu's accusation, but with several swords pressed into my belly and nowhere to run, there wasn't much I could do. Cartu simply tied my hands, put a rope around my neck, and hauled me off to face the king's justice."

"What did Ateron say?"

"I didn't see him. I was chained hand and foot, and thrown in the dungeon." He grimaced. "It sounds so medieval, but the hole they tossed me in was as primitive a place as you can imagine."

She hunched her shoulders and shivered. "How long were you in the dungeon?"

He dropped his hand from his jaw and took his seat again. "I don't know. When I was finally hauled out, Ateron told me because of the severity of my crime, I was sentenced to life as a slave. I was sold to the owner of a copper mine on the north side of the valley."

"But what about Renla, why didn't she come forward and tell Ateron what really happened?"

"She died of her injuries. I can't prove it, but I think Cartu found her in my room and beat her to death. She'd been making inappropriate overtures to me, and I was careful not to be alone with her. She set a trap for me and caught Cartu. To this day, I think he hates me for something I didn't do. I never encouraged Renla—*never*."

Injustice choked him. He glanced at Hadlee, and shame landed him a sucker punch. He was the last man on earth who had the right to complain about life's injustices. He dropped his head and rubbed the back of his neck.

"So you were supposed to spend the rest of your life in the mine?"

"Yeah. Life slaves go into the mine and never come back out."

"That's why you didn't know the date, isn't it?"

"Yeah."

"Didn't you ever try to escape?"

"I was taken into the mine blind folded. By the time it was removed, I had no idea where I was. My legs were shackled, and my movements in the mine were restricted and carefully monitored by whip wielding, sword toting guards."

She leaned forward. "If you were never supposed to come out of the mine, how did you get out after less than a year?"

He related the events leading to his change of ownership. "When I came out of the mine, it took weeks to get used to being in the light of day. I wore a blindfold over my eyes until they could tolerate the light. I got quite a sunburn the first month I worked in the stone quarry, but it was . . . nothing short of heaven to be out in the open again."

"Now, you know why I was climbing the trellis."

"I really do understand, except that's not going to help you get out of here. It's a sheer drop to the ground, and you're nearly five stories up."

She shrugged. "So, you went to work in the quarry. Why didn't you try to escape then?"

"I was working on it, but by then I knew finding a good escape route would take time, and the escape itself would take careful planning. That was nearly impossible to do with Daelo working me sixteen hours a day, and chaining me into my hut at night."

He grinned.

"What?"

"A couple of weeks before Ateron bought me. I managed to get hold of, and hide, a small finishing chisel. I used it to pick the locks on my shackles. I spent several nights roaming the base of the cliff on the south side of the quarry, looking for a good place to climb out."

"Did you find one?"

"Maybe, but I need a closer, daylight look, before I can be sure."

"So, it's not a place you saw on your tour."

"No, the northeastern side of Injanae was supposed to be the next stop on my tour agenda, but I never got that far, until I became a quarry slave."

She sighed, and stretched out her long legs. Turbulent thoughts troubled her face. "So how long have you been Ateron's slave?"

"I was brought to the palace just a few days before we . . . ah . . . met." The memory of that meeting reared its head like a deadly hooded cobra. Fearing it would strike, Ryder hurried on. "The king sent his goons in the middle of the night to get me. They took me straight to Ateron, who told me he had a job for me to do."

"Interpreting for me?"

"No. I didn't even know about you then. Ateron told me he bought me for my engineering skills." He lifted his arm in a sweeping wave. "My first project was to wall up this terrace."

"*You* are the one who closed me in?"

"I didn't know at the time why I was doing it," he said, explaining Cartu's reprimand and threat. "Being an *obedient* palace slave gives me a little freedom, something I need to continue working on a way out."

"Are you allowed to leave the palace unescorted?"

"Only with permission, and if it involves the construction projects I'm working on."

Hadlee's look of envy lifted his brows him.

"At least you have something to do to occupy your time," she said.

"You have something to do now too."

"What?"

"Ateron wants me to start teaching you Injanae."

The apartment door opened.

Taya came in with a cheery good morning. They returned her greeting as she crossed the apartment, plunked a heavy tray of food down on the table and started clattering through dishes in a tall leaf-patterned cupboard.

Ryder refocused on Hadlee. She lifted her chin. "You can tell Ateron I'm not going to learn the language."

"Aren't you?"

"No." She stood. "He may be able to keep me prisoner, but I won't cooperate with him."

"Are you sure he can't *force* your cooperation?" The intentional threat in his voice, made her stare at him, he slowly shifted his eyes to Taya, setting plates on the table.

She fell back onto the bench. "He wouldn't! Would he?"

"Your affection for Taya is all the ammunition he needs. And your attachment to her has grown, hasn't it?"

She nodded mutely, despair claiming her face.

Taya came out the terrace door, smiled, and invited them in to eat. Her smile disappeared as her eyes flew from Hadlee to Ryder.

"What would he do to her, Garrison?"

It hadn't escape Ryder's notice, that she never addressed him by his given name. "I don't know for sure, and it won't make either of us feel any better if I speculate. I just know he will use your affection for her against you, to get what he wants."

"Then that makes me . . . as much a slave as you are."

The truth of that fell on Ryder with the full weight of his own life sentence, leaving him speechless. He couldn't refute what she'd said.

Taya put a gentle hand on Hadlee's arm, and asked Ryder what was wrong.

"She's very upset about being held prisoner, Taya. Try to find something to divert her if you can. I wish I could stay, but I have to go to work."

He stood, still searching for the words to comfort Hadlee. The fear of an animal caught in a snare radiated from her. It ripped through his heart, dropping him to his knees. He grasped her shoulders.

She shuddered.

"Don't lose hope, Pilot. Pray for us to find a way out of Injanae. I promise you—even if it takes my life—I *will* get you out of here."

Glacial, Silver-blue eyes, bore into his. "I'm going to hold you to that promise, Garrison."

The afternoon was sliding toward evening when Ryder ducked through the doorway of Kytan's shop.

With a flash of dimples, Kytan waved him to a seat, and went back to waiting on his customers. Several minutes went by before the last customer left, and he was free to talk.

"Business is good, I see," Ryder said.

"It is, and I have even attracted some of the nobility's attention. I have commissions to make jewelry for two noble patrons."

Ryder grinned. "Then you may not have time for Ateron's request."

Kytan's dark eyes widened. "The king wants me to make something for him? Do you know what that will do for my business?"

"I hope it will make you the most sought after medal smith in Telquset. Maybe it will even make you rich enough to buy me," Ryder said wistfully, then quickly added, "but it's not what you think. The King's not in the market for a new crown. He wants nails, and lots of them."

"Nails? What for?"

Explaining Ateron's projects for the coming Lunar Celebration, Ryder asked for a slate, and drew the nails, and the kind of hammers he wanted. "You will need to make a hammer and some nails for Ateron's approval."

Kytan looked over Ryder's designs, asked questions, made a few notations, and assured Ryder he could do the job. After all the details were worked out, he leaned back in his chair. "With everything Ateron has you doing; do you still have time to think about getting out of Injanae?"

"I never stop thinking about that. Waking—sleeping—working; I'm always thinking about it."

"I think about it too. I want to leave here, and be baptized. I want to see all the wonderful things you told me about, like cars, and trains, and movies." Kytan's dimples danced. "If the king will hire me to make nails, my purse should allow us to start purchasing supplies for our escape."

The door of the shop opened, several people entered.

"You better get back to your customers. We can talk about the supplies we need when the samples are ready."

"I will have them finished for your inspection in a couple of days," Kytan said as Ryder ducked back out the door.

Sixteen

Hadlee spent another sleepless night, pacing the terrace. She was still at it when Taya walked out onto the terrace in the pre-dawn light. Taya's worried face brought her to a halt.

"Bath?" Taya asked in English. It was one of a growing number of English words Ryder was teaching her.

It made Hadlee smile. She nodded, and Taya went to arrange the early morning bath. Hadlee knew it would take at least thirty minutes for the guards to bring the gallons of hot water a bath required. She resumed her restless pacing. *Maybe a bath will sooth not only my body, but also my mind—at least enough to finally allow me to sleep.*

She stayed in the bathtub until the water began to cool. Taya called good-bye to her in English, from beyond the curtained bedchamber, and left for—what Hadlee now knew were—her usual morning errands.

With her wet hair wrapped in a turban, Hadlee dried off, and dressed. She pushed aside the heavy bedchamber curtain, descended the stairs, and walked without a glance passed the breakfast of hot bread and fresh fruit Taya left laid out for her on the dining table. Lying back in a mound of big pillows in the living room, she pulled the turban from her head, tossed it aside, and fanned her long hair out like the tail feathers of a peacock to dry.

The bath hadn't accomplished all she'd hoped it would. Although it had loosened the tension in her muscles, it hadn't loosened the hold of the dark thoughts that had consumed her mind all night and assailed her even now—giving her no quarter.

A slave without choices, that's what my life comes down to. Since the day Garrison killed Mama, I've been a slave to other people's choices. I wouldn't even be in Injanae if I hadn't been enslaved by Garrison's criminal choices.

She rolled her face into the pillow and gave into the tears she'd fought all night. Her heart insisted Ryder was the source of all the bad things that had happened in her life. As hard as she'd tried over the years to dismiss that feeling—and at times thought she had—it always seemed to resurface.

Needing his help now, tormented her. She pounded her fist into the cushion, *Why him of all people? Why?* The dark emotions meeting him again brought to the surface, consumed her—becoming her masters.

The urgent need to reassure and give Hadlee hope, brought Ryder to her door for his morning visit just as the city belfry chimed eight. He knocked, and entered.

"You look comfortable," he said to her averted face, admiring her fanned out hair. "But it doesn't look like you've eaten anything." He surveyed her untouched breakfast and savored the aroma of the bread. When she didn't answer him, he walked over to her and looked down at her with concern. "Are you feeling alright?"

"Tell me"—she turned her head, and looked up at him with teary eyes—"how did *you* feel the day you were taken into the copper mine; knowing you would never come out again. Was it worse than the day you were put in prison for killing my mother?"

The question hit him like an unfair blow below the belt.

She tilted her head in a considering way. "Of course it must have been worse. After all, you weren't sentenced to life in prison for killing my mother were you? Well, I feel like that!"

His heart dropped into the dungeon. His throat closed. This moment had been barreling at him since he climbed Farlana, and still, he was completely unprepared for it. He wanted, needed, more time to get to know her—to let her know him. The grief that vibrated in her voice told him, his time was up.

He sank onto a gilded bench next to her, desperately searching for the strength he needed to pull his courage out of the dungeon and force his voice to work despite his closed throat. "I'm truly sorry you are in this situation. Please, believe me, I—"

"Tell me, *Ryder*—since I've always wondered—how did you get your name. It really suits you."

"You . . . want to know how I got my name?"

"Yes, it's not every day you meet a guy named Ryder, especially one like *you*."

"My father was one of the Rough Riders. He went up Kettle Hill with Teddy Roosevelt. He was wounded and decorated for his bravery."

"You must be very proud of him, and it makes a kind of sense—you know." She plucked at a long damp strand of hair. "A Rough Rider fathering a Death Ryder."

He flinched.

She peered up at him. "I've always thought of you as Death Ryder. I'm sure that sounds childish"—she shrugged—"but then, that's what I was when you killed my mother."

Ryder's gut twisted. He willed himself to look into the pain-wracked eyes of his dragon. "You have every right to hate me. My irresponsible—"

The word "irresponsible" brought a look of utter contempt to her face and stained his with shame. He grappled with it, forcing himself look at her squarely and resolved not to minimize his accountability.

"My *criminal* actions robbed you of your mother. I know the prison time I served for her death must seem woefully inadequate to you. I will never be able to tell you how eternally sorry I am for what I did. Every day I'm sorry for it. I know there's no restitution I can make, and it weighs on my soul. I—"

"You really don't know how much you took from me, do you? Tell me, who started the letters between you and my father?"

"Your father did," he said, grateful for a chance to praise her father. "His forgiveness changed me. With his help, I sought repentance and through the Atonement found forgiveness."

"Yes, I know—I found your letters," she spat the words out like something vile from her mouth.

He balked. "Your father let you read my letters?" He'd assumed their letters were confidential. During his struggle for forgiveness, he'd poured his heart out in them, and then with all his dreams, once he was released from prison.

"No, he didn't. I didn't know about your letters or my father's *close relationship with you*, until after Dad—died."

He stared at her in disbelief. "Your father's . . . dead?

The look on her face told him it was true.

"I . . . didn't know. I wondered why my last letters . . . came back." He blinked back tears. "I'm . . . so sorry. Your father was my hero. He was the most kind and loving man I have ever known."

"Well, isn't it nice—that at least one of us knew him?"

Ryder shook his head, trying to clear it. James MacLean's death was a crushing blow. He couldn't seem to grasp what she was saying. "Surely you felt—"

"Abandoned."

"What?"

She sat up, pulled her heavy tresses over her shoulder, separated them into three even parts, and began weaving her damp hair into one thick rope. "I really need to ask Taya for some scissors, it would be better to cut my hair off since I'm staying here for the rest of my life. It's just too hard to wash and dry it in this primitive place."

"No!" The word burst from him without consent. Her hair was so spectacular, so different from the popular cap like crops of the day, falling in silvery waves to her waist.

She gave him a scathing stare.

He dropped his eyes, focusing on her flying fingers. They worked the braid, crossing one part over another, pulling it tight, and then repeated the process. The acceleration of her fingers seemed to mark the pace of her growing hostility as she braided her way down to the end.

"After you killed Mama, I was sent to Salt Lake to stay with Aunt Ann's family. She's Mama's older sister. I was only allowed to come home the day of Mama's funeral. Then I was taken back to Salt Lake. My father decided not to keep me. He gave me to my aunt. I cried myself to sleep for months. For a year, I wrote him every day. When he called, I begged to come home, but he told me my aunt's house was now my home. So forgive me, if I don't *know* how kind, loving, and heroic my father was—he abandoned me!"

Ryder's face was as gray as the burnt out logs laying on the edges of the fire pit. "I didn't know he—he never told me."

"Oh, don't imagine my aunt and uncle were unkind to me. With a houseful of sons, they were happy to have me become *their* daughter. Except, they treated me like a china doll—one that might break at any moment. Enduring their pity was . . . awful, and accepting their love—impossible, when all I wanted—"

Her eyes overflowed. She brushed at them impatiently, took a breath, closed her eyes, took another breath, and slowly opened them. The action seemed to compose her.

Battling to hold on to his own rapidly diminishing control, Ryder forced his own breathing to slow, dropped his eyes from her tragic face and followed her hand as she picked up a leather tie off the pillow next to her, wrapped it around the end of her finished braid, jerked it hard, and tied it tightly. *That's just what she'd like to do to my throat,* he thought, unable to swallow.

She flipped the finished braid behind her back. "All I wanted was to go home to my dad. I prayed every night that he would come and get me. Instead, there were infrequent visits from him that grew further, and further apart."

The sharp spurs of conscience gouged him, thinking of the wonderful relationship he'd developed with her father through countless letters.

"The last time I saw him, he came to tell me he'd given up his job as a professor, and had accepted an offer to work on a dig here in Peru. The distance he put between us didn't lessen my prayers or diminish my faith that one day we would again be a family. With that hope, I went to college determined to become an archeologist. In my heart, I truly believed he would want me if I could understand his passion and work with him." Her chin quivered. "He died here of some strange fever, just after my second year of college."

Her words were indefensible punches raining down on him. "I'm so sorry—so sorry," he said, knowing how pathetically inadequate the words were.

She leaned toward him. "Please, spare me your pity."

The herbal scent of her hair invaded him, becoming a memory he would always associate with her.

"Being my parent's only heir, I inherited our home in Provo. I went back to clean it out and sell it. I spent a week going through the lives of my parents. Sorting through their earthly possessions taught me how little I knew them and now couldn't, especially my dad. When I found your letters in the back of Dad's desk, I debated for days whether to read them or burn them. I—"

The city belfry's booming chimes silenced her.

Ryder welcomed the reprieve. His emotional control was almost gone. He drew on his last reserves of courage. *I can't escape what justice demands. I have to know and feel everything she's suffered—because of what I did.*

The final reverberating chime of the clock died away.

Her mouth trembled. "I made the wrong choice. I burned your letters *after* I read a few of them, and learned how close you and my father were. Then I packed my bags and took a train to California. I decided to leave everything that reminded me of my father behind—including my faith."

Her grief-stricken eyes convicted him. He dropped his head and rubbed his neck. *No more, please!* The urge to run was strong, but his conscience forced him to keep his seat.

"You robbed me of every precious thing in my life; my childhood, my faith, and my whole family—my mother—my father—and our baby."

His head snapped up. "What baby?"

"You really don't know, do you?"

"What baby?" He was on his feet.

She leaped to hers, standing toe to toe with him, glaring up at him, tears coursing down her face from the terrible wounds he knew he'd inflicted—wounds that had never healed.

"Did you ever stop to wonder why we were outside of that soda fountain? We were celebrating. Mama had just told me about the baby." She choked on a sob, her eyes demolishing him. "She had three miscarriages after I was born, and my parents thought they weren't going to be able to have more children, because she couldn't carry them passed the first two months. We were going home to make a special dinner and tell Dad the news. Mama was four months pregnant!"

Her words raked his soul, just as her fingers had raked his face, twelve years ago. His hand clutched his cheek. He backed away from the dragon's devouring fire and slammed out the apartment door.

Seventeen

Shaking with the force of her unrelenting grief, Hadlee collapsed into the pile of cushions after Ryder bolted from the apartment. She sobbed with all the grief her heart held until Taya came in and found her.

For as long as she could remember, she'd believed confronting Ryder Garrison with all his crimes would somehow heal her wounded heart. At the very least, she hoped to wound him and thereby ease her continuing need for justice. *He deserves it—he does. Why should he be free of the suffering I will never escape? After all, he's the one that caused it, and spending a few years in prison can't begin to make up for all he took from me.*

As Taya pulled her from the cushions and coaxed her up the stairs to her bedchamber, reality's brute frankness scorned her. Confronting Ryder hadn't made any difference. The anguish contorting his face, just before he bolted, should have brought her some satisfaction—it didn't. *Why don't I feel better?*

She was still crying and shaking when Taya drew up the covers, sat on the bed, and held her hand, murmuring words she couldn't understand.

Taya did her best to comfort Hadlee. She hummed a soothing lullaby, and lightly massaged Hadlee's temples. Knowing the exhaustion of tears would subdue Hadlee, Taya patiently worked and waited. Finally Hadlee quieted. Her breathing became relaxed and even. Taya let her humming die away, and lifted her hands from Hadlee's temples. Once she was sure Hadlee was asleep, she went to find Ryder.

After an hour of searching for him, worry drove her to the king.

Ateron's private meeting with Darvoe, the royal high priest of Ansuetra, had gone just as planned. He stood. "Please accept my congratulations on the return of your powers by the council. I won't challenge their decision, so there will be no need for the councils' further interference."

Darvoe rose, accepting Ateron's congratulation with a skeptical smile. "Only through the power of my office, can Ansuetra be appeased. I am relieved you understand and support that."

"Of course," Ateron said, walking with Darvoe to the door of his private judgment chamber. "And thank you for honoring me by accepting my invitation to hold the Lunar Celebration in my rooftop garden. I am sure the lunar ritual will appease Ansuetra, prove our united devotion to her, and the trembling of the earth will cease."

"The sacred lunar rites will certainly dispel the fears of the people—ensuring their confidence in both of us will grow." Darvoe's pitted face mirrored Ateron's ingratiating smile. "We will need to meet again as the time draws near to discuss your part in the ritual."

"Whenever you wish," Ateron said, and inclined his head in a gesture of respect as he closed the door behind the priest. He flopped down on his couch and shared Cartu's cunning grin. "When all my plans have come to pass, I will hold Darvoe's priestly scepter and give you the pick of his concubines—if you like."

"I have no desire for Darvoe's leftovers. You know what I want."

"Yes, yes and things are moving along to that end, are they not?"

A knock fell on the door.

Cartu hastened to open it.

Taya bowed. "Sire do you know where I can find Ryder? Hadlee is very upset and I don't know what to do for her."

"I am sure he is working either on the roof, or the stairs."

"Excuse me, Sire, but I have looked."

"Cartu, have Pel locate Ryder," Ateron said with an unconcerned wave of his hand. "I want to know as soon as possible the source of Hadlee's distress."

Eighteen

Blind to everything around him, Ryder fled. He didn't hear the roar of the falls, or pause to look at them. He passed unchallenged through the city gates. The token he still wore clipped to his collar from the previous day's visit to Kytan gave him passage. He'd meant to return it to Huld this morning, but in his anxiety to see Hadlee, he'd forgotten. Now it was his passport to go wherever he wished.

He briskly strode down the road in the direction of the stone quarry, desperately needing to be alone, in a place he couldn't be found, before the dragon incinerated him. Before he touched Hadlee's agony, and grief, and faced his responsibility—for all of it. In a few minutes, the people, vehicles, and animals on the road thinned out. He picked up his pace, jogging, and then running full tilt, pushing himself as fast as his long legs and hard muscles would let him.

Miles went by before he noticed his tunic was saturated with sweat. He veered into the forest at a dead run, heading for the lake. Branches of trees and bushes slapped and scratched him. The wounds they inflicted went unnoticed. Reaching the lake, he stopped only long enough to remove his belt, kick off his short boots, and peel off his clinging tunic, before he dove into the water.

The lake was as cold as Hadlee's eyes, as wide as her suffering, and as deep as her grief. *If I sink to the bottom before I make it to the other side, at least she will have some justice.* He tore his mind from that temptation, and focused on each stroke, each kick, each breath, pushing himself hard.

The torrent of pain building inside him couldn't be denied much longer. He struggled to hold on for the last quarter mile. Near exhaustion, his feet found the bottom of the lake. He hauled himself out of the water, stumbled into the trees, and collapsed on the mossy ground.

The woodland creatures were startled into silence by a primeval cry. Ryder's sobs came in bone racking shudders. Finally, he understood the enormity and full fury of his dragon. The pain was so intense he was tempted to escape it. He could do it too, had done in the past. He could retreat into his mind. His memories, so complete and vivid, could take him out of the present.

He wrenched his mind away from that escape. *I deserve to feel all Hadlee's suffering and grief.* The extent of Hadlee's losses overwhelmed him. He hadn't known them, so no justice had been exacted from him for them. He opened his soul, owning all of them, suffering a depth of anguish and sorrow he'd never known, *but Hadlee has,* his soul cried.

Being forgiven by the Lord and James McLean hadn't eradicated the consequences of his actions, and he'd never truly considered the extent of them. *That's what the dragon is; the consequences Hadlee has, and always will, live with. That's why her eyes have never stopped accusing me.* Facing the depth of grief in her eyes over all her losses was more terrible than anything he'd ever imagined.

In his mind, he watched grief spill down her face as she told him about the baby. *Why wasn't I told about the baby?*

Taking one life had devastated him. Now, to know Hadlee's mother was carrying a longed for child, put him in hell. For what felt like eternity, he was crushed by the weight of his responsibility for that crime, before another terrible truth intruded.

Not only did the baby lose its life, but in a very real way, Hadlee lost hers too. He'd gone home like the prodigal son, after serving only a few years of his sentence, to a loving family who helped him fulfill his dreams. Hadlee—on the other hand—had never gone home. For the past twelve years, she'd lived in a prison he'd made for her.

"Why James, why did you send her away? Why did you spend more time trying to help me than your own daughter?" he shouted the unanswerable questions, splitting his knuckles against the trunk of a tree.

In that moment, he hated himself for never finding the courage to ask James about Hadlee, admitting his desire to know about her had often pricked his conscience. He searched his heart. *If I had asked James, would it have made any difference in her life?* That unanswerable question tore through his soul with brutal condemnation.

Everything he'd robbed her of overwhelmed him, bringing intense, unrelenting agony. In the long hours that followed, the final cost of his actions came to torment him. He'd cost Hadlee her faith. The only thing that could truly help her bear her grief, cope with her terrible losses, and overcome them.

By mid-afternoon, the search for Ryder widened, with most of the King's bodyguards scouring the city for him. Searching house-to-house and stopping at each shop, the guards eventually came to Kytan's shop.

He couldn't disguise his concern when he learned Ryder was missing. He admitted he knew Ryder, but truthfully stated he hadn't seen him since yesterday. After the guards left, Kytan closed his shop and trailed the guards as they continued scouring the city for Ryder.

Early in the evening, the guards learned Ryder had gone through the city gates that morning with the proper token attached to his slave collar—allowing him passage—and had taken the road toward the quarry. When Pel reported this to the king, Ateron sent a contingency of guards after his errant slave, confiding to Cartu, "Ryder tries my patience too far. I can't allow him to think he is indispensable to me."

Cartu inclined his head. "If you will allow me to instruct him, I am sure I can bring him to an understanding of his worth."

"Yes." Ateron's eyes narrowed. "Inform me as soon as he is found." He rose from the comfort of his couch and stretched. "Won't it be nice, when we can dispense with the services of so troublesome a slave?"

Cartu gave Ateron a gargoyle smile. "It will give me great pleasure to rid you of him, whenever you wish."

The day was gone before Ryder's emotions were spent. They left him desolate and empty. He lay on the muddy ground, unable to move or think, not wanting to feel.

The sun disappeared behind Farlana. He shivered in the cool of the evening, knowing he had to confess his crimes to the Lord. Beaten by shame and guilt, he pulled himself into the position of total submission he'd learned so well as a slave. His pain returned, and his heart hurt with an intensity that made him shake.

He'd willingly sought to do battle with the dragon that continually tormented him, and, incredibly, the Lord brought Hadlee to Injanae so he could. Now the stark understanding that he couldn't slay the dragon by simply asking for Hadlee's forgiveness assaulted him. The consequences of his actions had grown into a dragon of monstrous proportions. One, he realized, Hadlee had been doing battle with for as long as he had.

He knew he needed the Lord's help to slay the monster he'd created, but feelings of unworthiness battered him. Hours passed while he wrestled with that nemesis, feeling he didn't deserve heaven's help, *but Hadlee does,* his heart insisted. Holding on to that conviction he prayed.

"I know I deserve the pain and guilt I feel, but Hadlee doesn't deserve to continue living with the consequences of my actions. All her losses can be laid at my door. Please tell me what I can do to begin to make up for all I've cost her."

His soul longed to find a way to make restitution, but he knew his crimes were irrevocable. "If the only thing I can do is get her out of Injanae, help me find the way to do that, but even more than escaping this valley, she needs to heal and find peace. I want to help her, but how can I, when I am the cause of all her suffering?"

The night's darkness deepened, he shook with cold, but stayed on his cramped and aching knees, his face in a growing mud puddle made by his tears. In the blackness of his despair, he confessed his willingness to do anything to help Hadlee overcome the losses and grief he'd brought into her life.

An icy shudder crawled over him.

"I don't care what it costs. I will pay any price to give Hadlee back her life, her choices, her freedom, and her peace. Please show me what to do."

The moon rose in the east and set over the top of Farlana without notice. He prayed with a depth and intensity he'd never felt before, knowing, unless Hadlee found peace, he never would. Her peace could only come from one source. Only the Master Healer could give her peace. With all his heart he wanted to help her find the Master again. He prayed heavy tears over that desire.

Ateron smashed a costly ceramic pot in his opulent apartment when Cartu woke him in the wee hours of the morning, reporting the guards' failure to find Ryder. "It is now in your hands, Cartu. Find him. Remember I still need him and handle him with care."

"Sire, do not distress yourself over this worthless slave, I will find him, and teach him obedience."

The first pale rays of sunlight streaked the sky as Ryder closed his prayer. His body ached from the long hours of being doubled over, but he stayed in his humble position waiting, longing, listening. Understanding finally touched his mind, illuminating it like a flickering beam of light in the black depths of a cave. Assurance grew in his heart. Guidance would come as he sought his way along this fiery path.

He struggled to his feet, stiff and sore in every muscle and joint, but knowing that would pass. The pain in his soul was something else. He knew that scorching agony would be there for a long time. *Only the Lord and Hadlee can remove it. Even then, the irreparable consequences of my actions will always be a scar on Hadlee's life—and mine. Learning to live with that burden will take time—maybe a lifetime. Right now, I have to focus on what I can do.* He committed himself, with the guidance of heaven, to getting Hadlee out of Injanae.

It took several minutes for the circulation to return to his throbbing limbs and joints. Massaging and shaking his muscles to loosen them, he walked the lake's shore until the numbness tingling through his arms and legs was gone. With absolute commitment, he dove into the lake and set out for the far shore.

Nineteen

Taya's apprehension and distress grew throughout the night as she thought about the two people she'd grown to love. There was something wrong between them. She always felt it when they were together. Hadlee's eyes would go cold for a moment when Ryder came into the apartment. Most of the time she hid it, but it was always there.

Is that the reason Ryder is missing? Frustration stung her like an angry bee. Hadlee wouldn't stop pacing. She refused to eat, and there was no word on Ryder.

By mid-day, Taya's distress overflowed. Collapsing into a pile of pillows, she wept.

Her misery brought Hadlee to her. They sat in the cushions, held onto each other and cried.

Taya wept with frustration. She longed to convey her concern for Ryder, understand why Hadlee was crying, and find a way to comfort her. Too much anxiety, through a sleepless night, took its toll. Cuddled in the cushions like two abandoned kittens, they slept.

Kytan left his weary vigil at the city gates when the guards returned from the quarry in the wee hours of the morning without Ryder. He went home, fell into bed and tried to sleep for a few hours, before another long business day started.

A loud commotion in the street below his window woke him from an uneasy slumber. Pushing open the shutters to the midday sun, he blinked against it and called to a man in the street. "Friend, what is all the excitement?"

"The chancellor and the king's guards have caught the big slave! They are nearing the gate and everyone is gathering there to watch them bring him in—it ought to be very entertaining." the man shouted above the growing din.

Kytan ran through the streets, pulling his tunic over his head. Panting, he reached the crowd at the city gates just as Chancellor Cartu entered. He rode a llama, smugly jerking Ryder along behind him with a rope looped through the gold ring encircling his throat. Ryder's hands were chained behind his back, and his legs were shackled, forcing him to run in short jerky steps to keep from falling and being dragged.

The crowd laughed, and taunted him.

Kytan turned away, fear choking him. *Will you still be alive by nightfall my friend?* Moving against the crowd, who followed in the wake of the armed procession, intent on enjoying the spectacle all the way to the palace, he raced back to his shop.

Slamming the door behind him, Kytan fell to his knees, and pleaded for Ryder's life.

The feel of rough fingers stroking her cheek, woke Taya. She peered through the deep evening shadows into a face that was much too close to hers. Her eyes widened when she recognized who was leaning over her. She recoiled from his touch, pressing backward into the big pillow.

Hadlee moaned, and snuggled deeper into the cushions.

"Come with me and bring your healing herbs. Ryder needs them after the punishment he received," said Cartu, pulling her from the cushions.

She pressed her lips together, fighting panic's stranglehold. Her hand slid into her tunic, grasping the handle of the long slender blade that was her constant companion, and found courage. "What did you do to him?"

Cartu grinned. "At the king's request, I instructed him with a rapa."

Hastening into her supply room, Taya gathered pouches of herbs into a leather bag. Shutting the apartment door softly behind her, she asked, "Where is he," but knew before Cartu answered.

"Pel will take you to him," Cartu said, running his hand down her glossy hair. She pulled away from him with a shiver, grateful to be left in Pel's care.

She turned to the king's stalwart captain. "I need to go to the supply room and the kitchen before we go down."

Pel nodded. "I have been instructed to help you procure anything you need."

As they hurried to the supply room, she asked, "How badly did Cartu beat him?"

"Cartu is always excessive, but Ryder should not have left without permission. He had to be punished," Pel said, his voice heavy with resignation.

Taya stopped. Her fingers grasped his arm. She searched his face and found a surprising admiration there.

"Ryder took his punishment without a sound. It made Cartu very angry, so he kept lashing him. The king finally stopped him. I have never seen a man take that kind of punishment and keep silent. He has won the respect of many today."

Taya bit her lip, and stepped up her pace. Still, it took nearly thirty minutes to collect everything she needed. By the time she enlisted a maid to help Pel carry all the supplies, and they were on their way down into the dark, dank cells under the palace, she was trembling with apprehension.

Pel stopped in front of an iron-reinforced door and unlocked it.

Lifting a torch from a wall sconce, Taya slipped into the cell, pushing the door closed behind her. The light from the torch was inadequate to lift the darkness enough to see Ryder clearly. She walked over to him lying on the hard dirt floor, dropped to her knees, and whispered his name, unable to hold back the tears.

His face was turned away from her, but his back was now clear in the light of the torch. It was covered with blistering welts, and bruises. In dozens of places, his skin was broken and bloody.

He turned his face to her, and whispered hoarsely, "An angel of mercy has come to me."

Wiping her flowing eyes with her sleeve, she brushed his hair away from his face and laid her hand on his cheek. "I have brought medicine for the pain," she said, and hurried back through the cell door.

Knowing the gossip the maid would spread if she saw Ryder; Taya took the maid's tray and dismissed her. The plump maid expressed her reluctance to walk back through the dark tunnels of the dungeon by herself. Taya conveyed her sympathy, inwardly sighing with relief. It gave her an excuse to send Pel back with the maid.

"Pel will take you back," she said, looking up at him.

He nodded and led the maid down the long tunnel.

Striding along the dim corridor of the dungeon, Pel struggled within himself. His pace forced the nervous maid to run in order to keep up with him. The endless stream of questions she plied him with about Ryder, registered in his mind as nothing more than a buzzing in his ears.

Ryder knew he would be punished for leaving without permission, every slave knows that. Pel frowned, and the maid went silent. *Why did he run, and why did he walk right up to us on the road, letting us shackle him without any resistance and drag him into the city?*

Pel had chained more men than he cared to remember to the dungeon wall to receive a lashing, and all their eyes held fear, but Ryder's hadn't. After he pulled the chain tight, stretching Ryder's long arms taut above his head, he managed to slide a wooden stick between Ryder's teeth, while Cartu tore the tunic from his back. Ryder nodded his thanks and turned his face to the wall.

It took Ryder's blood before the king's anger abated, but it was obvious to everyone Cartu's ferocity hadn't been satisfied. He wore out the rapa without as much as a sound from Ryder. His only indication of pain was the grip he held on his chains, the tightness of his muscles, and the heaviness of his breathing.

It was no secret Cartu hated Ryder, but Pel didn't believe Ryder had attacked Cartu's wife. Everything he saw in Ryder—since the day he'd met the big slave—told him Ryder was a decent man. He knew Cartu well enough to believe Ryder had been sold into slavery through his lies.

The frown deepened on Pel's intelligent face. *I was a fool not to have listened to my father.*

When he won the position of Captain of the king's bodyguards, through many strenuous tests of arms, he was elated to hold such a position of trust and respect. Seven years in the king's service taught him to despise Ateron, and hate Cartu. He wanted to leave Ateron's service. Unfortunately, Hadlee's arrival had forestalled him. *Ateron won't release me—not now. Anyone who knows about Hadlee may be irrevocably bound to the king, and in honor—no matter how I feel—my duty is to do Ateron's bidding.* His lips tightened into a grim line. *But taking orders from Ateron and Cartu is getting more impossible every day.*

They reached the ground level. He nodded to the jittery maid. She bobbed her head and ran up the stairs.

Ryder's eyes followed Taya as she lit the cell with torches from the passageway and then quickly carried in her supplies.

She knelt beside him. "I have some herbs I want you to take. They will help with the pain and make you sleep."

"You are truly an angel of mercy."

Undoing a small pouch, she emptied the contents into a cup and added water. Holding his head, she spooned the pungent, bitter tasting concoction into his mouth. Uncomplaining, he took every mouthful, praying his stomach wouldn't reject it and hopeful it would take the edge off his pain.

She set the cup aside and poured water through a cloth filled with herbs into a basin, explaining what she intended to do. "I am sorry to hurt you, but I must clean your back with this herb rinse. Then I will put a paste of herbs on that will sooth the welts and bruises, and help close the lacerations in your skin."

"Don't worry about hurting me," he said, softly. "I can't tell you how grateful I am for your kindness."

She sponged the cool herb rinse over his back with the lightest touch, but his muscles jumped, and he couldn't keep from clenching his fists.

"Why did you run away? We have been so worried, so afraid."

"We?"

"Yes, Hadlee paced the terrace all night, this morning she pointed at the door and said your name. When I couldn't make her understand you were missing, we sat in the cushions and cried, until we finally fell asleep this afternoon."

Causing Hadlee and Taya to worry added the pain of guilt to Ryder's bruised face. "Taya I need you to give Hadlee a message for me. Tell her . . . Ryder will be back soon. Can you do that?"

It took some practice for Taya to learn the English words and more to remember them. "I will tell her," she said, washing the last of the dried blood from his back. "Can you sit up? I want to put a mat and a blanket under you."

Shaking, Ryder pushed himself up and sat. "There is nothing quite like a beating to show a man how weak he really is."

"Cartu is a monster," Taya said, spreading two reed mats end to end, topping them with a thick blanket of llama hair, and adding a pillow. "I have never seen so many rapa stripes on one person's back," she said, helping him position himself on the blanket.

"Well, you have to admire a man who loves his work and can do it with such skill," Ryder said, with a faltering grin.

She looked at him as though he might be delirious. It told him, his sarcastic humor was lost on her. Concern puckered her brow, while she mixed herbs into a paste to spread over his blistered back.

He wrinkled his nose, nearly gagging over the noxious smell of the herb poultice.

"I am sorry this is going to cause you more pain, but it needs to be done."

Even with her delicate touch, the pain produced a heavy sheen of sweat that ran down his face and neck. He set his jaw and turned his face away.

When Taya was done, she laid a large cloth over his back, and then covered him with three llama hair blankets. Dipping another cloth in water, she washed his neck, arms, and hands then turned his face to her, gently wiping away the dirt, sweat, and tears.

Pulling forward a tray of food, she offered him some bread.

"I'm not hungry."

"You need to eat. Your body needs the nourishment."

Unable to refuse the concern in her eyes, he ate bread, a little smoked fish, and drank several cups of water.

When she seemed satisfied with his effort, she ran a hand lightly over his hair, and again asked, "Why did you run away?"

"I didn't really run away. I just needed some time to work through . . . something. It upset me, and I needed to be alone—to pray. I was returning to Telquset when Cartu and his men caught up with me." He freed his hand from under the blankets, reaching for hers. "I would never leave Hadlee here at Ateron's mercy. Please, believe me."

She searched his eyes. "I do," she said, squeezing his hand.

He slurred a relieved sigh as Taya's powerful potion clouded his mind, induced drowsiness, and eased his pain. "How long . . . do you think it will be . . . before I can . . . go back to work?"

She patted his hand. "I will ask the king to move you to your quarters tomorrow—then we will see. You should be better in a few days."

He tried to reply, mumbled something, and finally quit fighting the urge to drift away. His eyes lids were just too heavy to keep open. He let them close.

Taya put his hand back under the blankets and sat beside him for several minutes. When his breathing became slow and deep, assuring her the herbs were doing their job, she leaned down, kissed his cheek, moved the tray of food and water within easy reach, gathered up her equipment, took a torch, and pulled open the heavy door.

Twenty

Hadlee awoke in darkness, listening to the belfry toll eight
times. Stiff necked from sleeping in the cushions, she
trudged out onto the terrace, hoping the night air would
bring relief to her throbbing head. Embracing the shroud of
frigid air that engulfed her, she gazed into the dusky mask of
the sky, alternately massaging her neck and temples.

Will I ever get out of here and fly again? She tried to
imagine the feel of a plane speeding down the runway toward
take off, but her wounded heart held her down, refusing to
allow her to take flight. Her physical and emotional
exhaustion deepened the spiritual darkness in which she was
lost. She knew of only one solution. Slipping to her knees,
she prayed.

It was so hard to start. She knew, with a stabbing pang of
conscience, what she'd done to Ryder was wrong and very
cruel. The anguish in his eyes just before he slammed out the
door, told her what she said to him, hit him like a bullet—
fired pointblank at his heart.

"He took everything I loved, and I finally exacted a little
justice for myself." Her motive, she acknowledged, was to
hurt him. "I've always wanted to, and I finally succeeded. I
took something precious from him—I took his peace," she
confessed.

That dreadful admission made her falter. Several minutes
passed before she could continue her prayer. It was chilling
to find herself in the position of having willfully hurt
someone, but she rationalized, "Don't I deserve to exact a
little justice for all my suffering?"

A strong impression pressed in on her to apologize and seek his forgiveness. She acknowledged the feeling, struggling through a deep quagmire of resistance in her heart, before committing herself. "I'll . . . try."

Everything she knew, and was taught as a child, told her she needed to forgive Ryder, not try to take revenge. Yet that demon had lurked in her heart since the day her mother died. She stayed on her knees, trying to banish the demon, but its talons went deep.

Her struggle for release produced a veil of self-recrimination. It cloaked her in barbed hypocrisy and allowed something more ugly and terrible, than what she'd done to Ryder, or even what he'd done to her, to crawl out of the black hole in her heart. Guilt was its name, and she realized it had lived there for a very long time, buried deep. Over the years, she'd ceased to think about it.

The accusation it threw at her—leveled her.

The city belfry tolled the hour again before a torch pierced the darkness of the terrace.

Prone and shivering on a stone bench, Hadlee pinched her eyes closed against the light's revealing intrusion. She felt a gentle touch on her tear-damp cheek and opened her eyes to Taya's distressed face.

"Ryder will be back soon," Taya said.

Hadlee gasped.

Taya repeated the English words again.

Hadlee sat up, clutching Taya's hand. Her heart lurched with guilt and shame. *He's coming back!*

Twenty-one

Peace touched Kytan as he prayed. An idea came. He lit torches and stoked the fire. Working through the night, he produced dozens of nails and finished the hammer he'd started the day before.

He wrapped the handle of the hammer in a long strip of llama hide to the tune of early morning food venders calling out their wares and the creaking of their heavily laden carts being pushed down the street. Examining his work with a critical eye, he nodded his head.

Sending a prayer heavenward, he left his shop and hurried through the growing crowds out doing their morning shopping. The greetings he returned to the acquaintances he met were short, almost curt, his mind focused on a single thought. *What has the chancellor done to you, Ryder?*

That question grew ever more urgent during the hour he waited in line at the tradesman's gate before it was his turn to talk with Tensar the trade steward.

"I am a metal smith," he said, when he had the steward's attention. "I was given a small commission by the king, through his slave Ryder. I have brought samples of my work for Ryder's approval."

The shrewd steward eyed him with interest. Kytan knew the hook was set. Anyone connected with Ryder was news today.

Tensar handed his responsibilities off to another servant. "Come with me. I am sure the chancellor will want to speak with you."

Weaving through the palace's busy corridors filled with servants and slaves, Tensar finally opened the door to a large chamber built into the cliff side of the palace. A host of silent people filled rows of wooden benches facing a dais. Chancellor Cartu sat on the dais in a finely carved chair, his feet resting on a padded footstool.

The spindly steward motioned for Kytan to take a seat, sat beside him and quietly probed, "Do you know the slave Ryder?"

Kytan sized up the steward, and shrugged. "I have little interest in slaves. I am only interested in being paid for the work the king's slave commissioned me to do."

The rabid curiosity in the steward's face waned with Kytan's dull response. He rose, told Kytan he would have to wait his turn for the chancellor's ear and left.

Fighting impatience and fear, Kytan listened to the pleas of many unhappy people before it was his turn to approach the dais. He went down on one knee, bowing his head.

"What is your business?" Cartu's bored voice inquired, without looking at him.

"Excellency, a slave from the palace came to my shop asking me to make nails for a job he is doing for the king. He was supposed to return this morning to approve my work. When he didn't, I thought I better bring the samples for inspection. May I be directed to the slave named Ryder?"

The chancellor straightened in his chair and put his feet on the floor.

Kytan hid his fear, and stoically underwent the chancellor's piercing inspection.

"The slave, Ryder, can't be seen today. However the king will want to see what you have brought," he said gesturing at Kytan's leather pouch. He motioned to a guard standing beside the dais. "Take his man to the king."

If Kytan hadn't been so afraid for Ryder, he would have enjoyed this adventure into the mysteries of the palace. As it was, his heart wouldn't stop pounding painfully in his chest. His mouth was dry and his palms clammy. He hadn't counted on being sent to the king.

The guard stopped at a set of gilded doors and knocked.

Thinking of Ryder gave Kytan courage. He walked into the king's presence with a confidence he was far from feeling.

Ateron sat at a small gold table looking more bored than Cartu, rolling a set of dice. Languidly he arose, when Kytan stopped at the foot of the dais and strolled to its edge.

Kytan dropped to his knees, put his hands together and his forehead on the floor.

"You may rise and tell me who my chancellor has sent to me today," the king said, accepting Kytan's show of respect.

Kytan obediently rose to his feet—as free men were entitled to do after demonstrating their allegiance. "Sire, I am the nail maker your slave, Ryder, commissioned. He was to come this morning for the samples. When he didn't, I thought I better bring them to him. Forgive me for troubling you with this small matter."

Ateron pursed his lips and silently paced back and forth, making Kytan's heart beat faster with each pass.

"Ah!" He raised a finger, pointed it at Kytan and said, "You are Kytan, are you not?"

"Yes, Sire, I am."

"Ryder speaks highly of your skills. How is it you know my slave?" he asked, sitting back down in the padded comfort of his gilded chair.

Kytan unfolded his service in the copper mine with a growing sense of uneasiness as the king closely questioned him about his relationship with Ryder.

When he finished, Ateron tapped his ringed fingers on the table for several nerve-racking moments, holding Kytan's eyes. "I think you should see your—*friend*. Only he will know if the work you have done on the hammer and nails is adequate."

With a silent prayer of gratitude, Kytan thanked the king and went with the bulky, ill-favored guard named Po. They climbed an additional two and a half levels of narrow stairs, from the king's public judgment chamber on the second floor, turning left into an equally narrow hall. Po stopped at the first door on the left and unlocked it.

Light pouring through a terrace door lit a mattress with a covered form, lying on the floor. Kytan glanced over his shoulder as Po closed the door behind him, staying in the hall. In three strides, Kytan was on his knees near Ryder's head, examining his pale face and the purple bruise that spread across his right cheekbone, slashed by small scratches.

Not wanting to wake him, Kytan laid his hand lightly on Ryder's head and whispered, "I am very grateful you are alive. I have prayed very hard for you."

The clanking release of the door latch turned Kytan's eyes to it.

An angel entered the room. Sunlight from the terrace made her light copper skin glow. Her glossy black hair swirled around her hips as a breeze coming in from the terrace caught it. The delicate gold band encircling her throat, with three suspended green jewels, proclaimed her a healer and personal servant of the queen. Kytan lost himself in her large velvet eyes. He had never seen anyone so lovely.

She frowned at him, making him feel absurdly guilty.

"Who are you?" she asked suspiciously.

"My name is Kytan. I am Ryder's friend. I came to learn what happened to him. I saw Cartu drag him through the streets yesterday. I feared the chancellor would kill him for running away."

The angel seemed to consider this before setting a large tray on the table and sitting down on the other side of Ryder. She whispered, "I am Taya, Ryder's doctor, and Cartu certainly wanted to kill him. He beat Ryder with a rapa until the king stopped him." Tears clung to the long lashes of Taya's beautiful eyes. Her soft mouth trembled, "He is my friend too."

"Quit mourning over me."

Kytan and Taya jumped like startled children.

"I'm not dead, or dying."

Kytan looked down into Ryder's open eyes as he shifted from his stomach to his side.

Ryder reached his hand out from under the blankets and took Kytan's. "What are you doing here?"

Before Kytan could respond, Taya said, "I am sorry to interrupt your visit with Kytan, Ryder, but I need to change your dressing and get back to Ha—my other duties."

A light flush stained her cheeks, adding to her beauty. Kytan held back a sigh.

Recovering herself, she turned to him. "You may not want to watch this."

"I've been told it's pretty gruesome," said Ryder.

"Why don't you wait in the hall until I am done treating Ryder's back," Taya said.

"I worked hard to get in here to see you, and I intend to stay," Kytan said to Ryder, relating his fears and the inspiration that led the king to allow him to visit Ryder.

Taya looked at Ryder. He nodded and rolled onto his stomach. She removed the cloth that covered his back.

Kytan drew in a sharp breath.

Ryder laughed and winced.

Kytan grimaced. "You must be in a great deal of pain."

"Only when I laugh—I did try to warn you."

"So did I." Taya dipped a clean cloth into a bowl of herb rinse and gently washed Ryder's back.

Ryder squeezed his friend's arm. "I'll be okay in a few days. I feel much better than I did last night. Taya is an amazing doctor and a beautiful angel of mercy."

"Hush!" Taya blushed, reaching for her pot of paste.

"Yes"—Kytan riveted soulful eyes on her—"she is."

Ryder choked on a laugh that made him wince and groan.

Taya's eyes flash disapproval at Kytan.

He flushed, and asked, "Ryder I don't believe you ran away. I know you wouldn't leave without me. What really happened?"

"I needed time alone to pray. That's impossible to do in this place. I knew when I left there would be consequences, but I just didn't care. I needed solitude to find answers."

"Please, the next time you need solitude, come to my shop. My room is always available to you, and I promise, I won't disturb you."

"Yes, please listen to him." Taya touched Ryder's cheek. "Don't let Cartu hurt you again. Don't frighten us again."

Their pleading concern added additional lines to Ryder's pain pinched face. "Forgive me for causing you to worry. The next time I run, I *will* be leaving Injanae, and I'm taking both of you with me."

Taya's eyes widened, but she said nothing.

Kytan's heart leaped. There was more going on here than Ryder was disclosing. *What caused you to need solitude so desperately that you ran and . . . is this angel really coming with us when we leave?* Those questions trembled on his lips. He pressed them together, knowing when Ryder was ready, he would tell him.

Taya covered Ryder's back with a clean cloth, stood, and reached for his blankets. Kytan stood too, helping her cover

Ryder. "I think it is time for you to go," she said. "I need to give Ryder more pain and sleeping medication now."

"Can you come back tomorrow? I want to see the nails and try them out."

"Will he be able to get up by then?" Kytan asked Taya.

"I don't know, but come anyway."

He knelt and grasped Ryder's hand, "I will be back in the morning. If you are well enough, we will try them." He stood and headed for the door.

"I will be right back to give you your medicine, Ryder. But first I want to talk with Kytan for a moment," Taya said, and followed Kytan out of the room.

Taya glanced at Po, still standing outside the door, "I will take him down," she said to Po. He nodded, and she leading Kytan down the stairs.

She covertly appraised him as they stepped aside on the third floor landing and paused—making way for three slaves coming up. He was taller than Hadlee, and well built, with powerful shoulders and arms. His simple attire was clean and neat. A thick braid, secured with a copper clasp, fell below his shoulder blades. His wide set, ebony eyes were a window to an honest, open countenance.

She dropped her eyes and admired his strong hands as the slaves came level with them. As soon as the slaves went by, they continued down the stairs. When they reached the first floor, she stopped and whispered, "I will be at the servant's entrance tomorrow at nine bells. Meet me there. I will bring you back to see Ryder. Stay out of Cartu's way. He hates Ryder and will do anything to hurt him, and that includes hurting anyone Ryder cares about."

Kytan nodded and whispered back, "How long will it take for Ryder's back to heal? It looks terrible."

She gave him a shy smile; glad Ryder had such a concerned friend. He returned it with a wide one that displayed a delicious pair of dimples, making her heart race.

"It will take a few more days before his pain diminishes and longer for his back to heal. Having you come to see him will lift his spirits. So, I will see you tomorrow," she said, and hurried back up the stairs, surprised to find herself hoping Kytan might become her friend too.

Reentering Ryder's quarters, Taya mixed herbs with water and then knelt beside him.

"What did you need to talk about with Kytan?" Ryder grinned inquisitively.

Taya felt the blush rise on her face. "I was just telling him I would come to the servant's entrance tomorrow morning to bring him up here. The less he is exposed to Cartu and Ateron, the better."

"I agree," said Ryder, shrinking with unconcealed distaste from the cup she held. "You know I'm really feeling much better. I don't think I need medicine right now—maybe tonight."

Glowering at her rebellious patient, Taya said, "You must be feeling better if you are in the mood to argue with me, but you will take the medicine."

She pressed the spoon to his lips. Reluctantly he opened his mouth and gagged down the first spoonful.

Escaping the boredom of his duties, the king spent a pleasant hour in the nursery with his two young sons. Cusi and Tupa were his greatest treasures, his dynasty, his immortality, and he guarded them fiercely. He spent another enjoyable hour in the Queen's rooms. Telsua was the loveliest woman of high rank in the kingdom. She added to his pride and dignity with her stately grace and delicate beauty. She was quietly supportive and never interfering. In fact, he considered her the perfect wife.

He left her fourth floor apartment with regret, boarded the slave operated, manual elevator, Ryder constructed for his convenience, and went to have lunch with Cartu on the terrace of his own apartment.

They ate grilled pig from a recent hunt, with potatoes, and vegetables marinated in herbs, while they discussed the morning's events, washing down their meal with large quantities of golden berry wine.

"What did you think of the medal smith I sent you this morning?" asked Cartu, cutting a thick slice of bread.

Ateron chuckled and reached for his wine. "Do you know he is a friend to my most troublesome slave?"

Cartu frowned. "How did they become friends, when he is not a slave? He greeted me as a free man."

"Yes, he is a free man." Ateron's chuckle deepened. "But that can change." He outlined Ryder and Kytan's friendship; then fixed Cartu with his deadly piranha eyes. "You can see why I need you to keep track of Kytan. It is essential to know all the ways someone can be controlled. I believe Kytan will provide the additional leverage I may need to keep Ryder subdued until his usefulness to me has ended."

Dal, another of the king's bodyguards, acting as a waiter, came out onto the terrace with a tray of cheese and fruit. His conduct indicated a certain familiarity with this domestic chore—and in fact, he was. If he felt being used as a waiter was demeaning, nothing in his dull features, or manner revealed it. This unusual duty was the result of Hadlee's arrival in the palace. Since that day, no servant, or slave had been allowed to set foot on the king's private level.

The king and Cartu were silent while Dal removed the plates of cheese and fruit from the tray and carefully set them on the table. Ateron thoughtfully swirled the wine in his cup until Dal bowed and left.

The king set his cup on the table and looked at Cartu, soberly. "I fear Hadlee is as spirited as Ryder, she too may prove to be troublesome. But I have a feeling there is something between them. I saw it the first time they met—if that was the first time." He frowned. "You better instruct Pel to have the guards look in on Ryder and Hadlee when they are together. I may need more leverage to make Hadlee cooperate with my plans, and I have always felt the lightest cords are more useful than the heaviest chains."

Cartu lifted his glass in a silent salute acknowledging the king's subtle skills, though he rarely employed those means himself, preferring the method he'd used on Ryder.

Ateron again sipped his wine and came to a decision. "I want Ryder and Kytan in my judgment chamber tomorrow morning. I think Ryder has had enough time to consider his behavior, and Kytan needs my permission to start making hammers and nails." Worry rode Ateron's brow. "Preparations for the Lunar Celebration must not fall behind schedule."

"I will arrange it," Cartu said, and drained his cup.

Twenty-two

The hour was late when Ryder's door again opened. He listen to the soft footfalls of someone steal into his quarters. He smiled warmly at Taya when she found him sitting on the small bench, on the equally small terrace, outside his room.

"What are you doing up?"

He took her hand. "You have done your work so well I couldn't stay in bed. It's a very beautiful night, and I'm sitting here counting my blessings."

"Blessings? Do you consider what happened to you a blessing?"

"Not particularly, but I consider having a doctor and friend like you a blessing." He brought her hand to his lips.

"You can't get around me like that," she said, smiling in spite of her harsh tone.

"The truth is, I'm going back to work tomorrow, so I decided I'd better get up and move around—see how it feels."

"You shouldn't go back to work for a few more days."

"I would certainly prefer not to. But Cartu came and told me I have an appointment with the king tomorrow morning, and as soon as it's over I'll be going back to work."

"Then I better treat your back and give you your medicine so you will sleep well."

"You've been wonderful, but I don't need any more medicine or herb treatments. Right now the cold air on my back is enough. I think I will sleep just fine if I sit here, count my blessings and enjoy this beautiful night."

Hands on hips, Taya favored him with a determined face. He responded with one of equal determination. The stalemate ended when she finally shook her head and shrugged. He slid over to the edge of the small bench and tugged her down beside him.

"I will never be able to tell you how much your kindness means to me. You're a good friend, and I was just thinking, I don't really know much about you. You're a doctor, so why do you wear the collar of a servant?"

Her face clouded. A storm brewed in her eyes, broke and finally dissipated before she spoke. "My mother's family is distantly related to the king."

"Wow. How closely—wait, that makes you the nobility. Then why are you a servant?"

She laughed humorlessly. "My relationship to Ateron is one of a third or fourth cousin, but because my mother married a commoner, I am considered a commoner."

"Why did your mother marry so far beneath her?"

"Many members of my mother's noble family are healers—of one kind or another. When Mother started studying herbal medicine, she made many trips into the valley to gather herbs and plants so she could learn how to use them. She met a young farmer, who loved the earth and plants as much as she did. He taught her many things about the plants in Injanae—things not even her family knew. They grew very close. My mother always told me he was a good, kind man who treated everyone with dignity and respect—not to mention he was very handsome."

"Then your mother didn't marry a commoner. She married a prince. There aren't enough men with those qualities."

"Yes, but they weren't the qualities that mattered to my mother's parents. When my mother came of age, they married. Her family disowned her for it, but Mother didn't care. She and my father were very happy together. My father farmed potatoes, corn, cotton, and herbs. My mother started a business selling the herbs, and treating people with all sorts of sicknesses and complaints."

"It sounds like a good life."

"It was—until my father died."

A night bird commenced its haunting evening recital.

Taya smiled faintly at the raven colored bird, sitting on the terrace rail, closed her eyes and drew in a soft breath.

Ryder listened appreciatively with her to the dark bird's plaintive song, waiting for Taya to continue.

She opened her eyes and said, "I was only seven, and I don't know how he died. My mother never would talk about it. All I remember is how much she cried." She brushed a hand across her eyes.

Ryder's arm encircled her, pulling her close.

"We were left on our own, but Mother was such a good doctor, we did well. Because of her skills, even the nobles started coming to her. One of her first noble customers was Cartu. I was nine when Cartu first came to get herbs. After that, he came frequently. My mother was always afraid of him and hated his patronage."

"I can understand that. Cartu is an evil man."

"I learned that the second time he came. My mother argued with him, and he struck her."

"That's certainly Cartu's style. So, where is your mother now?"

"Dead—murdered. I can't prove it, but I am sure it was Cartu." She leaned into his side as though seeking protection from the memory.

His arm tightened. "That doesn't surprise me, but why would he kill your mother?"

"He was always asking for very dangerous herbs and potions. He got her to give them to him by threats."

"What kind of threats?"

"I think he threatened to hurt me, so she gave him whatever he wanted. He killed her to silence her about the potions he forced her to give him."

"Murder is something Cartu wouldn't hesitate to do if it served his needs. He's a man who enjoys inflicting pain," Ryder said, his back throbbing.

"Yes and the pain he inflicts isn't always physical. He enjoyed tormenting my mother and me."

Ryder nodded. "And now you have to put up with seeing him on a daily basis, but how did you ended up here?"

"After my mother died, her brother, Tulas, came and got me. I was allowed to be a slave in his house."

"*A slave?* Was he trying to get back at your mother by treating you like that?" Ryder's incredulous voice silenced the night bird's mournful song.

"I don't know. I was just sixteen and grateful someone related to me wanted me. If my uncle hadn't taken me in, I would have been sold in the slave market."

"Is that the solution for orphans in Injanae?"

"For the common people, it is." Taya sniffed. "So I was very fortunate to be taken in by my uncle, even as his slave."

Ryder's brow puckered. "But how did you go from being a slave in you uncle's house to a servant in Ateron's?"

"Tulas invited the king and queen to dine in his home. During the meal, the queen became ill. Tulas sent for me. I listened to the queen's complaint and mixed her a potion. She felt better almost immediately and asked to buy me to treat the royal family."

"So, now you belong to Ateron."

"No. Tulas wouldn't relinquish ownership. He told Ateron that regardless of my birth, I was still family and it wouldn't be right to sell me. Instead, he allowed Ateron to persuade him to let me come and serve the queen by offering to pay him for my services. Tulas never could turn down an ongoing, moneymaking proposition, so he agreed."

"And of course you had no say in any of this."

"No, but I have been very happy serving Queen Telsuea."

"If you are actually a slave, why do you wear the collar of the queen's personal servant?" He touched the delicate gold band that graced Taya's neck, making the green jewels dance.

"The queen asked Ateron to allow me to wear the collar of a servant rather than a slave, because of my skills."

"I only met the queen once, but she seemed like a genuinely good person."

"She is a wonderful lady, and I would be happy and count it a blessing to spend my life in her service. But now—that won't happen," Taya said with a finality that accelerated Ryder's heart.

"Why?" he asked warily.

"A few months ago Ateron presented a proposal to Tulas. He accepted it and the formal negotiations began."

Apprehension's cold fingers slid across Ryder's skin. "What's the proposal about?"

"Cartu . . . wants me."

A hard shiver shook her. It skidded across Ryder's raw back like the bite of a rapa. He hugged her protectively while he did battle with a murderous anger. "Has Tulas agreed to let that monster have you?"

"Not have—buy."

"I don't understand. Why is your uncle willing to sell you to Cartu when he wouldn't sell you to Ateron?"

"When Ateron presented Cartu's proposal, he reminded Tulas he could also claim me as family, and as the king he could simply take me from Tulas."

"Why didn't he just do that?"

"Because he would rather have the deal look like a private matter between Tulas and Cartu. You see, throwing his weight around in petty, private matters makes Ateron look bad in the eyes of the nobles—whose support he needs. He had to persuade Tulas to agree to sell me, willingly. The reminder of his claim on me was enough. Tulas took the hint, and rather than get nothing for me, he agreed to sell me. In return, Cartu agreed to all the proper legal conditions to soothe the family's dignity. Including paying an agreed upon purchase price."

Ryder snorted. "And just how much money does the family dignity require?"

"I don't know, but fortunately for me the initial price Cartu offered was rejected. Apparently, it wasn't enough to compensate Tulas sufficiently to make up for what the king pays him for my services."'

"So as long as Cartu and Tulas haggle over a price, you're safe?"

"Yes, and fortunately the law doesn't allow Cartu to buy me or have me—in the way he wants—until I turn eighteen. There is a specific legal agreement Cartu must enter into to buy me as a . . . concubine," she said, gagging on the word.

Ryder's jaws clenched with fierce protectiveness.

She put her hand on his outraged face and gave him a wicked grin. "I lied about my age when Tulas took me in. I told him I was thirteen instead of sixteen. I knew it would protect me longer, and since I am small and wear very loose clothes, no one knew."

Ryder's fierceness faded. He returned her grin, his full of admiration. "So when will you, supposedly, be eighteen?"

"Seven more cycles of the moon must pass before my twenty-first birthday—when everyone believes I will be eighteen." Her smile faded. "But . . . Ateron told me the day Hadlee came; the price was all but settled. He said as soon as it was, and the legal agreement was signed, he wasn't going to make Cartu wait any longer to have me."

Fear pounded in Ryder's chest.

Taya's lips quivered. "I am so thankful Hadlee came and needed my skills. I was going to end my life that day, but Gidlo came and took me to the king's lodge to treat her before I could." Her back straightened, and she looked at Ryder with unwavering resolve. "Cartu will never have me. I *will* kill myself the moment Ateron decrees I belong to him," she said with deadly calm, sliding her hand into her pocket.

Ryder's eyes burned into hers. "I don't ever want to hear you talk about killing yourself again. I'm going to get you out of here before Cartu can lay even one finger on you. I promise. I don't know how yet, but I will."

The necessity of taking Taya with them had come to him in the pain laden hours of the previous night. She couldn't be left behind to take the blame and the inevitable consequences for Hadlee's escape. Now, her predicament made taking her even more imperative.

"For the moment I think you're safe," he said thoughtfully. "The king needs you to stay with Hadlee and take care of her until he's ready to let her out of her cage. He also seems to need her cooperation—for whatever he's planning—something she won't give him if he hurts you. Whatever he's up to—and I have a nagging hunch—it's part of this Lunar Celebration. I think we have until then to make our escape, and it's time we started planning."

"Yes." Taya grasped his hand. "I want to leave—I *must* leave."

He breathed easier with the flicker of hope escaping Injanae sparked in her eyes. "Promise me you won't do anything to hurt yourself."

"I know you will do everything you can to get me out of Injanae, and I believe you are right. Now that I am responsible for Hadlee's care, the king won't let Cartu have me until the celebration is over. So I will give you this promise"—her velvet eyes hardened into flint—"I won't hurt myself, unless we can't escape Injanae by then."

It wasn't all Ryder wanted from her, but the stubborn set to her mouth told him it was the most he would get. He nodded grimly.

They drifted into a companionable silence, enjoying the melancholy music of the night bird, who again took up her song.

When the belfry rang eleven, Taya stood. "You need your rest if you are going back to work tomorrow."

"I will come to the apartment early. I need to see Hadlee before the king or his men can waylay me."

"Alright—oh, I am supposed to meet Kytan and bring him up here at nine bells."

"I'll meet him. The king wants to see him too."

Twenty-three

The joyful morning birds were always Ryder's alarm clock. He woke to their loud, cheerful anthems, listening and thinking. As much as he needed and even wanted to see Hadlee, he knew the encounter was likely to be more painful than his lashing. He rolled off his mattress and onto his knees.

The sun wasn't quite up by the time he arrived at the door of Hadlee's hall. Numo, one of the night guards, sat in a chair, his double chin resting on his chest, dozing. Ryder pushed back the tapestry hiding the door to Hadlee's hall, turned the key in the lock, slipped through the door and walked softly down the hall.

Shur, responsible to guard Hadlee's apartment door, snored like a freight train on the floor beside it. Ryder shook his head and then decided the slothful security might turn out to be a blessing. Easing the apartment door open, he crept through, shutting it softly behind him.

He met Taya coming out of her room.

She jumped, clutched her heart, and whispered, "Ryder, you scared the life out of me. You said early, but the sun is barely up, and Hadlee is still asleep."

"Good," Ryder whispered back. "I was hoping for a little medicine this morning, just something to help with the discomfort of wearing my tunic."

"Sit down, and I will get the medicine. Then I want to put an ointment on your back.

He held up his hands. "I don't think I need any—"

"It is something different. It doesn't smell bad and it will protect your back from your tunic rubbing against your skin," she said, quickly.

"Okay, but let's go out on the terrace, and make this fast and quiet."

He straddled the bench farthest from the terrace door, while Taya got the medications. He wasn't looking forward to taking off his tunic. Putting it on had required an excruciating skirmish. One the coarse cloth rubbing relentlessly against his bruised and broken skin was still waging.

She came out with her tray and handed him a cup. "This will ease your discomfort, but only for a few hours. You will need to take more by noon. Now let's get your tunic off."

"First, go check on Hadlee. I want to be sure she's asleep," he said, and then swallowed the vile tasting potion in one, gagging gulp.

Taya shook her head, but went in to check on Hadlee. "It is alright," she said, coming back out onto the terrace. "Hadlee is still sleeping soundly."

It was marginally easier with Taya's help to take off the tunic. Letting out a breath of relief as soon as it was over his head, Ryder demanded to see and smell the concoction she wanted to put on his back. He was pleasantly surprised by its faintly minty scent and willingly consented to the treatment, letting Taya pat the ointment gently over his raw back.

"Why didn't you use this the first night? It smells nice and feels cool."

"Because the other takes the swelling down, helps heal the bruises, and seals the wounds." She paused to examine one particularly deep laceration. "I will need to put—"

They saw her at the same moment.

Hadlee tilted her head, walking toward them. "What's wrong with your back?"

Ryder bent sideways, grabbed his tunic from the floor of the terrace and fumbled to find the opening at the bottom.

His frantic efforts only succeeded in propelling Hadlee forward. She reached the bench before he could find the sleeve holes, grabbed the tunic, jerked it away, and backed up.

He sprang to his feet. "Pilot, give me my tunic."

Her eyes ran over his sculpted torso and arms in a long, searching stare, stopping at his throat.

He swallowed, feeling the sting of the vertical rope burn, running above and below the gold band around his neck.

"What happened to your throat?" she asked, raising her eyes to his scratched and bruised face.

"Give me back my tunic."

"I will, after I see what Taya's doing to your back."

He cautiously stepped toward her, holding out his hand. "Give it to me."

She backed toward the terrace wall. "Show me your back, or I'll toss it over the wall."

Keeping his eyes on her, he spoke to Taya. "Get something to cover my back."

"No."

His head swiveled to face her.

"She should see it, and you should tell her what happened and why. She should know what her words cost you. And don't try to tell me it wasn't something she told you that made you leave."

"Don't do this to me, Taya."

"She will find out. So you might as well get it over with."

He dropped his head, and shoulders drooping, growled at the girls in both languages. "Why are you being so stubborn?"

"I take it Taya's on my side," Hadlee said smugly. "So show me."

He shot smoldering aggravation at her from his burnished eyes. "Suit yourself," he said through his teeth, turned and walked back to the bench.

Hadlee's cry was almost a scream. She collapsed onto a bench. "What happened to you?"

Ryder talked with Taya for a moment, before she went to the door, picked up a bag of laundry and left.

"Why couldn't you just let it go?" He held out his hand, unwittingly displaying his split knuckles. "Now, can I have my tunic back?"

She brought it to him, her eyes on his hand. He realized what she was looking at, groaned inwardly, and quickly took back his tunic, jerked it over his head and down his back. The coarse fabric skidded across his skin. He inhaled sharply and turned his face away, blinking hard.

Sitting on the other end of his bench, Hadlee drew her knees up to her chest, hugging them. "What happened?"

"I don't want to talk about it. I—"

"Tell me what happened! I know how upset you were when you left here . . . the other day."

Ryder hung his head and ran a hand over the back of his neck. "Slaves aren't allowed to leave their work areas without permission, but I needed time to think so . . . I went AWOL. I had to be alone with what you told me, to face it, and accept my responsibility for everything I've done to you and your family. It was the only way I could start to deal with . . . everything you've suffered because of what I did."

"Where did you go?" her voice quivered.

"Across the lake; there aren't any people over on that side. Most of it belongs to Ateron. I was on my way back when Cartu and his mob caught up with me. I knew when I left there would be consequences. But at the time, I just didn't care."

"After what I put you through, why would you come back?" she asked, her voice laden with guilty astonishment. "Why didn't you just climb out, or hide, or fight?"

"Because, I'm not going to run away from you, or from what I've done, and I am not leaving here without you and Taya." He set his jaw with mulish determination.

"But they whipped you."

"No! Well, not with a whip. Cartu used a rapa. It doesn't cause nearly the damage a whip does. Slave owners here figured out a long time ago it's unprofitable and inconvenient for them to have to wait for a slave to recover from a lashing with a whip. A rapa provides them with a less severe alternative."

She scoffed her disbelief.

"It's true. A rapa is a long, flexible, hollow reed that grows by the lake. They cut them when they're about five feet long and six inches in diameter. The stock is split into several strands leaving about eight inches whole as a handle. It's like being switched with a multiple stranded willow. I've been hit with them before."

"Your back is completely crisscrossed with horrible red welts, or black and blue ones, and your skin is broken in more places than I could count. So you're telling me, you have been switched with a rapa like that before?"

He huffed out a breath and conceded, "No."

"It's my fault." Hadlee eyes brimmed. "I wanted to hurt you the way you've hurt me. I wanted you to hurt as badly as I have all these years."

"You didn't hurt me. My own choices hurt me."

"But I did hurt you and . . . I meant to." She blinked back tears and choked out, "I thought I would feel better if I could hurt you, but I didn't—I don't. I feel like a . . . *monster.*" Shame stained her face. "I'm . . . so sorry. Can you . . . forgive me?"

He stared at her, tongue-tied by her guilt and completely unprepared for her apology.

Tears overflowed at his silence. She jumped up and ran from the terrace.

He caught her hand as she reached the top of the stairs to her bedchamber. Sitting down on a step, he tugged on her hand until she sat on the landing above him. "I don't blame you. The whole time Cartu was lashing me, I felt I deserved every stroke for what I've cost you and a lot worse."

She shook her head violently, jerking her hand from his.

"I didn't know about the baby or what your life has been like—what your dad did, I don't understand that. I have even cost you your faith. I know everything you've suffered is my fault. I've known since the day we met again that I needed to seek your forgiveness. And I've been trying to find the courage to do it, but until you told me, I didn't know the full extent of my crimes. I had to be alone to face them. The pain I feel inside right now is so much worse than the physical pain I've been through."

Grief and guilt teamed up against him. He silently endured their thrashing, rubbing a hand over his haggard face.

"I know how you feel—inside."

The anguish in her voice confirmed that truth. Her suffering was different from his, but just as deep, and there because he'd put it there, something he needed to acknowledge.

He drew a fortifying breath. "I know there isn't any way to make restitution for what I've done. Nothing I can do will ever make up for what I've taken from you."

That acknowledgement overwhelmed him. Clenching his jaw, he fought a grim, silent battle before he could command his voice. "But I'm going to do what I can. I'm going to get you out of here, and I would like to help you find your faith again. I know it can get you through this. Please—please, let me help you. It feels like the only reason I have to be alive. I can't find the words to tell you how desperately sorry I am. If I could trade my life for your mother's, I would gladly give it up. You have every right to hate me, but someday I hope—"

The words stuck in his throat. He swallowed them, knowing he didn't deserve her forgiveness. Nothing he did could merit that. Still, he hoped someday she would forgive him, if not for his sake, then for her own.

The weight of her silence pressed down on him. He dropped his head and rubbed his neck.

She touched his shoulder.

He started, astonished as much by her touch, as by her haunted expression.

"You have as much reason to hate me as I ever had to hate you. I let you take all the blame."

He recoiled as though she'd slapped him. "What are you talking about?"

"What do you remember about me the day my mother died? When you first saw me, before my mother jumped in front of the car to save me?"

The last thing in this life he wanted to do was relive that day again. His gift for perfect recall—in this case—wasn't a blessing; it was a curse. It had taken years to keep that memory from replaying itself repeatedly in his mind every day. Even when he finally mastered it, he couldn't control the nights he dreamed it and woke in a heart throbbing sweat.

The dragon's eyes probed his, giving him no quarter. Slowly, the fierceness in her eyes faded. They lost their focus, and he knew where she'd gone. Dread rolled through him, merciless and hard. He took a breath and went there too.

"I was speeding along the street when I saw the soda fountain and decided to stop for an ice cream cone. I jerked the wheel, took the corner too fast, almost overturning the car, and there you were in the road."

"What was I doing?"

He concentrated, replaying the moment. "You were skipping, or dancing, you were—happy."

"Yes, I was happy. So happy I didn't mind my mother. I danced out the door of the soda fountain while she paid for my gumdrops. 'Don't cross the street without me,' she said. I was at the curb when she came out. She said it to me again, in her, "you better mind me" voice, but there were no cars in the road—so I didn't mind her. I decided to skip across the road and open the car door for her. The door handle usually needed to be wiggled to make it work. I didn't want her to have to fumble with it and juggle such a big bag of groceries too. It was all I could think of to do, to take care of her—because of the baby."

Ryder yanked himself back to the present, dumbfounded and cold all over. His heart hammered as much from having to relive that catastrophic experience, as by what she'd just disclosed.

"I killed my mother and the baby as much as you killed them. Both of us chose to do something we knew was wrong. Either one of us could have prevented what happened, but it took both of us to kill them." Tears swamped Hadlee's huge eyes. She sucked in deep shuddering breaths. Her trembling betrayed the devastating damage her confession to him was doing inside her.

Ryder tried to breath, tried to speak, but the weight of her confession and the burden she carried, one he knew he was responsible for bringing into her life, suffocated him.

"All these years I've blamed you and let everyone else blame you too. It wasn't until I felt no satisfaction in hurting you that I finally faced myself and acknowledged it was as much my fault as yours. I am the one who should have died that day, not them. My disobedience should have cost me my life, not theirs. I deserve everything that's happened to me. Maybe that's why my dad sent me away, because he knew it was my fault and he hated me for killing Mama."

Ryder gasped a breath. "Don't do this; it wasn't your fault. You were just a little girl trying to do something helpful for your mother."

His words seemed lost on her. Her body began to quake convulsively. Guilt and grief marred her face. She struggled and lost the battle against the volcano of explosive tears that erupted.

Her guilt was as raw as his back and infinitely harder for him to bear. "Don't," he pleaded, pulling her into his arms.

She pushed against his chest; then grabbed the front of his tunic, burying her face in his shoulder. His tunic pulled tight across his back, searing it, but nothing felt more painful to him than her guilt.

Holding her against him, he rocked her like a child. She wasn't going to let him dismiss or minimize her responsibility for her mother's death, and the guilt it invoked was unbearable. Nothing he did now could keep her from falling into that paralyzing pit of despair—he knew all too well. The only thing he could do was hold on to her—and go with her.

The door cracked opened, Shur stared at them for several moments, before quietly shutting it again.

His news put Ateron into a very good humor. "I told you there was something between them. The silken cord is much stronger than I imagined," he said to Cartu.

"And that makes it all the more likely they will—or are—plotting an escape."

"I have no doubt, and any attempt at escape could spoil my plans. You better instruct Pel to tighten security. Have the guards increase the number of times they look in on Hadlee, whenever Ryder is with her. I would ask Taya to tell me everything that goes on, but she is more likely to be part of the plotting than a reliable spy."

Cartu's eyes lit with a particular gleam that always chilled his sovereign. "When she is mine, I will teach her obedience."

Twenty-four

Ryder rocked Hadlee as years of suppressed guilt and shame poured out of her. Completely drained, she leaned against him, a rag doll in his arms. After her breathing slowed and she quit hiccupping sobs, she lifted her head from his shoulder.

Her eyes widened with astonishment at the depth of anguish and remorse that flowed down Ryder's face. Her finger caught a tear as it dripped off his cheek. Abruptly, she wrenched herself out of his arms, unable to bear the sight of his torment.

She jumped to her feet and stumbled to her bedchamber. Her shaking fingers took hold of the curtain, parting it. She paused. Her voice quivered over her shoulder, "I don't want to hurt you anymore. I deserve all the unhappiness and pain I've suffered, and the guilt I feel." She sniffed and wiped her eyes with the sleeve of her tunic.

"Do you believe we can be forgiven, Hadlee?"

The unexpected sound of her name coming from his lips jerked her head back toward him.

"Do you believe in Christ's Atonement?"

Her eyes dropped. "I told you I lost my faith to hurt you."

Hope rang in his voice, "Are you saying you didn't lose your faith?"

"Actually, I did leave the church for almost a year." She walked back and sat down again on the landing, "It wasn't because I didn't believe. I was just so angry about everything. It was all so unfair. I felt like the Lord and everyone I loved had abandoned me." She shivered and hugged herself.

"I'm so sorry. It sounds so pathetic to keep saying that, but there just aren't words to express my regret." Ryder wiped his face with his sleeve. "I can't even imagine what it was like for you to lose your dad too."

"It was the darkest time of my life." Her face puckered, but she held back the tears. "I shut it all out by flying as many hours as David Willard would let me, but that wasn't enough. I started doing air shows and stunt flying on the side. Then I was almost involved in a mid-air collision. It wasn't my fault, but I came within a heartbeat of losing my life. It made me stop and really look at my heading, or rather, my lack of one. I went back to church and managed to lock my bitterness away in the same vault I hid my own guilt."

Poignant empathy filled Ryder's eyes.

Shame dropped hers.

She twisted her braid. "I do believe in the Atonement . . . Ryder," she said his name tentatively, "even if I haven't allowed it to help me." Her eyes came up. "How could it help me, when for the past twelve years I have refused to acknowledge my own guilt?"

Relief, like a cleansing shower, washed over Ryder's face. "Then let it help you now—help us." He got to his feet. "We could begin the repentance process together. If we let the Atonement help us, these wounds we've carried for so long will finally heal. Then we can be at peace and move on with our lives."

He held his hand out to her in a gesture of solidarity. She hesitantly put her fingers in his. He pulled her to her feet, led her out onto the terrace and knelt.

"Prayer is always a good place to start."

Hadlee dropped to her knees. They bowed their heads and took turns praying.

Seeking forgiveness and pleading for mercy was an awkward, tender experience that left their faces wet. First, with the bitter, jarring tears of guilt and shame, and then with the gentle bathing ones of broken hearts and contrite spirits, invoking the beginning of cleansing. By the time they left their knees, hope had begun its patient work.

They smiled bravely at each other.

"Do you think I'll ever know if my parents have forgiven me?"

He took hold of her shoulders, "I'm sure of it, but it may take some time. Be patient and keep praying." He looked at her thoughtfully. "You know, we ought to start studying the scriptures."

"You have a set of scriptures with you?"

He pointed to his head. "They're all up here. I was a missionary, and I learned a lot of scriptures, especially about repentance, mercy, and forgiveness."

She sighed. "I need that kind of wound treatment."

"I do too. So this evening I'll be back, for scriptures, prayer, and language lessons."

"Language lessons," she said with a grimace.

"Don't look so glum. Learning Injanae is the only good thing Ateron has ordered so far. The more you can communicate, the less you'll feel like a prisoner."

"I don't know about that, but I'd love to be able to talk to Taya. I can't begin to tell you how tired I am of charades!"

The sound of light footsteps crossing the apartment announced Taya's return. They hastily wiped their faces again. She came out onto the terrace, looking at them anxiously. They gave her the same brave smiles they had given each other.

"Ryder . . . is everything okay?" she asked.

"No, but Hadlee and I have agreed to work on our problems. I'm hopeful things are going to get better."

"Good. Now I want to finish treating your back."

He shook his head.

Taya looked at Hadlee, pointed to his back, took his arm, and tried to pull him over to a bench. She couldn't budge him.

"What was Taya doing to your back when I interrupted?" asked Hadlee.

"Applying one of her herbal remedies. She's been my doctor since Ateron threw me in the dungeon. I'd be in a lot worse shape if it weren't for her. She's my angel of mercy," Ryder said, smiling down on the angel who continued to tug on his arm.

"You need to let her finish." Hadlee took his other arm, unsuccessfully adding her own efforts.

"No, really, I'm alright," he said, but they kept tugging.

Their stubborn persistence convinced him he wasn't going to win this one either. "Women," he muttered, letting them lead him to a bench, push him down onto it, and help him off with his tunic.

He looked up at Hadlee as she stared over his shoulder at his back. She bit her lip and sucked in a ragged breath. "Ryder, tell Taya I want her to teach me how to take care of your back."

"Pilot, you don't need—"

"I do need to." She dropped to her knees in front of him. "I'm responsible for this and I need to do something to make restitution for my—*hate.*" Her face flamed.

His jaw tightened. "Alright."

Ryder interpreted as Taya instructed and Hadlee worked. He noticed Hadlee stopped several times to wipe her eyes while she treated—what she frankly told him was—"the ghastly evidence of my animosity." When she was done applying the ointment, Taya gave her a soft, gauzy fabric, instructing Ryder to tell her to wind it around his back and chest, and then up over his shoulders to hold it in place.

"It will protect you against the rubbing of your tunic when you move," Taya said.

Hadlee tied off the gauze, and they helped him back into his tunic. He stood, took their hands, and brushed a kiss over each girl's knuckles, formally expressing his thanks.

Hadlee pulled her hand back and turned away, but not before Ryder saw the guilt puckering her face. He caught her arm. She looked over her shoulder at him.

"I'll be alright." He smiled, turned to Taya and said, "Now I have to meet Kytan, and I desperately need my breakfast."

Whispers and stares followed Ryder's descent down the service stairs and out the slaves' exit. He cheerfully said good morning to everyone he met, but it required real effort to keep the pain off his face. His back was still agonizingly sore, even with the herbs and wrapping. Without a doubt, he knew it was going to be a long, miserable day.

The belfry finished ringing nine times before Ryder saw his friend approaching the gate, carrying a big leather pouch.

It was easy to spot Kytan in a crowd. He was the tallest man Ryder had seen in Injanae, toping six feet by a couple of inches. His obvious dismay when he saw Ryder waiting for him, made Ryder sputter a laugh. "I can tell you're disappointed not to see my fair doctor."

"Well . . . ah . . . I just didn't think you would be up so soon," said Kytan, recovering his countenance. "I am— amazed." He looked Ryder over with a skeptical brow. "Should you be up?"

"I'm starving, why don't you come and have breakfast with me, compliments of the king, and I'll tell you all my troubles."

"Hmm, eating the at the king's table, how can I refuse?"

They went back through the slaves' entrance, down several narrow passages and into the kitchen.

Ceeona's round face scrunched up in delight. "Every slave in the palace knows how bravely you took your punishment, Ryder, and everyone is proud of you." She patted his arm. "So how are you feeling?"

Taking her hand, Ryder said, I'm okay, but starving. I know it's too late for breakfast, but could we raid the Kitchen?"

Ceeona loaded a platter with smoked fish, potatoes, berries, cheese, and fresh bread. She handed it to Ryder with a wink, and then gave Kytan a jug of water and two cups.

Eating took all Ryder's concentration. He hadn't eaten a substantial meal in three days. Kytan's dimples danced with appreciation as Ryder consumed a vast amount of food.

When he'd taken the edge off his appetite, Ryder said, "You and I have an appointment with the king in a little while, and as soon as the interview is over I'm going back to work. My unscheduled vacation is over."

"That may be, but can you make it through a day's work? You look like a man holding himself in pretty tight control," Kytan said, swallowing a mouthful of pungent cheese.

"It would be a relief to take my tunic off. But I don't intent to walk around shirtless for the next several days displaying Cartu's handy work just for my own comfort. Taya is giving me herbs for the pain, and it won't be long before I can forget all about this. Now, I'd like to see the hammer and nails."

Kytan pulled them from his bag and handed them across the table to Ryder. "What do you think?"

Ryder turned the hammer over in his hands and inspected the nails. "They look good—real good. Let's go to the construction site and try them out."

They only managed to hammer a few nails before the king's summons came.

Kytan was told to wait while Ryder was admitted into the king's judgment chamber. Composing his features, Ryder strode boldly down the length of the hall to the dais, knelt and put his forehead on the floor. The weight of the king's silence pressed down on his lacerated back until Ateron condescended to break it.

"The unpleasantness we have all suffered because of your actions will not happen again. I trusted you, and you broke my trust. That is something I told you I would not tolerate. Because of that, you are no longer allowed to leave the palace grounds unescorted." He paused, and Ryder listened to him pace. "If you have anything to say for yourself you may raise your head and speak."

Ryder raised a blank face and staunchly held onto it. Cartu stood behind the king, idly flicking a rapa. Ryder rolled his shoulders, easing the tug of his tunic across his burning back, and forced his eyes to meet Ateron's. "I deserved my punishment for breaking your trust and leaving without permission."

Looks of startled surprise appeared and vanished with equal speed, on the faces of the king and Cartu. The latter frowned, but Ateron nodded his approval at this straightforward admission and then warned, "If there is another breach of trust, I will instruct Cartu not to be so gentle with you." He motioned to Cartu. "Bring Kytan in. After he shows us the nails"—he glared at Ryder—"you will go back to work."

At the end of a short demonstration of the nails' strength and the hammer's power, Ateron asked, "How quickly can you produce the nails and hammers Ryder needs, Kytan?"

"My forge is small, but I will do the best I can."

The king pursed his lips. "I see. What you need is a bigger forge, and an assistant."

Under the king's directive, Kytan took charge of the king's forge. By the end of the week, with the help Idon and the forge slaves, hundreds of nails and dozens of hammers were ready for Ryder's crew, and the stairs began their ascent.

Twenty-five

Making his way through the dinner line in the slave's hall, Ryder mulled over the past few weeks. He looked forward to every visit with Hadlee. She was sharp minded, and already picking up basic phrases in Injanae. He was equally impressed with her scriptural knowledge and insights. Scriptures and prayers were a bond of comfort and hope growing between them. Still, the time they spent together was often somber and usually a little tense—if not awkward. There were moments when her eyes expressed so much grief it wrenched his heart all over again.

He dug into a mound of potatoes. His heart still yearned for the healing of her forgiveness, but he was grateful the passing weeks had at least healed his physical wounds. According to Hadlee and Taya, the only remaining signs of his lashing were some yellowish patches where the bruising was the worst and a few thin red lines left by the bite of the rapa. Now entirely pain free, he informed the two most stubborn women he'd ever met that their daily inspections of his back, which he'd endured because he couldn't fight both them, *or even one of them,* he admitted—were done.

The irony wasn't lost on him. The lashing *had* turned out to be a very painful blessing, accomplishing the impossible. It breached the barrier of Hadlee's hate, broke down her defenses, and he shamelessly used her guilt to get her to open up about her life.

"After I got used to living with my four male cousins, I found it had certain advantages and included a good deal of intrigue," she told him one dismal rainy night.

"For instance?"

She related a string of comical adventures, and scrapes she'd got into with her cousins. They made Ryder laugh, and explained, in his mind, how she gained her adventurous, confident and very outspoken nature.

"So what made you become a pilot?"

"When I turned fourteen, Uncle Bill took me up in one of his airplanes as a birthday surprise. He owns an airfreight business. I didn't really want to go—and said so. His disappointment made me change my mind."

"And your life?"

Her eyes glowed with the memory of that first flight. "Yes. I fell in love as soon as we took off. My uncle's a great pilot. He did some loops and deep dives that made me feel more alive than anything had since Mama died. From that moment on, I knew I wanted to be a pilot."

His lips twitched. "How did your aunt take it?"

A rebellious glint replaced the glow. "My aunt was indignant, 'refined young ladies don't become pilots,' she told me."

A blustery gust of wind whistled in through the terrace door, which Hadlee always left cracked open. She said it made her feel less like a prisoner. It blew her hair around her face like silver streamers and spattered the floor with rain.

Ryder jumped up and secured the door's latch against the wind, urging her to continue.

"My aunt finally gave in, when she saw how happy flying made me. She agreed to let Uncle Bill give me lessons. I was so good—he let me solo at sixteen and hired me to fly the regular hop up to Ogden and back that summer."

A smile touched Ryder's heart, the nickname he'd given her definitely fit.

"When I ran off to California, David Willard hired me because I could out fly all of his other pilots."

Her reasons for running away to California settled into the room like the dark, threatening clouds outside.

"How did you end up in Peru?" Ryder asked, hoping to disperse them.

"David accepted a contract to fly supplies into an Incan dig site. A good friend of his was one of the men sponsoring the dig, and the money he was offered—for two months work—was too good to pass up. He told me he needed his best pilots because of the risks involved in flying through the Andes. He paid me almost half a year's salary to come, and he made the four of us, who accepted the job, train with parachutes."

"And that saved your life."

"It did. But when we first started the training, I was so confident of my flying skills, I thought it was unnecessary. Thankfully, David insisted."

"Did you have a choice about taking on this job, considering the risks?"

"Yes, but I couldn't pass up the chance to see the country that stole my father from me. I hoped if I saw Peru I would understand my dad better."

"And do you, now that you have?"

She shrugged, leaned back against the sofa and stretched out her long legs. "I really wanted to see the digs Dad worked on, but they were too small and remote. I settled for seeing the spectacular sights I could get to easily by plane. David arranged for the plane I crashed and gave me three days to go wherever I wanted. I loved what I saw, so maybe I do understand my dad better."

That knowledge brought Ryder a small measure of comfort. He finished dinner, deposited his dishes in the washtub, and headed down to the hot springs bath to clean up before giving Hadlee her evening language lesson. His growing insights into Hadlee's life were always bittersweet experiences. They brought intense guilt, painful understanding, and boundless admiration.

After an hour of forming the tongue twisting words of the Injanae language, Hadlee begged for a break. Giving Ryder a tentative glance, she said, "I've told you a lot about my family. I think it's time you told me something about yours." She smiled at his look of surprise.

Without hesitation, he answered, "I have two sisters. Hannah is two years younger than I am. She got married just before I graduated from college. Her husband, Clint Gilbert, is the son of our ranch foreman. My baby sister, Jessie, graduated from high school a month after Hannah got married. I don't know what she's doing now. She's a cowgirl through and through and wasn't particularly interested in going on to college."

"What about your parents?"

"Well, it wasn't love at first sight, if that's what you're asking."

"Oh?" She pulled her knees up and leaned forward.

He told her the tale that resulted in the marriage of the last, half Nahtow Indian princess, and the six foot, nine inch, green eyed, redheaded, Irish, U.S. Marshal. Their adventure kept her on the edge of her seat, and as Ryder described his mother, she saw his Nahtow heritage in the unique color of his eyes and high cheekbones.

Ryder concluded his parents' adventure, slouched back against the sofa and puffed out a disgusted breath. "I've been a big disappointment to them. They should have named me Rough—that's what I've been for them."

She touched his sleeve. "That should have been my name too. Raising me was no picnic for my poor aunt and uncle. I deliberately got into trouble with my cousins because I was so angry about being sent to live with them. Every one of the Brannigans took me into their hearts and loved me, but I couldn't accept it. Somehow it felt like a betrayal of my family to be happy when my mother was dead, and my father was so distant and sad."

Her admission plunged them both into melancholy. They traded glum expressions. Their gloomy mood brought the one question that had gnawed at Hadlee constantly over the years to the forefront of her mind. She gathered her courage, deciding there would never be a better time to ask. "I'd like to know something—" Her courage wavered, and she shook her head.

"What?"

She didn't answer.

"What do you want to know? I'll tell you anything," he said without reservation.

"It's just—I have never understood why you stole your uncle's car and came into town for something as . . . insignificant as an ice cream cone."

Shame fired his face.

Seeing his discomfort, she quickly added, "You don't have to tell me."

He held up his hand. "I do have to tell you. You are the one person in the world who has the right to know." He sat up, squaring his massive shoulders. "I have a photographic memory."

"Really?"

"Yeah."

"Is that why you can quote so many long passages of scripture?"

"Uh-huh, and my memory isn't only visual, it's auditory too." He mimicked the voices of Jack Benny, and Jimmy Durante with perfect timbre and intonation.

She fell back into the sofa pillows and laughed. "You're very good, but can you truly remember everything you see and hear?"

"Yeah and when what I'm seeing or hearing is intense, or emotional, my memory goes into overdrive. Everything seems to slow down and move in slow motion while my mind takes in every last detail of the experience."

"That must be a wonderful gift."

"You might think so, but it's gotten me into a lot of trouble."

"How?"

"I jumped a few grades in school because of it. That led to my association with guys a lot older than me." He blew out disgust and admitted, "I fit in real good because of my size, and I liked their acceptance. They were a bunch of ranch kids, wild and pretty reckless. I started sneaking out at night to go into town with them. I got drunk a couple of times and tossed into jail. I had a colorful juvenile record by the time I was thirteen."

"You didn't." Her reproachful stare blistered him all the way to his ears.

"Needless to say my parents weren't happy. Actually, they were beside themselves, trying to figure out what to do with me." He grimaced. "My dad started locking me in my room at night, but before he could get bars on my window, I got out, *one—last—time.*"

"I take it something happened that night."

"Yeah. I climbed out my window, met my buddies on the road, and we drove into town. It was about two in the morning." He paused and looked away, his expression conveying his shame.

"Ryder, you don't have to tell me this."

"Yeah, I do. You have the right to know what led up to your mother's death." He looked down at his hands. "One of my friends brought his twenty-two rifle. We shot out the windows in several cars. We thought it was so—*funny.*" His fists clenched. "At first, I didn't do any of the shooting, but my buddies urged me, so I took my turn. I shot out the side window of a car. The glass shattered and a girl started screaming."

Hadlee gasped and hugged her knees. "Did you hit her?"

"No, thankfully, but the glass cut her arm up and she needed a few stitches."

"What was she doing out in a car—oh!"

"That's right. Her boyfriend jumped out of the car as we sped off. We beat a hasty retreat out of town, not knowing he'd gotten our license plate number. The sheriff was downstairs with my dad when I got up the next morning. My three *buddies* gave me up as the shooter, and the sheriff hauled me off to jail. That's where I should have stayed, except my dad's a pretty big gun in Glenwood Springs. He paid for all the windows we shot out and made a deal with the girl's family. I can only imagine what that cost."

Hadlee's tight lips and shaking head delivered a stinging lecture. What he'd done wasn't just a juvenile escapade. No, it was genuine criminal mischief.

He hung his head and ran his hand across the back of his neck. "I know I should have been kept in jail like my buddies for that crime. I wasn't, because my dad also made a deal with the county prosecutor, and that's where your mother's death began."

"I would say a former U.S. Marshall is a pretty big gun. I'm not surprised he had the power to make a deal to keep you out of jail." She tried and failed to swallow that bitter injustice. *If you'd just been kept in jail, Mama would still be alive.* She stopped, choked by her own hypocrisy. *And if I'd just been obedient, she would be alive. But he was old enough to know better,* she rationalized. *But so was I,* her conscience reminded her. *My deliberate disobedience was just as much to blame for Mama's death as his choice to steal a car.*

"I didn't know about the deal my dad made when he came to get me out of jail. I can't begin to tell you how scared I was after a week in a cell. I was so relieved when the sheriff opened that door, and my dad jerked his head and said, 'Let's go,' that I didn't care where we were going as long as I wasn't staying in jail. We got in the truck and started driving. We drove all day. Dad didn't say a word to me, and I didn't dare ask him anything. When I figured out where we were headed, I was really scared."

Hadlee stretched her legs back out. "But you were just going to your uncle's, why were you afraid of that?"

He blew out a breath. "My uncle Jared raised five boys, and some of the stories I heard from my cousins when I was growing up—well, I was about to learn the truth of them."

"What did he do to you?" she asked, and then held up her hand. "Don't answer that."

"Don't waste your pity on me, I don't deserve it. If you want to understand what happened the day of the accident, and why, I'll finish this story—it's up to you."

She hesitated, scrunching the edge of her tunic between her fingers. "I need to know."

"Alright—just keep in mind everything that happened to me I brought on myself, by my own bad choices," he said, and continued with the story. "When we turned down the road to my uncle's farm, I broke down and started pleading with my dad not to leave me there. He didn't say a word. My uncle was waiting for us when my dad stopped the truck, got out, and told me to get out too. I didn't budge. He reached in, hauled me out, dumped me onto the ground, and looked at me with a face I'd never seen before.

"He said, 'You've broken your mother's heart. She's cried endless tears over you. She did everything she could to love you and treat you with kindness, and I did everything I could think of to teach you right from wrong. Your mother and I have worn out our knees praying over you, and nothing we've done has helped you. Maybe we were just too soft on you, but that's about to change. After the stunt you just pulled, I've decided it's time for a new approach with you.' He turned to my uncle and said, 'Don't spare him, Jared, he doesn't deserve it,' and got into the truck. He leaned out the window, fixed me with a dead-eyed stare, and said, 'I am ashamed to call you my son.'" Ryder's voice broke on the words.

An eerie chill shivered over Hadlee. He was literally speaking his father's words, using, what she could only assume, was his father's voice. It made the whole thing so real, so tangible, so awful. Even more awful, the sympathy she felt was all for Ryder's parents. Her little rebellions growing up were nothing compared to his criminal behavior. It took a concerted effort to keep the contempt she felt for him at that moment, after hearing the despair in his father's voice, from leaping off her tongue. She pressed her lips together.

"Every word he said was true." Ryder confirmed her contempt. "There was a rebellious streak in me wider than the state of Texas, and a will to match. I rejected every gentle effort my parents made to help me see the error of my ways. I thought my amazing gift made me so much smarter than anyone else. So, of course, I didn't need church, or school or my parents to tell me what to do."

She swallowed the stinging words threatening to escape her mouth. *Maybe having perfect recall isn't such a great gift, not if you become a criminally, disrespectful know-it-all.*

He cleared his throat, fighting the emotions that tugged at his face and pushed back the strand of hair that habitually fell over the scar on his left temple. "Only a few people know the whole story of what happened during the time I spent at my uncle's farm, and I'm not trying to enlist your sympathy by telling you now. But what happened did influence my decision." He held her eyes, "Just remember there's no excuse for what I chose to do that day."

His expression and tone of voice, ratcheted up Hadlee's pulse rate and almost made her stop him . . . almost. She bit her lip and tried to dislodge the ugly claws of fear that gripped her.

"My uncle, all six foot eight and three hundred pounds of pure muscle, looked down at me and said, 'I understand it is your birthday today, and we need to start this new year of your life off right. So I'm going to give you the gift of a little education.' "

Hadlee reached for a pillow, hugging it like a shield, a protection against an unknown, but eminent horror. His voice had changed. Now she was listening to the cold, harsh tones of his uncle Jared. She wondered if he even knew he was doing it, or if that was just how his uncanny memory worked.

"He picked me up off the ground by the front of my shirt, and hauled me off to the barn. If you will remember, I was over six feet myself by then, but I was mostly just skin and bones, it took me a few more years to fill out."

She bobbed her head. He had been kind of gangly, and for a moment she wondered how long it took him to develop the body builder muscles so evident now. As he continued, she reminded herself to think of him as he was at fourteen.

"Jared hauled me into a horse stall, closed the door and let go of me. I backed away from him until I hit the wall of the stall. He said, 'We're going to have a little chat before we start your education. You've brought shame on your father and to the good name of Garrison. No father should be ashamed of his son, and we're going to change that. I always start a boy's education off with one fundamental lesson in humility. I have a nice old friend here who has helped my five sons find humility, and it's going to help you too.' He took off a heavy leather belt, hung it over the railing, and reached for me."

Twenty-six

Ryder's lesson in humility made Hadlee cower into the corner of the sofa. The pillow she held was mangled beyond redemption.

"When he finally quit educating me, he dumped me onto the stall floor, right into a fresh pile of horse manure, and said; 'Now, son, I hope this first lesson has helped you understand the way things are going to be around here, and taught you a little bit more about humility.'"

A scornful sound erupted from Hadlee.

"Exactly." Ryder's face went cold. "All I really gained from that lesson was a massive amount of anger."

The belfry began clanging the hour. Hadlee wondered if she would ever get used to its constant, boisterous interruptions, but in this instance, she was grateful. The premeditated brutality of Ryder's uncle appalled her and made her remember all the terrible things she'd wished on him as a child. Worst of all, there was still a whisper in her heart that kept saying he deserved what he got because he brought it on himself. That thought made her flinch. *If he deserves what happened to him . . . then I deserve everything bad that's happened to me too.*

The bells finally fell silent.

"I can't believe your father knew what your uncle would do to you."

"He didn't. But at the time, I thought he did. Everyone in the family knew my uncle advocated corporal punishment, just not the extent of it. My dad thought a little *education* by Jared wouldn't be as bad for me as being shut up in prison with hardened criminals. He was afraid I would come out more hardened than when I went in."

"But you did end up in prison, and you didn't come out more hardened."

"Thankfully—because of your dad—I didn't. There's no telling what would have happened if I'd been sent to prison for just shooting out a car window."

"So you agree with what your dad chose to do?"

"No, but I understand why he did it. Although at the time, I thought he wanted me to suffer as much pain and humiliation as my uncle could inflict on me."

His face filled with the self-condemnation she'd just experienced and become all too familiar with in the past few weeks. An unexpected pang of real sympathy smote her, followed by a sharp dig of guilt for her judgmental and unforgiving heart.

"What it should have done was make me realize how gentle my folks were with me, but it didn't. I was so blind— not to mention ungrateful and stupid—all I felt was anger. I decided right then my dad was my mortal enemy, and what I'd just been through was *his* fault and I would never forgive him. I let that idea poison me like rattlesnake venom."

"I don't think anyone could blame you for feeling angry."

"You should blame me. If I had just faced the fact that my situation was my own fault, brought on by my own rebellious and even criminal actions, your mother would still be alive. Instead, I blamed everyone except myself for my situation— especially my dad. He put me in the nightmare I was living in, and I really didn't think shooting out a window, even if the girl needed a few stitches, was a crime so bad I should be put in jail, or subjected to my uncle's reform school."

"Did you really believe you shouldn't have faced any consequences for that?" she asked unable to keep the reproach out of her voice.

He groaned. "I know how that sounded, and that should tell you how far gone my conscience was."

Hadlee jumped as an ugly laugh burst from him.

"I have to hand it to Jared, he was good preparation for prison . . . being a slave in Injanae . . . and taking my licks from Cartu."

"How can you laugh about any of it?" Hadlee rubbed away goose bumps.

His eyes hardened. "You should applaud my uncle for dispensing a little justice. You're certainly entitled to it, and that was only the opening round in my education."

"If that was only the opening round, I don't want to hear any more."

"Alright." He shrugged. "It's up to you, but without the whole story you will never fully understand why I took my uncle's car, or wanted an ice cream cone."

"Oh, I think I've got the picture. You endured your uncle's cold, calculating cruelty until it drove you over the edge. You were running away that day weren't you?"

"Yeah, I was. You see, the deal my father made, not only included paying a hefty fine, but removing me from the state of Colorado for the length of the juvenile prison sentence I would have received."

"Which was?"

"One year."

"You were supposed to live with your uncle for a year?" She gawked at him, swallowing hard. "I think I'm beginning to understand."

"No. I don't think you do, not yet. You see, although my uncle's educational training was brutal, it taught me something about myself that left me without excuse in your mother's death."

She plucked at the mangled pillow she still held. "What could you have possibly learned about yourself from your uncle's brand of *education?*"

"After that first lesson, when I howled like a baby and sobbed for mercy, I decided I would never let Jared hear my pain, or see my humiliation again—no matter what he did to me. He gave me weekly educational instruction, and by the time I'd been there six weeks, he couldn't get so much as a sound or tear out of me."

"How did you do that?"

"I learned I could retreat so far into a good memory, reliving it so completely, that I could barely feel the pain Jared inflicted. That taught me if I could control my response to his lessons, I could control my actions too. I could make myself do whatever I was told, no matter how I felt about it. And that's what I did for the next three weeks. I was the most obedient, subservient kid you ever met, and I didn't receive any more education."

"Then *why* did you steal your uncle's car that day?"

Ryder hung his head and rubbed the back of his neck. That habitual gesture was something Hadlee now understood. He did it whenever he was embarrassed, uncomfortable, or ashamed.

"Four days before the accident, Jared decided it was time to test me."

"How?"

"He found fault with every job I did that day and made me do them over, and over. By lunch time, I was so angry and frustrated . . . I mouthed off—"

"And got another educational experience."

"Yeah, but what he gave me that day was a lesson in higher education. By the time he finished my instruction, I was nearly unconscious. He had to carry me into the house and up to the little attic room—that was my prison. He tossed me on the bed, and that's where I stayed, until he rolled me out at four in morning on the day of the accident, and told me I was going back to work. I decided that no matter how bad I felt, I wasn't going to let him see it. He worked me like a dog in the barn until the sun came up."

"I'm surprised you could stand up, let alone work."

"I retreated into my mind, but it took all the grit I had to maintain it. After breakfast, we went out into the field and started loading hay. I picked the bales up off the ground, tossed them up onto the flatbed my aunt was driving while my uncle stacked them, until lunchtime. By then, it was scorching hot and my control was weakening—actually, it was nearly gone. I'd never maintain it that long, and the pain that slipped in was so bad, I thought I would die."

She hugged the pillow, protecting herself from feeling the pain he must have endured. "I'm amazed you lasted until lunch, but how did you escape your uncle long enough to get the car?"

"With the help of my unsuspecting aunt, and the carelessness of my uncle. After we ate lunch in the field, my uncle wandered off to find a convenient bush. As soon as he was out of earshot, I begged my aunt to let me go cool off in the pump behind the house. I hoped it would help me get a grip on my waning control."

"More like preserve your life," she said, pity coloring her voice.

"Don't," he said, and told her how he felt when he looked at Jared's car. "I knew that car was the way out of my nightmare." He shook his head, his jaw rigid.

It was obvious to Hadlee that the stark, unguarded guilt he wore was threatening to overwhelm him. The pang of sympathy she'd felt before, grew into a painful throb in her heart, watching him hang onto his self-control with bulldog tenacity.

"This is the part you really need to understand," he said, spitting the words out with a depth of self-loathing she hadn't heard before. "Right then I felt a good old fashion tug on my conscience. I knew taking that car was wrong, but I chose to shut my conscience down. I'd been dreaming of my escape since the day I arrived, and although up until that moment, I didn't know how I was going to do it, I knew what I was going to do—if I got the chance." He paused, a faraway look in his eyes.

"What were you going to do?"

"I was going to head for California and catch a ship to Alaska. I'd read articles about how wild it was up there. I knew if I could get there, no one would ever find me, and I would never come back."

"Ryder, why wasn't there anything in your court proceedings about your uncle's abuse or the fact you took the car to escape him? The court records said you stole the car on a lark, intending to just grab an ice cream cone, and then head back."

"That's the lie I told the court, and since all I had on me was about forty cents, and the clothes on my back, the judge believed me. I didn't tell him—because I felt too ashamed to tell anyone—what Jared had done to me, or admit I was running away."

Hadlee focused on the mangled pillow, escaping the sight of the guilt that plagued him, and now her. The pillow reminded her of Ryder's educational experiences. She tossed it over the back of the sofa.

"The truth is—I had no intention of stopping in town. I knew my time was limited before Jared would have the police after me. I wanted to make tracks as far and fast as I could, but when I saw that soda fountain, I decided to stop for just a moment, and get an ice cream cone to celebrate my— *freedom.*" He dropped his head and rubbed his neck.

She again drew up her knees and hugged them. "So my mother died because of a disobedient daughter, and the desire of a battered boy to celebrate running away with an ice cream cone."

"Yeah," he admitted, then added, "But in my mind, your mother died because a willfully rebellious kid deliberately chose to do something he knew, and even felt, was wrong."

"We both did," she said with finality, buried with him in a coffin of guilt.

He nodded and looked away.

"I saw a picture of you and your dad the day you were sentenced," she said hesitantly. "You were yelling at him. There was so much anguish in his face and so much anger in yours. What happened that day?"

"My dad found out about the extent of Jared's educational program and went to the judge before he sentenced me."

"I'm surprised Jared's education wasn't obvious."

His laugh slid like ice down the back of her neck. "Jared perfected his technique on his five sons. Everything he did to me was covered by my clothes. But when a doctor examined me, the evidence was indisputable, and I confessed about why I took the car. That's what made the judge lighten my sentence."

The sharp clarity of complete understanding illuminated Hadlee's mind. A new perspective began to beat in her heart. "I bet your father felt terrible."

"He did. He even apologized for leaving me with Jared and asked for my forgiveness. I told him I would never forgive him, and I never wanted to see him again."

"Are you still estranged from your father?"

"No. Your dad's letters, and getting to meet him, changed everything."

Hadlee gasped. "You met my father?

"I only met him once—face to face."

"Where? When?"

"In Buenos Aires—near the end of my mission—he came to buy more supplies for his dig. I spent one of the most memorable hours of my life with him. I loved him, Pilot"—his voice broke; he dropped his head, blinking hard—"more than I can ever tell you." After several ragged breaths, he said, "He rescued me, and that's why I don't understand what he did to you."

"I don't understand it either. I've tried, but the best I can do is believe he truly thought it was in my best interest to give me to my aunt." She kicked her toe into the deep pile of the alpaca skin rug. "But I hated him for it, and yet, I did so many unkind things to try and get my aunt to send me back to him. When I fell off the roof and broke my arm, trying to run away, he came to see me. He told me he would come as often as he could, but no matter what I did, he wasn't going to take me back. He said he just couldn't raise me, and he loved me enough to give me to someone who could. I didn't believe him, and after that, I felt like every reason I had to live was gone." She forced a smile. "That is until my uncle took me flying."

A smile flickered and died in Ryder's eyes. An uneasy silence fell between them. He broke it, changing the subject. "You have an unusual name. I've never met another Hadlee."

Jumping at the opportunity to move away from the dismal memories and painful feelings her question had invoked, she said, "My name is a combination of my father's name, Haddon, and my mother's name, Leena." She smiled sadly. "Now that they're gone, I find it comforting to have both their names. Maybe someday I will do the same thing with one of my children—if I ever get married"

Ryder left the apartment that evening with no doubt in his mind about Hadlee getting married. *She's one amazing woman,* he mused, starting down the stairs to his quarters, *strong, smart, independent, courageous, and spiritual, not to mention drop dead gorgeous. In fact, I've never seen a more breathtaking woman.*

He took hold of the door handle to his quarters and stopped—gripping it hard—his heart suddenly hammering with an ugly premonition.

Twenty-seven

Ryder stood outside the king's forge, waiting for Kytan. He hoped another batch of nails would be finished soon because he was running short.

Five minutes passed before Kytan came through the door. "Your next batch of nails is ready," he said, wiping the sweat from his face.

"Good, now let's go have dinner."

"Dinner—what a wonderful word," Kytan said lengthening his stride to keep up with Ryder.

They joined the fast growing dinner line outside the slaves dining hall, moving slowly toward the smell of fish stew, and hot bread.

Ryder whispered to Kytan as they entered the dining hall, "I hope you don't mind too much, eating with a bunch of slaves."

Kytan's dimples did a jig. "Considering I was one—and at times still feel like one—I don't mind at all."

"Good. After we eat, let's go to my quarters and talk. There are things we need to discuss." He gave Kytan a meaningful look.

They downed dinner like starving men, waiting to talk until they reached Ryder's room. Upon entering, Ryder stripped off his tunic, poured water into the basin on the washstand, grabbed a washrag, and started scrubbing away the day's dirt and sweat.

"I see your back has finally healed," Kytan said, sitting on the edge of the stone bed-shelf.

"It has, I am thankful to say, and it is due to Taya's excellent care." Ryder glanced toward Kytan.

Kytan sighed, "Taya."

The quality of that sigh put a grin on Ryder's face. "I've only got a few minutes before I have required duties, and I want to spend them talking about our escape. To get out of here—and take Taya with us—we have to find the easiest place to climb out of this valley. I can think of one place, but it's near the stone quarry and that's pretty far away. Do you know of any place closer to Telquset?"

"I know the area around Telquset very well and I can't think of any place where the cliffs aren't just sheer faces." Kytan frowned. "Maybe I should ask one of the historians. If anyone has attempted to leave Injanae by climbing the cliffs, they might know where."

Ryder finished drying off, and shook his head. "It would be very dangerous for you to start asking question about leaving Injanae." He pulled clean clothes from the chest at the end of the bed and started to dress. "No, I think we should just start by getting some supplies together. That needs to be done slowly, so no one suspects what we're doing." He gave Kytan a wry face. "I should say what you're doing. As you know, I can't leave here without ten armed guards at my heels, not to mention I haven't got any money."

"Fortunately, I am being very well paid. So, what do we need?"

"First, you need to start buying good quality rope. We will need at least a few hundred feet, in the longest lengths you can find. Buy it slowly—from different vendors. You can also start making climbing hammers, pitons, and carabineers. I'll draw them for you." Ryder finished dressing, combed his long hair and pushed it behind his ears, securing it in place with a clean headband.

Kytan cocked his head. "If I didn't know better, I would say you just cleaned up to go see a woman."

"Matter of fact, I am."

"Who is she?"

"I believe you've met her."

Kytan's face fell. "Do you have feelings for Taya?"

"I certainly do. She's beautiful, smart, talented, gentle, and completely wonderful." Ryder heaved a soulful sigh. "Any man would be fortunate to catch her eye."

"Does she have feelings for you?" Kytan asked in a dejected tone.

Ryder had never seen Kytan so downhearted. With a concerted effort, he kept the mischief off his face. "She does," he said, standing over Kytan. "We are as devoted to each other as any—brother and sister *you* will ever meet, *and if you hurt her,* I may not be able to forgive you."

Kytan's mouth fell open. "You aren't in love with her?"

"I *do* love her, and that is why I am warning you." He poked his finger into Kytan's chest. "If you want to court her, you better be very serious about it. I won't allow you, or anyone else, to hurt her. She's been hurt too much in her short life already."

Kytan looked like a man who had just escaped a death sentence. He assured Ryder of his genuine desire to woo Taya and flooded him with questions.

"If you want to know more about her, you will simply have to win her confidence. Now I'm afraid I need to go." He started for the door, not wanting to be late for Hadlee's language lesson.

"Wait, I have something I want to give you." Kytan put a fabric bag in his hand. "Thank you for all you have done for me. You kept me alive in the mine by giving me your protection and friendship, teaching me the gospel, and helping me find the courage to hope for a better future. I owe you more than I can ever repay."

The bag felt heavy in Ryder's hand. His brows lifted. "What is it?"

"Open it. I must know if it fits."

Ryder untied the strings and turned the bag over. An intricately worked gold armband fell into his palm. "Wow. This is a gift fit for a prince," he said, holding it up to the light.

Heavy strands of gold were intertwined in a complex series of braids that looped and swirled around a stunning silver-blue agate infused with clouds of gold. Ryder slid it up his arm, passed his huge bicep. "Thank you, but you must know you kept me alive in that mine too, and gave me something I've always wanted"—he extended his hand—"a brother."

Kytan gripped his hand. "Yes, that is what we are— brothers."

"There is one more thing I should mention—brother. Don't let anyone, and I mean anyone, know about your interest in Taya. I can't explain it right now, but it would be very dangerous to both of you."

Kytan searched Ryder's grim face, his own becoming a mirror of his brother's, and gave his word.

Ryder slipped through the door of Hadlee's apartment and stood transfixed by the contrast of the platinum and midnight hair that adorned the heads leaning over the large dining table, examining yards of green cloth.

He sighed just looking at them. *They are such a feast for the eyes.*

He let his eyes admire them.

They are remarkable, and for far more than their beauty. Every day they demonstrate strength of character against the evil that threatens them. A fierce protectiveness pulsed in his veins. *No matter what it costs me, I'll protect you both and get you out of here,* he silently promised them.

They looked up in unison and smiled.

He couldn't catch his breath. *They have no idea how spectacular they are.* They walked over to him, immediately spotting his armband. He took it off and let them examine it.

"Where did you get this?" Hadlee asked. "It's the most exquisite thing I have ever seen."

"My friend Kytan made it for me." He repeated this to Taya, and felt gratified by her heightened color.

"He truly has a wonderful gift," Taya said reverently.

"How did you and Kytan become friends?" asked Hadlee.

Ryder unfolded Kytan's noble gesture in serving his father's sentence, and the bond that grew between them in the mine. "The day he finished his father's sentence, and left, was one of the worst days of my life."

"I wish I could meet him. He sounds like a man worth knowing." Hadlee nodded at Taya. "And Taya's rosy cheeks tell me, she thinks he pretty swell too."

"They met over my beaten body." Ryder grimaced, accepting the armband back from Taya. "I think it was interest at first sight, maybe more."

He slid the armband back in place just before the door opened. Ateron, with Cartu in tow, walked in. Ryder dropped to his knees.

"I think it is time to see how Hadlee's language lessons are progressing," Ateron said without preamble, sauntering across the living room and settling onto a sofa.

Hadlee became an ice sculpture as Ryder explained the king's visit. He winked to reassure her. She turned her frozen face to the king and gave him a short recital.

Ateron listen with a growing smile. "She is making excellent progress," he said to Ryder, after she finished. "Now that she has shown her ability to learn our tongue, it is time to teach her what she will be saying as Ansuetra at the Lunar Celebration."

Ryder blinked. "Hadlee is supposed to pretend to be the Moon Goddess at the celebration?"

Ateron's chuckle moved like shards of glass down Ryder's spine. "She will not be pretending."

He gazed at Hadlee with a lingering appreciation that tightened Ryder's jaw. The blue tunic and slacks she wore— something she'd made to pass the time—accentuated her magnificent eyes, long legs, and cool blond hair.

"You and Taya will help her become Ansuetra. With Hadlee's excellent sewing skills, she will design and make a dress fit for Ansuetra's debut on the first night of the Lunar Celebration. I will have the fabric brought up, but it is not to be worked until I approve the design, which I want to see in one week's time. Taya will help her make her gown, and you will teach her the lines Ansuetra will say."

Taya put her hands together and bowed her pale face to them, submissively.

Ryder mechanically did the same, resisting the urge to shake Ateron's proposed madness out of his head.

Ateron rose and strolled languidly toward the door. "Tell Hadlee, two lives will depend on her ability to convince Darvoe and the nobles, she *is* Ansuetra. If she fails—*two people will die.* And if she doesn't cooperate, you and Taya will suffer the consequences." He paused. "And she will be compelled to watch."

Anger so intense his muscles pulsed, boiled in Ryder's veins. Ateron's threats infuriated him, but he was powerless to do anything—at least for the moment. He forced his muscles to relax and his face into its usual state of dull neutrality, before he raised his head from his hands.

Ateron nodded for Cartu to open the door, but Cartu's eyes were fixed on Ryder. "Where did you get that armband? Who did you steal it from?"

Ateron held out his hand, Ryder removed the armband and handed it to the king. Again, it was carefully examined, passed from one set of curious hands to the other and back again.

"This is a very remarkable ornament. Where did you come by it?" Ateron asked.

"It's a gift from"—Ryder tasted the betrayal—"Kytan."

Handing the armband back, Ateron continued to stare at it thoughtfully. "Your friend's talent would be very useful in accentuating Ansuetra's gown and beauty. Therefore, you and Kytan will meet with me tomorrow morning. I will give you the lines you are to teach the Moon Goddess, and you can introduce Kytan to her." He paused tapping his lower lip, "You may also come during your working hours when you are needed to interpret for Hadlee, while she and Kytan design her gown and jewelry. But that should only take a week." He paused. "Also, plan a daily morning and evening language lesson with her." He motioned for Cartu to open the door. "And Ryder . . . take good care of that armband, it would be a shame if you . . . lost it," he said, going through the door.

It looked to Hadlee like Taya and Ryder had been turned to stone. They remained absolutely still, staring at the door after it closed. She bore their statuary stance for as long as she could stand. "Ryder, what did Ateron say?"

Slipping the armband back into place, Ryder stood and faced her with hooded eyes. "I need to talk with Taya for a while—then I'll tell you everything."

Hadlee marched onto the terrace and threw herself down on a bench. The conversation between Ryder and Taya was moving too fast for her to make out many words, but she only half listened. Lying on her back, she looked up at the stars, forcing herself to take slow, calming breathes of the damp night air. *Whatever just happened rattled both of them, badly.*

The waiting was torture.

She jumped up, and began pacing. It had become such a habit that she could do it in the pitch black of the night and never run into any of the stone benches or large decorative pots of exotic plants. She was at the far end of the terrace in her route, when Ryder and Taya finally came out. She stopped and dropped onto a bench.

Ryder placed torches in the wall sconces, bathing the terrace in a softly swaying light. He sat down next to her, leaving room for Taya.

"So?" she asked.

"You know these people worship the Moon Goddess, and because they do, they live by a lunar calendar. On the first night of the full moon—five full moons from now—the people will celebrate the four hundredth anniversary of being brought by Ansuetra into Injanae. There will be a great Lunar Celebration to honor her. Taya says up until five years ago, the high priest chose two people to be sacrificed to Ansuetra during this annual celebration."

Hadlee gasped revulsion. "So what happened four years ago that stopped that ghoulish ritual?"

Ryder explained the history of the power struggle between the kings and the high priests, detailing what Taya knew about the loss of the high priest's power. "Essentially, Ateron solved his power struggle with a senile old high priest, named Lontae, by conning him into changing the oppressive religious rites and rituals. Then he preyed on the old priest's fears of the younger priest's efforts to usurp his power and convinced Lontae to give the council guardianship of his office, virtually surrendering all the power the priests held."

"And that's when the sacrifices stopped."

"Right; and the people were ecstatic over the changes. No longer were they forced to pay the high prices demanded by the priests to intervene on their behalf with the goddess, and live under the harsh dictates and cruel rites of the priests. That made Ateron vastly popular, and protected his power until Lontae died and Darvoe became the new high priest."

"Did the power of the priests' automatically return to Darvoe when he became the new high priest?"

"No. Darvoe had to petition the nobles' council for the return of the priests' powers, which he did. However, the conflicting voices in the noble's council—something Ateron continually encourages—prevented a majority of agreement in that volatile body, effectively blocking Darvoe from regaining the power to reenact the religious rites that terrorized the people, and threaten the king's preeminence."

Hadlee grimaced. "No wonder Ateron struts around like a high and mighty peacock. He rules Injanae with an unchecked hand, and a ruthless one, I might add."

"Yeah, up until a few weeks ago—he did."

"Oh?"

"Most of the people in Injanae are very superstitious. All the tremors Injanae has suffered over the past couple of years have helped Darvoe convince the nobles' council his intervention with Ansuetra is vital in preserving Telquset. His campaign has been so successful that recently the council reinstated his power, leaving Ateron with no recourse. The sacrifices will happen again at this coming celebration."

"You're telling me, Ateron is being forced by Darvoe to hold the sacrifices against his will? I don't believe it. He seems barbaric enough to enjoy that kind of spectacle."

"I don't think Ateron cares whether anyone dies. He just doesn't want Darvoe to hold as much power over the people as he does."

"And the sacrifices will give Darvoe that much power?"

"Yeah. In fact, there have been times in Injanae when the high priest has been more powerful than the king. The council's backing of Darvoe puts him in the preeminent power position. So of course, Ateron has to do something to counter that. He needs to stop the sacrifices in some spectacular way that will discredit Darvoe."

"So what spectacular trick is he going to do that will—"

Ryder's expression made the question die on her tongue.

Her jaw dropped. "Oh . . . no—*no!* Is he nuts?"

"I'm afraid that's a given, but don't confuse insanity with cunning. He's a man who has a great deal of that. Taya's heard some pretty chilling theories about Ateron's ascension to the throne, and the death of his first wife."

"He can't possibly get away with passing me off as a pagan goddess!"

"First, I think he can get away with passing you off as Ansuetra. No one in Injanae has ever seen anyone like you. Even Taya thought you were a goddess when she first saw you."

"But what about you, you're not like the people here either. They didn't think you were a god when you came, did they?"

"No, they didn't, because I was introduced right way as an outsider, which brings me to my second point. That's why you are being kept hidden."

She jumped up, walked to the wall and back again, hugging herself. "How am I supposed to make anyone believe this farce? I'm no actress, and I don't speak enough of the language to convince Darvoe—or anyone else for that matter—that I'm Ansuetra."

"To begin with, you'll need to keep learning the language. That's why Ateron came here tonight. He's written a script for Ansuetra, and wanted to know how good your pronunciation is. Unfortunately, it's very good, and I'm supposed to start teaching you Ansuetra's lines as soon as he gives them to me tomorrow."

Hugging herself tighter, Hadlee rigorously shook her head.

"If it's any comfort, the fact that Ansuetra's part is scripted must mean you will be acting in a highly controlled situation—it has to be. If this con doesn't work, Ateron might find himself in a lot of trouble. He can't afford to put you in a position where anyone will discover you aren't Ansuetra."

"You can't be sure of that. And even if it is a controlled situation, what happens if I do something wrong like . . . miss a line, or worse—*panic?*"

He stood and took hold of her shoulders. "You're a pilot. You fly through the air and jump out of planes. How can you be afraid of a little thing like acting?"

"Because if I understand this right; I do anything wrong, and two people are going to die!" She pulled away from him. "I won't do it—*I won't!*"

He shrugged "Okay. I'll tell Ateron in the morning."

Her shoulder's drooped with resignation and she growled, "You know perfectly well he has two very big pieces of ammunition to use against me to make me do this. He did threaten you and Taya, didn't he? I may not understand much of the language, but I'm not blind. Taya's face went dead white, and your jaw was so tight I'm surprised you didn't break any teeth. What did he say?"

"Just what you think he said, and there's no point in dwelling on it."

"So he said he would hurt you and Taya if I don't cooperate."

"Yeah. Now can we just let it go?"

She took hold of his arm. "There's more, I know there is. Stop playing the over protective Boy Scout, doing your duty to shield me, and just tell me."

"Fine," he said through his teeth. "Ateron said you'll get to watch him punish us."

Her outrage tore through the night air, causing more than one citizen down in the street to stop in fright.

Ryder reached for her.

She backed away, leaning her head against the wall. "I am a slave with no choice—*no choice.*"

He laid his hand on her shoulder. "None of us have, but we can use the time to plan and prepare for our escape."

She shrugged his hand off and straightened. "And just how are we going to acquire all the things we need for a trek up a sheer cliff and then a mountain. I bet you're watched constantly since you went AWOL, Taya too. You two are sitting on Ateron's big secret, and he's not going to take any chances."

"True, but there's one more player in this game you haven't met yet," Ryder said like a gambler with a card up his sleeve.

"Who?"

"You're going to get your wish."

"What wish?"

"Kytan's gift has just landed him in the middle of this nightmare. Ateron is going to commission him to make jewelry for Ansuetra. To do that, he has to meet you."

Hadlee groaned, "And that will put him in as much jeopardy as the rest of us, won't it?"

"Yeah, but he's as eager to get out of here as we are and willing to take some risks to do it too. He'll be our ace, free to move around the city, which will allow him to buy supplies and equipment for our escape. So tomorrow, after you meet Kytan, we're going to start making our own plans."

Twenty-eight

Loud pounding on the door to his shop woke Kytan. Pulling on his tunic, he opened the door to the King's formidable bodyguard, named Sual.

"You are to be in the king's judgment chamber by seven bells." Sual tossed a small copper token at him.

Kytan fumbled with the unexpected object, before securing it.

"Give that to the servant at the king's gate. He will escort you in," Sual barked, and stalked off, without any further explanation.

The belfry chimed the sequence for six fifteen, before Kytan left his shop. Anxious to be in the king's judgment chamber on time, his long strides ate up the distance to the palace, while he worried and wondered about what Ateron wanted.

At the king's gate, he joined the long line of people hoping for an audience with various palace officials. The length of the line made him doubt he would get through it before he was due to meet the king.

He fidgeted with the copper token, watching an elderly man in the king's livery shuffle along the line, questioning the people. When the servant reached him, he asked without interest, "What is your business?"

Kytan handed him the copper token, telling him what Sual had said. The servant immediately ushered him through the gate.

He was surprised when he wasn't taken to the king's common judgment chamber on the second floor. Instead, he was turned over to the solemn captain of Ateron's bodyguards, who led him up the same set of stairs he used when he'd visited Ryder. He glanced down the hall at the closed door of Ryder's quarters when they passed that landing, and followed Pel on up half a level.

The hall Pel led him through was rich with grandeur. Colorful glazed tiles in geometric patterns finished the floors. The finest gold plaques and detailed tapestries he'd ever seen graced the upper half of the walls, depicting scenes from the history of Injanae and particularly the events of the king's life. Large, airy alcoves held shoulder high ceramic pots, gold statuary and comfortable chairs, set on deep alpaca fur rugs.

His feet lagged, trying to take it all in.

Pel called him sharply to attention twice before they reached the closed doors of the king's private judgment chamber.

"Sit here and wait," Pel said, indicating Kytan should sit on a gold inlaid bench.

Kytan sat gingerly on the edge of the bench. His eyes ran over the gold plated door and back to the magnificence of the hall.

Pel turned to the heavily armed guard standing next to the door. "Moran, this is Kytan. The king is expecting him and should call for him in a few minutes."

Moran nodded, and Pel walked back down the hall.

Ryder knelt at the bottom of the king's dais, listening to Ateron outline the whole plan for the Lunar Celebration with growing amazement. *He certainly doesn't lack ingenuity or guts.* It was a bold plan, and one that hung completely on Hadlee's ability to learn the language and act out her part.

The king came to the end of his lecture, motioning with his hand. Cartu put a scroll into it. "Do you read our written language?" he asked

"No."

"No matter." Ateron handed him the scroll. "Taya, or Kytan—if he reads—can tell you what it says, and you can teach it to Hadlee. This scroll is not to leave Hadlee's quarters. Taya is to assume responsibility for it and will be held accountable for keeping it safe. See that she understands the importance of this responsibility."

Anger at the veiled threat against Taya, kept Ryder's eyes lowered. Unsure he could command a civil response, he merely nodded his understanding.

"Good, now if your friend has arrived, he can join us." Ateron motioned to his chancellor to admit Kytan.

Kytan's overwrought nerves made him jump when Cartu opened the door and barked his name. He meekly followed the Chancellor into the king's judgment chamber. Seeing Ryder, he immediately felt calmer. He knelt beside Ryder, put his hands together and touched his forehead to the floor.

The king accepted his allegiance, allowed him to raise his head, but didn't indicate he could stand.

An alarm sounded in Kytan's head. Glancing at Ryder's blank face, he let his go blank too, before meeting Ateron's eyes.

"Kytan, it has come to my attention that you have great talent," said Ateron, gesturing at Ryder's armband.

Kytan dipped his head, accepting the compliment.

"I need your skills for a very special project. Are you willing to serve your king?"

Put like that, he couldn't refuse. "Of course, I am your servant in anything you wish me to do."

"I am gratified to hear it, but I must become your patron and have your oath, before I can give you this commission."

The king's words were a lightning bolt of understanding. *That's why I am still on my knees.*

To enjoy Ateron's patronage, he would have to become a member of the king's house and renounce his status as a free man. A distinction many men sought. As the king's personal artisan, all his needs would be provided for, and if he pleased Ateron he would be well rewarded, living in a manner far above the station of a common man. However, he would no longer be allowed to sell his skills to others, or decide on his own projects. That right would belong exclusively to the king.

The pounding of his heart slowed. He took a calming breath and told himself, *it doesn't matter. I am not spending* the rest of my life here and hopefully not even many more moons.

"Will you pledge your talents to me with an oath to faithfully carry out the commissions I entrust to you?"

Kytan felt Ryder shift uncomfortably beside him, but didn't dare look at him. Blank faced, he met the king's eyes squarely. "I so swear."

"Good!" Ateron's smile beamed down upon him. "Ryder will explain your commission. You are to do the work I require in your shop—*in complete secrecy.* I can provide most of the materials you will require and funds for those things I can't supply. You are required, from this moment on, to leave word with Pel so I can find you at all times. Everything you see and learn today is not to be spoken of—to anyone. You wouldn't want a lesson in obedience like Ryder had."

Kytan swallowed fear.

"And of course you must continue to provide nails, and anything else Ryder needs for my construction projects, which require your skills. Chancellor Cartu has arranged for you to have the collar of my personal artisan attached by Idon, tomorrow.

Kytan put his hands together, and bowed to the floor, his head reeling from this unexpected punch.

"Taya," Ryder called softly as he and Kytan entered the apartment.

She came out the door of her supply closet, juggling several pouches of herbs and a kettle. "I didn't think you would be here so early," she said, losing her grip on one of the pouches.

Kytan jumped forward catching the falling pouch. "May I help you," he asked, taking the rest of the pouches and kettle from her hands. "Where do you want these?"

She pointed to the dining table on the other side of the room.

Kytan went and set them down.

She frowned slightly, her cheek growing rosy. "Thank you, Kytan," she said, throwing Ryder a stern look for his dancing eyes.

"Is Pilot awake yet?" Ryder asked.

Before Taya could answer, the curtain at the top of the stairs parted.

Kytan looked up. His mouth fell open, his knees buckled, and he went down hard. Clasping his hands together, he put his forehead on the floor.

Hadlee looked down on this spectacle, glared at Ryder, and rolled her eyes. A clear indication the last thing she wanted this morning was a worshiper.

Ryder spread his hands and shrugged.

Lifting her chin, Hadlee descended the stairs with regal deportment, again wearing the blue tunic and slacks she'd made.

Ryder's heart did a painful flip-flop.

Stopping in front of Kytan, she dropped to her knees, clapped her hands together, and put her forehead on the floor too.

Ryder choked.

Taya covered her mouth, her shoulders shaking.

Hadlee remained motionless for several seconds then raised her head just an inch.

Ryder's face puckered with the effort it took to keep from laughing, waiting for Kytan's reaction to the long strands of Hadlee's hair lying across his clasped fingers.

Slowly Kytan's head began to rise. He looked wide-eyed at the pale strands of hair draped over his fingers, before raising his eyes farther.

Laughter sputtered from Ryder when his brother encounter startling silver-blue eyes, staring at him only inches from his face.

Kytan gasped, quickly lowering his head again.

Taya, gripped in her own irreverent struggle, bumped against Ryder, trying to keep from falling over. Unable to breath, he put his arm around her, and they tumbled into a pile of pillows, eyes streaming.

Kytan raised his head again, encountering not only the impossible blue eyes, but a dazzling smile too.

The goddess sat back on her heels and extended her hand. "It's nice to meet you, Kytan. I am Ansuetra, Goddess of the Moon—but you can call me Hadlee."

With a dazed expression, Kytan sat back on his heels too, and reached for her outstretched hand, shaking it just as

Ryder had taught him. "Thank you, Hadlee. I am honored to meet you."

The goddess gasped, jumped to her feet, and glared accusingly at Ryder. "You didn't tell me he could speak English! Oh Kytan, *you* are a gift from heaven." Extending her hands to him, she pulled him to his feet and hugged him.

Ryder's laughter died instantly as Kytan enthusiastically returned the Moon Goddess's embrace.

Turning her back on the scoffers, Hadlee led Kytan toward the terrace. "Don't mind them." She waved her hand at Ryder and Taya. "Good servants—even for Ansuetra—are hard to find."

Kytan's dimples flared over his shoulder at his now silent brother.

Ryder stood up, pulling Taya with him. She immediately followed the others out onto the terrace. He stayed where he was, frowning over the strong emotion that gripped him. Absently he began looking through the pile of cushions for the scroll he'd dropped—when he and Taya fell into them— trying to rid himself of the unwanted feeling.

He retrieved the scroll and put it down on a gilded table. Still fighting the grip of the unexpected sensation, he went to join the others. He almost ran into them on their way back in before he became aware of them.

"We are going to have breakfast," Taya said, starting for the door. "I will be back in a few minutes with everything."

Kytan tagged after her. "May I help you?"

She gave him an encouraging smile, and they went out the door together.

Ryder watched them leave, with a pensive look.

Hadlee touched his arm. "What's the matter?"

He gave himself a hard mental shake. "It's nothing," he said, following her out onto the terrace.

They strolled down its length, stopping to sit on the bench next to the flowering trellis vine.

"I really like Kytan, and it is going to be very nice to have someone else to talk to."

Ryder's brows contracted.

Hers rose, and she quickly added, "I didn't mean I don't appreciate talking to you, but you aren't here very much. Kytan's work on the jewelry will give me another person I can talk to, and not only will I get to know him, but I can finally get to know Taya better too. There are so many things I would like to know about her."

Ryder forced a smile. "There is a lot about both of them you should know, and I think it's great you'll have someone else to talk to. I forgot to tell you last night that you and Kytan are to collaborate on both the designs for the jewelry, and the gown the king is expecting you to make."

"I'm supposed to design and make a gown for Ansuetra?"

"Ateron is very impressed with your sewing skills." Ryder gestured to her outfit, and explained Ateron's dictates about the gown and the delivery of the fabric. "Taya can bring you a slate and some chalk so you can start working on it today."

"What about Ansuetra's lines?"

"I left them in the living room. After breakfast we'll go over them."

"I'm rather anxious to know what I'm going to be doing. Could you read them to me now, while we wait?"

"Unfortunately, I only speak the language, I don't read it. Most slaves aren't taught to read or write. Kytan will have to read them to you, and that brings up another matter." He looked at her squarely. "Ateron doesn't know Kytan speaks English. If he did, I probably wouldn't be coming here anymore. He would be happy to know I'm not needed as your interpreter. Then he could work me sixteen hours a day." He paused. "You can be rid of me—if you want."

Her eyes scoured his carefully neutral expression. "You think I *want* to be rid of you." It wasn't a question.

"I just thought—"

"Breakfast is here," Taya called, coming through the door.

"Great," Ryder said, standing.

Getting to her feet, Hadlee put a restraining hand on his arm and hissed, "We're not finished with this."

Twenty-nine

A fragrant smorgasbord of warm bread, baked fish, fried potatoes, and fruit was passed around. When everyone's plate was filled, Kytan asked, "What is going on? I feel like I have just come in late to a play and missed half the story."

"Up until this morning, I didn't know the whole story either," said Ryder. "Maybe we better start with how you got here, Pilot."

Hadlee recounted her entrance into Injanae, answered Kytan's numerous questions about airplanes, avoided Ryder's eyes when Kytan asked if that was why Ryder called her Pilot, and ended with, "My biggest frustration during my first week here was that I couldn't talk to anyone."

"That's the other reason the king bought me," Ryder said. "He hoped I would be able to talk to Hadlee."

"Why didn't you tell me any of this?"

"I was going to tell you before we made our escape, but the less you knew, the safer you were. Now your life is in as much danger as the rest of us."

Kytan's frown made Taya ask what was being said. He explained, and she said, "I agreed with Ryder after I met you. We knew it would be safer if you didn't know about Hadlee."

The belfry in the palace courtyard, chimed eight.

"I don't know how much time I have before my *master* will haul me back to work, and I need to tell you about Ateron's plan," Ryder said.

They rose, and went out onto the terrace. As they filed out, Ryder picked up the scroll.

Hadlee and Taya settled on a bench near the trellis. Kytan and Ryder sat on another bench facing them. Ryder briefly explained Ateron's plans for hosting the Lunar Celebration, and why, in his and Taya's opinions, Ateron didn't want the sacrifices to happen.

"Wait a minute"—Hadlee lifted a hand—"who is being cast to play the victims in this farce?"

"Darvoe is the one who will decide that. He will choose them at least three or four days before the Lunar Celebration, because they have to go through the purification rites before they can be sacrificed," Kytan said.

"But they aren't going to be sacrificed. That's where Ansuetra comes in." Ryder inclined his head to Hadlee. "Right now, Pilot, I'm in the process of clearing out an old tunnel that starts in the hallway, just outside your door. It goes through the cliff, ending at a small balcony above the rooftop garden. That's where you will make your appearance and stop the sacrifices. Ateron is keeping that job a secret. Only his bodyguards are working in the tunnel."

"So that is where the big hole in the hall leads," Taya said, after Kytan interpreted for her.

"It is, and according to Ateron, everyone has forgotten the tunnel is there," Ryder said.

Hadlee frowned. "Why was it forgotten?"

"Because about two hundred years ago, part of it caved in. Ateron said his ancestor felt it wasn't worth reopening, and had the balcony and hallway entrances bricked over—to keep the royal kids out of it—and over time it was forgotten."

"A forgotten tunnel between my apartment and the rooftop balcony certainly makes a perfect conduit for Ansuetra's dramatic entrance," Hadlee said, her frown deepening.

"It will be, once I open the tunnel all the way to the balcony wall and put in a concealed door—"

"Where I will magically appear and stop the sacrifices." Hadlee rolled her eyes. "How very theatrical, but how will I know when to come through the concealed door?"

"I'll make a peep hole, so you can see everything that happens on the sacrificial platform below the balcony. I'm sure Ateron has a particular moment he wants you to appear—"

"Just in the nick of time for the victims, no doubt."

"Yeah, but what I haven't worked out yet is how to hide your entrance through the door, and then call attention to you after you come through it."

"It all sounds very complicated, not to mention deadly." Hadlee's fingers twisted one long strand of hair.

"Admittedly, it's going take some practice. That's why Ateron wants me to have everything finished two weeks before the celebration," said Ryder.

"I don't see how we can rehearse if no one is supposed to see me."

"I'm guessing the rehearsal will be held on the night of the new moon."

Hadlee's teeth tugged at her lip, her head shaking faintly.

Ryder touched her hand. "Right now all you have to do is work with Kytan to design your dress and jewelry. Both of us can help you learn your lines. So, Kytan, if you will"—Ryder handed him the scroll—"read Hadlee her part."

Unrolling the scroll, Kytan silently read for several moments. He looked up and let out a doubtful breath.

Hadlee leaned forward. "So, what do I say?"

"I will do the best I can to interpret the words into English." He shrugged apologetically and began, "Stop! Why have you reinstated the sacrifices, Darvoe, when I told King Ateron they were to cease."

Hadlee sputtered and Taya snickered as Ryder interpreted the lines for her. He reprimanded Taya, then Hadlee. "You better get the giggles out now because when you do this, Pilot, it will be in deadly earnest."

Hadlee and Taya sobered, and Kytan continued, "Kneel, Darvoe, and explain your actions. I am outraged. It is not Ateron who has defied me, but you."

Something between a snort and a hiccup erupted from Ryder. "Well, now we know Ateron is a terrible writer," he said unsteadily. "It's really going to be a tough job to sell this, Pilot." He struggled to keep a straight face, but the laugh came out anyway. His outburst contributed to the downfall of the others.

Holding her shaking sides, Hadlee said, "Maybe it's a good thing I don't know the language well, or I would never be able to get through this ridiculous part with a straight face."

Recovering himself, Kytan held up his hand. "After you hear whatever explanation Darvoe gives, you say"—he struggled against his dimples—"silence! I will hear no more. Take him from my sight. He is no longer worthy to be my high priest. Only Ateron is worthy to hold the scepter of the high priest, only he listened . . . to my . . . voice . . . and . . ."

Kytan glanced at Ryder. They exploded; knocked each other off the bench, fell to their sides and roared.

Hadlee tried to catch her breath; collapsed into Taya, knocking her off the bench and on top of Kytan. He broke her fall and held her while she laughed herself to tears.

They were so overcome, they didn't hear Ateron enter the apartment and step with Cartu onto the terrace.

Hadlee saw them first and jerked up right. *"The king,"* she said urgently, scowling at him and his frowning companion, whose bug eyes stared at Taya.

Untangling herself from Kytan's arms, Taya hid the scroll under her as she too sat up.

Ryder and Kytan found their knees and lowered their eyes.

"It is gratifying to see all of you so happy, Ryder. I trust you have told them all about their duties, and my expectations."

"Sire, I haven't had time to explain everything yet. I thought it would be a good idea for Hadlee and Kytan to get to know each other, since they're going to be working together," Ryder said to the floor.

"It is now eight and a half bells, you may have till nine to finish your explanation. Your other work cannot wait any longer," Ateron said sternly, and turned on his heels.

The king's visit brought them back to the reality of their predicament. They sat on the terrace in glum silence, waiting to hear the door shut behind Ateron and his henchman.

Hadlee broke the silence. "Ryder, ask Taya why Cartu was staring at her. He didn't take his eyes off her, except to shoot bullets from them at Kytan. I didn't like it—it was chilling."

Kytan looked from Ryder to Taya. Before he could ask, Ryder said, "I'm sorry, that explanation will have to wait. You can ask Taya to tell you about her situation after I leave—if she wants to. I don't have much time left and there are still some things we need to go over. Kytan you will need to interpret for Taya and Hadlee."

Ryder looked around, but couldn't find the scroll until Taya pulled it out from under her. "Thank heaven you are such a bright girl. If the king had seen that scroll, while we were all behaving like idiots, I'm not sure what would have happened."

Taya started to hand him the scroll.

He held up his hand. "Ateron has put you in charge of the scroll's safe keeping. It's not to leave the apartment. You will be held accountable for keeping it safe."

Hadlee's arm encircled Taya's shoulder, when Kytan told her what Ryder had said.

"There is also something I want you to take care of, Pilot." Ryder slipped the armband off, apologizing to Kytan, "I'm sorry, but for now it's better if Hadlee holds onto this. Ateron already made a remark about my losing it. I can't wear it while I work, and it wouldn't be safe to leave it in my quarters."

Hadlee cradled it in her hands. "I'll take good care of it for you. I promise."

"I know you will." He smiled and turned to Kytan. "The instructions the king gave me last night made me realize he isn't aware you speak English." His eyes shifted to Hadlee, his face unreadable. "Do we tell him or don't we?"

"I think it would be better, mostly for me, if he doesn't find out. I like having both of you to talk too."

Ryder let out the breath he was holding and smiled his gratitude.

"Why don't you want the king to know I speak English?" Kytan asked.

"I believe once he knows you can talk to Hadlee—and act as her interpreter—he won't let me come here anymore. I'll spend all my time working on his projects, and we need time together to plan our escape. That means you and I need to be careful to speak only Injanae when we're out of this apartment."

Nodding his agreement, Kytan told Taya.

"The king also gave me a schedule for your lessons, Pilot. I'll come for an hour each morning at eight bells and again in the evening at nine. So I'll be back tonight. Oh, and I have permission to come whenever you and Kytan *desperately* need to communicate." He grinned. "Lunchtime would be good."

"I think that can be arranged," Hadlee said dryly.

"Kytan, why don't you and Hadlee go over the first few lines of the . . . ah . . . drama, then when I come back, you can read the whole thing to me so I can help too."

Kytan dimpled at Hadlee and nodded.

Ryder held up a finger, using it to punctuate his words, "I can't say this strongly enough. Be very, very careful. The door to this apartment opens without warning all the time, today was a great example of that." He turned to Hadlee. "Pilot, if there are things you need to discuss with Kytan, come out here, and have Taya stand in the entrance, so no one can take you by surprise."

He switched languages, and Kytan immediately did too, interpreting for Hadlee—in a rhythm they quickly established to keep everyone involved in the conversation.

"Taya, if you and Kytan need to talk, have Hadlee watch. The danger isn't just what language we speak; it's what we talk about too. If Cartu or Ateron hears anything that makes them uneasy about us, they could make it a lot harder than it's already going to be for us to get out of here."

Three grave faces accepted Ryder's orders with nods of agreement.

Ryder stood. "When I come back tonight we'll do some planning of our own. Until then, each of us needs to diligently do what Ateron has assigned us. Let's not give him cause to doubt our compliance." Their somber acceptance of his orders lifted the corners of Ryder's mouth. "I'm going to miss spending the day with all of you. Enjoy it and get to know each other."

He turned to leave, the weight of responsibility heavy on his brow. Taya stopped him with a hug. His huge arms swallowed her. She turned in his arms and reached out a hand to Hadlee.

Ryder opened his arms in invitation.

Hadlee hesitated, and then let him draw her into the hug.

Kytan jumped up, joining the group.

Ryder's long arms gathered them close. They held on to each other letting the minutes pass, drawing courage, sharing strength, growing in hope. When the tower bell rang nine, they broke apart, filled with a sustaining comfort.

"Let's pray before you go," Kytan said, dropping to his knees. The others followed suit, and Kytan offered the prayer.

Thirty

After Ryder left, Taya went into the depths of her supply closet, and brought out two large slates and several pieces of chalk. She handed them to Kytan and Hadlee. They went out onto the terrace, and spent an intensive thirty minutes bouncing ideas off each other about Ansuetra's costume and jewelry. Taya stood guard in the doorway until they came back in and sat at the dining table to work on their ideas.

Kytan tried to keep his mind on his work, but he wasn't as interested in designing jewelry, as he was in learning more about Hadlee, and particularly, Taya. After drawing some initial sketches, he expressed his desire to Hadlee. Thanks to her own eagerness to know more about Taya, they set aside their tasks and indulged their curiosity.

Taking Ryder's warning to heart, they were careful to watch the door that opened a crack at random intervals, allowing the guard to listen for a few seconds.

"Ryder was right," Taya said, after the door shut for the fourth time. "They must have orders to keep a close eye on us."

Hadlee scoffed. "Let them, they won't catch us doing anything wrong."

However, the conspirator's vigilance waned as they became engrossed in Taya's history. Kytan and Hadlee's highly emotional responses to Taya's plight and deception caused them to forget about watching the door. Fortunately, the next time it opened a stunned silence had overtaken them with Taya's confession of what she intended to do to herself the day Hadlee arrived.

They sucked in a collective breath of guilty relief as the door clicked closed. Kytan and Hadlee immediately demanded the same promise from Taya, Ryder had. She stubbornly gave them the same response Ryder received.

Her refusal prompted Hadlee to confess, "I've felt sorry for myself ever since I landed in Injanae. Now I understand—at least in part—why I'm here, and I'm grateful my coming kept you from doing yourself any harm, Taya. Please don't think of hurting yourself anymore. I believe with the four of us working together, we can escape Injanae."

Taya's expression softened as Kytan interpreted what Hadlee said. She squeezed Hadlee's hand. "Now maybe we better get back to doing what Ateron expects us to be doing in case he drops in to check on our progress."

Hadlee nodded agreement after Kytan interpreted, and they all went back to work.

The next time the door opened, Pel stepped in, handed Taya a large bundle and spoke to her for a moment.

As soon as Pel closed the door, Kytan told Hadlee the bundle held the fabric for Ansuetra's gown.

Taya quickly opened it.

Hadlee laughed, fingering her parachute. The soft silky fabric was as white as snow. No such color, or fabric, existed in Injanae.

Kytan and Taya ran eager hands over the cloth while Hadlee explained what it was.

"Well it is certainly the color of the moon," Kytan said.

"That's probably why he wants us to use it," Hadlee said.

Taya fingered the fabric. "And there is so much of it. I have never seen, or felt anything like it."

"Then why don't we make you something from it too." Hadlee grinned. "You can wear it as a sign of Ansuetra's favor," she said with a sweeping flourish of her hand.

"Do you think I could?"

"Absolutely, as a matter of fact as the Moon Goddess I intend to dispense my favor on a grand scale by freeing all the slaves." Hadlee smiled with grim satisfaction. "We're going to make a few changes to Ateron's script."

"No, Hadlee that would be very dangerous," Kytan said.

"Maybe so, but when I'm playing Ansuetra, he won't be able to do much to stop me unless he wants to give his whole plot away, and I'll bet my life on it, he won't."

Kytan's troubled eyes held hers. "You *will* be betting your life on it."

Hadlee shrugged.

They worked off and on for the next few hours on the design for the dress and jewelry, but as the hours ticked by, they often found themselves just sitting and talking, each wanting to know more about the other two. At first, Kytan deflected the girls' questions, reluctant to talk about himself, but they finally wore him down.

"My parents were very devoted to one another. Their only sadness was not having any children. After ten years of marriage, they gave up hope of ever having a child. When I was born, it was a miracle to them, but it was a hard pregnancy and birth for my mother. She was sickly for many years and died when I was fifteen."

Taya laid a comforting hand on his arm, giving it a consoling squeeze.

He gave her grateful dimples, and sadly said, "It changed my father. He began to look at me with resentment, blaming my birth for her death. My mother was his whole life. Losing her made him very bitter. He began drinking, and then started gambling. Eventually he spent more time gambling than he did working." Kytan went on to relate the events leading up to his enslavement, explaining, "I hoped by serving his sentence, he would resent me less, and it would be a way to honor him." He bowed his head, struggling silently with his grief.

Taya took his big hand in both of hers. "What you did was very brave and noble."

"It didn't feel that way. That first work session in the mine was the worst experience of my life. I had never worked so hard or been treated so harshly. My back wore at least a dozen rapa stripes by the end of my shift. When the slaves on my crew were finally allowed to eat and sleep, I couldn't do either. I sat on the ground—and cried," he admitted, shame faced.

"I would have too," Taya said consolingly.

His dimples lit for a moment. "Then I felt a hand on my shoulder, it was Ryder. He said, 'I know exactly how you feel.' We spent most of our sleeping time talking. I answered all his questions about Injanae, in turn, he told me about America, his home, and his hopes and dreams. When we went back to work, he taught me what to do and how to do it. He protected me until I could handle the workload. He even took the blame for some of my mistakes and the rapa stripes too. Our friendship gave us the strength and courage to endure the long hours of back breaking labor, the brutality of our guards, and always—the darkness." He paused and blinked. "It was a terrible place, but it gave me the greatest gift I have ever had."

"What?" asked Taya.

"A brother."

"That's just what Ryder said about you," Hadlee said, when he translated for her.

Kytan's dimples warmed. "We may not share the same blood, but we have one heart."

When pressed about her life, Hadlee shared the same comical adventures of growing up with her cousins as she had with Ryder. She disclosed nothing of her parents' deaths. Except to say they died by accident.

Thirty-one

Squeezing water from his long hair, Ryder left the hot springs bath, dried off, and put on clean clothes. He'd worked his crew hard today, but not any harder than he worked himself. He was confident the stairs would be finished in a couple weeks. Then work on the sacrificial platform and altar bases could begin.

He combed through his wet hair mulling over his biggest worry. Ateron's bodyguards were making little progress in the tunnel. They weren't happy about breaking boulders and hauling rock. *I need to spend more time in there—a lot more time—but I can't do that until the stairs are done. And if I spend all my time in the tunnel, when will I get the platform done or find the time to repair the balcony and the stairs leading to it.* He frowned over the dilemma. *I wonder how much of the tunnel is blocked.*

The two story stone staircase, behind the wall in Hadlee's hall, leading up to the tunnel, was in good shape, but then, that part was built next to the cliff, not into it. A heavy door closed off the tunnel at the top of the stairs. Everything passed the door was inside the cliff wall.

The first half of the tunnel held just loose rubble which was easily pushed aside. Now, large rocks and boulders blocked the passage. They had to be broken up before they could be moved, and every foot of the tunnel had to be braced.

Not knowing how far the cave-in went or how much time it would take to clear it and brace it, to make it safe for Hadlee's use, nagged at Ryder.

Thinking of Hadlee made his heart turn over. Battling his guilt continued to be a relentless, vertical climb. He offered a silent prayer of gratitude for her willingness to keep him around now that Kytan could be her interpreter, but he didn't delude himself. *Just because she's willing to continue putting up with me, doesn't mean she's let go of her guilt, or the resentment she feels for me. It's there in her eyes too often to believe anything else;* he lectured himself, tying on a clean headband.

He thanked Oswan for the shave and left his dirty clothes with the laundry slaves. *No, there is still a long way to go before I can hope for her forgiveness.*

When she'd joined the group hug, a spark of hope had shot through him. He let that spark flare to life, reliving that tiny joy. Then watched it flounder in the wake of the other emotion he'd experienced when she'd hugged Kytan.

That had blindsided him.

Trudging up to Hadlee's apartment, he gave himself another stern lecture.

Kytan and Taya pressed Hadlee to tell them about life in the United States as they ate dinner.

Listening to Hadlee talk about telephones, cars, and electricity, kept Taya on the edge of her seat. "Your world must be so wonderful," she said dreamily. "I hope we get to see it."

"You will." Ryder clicked the door latch into place, his expression accusing them of carelessness.

They fell over themselves with apologies.

It didn't lessen the frown between his brows. "You can't let this happen again," he said gruffly to the penitent conspirators. He took a deep breath and blew it out. "Sorry, I'm just tired. It's been a long day."

Hadlee murmured sympathy and coaxed him into a pile of cushions. Taya asked if he wanted anything to eat. Kytan inquired about his day.

His frustration faded with their efforts to soothe him. He settled back against the cushions, and ate some warm bread, then told them briefly about the progress on the stairs.

The conspirators inhaled relief when he finally smiled and said, "Now to more important matters. Pilot, can you recite the first line of your speech?"

A guilty look spread across Hadlee's face. "I'm sorry. We spent so much time just talking that we didn't work on it, but I did work on the design for the gown." She brightened, reaching for her slate. "What do you think?"

He dusted the breadcrumbs from his fingers into the fire pit, before taking the slate and studying the two different designs she and Kytan had worked on. "I like this one," he said, pointing to the one that looked like something from Greek mythology.

"That is my favorite too," Kytan said. "But I don't think Hadlee's satisfied with either one."

"Not yet." Hadlee thoughtfully considered the designs. "After all, I've only been working on the designs for a few hours. I just need more time."

"You have until the end of the week. Remember that's your deadline." Ryder turned to Kytan. "Ateron wants the jewelry designs by the same deadline."

"I am sure we will both be ready by then." Kytan showed Ryder some of his ideas that Hadlee liked.

He clapped Kytan's shoulder, "You're making good progress."

"You will never guess what the dress is going to be made from." Taya danced over to the table and held up a corner of the parachute.

Ryder's jaw dropped, and everyone laughed. "Is that what I think it is?

"Uh huh, it's my chute," Hadlee said, and told him why they thought Ateron wanted to use it.

"Well you can't argue with any of his reasoning. But enough of Ateron and his plans, let's talk about our plans."

The fire danced brightly in the fire pit, and everyone but Taya had settled comfortably into the mounds of pillows scattered in front of it.

"Come sit down, Taya," Hadlee said, patting the cushion next to her.

"Shouldn't we go out on the terrace to talk about our plans?" Taya asked.

Her question jarred Ryder out of the comfort of his cushion. He hesitated, it felt wonderful to lean back into the enormous pillow and relax, but he'd just warned them about being careless. "Well, since I'm facing the door, I'll watch it. If it opens, I'll point my finger at you, Pilot, say the first line of your part and ask you to repeat it. Hopefully anyone opening the door will think we're rehearsing your lines."

"Okay. Now, I think the first thing we should do is list all the equipment and supplies we'll need to make our escape," Hadlee said.

Taya nodded agreement. "And we need to write them down so we can check them off as we go."

"Writing everything down could be dangerous, suppose the list fell into the wrong hands," Kytan said to Taya, and then Hadlee.

"Not if I write it in English." Hadlee grinned. "We could write it on the wall, and no one except Ryder and I would know what it said."

Everyone shared Hadlee's conspiratorial smirk, prompting her to get up, grab a piece of chalk, and head to the wall between the doors of the storage room and Taya's bedchamber.

"So what do we need?" she asked, chalk poised and ready.

"Rope," said Ryder. "Kytan and I have discussed this. I think we will need at least a hundred feet of good rope per person."

Hadlee wrote: *four hundred feet of rope*

They spent almost an hour discussing their needs, adding them to their growing list. Each time they were interrupted by a guard poking his head into the room, Ryder pointed his finger, said one of Ansuetra's opening lines, and Hadlee quickly repeated it.

As the hour grew late, Taya silently frowned into the dying fire.

Kytan noticed and asked, "What is the matter?"

"Where are we going to put all the supplies we acquire? Some of them can be stored here, as long as they won't attract any notice if the apartment is searched, but not all of them."

"She's right," Hadlee said to Ryder. "No one has searched it so far, but we can't be sure they won't."

"We will only store food and some bedding here, that shouldn't attract any notice if Ateron gets suspicious and starts snooping around," Ryder said.

"We can store the rest of our supplies in my shop," Kytan said to Taya. "I built a large hidden space between the ceiling and the upper floor. We can put anything in there that is too dangerous to hide here. It won't be found."

Taya shook her head. "But how do we get the things Hadlee and I are responsible to make—that are too dangerous to keep here—to your shop?"

"Uh . . . maybe I had better take a look at your room, Pilot." Ryder said after he interpreted for her. He got up and said to Kytan, "Watch the door. Whistle if anyone pokes their head in."

Hadlee jumped up and led the way up to her bedchamber. "What are you up to?" she asked pushing the curtain aside.

Ryder took in every detail of the elegant room. It was furnished with a suite of finely carved, gold inlaid furniture. A large bed, a tall wardrobe, a mirrored dressing table—accompanied by a matching chair—and a deep chest of drawers, graced the room.

After several moments of consideration, Ryder walked over, dropped to his knees on the alpaca rug and looked under Hadlee's freestanding bed. "This should do nicely," he said and grinned up at her. "I think you're about to need a new bed because you have a very bad back."

"But I don't"

"Oh yes you do. Come on and I'll explain," he said, going back down the stairs.

"So?" Kytan asked.

Ryder grinned. "We will have a nice large hiding place in a week or so, and Hadlee can give us her first performance as an actress."

"I don't think Hadlee likes your idea," Taya said, shifting her eyes from Ryder to Hadlee.

Ryder glanced back at her. Alarm was clearly etched on her face. "Now don't get upset, Pilot, but I need an excuse to make you a new bed. All you have to do is convince Ateron you're in pain because the bed isn't comfortable. I can make a box springs mattress with a compartment beneath it that will hold everything we need. The only way they will find it is if they tear the bed apart, and I don't think a search will come to that. So what do you say, Pilot? Will you do it?"

Hadlee blew out a reluctant, but consenting sigh, took several faintly faltering steps, while holding her back, and sat down stiffly on a low bench in the living room. "Well, what do you think? If I add a little subtle moaning maybe he'll believe me."

"I would believe you." Kytan said and Taya agreed.

"Okay, tomorrow, when the guards poke their heads in, try and let them see you're in pain," Ryder whimpered.

Hadlee snickered and Taya giggled.

The belfry chimed ten-thirty.

Kytan stretched and yawned. "It is time I went home."

"I think there is one more thing we need to do tonight," Taya said.

"What?" Hadlee yawned too.

"Take measurements."

"Of what?" Ryder asked.

"You two." Taya pointed at him and Kytan. "If Hadlee and I are going to make leather coats, pants and gloves to protect us from the climb out of here, we need your measurements." She went into her supply room and brought out her tape measure.

The looks of chagrin on the two men's faces made the girls grin.

"Don't tell me you guys are afraid of what the tape measure will tell us," Hadlee said picking up a slate and chalk.

A silent agreement passed between the men. Ryder grabbed the tape from Taya, and Kytan confiscated the slate and chalk from Hadlee. Lifting torches from their sconces, they headed for the terrace.

Ryder turned at the entrance, "Don't come out. Just tell us what measurements you want?"

After fifteen minutes of helping each other take their measurements, Ryder and Kytan came back into the room.

Snatching the slate, Hadlee and Taya looked over the results, written neatly in both languages. Their teasing comments drove the men to make a hasty retreat.

Thirty-two

Kytan yawned again as he and Ryder walked toward the servants' stairs. "I shouldn't have stayed so long."

"Nor should you go walking through the city streets alone this late," Ryder said.

"Well it can't be helped and I will be careful."

They turned into the stairwell and started down. "Why don't you just spend the night in my quarters?"

"I could, but I would rather sleep in a bed than on your floor."

Ryder stopped on the landing that led to his room. "We could go find the night steward, and requisition another mattress and some bedding for you."

"Could we?"

"Yeah," Ryder said, and they went down two more flight of stairs.

Olk, the night steward, was slumped over his desk, snoring noisily when they walked into his supply room.

"Apparently night duty isn't too strenuous," Ryder said, and shook Olk's shoulder until he roused the young steward, who didn't look old enough to hold the job.

"What do you want?" Olk asked in a sleepy voice, rubbing his eyes.

"A mattress and some bedding," Ryder said.

Olk automatically reached for a requisition order, paused, then dropped his hand and shrugged. "Take whatever you need, but return it in the morning or come back and fill out a requisition order."

By the time Ryder and Kytan had what they needed, Olk was again slumped over his desk.

They hauled the mattress into Ryder's quarter and laid it on the floor. There was a short, heated debate before Ryder convinced Kytan he was the one sleeping on the floor mattress. Kytan didn't feel right about it until Ryder demonstrated his problem with the size of the stone bed-shelf, and although Kytan was taller than the length of the bed-shelf, he conceded the argument, and took up residence on the bed-shelf mattress.

Ryder lay on the floor mattress with his hands tucked under his head, listening to the soft sounds of the night creatures, waiting for sleep to come.

"Are you still awake?" whispered Kytan.

Ryder yawned. "Yeah."

"We have to get them out of here, no matter what it costs us, we have to!"

"That we do, but if anything unforeseen happens to me; it will be up to you." Ryder rolled over in the dark, facing the shelf where Kytan lay. "I want your oath on it. If I tell you to get them out, or if you can find a way to do it without me, I want to know you will think of their safety before mine. Will you do that?"

"I will. Getting them out of Injanae is more important than what happens to either of us. So I will take your oath too. If you need to leave me behind, don't hesitate to do it. Do I have your word?"

"You do." Ryder rolled onto his back again and laced his fingers under his head. "I've decided the cliff face just south of the stone quarry is probably our best bet. I've only seen it in passing, and in the dark. Still, I think I could free climb that wall for quite a ways. The cliff face takes a dip there too, so we wouldn't have as far to climb."

"Do you really think Hadlee and Taya can do it? They aren't climbers, or men."

"That's my biggest concern." Worry contracted Ryder's brows. "At least they're pretty fearless—from what I have seen of them."

"But it will take more than being brave to make the climb."

The concern deepened on Ryder's brow. "Tomorrow I'll start teaching them some exercises to build their upper body strength. If we can get them to do the exercises regularly, I have no doubt they will be able to make the climb, by the time we are ready to go."

"I wish we didn't have to go that far." Kytan frowned over the side of the bed.

"Yeah, our biggest problem is the time it will take to get there and be high enough off the ground before we're found."

"How much time do you think we need?"

"Enough to get us beyond accurate arrow range."

"I hadn't thought about that." Kytan shifted on the thin mattress and tugged up his blanket.

"That's why I think the best time to go will be the night of the Lunar Celebration. From what I've heard, there will be a lot of drinking, and the drunker everyone is the less steady anyone's aim will be. Also, with everyone focused on celebrating, it might give us more time before anyone figures out we're missing, rounds up a posse and comes looking for us—at least that's what I'm hoping."

"I hate to wait that long. Did you see the way Ateron and Cartu looked at Hadlee and Taya today? The sooner we get them out of here, the better I will sleep."

"Amen, but right now I think they're both pretty safe. Ateron can't afford to make Hadlee angry by hurting any of us. If he does, she'll refuse to be Ansuetra. That alone should keep all of us fairly safe. It's kind of a double-edged sword. He is holding her hostage by threatening to hurt us, and she is holding him hostage by saying she won't cooperate if he does."

"That is a very dangerous game, and the longer we have to play it the more likely it is we will lose, especially if Ateron decides to hurt us just enough to keep us from being able to climb. I think we need to leave as soon as we can."

"I seem to remember you telling me we couldn't leave without careful preparation, and you were right. We can't climb out of the valley, or up Farlana, without the right equipment and supplies. Gathering survival and climbing equipment is going to take time. We can't do it very fast or someone is sure to get suspicious. Right now, while the lovely ladies figure out how to make our climbing clothes, you need to look for rope, and I need to take a closer look at our escape route." Ryder nodded to himself.

"How are you going to do that?"

"I need to go to the quarry to order the altar stones and arrange for the delivery of the platform stone, I'll do it then. It shouldn't be too hard to find an excuse to take a closer look at the section of the cliff face I'm interested in." Ryder yawned again and rolled to his side.

Kytan adjusted his pillow. "You know, I have never met two more beautiful or wonderful women. I would do anything for them."

Ryder closed his eyes. "So would I."

Thirty-three

Most of the week went by before Ateron learned about Hadlee's back problem. He had judiciously kept his visits to a bare minimum, not wanting to antagonize her. However, when Pel brought the report that he, and several of the guards, had seen Hadlee holding her back and moving painfully, he went to investigate, dragging Ryder away from work on the stairs.

He entered the apartment with his usual disregard for Hadlee's privacy. It couldn't have been a better moment. Hadlee was just standing up, after long hours of bending over the slate board. With a sigh, she massaged her tired back, turned to the king in a faltering way and let out a little groan of discomfort. Clutching her back with one hand as though enduring a spasm of pain, she gripped the slate in the other.

The performance wasn't lost on Ateron. "You are to ask Hadlee what is wrong with her back," he said to Ryder.

Ryder explained the king's visit.

Hadlee responded in a pitiful voice, walked stiffly to the king with a tired sigh, handed him the slate, and then accentuated her discomfort by easing into a chair.

Ateron studied the gown she'd just finished designing. He smiled his approval, and told Ryder to pass along his praise. Then demanded to know what she told Ryder about her back pain.

"Sire, Hadlee's back is very sore. It's been a growing problem for her. She isn't used to sleeping on such a hard bed. In her country, there is another kind of framed mattress, put under the usual one, adding extra softness to a bed.

Hadlee misses that kind of bed," Ryder said and added, "But given time, I'm sure she will adjust."

"Is that why you haven't told me about her discomfort?"

A slightly defensive tone flavored Ryder's response, "She hasn't complained too much about it, and I suspect in another month or so she'll get used to sleeping on a harder surface and be just fine."

"Do you know about these framed mattresses?"

"Certainly, I also used to sleep on one. When I came to Injanae it took me quite some time to get used to sleeping on hard surfaces and thin mattresses."

"Would adding another mattress help?"

Ryder shrugged. "Maybe, but it wouldn't provide the give a box springs mattress does because of the springs."

Baffled, Ateron asked, "Can you build one of these box springs?"

Ryder frowned thoughtfully and finally answered, "I could, but I would need Kytan's help with the springs. And I would have to work out what I would need to use for webbing and padding, and the casing for the mattress." His eyebrows lifted. "Do you want me to?"

Ateron's almond eyes shifted to Hadlee, who still rubbed her fictional sore back, "How long will it take? Your other work must not fall behind schedule."

Ryder blew out resignation. "I suppose I could build it in the morning and in the evening, during the time I am here teaching Hadlee her lines."

"Good. Tell Taya what you need. I will give her my authorization to requisition everything you require from my storehouse. You can begin tonight. I don't want Ansuetra making her entrance holding her back."

With the limited time Ryder could spend on the project, it took two weeks to construct the box springs. The need for llama hides for webbing, thick pelts of alpaca fur for padding, and canvas for the mattress casing, provided Taya with the perfect cover to requisition far more than was required for the bed. She and Hadlee at once started designing pants, jackets, gloves, and knapsacks.

By the time the box springs mattress was finished, a new double thick mattress of alpaca hair was also ready, compliments of the king. After Ryder and Kytan placed the mattress on top of the box springs, they all took turns trying it out. Hadlee was in heaven. Ryder was homesick for a real bed. Taya enjoyed bouncing on the bed, and Kytan put a box springs mattress on an ever-growing list of things he wanted to acquire when he got to the United States.

Ryder's expert engineering camouflaged the hinges on the side that opened, and with the sheet Hadlee constructed to cover the mattress, their hiding place, which now housed Ryder's armband and all the extra materials from the bed construction, was invisible. Still, they endured an anxious fifteen minutes when Ateron and his favorite pet—as Hadlee continually referred to Cartu—came to inspect it.

Ryder dropped to his knees on the stone floor in front of Ateron's dais, wishing for a rug. *I really should ask Hadlee to make some kneepads for me, since I spend so much of my time on them—assuaging a madman's ego.*

He lifted his eyes and listened to the king's compliments over the completed stairs. Ateron was particularly impressed with the ingenious way the last twenty feet of the stairs could be drawn up—eliminating access to the roof.

"Thank you." Ryder accepted the king's compliments, and anxious to get off his knees, immediately pressed his next agenda. "Sire, your bodyguards' lack of experience in breaking stone is hindering the progress of clearing the tunnel blockage. The only way I can ensure the job will be finished before the Lunar Celebration is to work there myself—full time. To do that, I need to employ Daelo's master mason, Lunal, to take over the work on the rooftop stage and balcony. With your permission, I can bring Lunal back with me when I go to the quarry to arrange for the delivery of the platform stone, altar bases, and benches."

Scowling, Ateron paced across his dais, but concurred with Ryder's assessment and had Cartu schedule Ryder's proposed trip for the following morning.

Just after dawn, Ryder climbed into a llama cart. Lul locked the shackles built into the cart's bed around his ankles; then climbed onto the seat of the cart and took up the reins. Six of the king's bodyguards mounted llamas, and the troop rode out of the palace courtyard.

Riding over the rough road in the crude cart made Ryder grit his teeth, *at least my hands aren't locked to the cart this time.* By holding onto both sides of the small cart and moving with its jarring motions as it fell and climbed in and out of the roads deep ruts, he was able to offset the cart's brutal bouncing.

He took his mind off the miserable ride by listening to the guards boast about their skills as warriors, and their victories in the many contests of arms they engaged in to keep themselves proficient in their art.

Lul crowed over his latest victory in the most recent contest of arms.

Norr, whom he had bested, scowled, leaned across his saddle and asked Ryder, "Are you a warrior among your people?"

"No. I'm an engineer. I prefer building to fighting."

Toba, riding on the opposite side of the cart from Norr, made a derisive sound.

Lul looked over his shoulder at Ryder. "But there are warriors among your people, aren't there?"

"Yeah."

"Are they as good as ours?" Toba asked.

"Yes, tell us about the skills of the warriors in your country," Lul said, slowing the cart as they came to a particularly rough section of the road.

Ryder did his best to explain about guns, planes, bombs, and warfare in the outside world. The guards scoffed and shook their heads, expressing their disbelief in the strange things Ryder described. Still, they were entertained by his stories and asked many questions, which helped keep Ryder's mind off his aching backside as the miles passed.

It was almost mid-morning before the troop came to the place in the northeast cliff that Ryder was interested in looking at more closely. The base of the cliff sat fifty yards off the road, obscured by a thick stand of trees. Coming abreast of the spot, Ryder told the guards he needed a few minutes privacy to answer the call of nature.

Lul reined in the llamas and tugged them to a stop. He wrapped the reins around the brake, stepped into the cart and unlocked Ryder's shackles. "Do I need to send someone with you?"

Ryder shrugged. "If you're worried I'll run off, you don't need to be. Believe me, I've learned my lesson and don't want to repeat it. Besides, there's no way out of Injanae, is there? So what would be the point?"

Lul gave Ryder his gold-toothed, jack-o-lantern grin, "Make it quick."

"I'll be back before you know it." Ryder hopped out of the cart, and without a backward glance, headed into the trees.

As soon as the trees blocked his view of the road and guards, he rushed through the dense undergrowth to the base of the cliff. He scanned the face of the cliff until he spotted what he was looking for. His fingers eagerly curled over a narrow ridge of rock. A daredevil joy he hadn't experienced since he climbed Farlana—pulsed through him as he started to climb.

He knew he couldn't go above the trees, but he wanted to look upward as far as he could. *Without a doubt, I can free climb this wall a long way, and it has to be at least a hundred feet shorter than most of the cliff walls that encircle the valley.*

Scrambling back down, he looked around for something to mark his position. He had to be able to find this spot again in the dark. Using a couple of large broken logs, he positioned them at the base of the climb, crossing them like an X, before he headed back to his guards.

Anxious to be back in Telquset for his evening visit with Hadlee, Ryder hurried through his business at the quarry. He refused Daelo's invitation to stay and eat supper, and accompanied by Lunal, he and his guards were back in Telquset an hour after sun down.

Ateron listened attentively to Ryder's report on the first delivery of stone Lunal needed to start work on the rooftop stage, and the timetable he'd established for the completion and delivery of the benches and altars. "Your arrangements are acceptable." The king flicked his hand in his usual gesture of dismissal. "You may go."

Thirty minutes later, bathed and shaved, Ryder bounded up the stairs to Hadlee's apartment; eager to share his optimism about the place in the cliff face he now felt sure was their way out of Injanae.

Thirty-four

Hadlee changed tunes. This time humming the melody to "Only You", one of her favorite love songs, and tried to teach Kytan a different dance step. An easier one—she hoped. Intently watching their feet, while Taya stood guard at the terrace entrance, Hadlee pushed her toes against Kytan's trying to get him to move his feet in the correct pattern, and in time with the rhythm of the tune.

"It might go better if he saw a demonstration."

Hadlee whirled around, surprised to see Ryder leaning against the terrace door, a Cheshire grin growing on his face. He'd told her the previous night it was unlikely he would be back in time from the quarry for his usual evening visit.

She raised a skeptical brow. "Oh, and I suppose you—"

He pushed off the doorframe, "Yeah, I can." He bowed gallantly, and began humming an introduction to "Only You". His left hand engulfed hers, and his right one spanned the entire back of her waist.

The startling realization she couldn't see over his shoulder, heightened her awareness of his colossal size. It invoked a disconcerting sensation she'd never experience before. With the exception of her uncle and cousins, she stood eye-to-eye, or higher, with most men and had never danced with a man whose shoulder she couldn't see passed.

The strange sensation of being short struck her. She struggled to keep the puzzling sensation, and the odd feeling fluttering in her stomach, from finding expression on her face as he began to sing and move her across the terrace.

"Only you, are the song, my heart can sing.
Only you, know the words, to my melody.
Sing them for me, in your harmony,
Forever with you, my heart's in tune."

His voice surrounded her in deep, soft mink. It was rhythm and blues, slow and intense, strong and compelling—captivating.

She glanced at Kytan staring at them wide eyes in the flickering torch light, and Taya, standing in the doorway with her hand over her heart. Inexplicably her own heart accelerated.

"Only you, are the dream, there in the night.
Only you, haunt my mind, throughout the daylight.
Waking or sleeping, it's always true,
My vision of love, is, ever you."

Not only could he sing, but Hadlee also became keenly aware of how easily she followed his lead. They moved flawlessly in and out of the benches, pots, and planters that were artfully placed around the terrace. He guided her effortlessly with the gentle pressure of his fingers, or the heel of his hand against the back of her waist.

The man can dance, she marveled. Surprised a man of Ryder's size could be . . . *graceful? Yes, graceful.*

A smile ruptured her carefully composed expression. Gazing up into his face, the revelation hit her with stunning force. *Ryder Garrison is a very handsome, charming man.*

It was a shocking realization. She immediately tried to deny it, but it was impossible to push the reality away while he danced her so skillfully around the terrace.

Heat grew in her face as his melting voice—and the words of the song—seemed to caress her.

"Only you, are the heart, I long to keep.
Only you, have the soul, that makes mine complete.
Our hearts and souls, were meant to entwine,
Until they become one—for all time."

She tore her eyes away from his simmering gold ones, stopping abruptly as they danced passed Taya. "Why don't you take Taya for a spin?" she said, taking her hand from his.

Ryder and Taya exchanged comical expressions. Their size difference made it ridiculous for them to be dance partners. Ryder resolved the problem by picking Taya up, holding her tightly, and dancing around the terrace. She giggled, and Kytan's dimples did a jig, while Ryder hummed an interlude. He ended the dance setting her down next to Kytan.

"Ryder, are the words, 'our hearts and souls were meant to entwine, until they become, one for all time,' a proposal of marriage in the United States?" asked Kytan in English.

Ryder stole a glance at Taya, and answered Kytan in the same language. "I suppose, in a way, they are. If you want to become one for all time, in heart and soul with someone, that—in my book—does equal marriage, but it's not the way most American men make a proposal of marriage."

Hadlee turned away and walked over to the trellis vine, feeling the imprint of Ryder's hand on her back, still seeing the look in his eyes as he sang those lines to her. A slow burn flared in her cheeks. She stepped out of the torch light and into the concealing shadows of the trellis vine.

"Hadlee," Kytan called. "Ryder says there are more verses to the song, and he will sing them if you will dance with him."

"I think we should get back to work on my part. I'm not doing very well, and—"

Three voices of protest overruled her.

She exhaled a slow breath, put on a consenting expression and walked back to Ryder, forcing her body to relax as he drew her into his arms.

His intoxicating voice again sang in her ear while he lightly moved her across the terrace.

"Only you, are the life, I want to live.

Only you, are the one, I'll willingly give.

All that I am, and all I hold dear,

From this moment on, through, endless years."

Each word was a barb in her skin. He spun her around, dipped her, and looked soulfully into her eyes as he sang the romantic lyrics.

"Only you, are the home, I'm searching for.

Only you, hold the key, to unlock that door.

Open to me, be my family,

Together we'll be, eternally."

Cold fingers of panic had her firmly in their grip by the time he brought her upright. She spun herself away from him, grabbed Taya's arm and pushed her toward him.

With hardly a missed step, Ryder swept Taya up into his arms again. Dancing her across the terrace, he hummed the interlude and made a key change, before finishing the song.

"Your words my song; your heart—my eternal home.

Your love my life; you're the soul I need to be whole.

There's only one clear vision for me . . ."

They danced passed Hadlee. She tried, but found she couldn't look away when his flaming eyes locked with hers.

In a silken voice, he crooned the last line, "Forever my love, I'll always see . . . only you."

Hadlee tore her eyes from his while his voice resonated on the last steamy note. Holding it out, he finished the dance with a whirl and a dip for Taya.

Kytan broke into applause. "Now I have one more thing to put on my list, but I won't have to wait to learn to dance. Hadlee, will you keep trying to teach me?"

"Sure, but now we really should get back to business."

They went into the living room, escaping the rapidly cooling night air and built up the fire. Hadlee sat as far from Ryder as the furniture allowed, listening to each chiming sequence of the tower clock with increased longing for the one that would signal the end of his visit.

When the men finally departed, she feigned a yawn, refused Taya's offer of herb tea, gave her a hug and sought her bedchamber—retiring to the only real privacy she possessed.

After changing into a floor length shift, she pulled out the heavy gold comb that held up her long locks—another gift Ateron had pressed her to take before she learned she was his prisoner—letting the thick tresses fall down her back. Sitting at the dressing table, she pulled her hair over her shoulder and began combing it out, trying to untangle her thoughts.

Seeing Ryder as a handsome, charming man felt like a sin. *The very idea I could see him as interesting, or attractive is such a betrayal of my mother.* Her comb jerked to a stop on an ugly snarl of guilt.

She confronted the painful tangle; worked through it by reviewing the past few weeks, and truthfully concluded seeing Ryder in a different light wasn't a betrayal. *It just means I'm beginning to let go of the resentment I've always felt for him.* She considered that and nodded. *At least I don't think of him as Death Ryder anymore. Now, I think of him as a . . . partner, working with me toward some very important common goals. We both need forgiveness, and we're helping each other seek that. We're also working together to get out of Injanae.*

Having resolved the tangle, she continued combing her hair without finding anymore. *It's all right to see Ryder a little differently. Achieving our common goals is vital to both of us. And that's the full extent of the relationship I intend to have with Ryder Garrison,* she resolved, combing the last strands of her hair.

Dividing it into three equal parts, she began braiding. An unwelcome question halted her fingers. *I know how I feel, but how does he feel? The song was certainly romantic, but I can't blame him for that. After all, he just took up singing what I was humming. No,* she puzzled it out; *it was the look in his eyes and the tone of his voice as he sang it to me that was so disturbing.*

She banished his eyes and the haunting sound of his voice from her mind, again braiding her hair. *I'm being absurd. It's positively ludicrous to think the man that killed Mama could have any interest in me romantically.* Her shoulders shook on a silent laugh. *Not even Ryder has that much audacity.*

Finished braiding, she secured the end with a tie, and covering a yawn, crossed the room to her bed, climbed in, blew out the lamp, snuggled down into the pillows, and closed her eyes.

The romantic tone of Ryder's voice, and the intensity of his eyes, came unbidden into her mind. She punched her pillow and rolled over. *That settles it. I definitely need to maintain a discreet distance on every level with Ryder.*

She'd learned from sad experience that being even a shade passed polite could give a man the wrong impression and invite attention she would then have the unpleasant task of discouraging. *I certainly don't want to give Ryder the wrong impression. He already feels too responsible, guilty, and sorry for me. I am not going to encourage him in any other delusions.*

Thirty-five

Kytan leaned over the edge of the bed and confided, "Not only do I need to learn to dance, but the way Taya looked at you while you sang made me so jealous, I will have to spend all my spare time learning to sing too." He paused and pleaded, "You will help me won't you?"

Ryder stopped fluffing his pillow and snorted. "Yeah, I'll teach you to sing, but you just want to learn to dance so you can have a legitimate reason to hold Taya in your arms."

Kytan pulled the pillow from under his head and threw it down into Ryder's face. "Oh and I suppose you hated every minute you were holding Hadlee in yours."

"That was different." Ryder tossed Kytan's pillow back up to him. "We were just demonstrating for you."

"Teach me a song."

"Now?"

"Yes, but it needs to be something easy, something I can sing to Taya in Injanae."

"Hmm . . . how about starting with a hymn?"

"What is a hymn?"

"A religious song, sung in church."

"That isn't what I had in mind, but I suppose it is a place to start."

Ryder sat up and sang "Abide with Me" in Injanae.

Kytan sighed, "It is like a prayer."

"That's what hymns are, prayers we sing. And it's a good place to say good night."

"Okay." Kytan leaned up and blew out the candle on the small shelf above his head.

Ryder flopped back down, rolled onto his side and closed his eyes, but found he was far too wound up to sleep. He relived the dance with Hadlee. *We dance really well together, and that smile she gave me means she enjoyed it as much as I did.*

He basked in that smile again; then watched it fade. His brow wrinkled. *She did seem anxious to let Taya take her place. Why?* He replayed it and groaned. *The song was much too romantic, and I sang it romantically because . . . that's the way I felt holding her in my arms.*

He couldn't deny it.

She must have seen it in my face, or heard it in my voice, and felt . . . uncomfortable, no—disgusted! She probably thought I was making a pass at her. The certainty she could have easily taken the way he sang and danced with her like a pass, dropped on him like the blade of a guillotine.

That's why she was so distant the rest of the evening. Was that actually what I was doing? The horror of the idea and how she would view it, steam rolled over him. *But that's not how I thought of it at the time. Still,* he admitted, *I did get lost in how wonderful it felt to dance with her.*

He rolled onto his back and laced his fingers behind his head. *Idiot, I deserve another round with a rapa. I may have just destroyed—with one dance—the trust that has taken weeks to build. How long will it take to repair the damage I've done and put her at ease with me again?*

He wrestled with that question far into the night.

Thirty-six

After weeks of breaking boulders, moving rocks and shoring up the tunnel, Ryder finally punched a hole through the blockage into open space. He widened the breach just enough to poke a torch and his head through. The foul air made him pull back, choking and coughing.

For the next hour, his six-man crew carefully worked to enlarge the opening. When he could put his shoulders through, he told the guards it would be a good idea to let some air circulate into the dead space before they continued. He came out of the tunnel and into Hadlee's hall with his worn out men, relieved the end of the arduous rock breaking work was in sight.

Glancing at the door to Hadlee's apartment, he decided he was too dirty, and it was too late to visit. A tug of regret pulled at him as he turned away. It was especially frustrating to miss a visit now that Hadlee seemed to be softening toward him. She'd been less guarded around him for the past few days. The care he'd taken not to alarm her in anything he did, or said, was finally paying off.

Since the night he'd danced with her, she'd maintained a cool demeanor and noticeable distance with him, while her companionship with the others grew. She laughed, talked, kidded them, and often shared hugs. But with him, she was careful and slightly withdrawn.

He noticed the only time her guard dropped with him was when they engaged in gospel discussions with Taya and Kytan. She always seemed to warm a little, letting go of her careful reserve in her enthusiasm as a missionary.

A swell of joy expanded his heart. Seeing Taya and Kytan absorb the gospel was as wonderful as watching their love for each other grow. A pang of envy dimmed his joy. He shrugged it off, and followed his crew down the hall to the door.

Lul asked if everyone was out. He said they were, and Lul locked the door, taking up his position as night guard outside the hall door.

Striding down the king's hall toward the servant's stairway, Ryder firmly reminded himself he needed to continue his careful restraint with Hadlee, *if for no other reason than to keep our relationship in proper perspective in my own mind.*

Self-mockery chided him.

Where Hadlee was concerned, his mind just wouldn't leave him be. At times, he felt like beating his head against the walls of the tunnel. As hard as he tried to keep it from happening, that relentless song would start up in his head; he would become aware he was whistling, or humming "Only You", and just like that, he would be dancing with her again, the memory moving through him more vivid than a movie. *I have to get control of my wayward mind, or is it*—he immediately blocked the thought.

Last night she rewarded him with a lukewarm smile, after prayers. It was the first one she'd offered him since they had danced. The impact it had on him was way out of proportion to the event.

I have to stop the ridiculous emotions that keep bombarding me. He smacked the wall of the stairwell with the palm of his hand as he descended the half flight to his quarters. *It's obvious where they're coming from. I need her forgiveness, and every little gestured of kindness she makes to me fuels the hope that she's beginning to let go of her resentment and forgive me.*

He met Pel coming up the stairs to check on night security and told him about breaching the blockage in the tunnel. Pel assured him he would inform the King and Ryder continued down.

What I feel for Hadlee is empathy for her guilt and the terrible situation she's in, he told himself, turning into the hallway of his quarters. *Isn't it understandable and even right, to feel compassion for her and treat her with kindness? Isn't it also completely reasonable to feel tenderly toward her in her quest for forgiveness and peace? Of course, it is;* he assured himself. After all, he, of all people, should feel that for her.

He pushed quietly through the door to his quarters, knowing Kytan would already be asleep. *As for my desire to protect her, well, any decent guy would feel that way, given the situation,* he nodded with certainty.

The dim light of a candle confirmed Kytan's slumbering state. Ryder quietly latched the door shut behind him. *All of it put together is what's confusing me. I just need to keep in mind that everything I feel for Hadlee has its roots in my own guilt and quest for forgiveness, including the need to make some small restitution by easing her burdens until I can get her out of here.*

On the washstand, he found a washcloth and clean towels set out next to a pitcher of water and a basin. He poured water into the basin, tugged off his tunic and began to wash. *Not visiting Hadlee tonight is for the best.* He shivered as he scrubbed with the cold water. *Until I can get control of myself and quit overreacting to every little gesture she makes toward me, it's better to limit the time I spend with her.*

He reached for a coarsely woven towel and rubbed himself dry. Exhausted, he stretched out on his mattress, knowing the strenuous labor of the day would soon put him to sleep. *With any luck, I'll be too tired to dream.* That was another ongoing problem. He couldn't seem to escape Hadlee even when he slept.

The following morning, after breakfast was finished, the object of Ryder's confusion fixed him with her best conspiratorial expression. "We need you to try on the jacket I—we, just finished for you," Hadlee said, going up the steps to her bedchamber to get the coat.

"Wait. I don't think you should bring it down. I'll come up." He followed her up the stairs with Taya and Kytan hard on his heels.

She deftly opened the hiding place in the box springs and pulled out the enormous alpaca skin jacket. Holding it by the shoulders, she helped him into it.

He was immediately encased in the warmth of the thick fur. After tying the laces up along the front, he turned in a circle, moving his arms back and forth, and over his head to check for comfort and the ability to move freely.

"It's terrific," he said running his hands over the supple alpaca hide. "Is mine the first one done?"

Hadlee helped Taya pull three other coats from the hiding place. "We're making great progress. We're almost done with your pants too. We'll do your fitting for them, tonight."

Apprehension claimed his face.

Hadlee rolled her eyes. "I'm sorry, but pants are a little more technical than a simple raglan sleeve jacket. If you want them to fit and be comfortable we will need to have you try them on." She shook her head, making her long ponytail swing from side to side. "It won't be that bad. Ask Kytan, we did his fitting yesterday."

Kytan shrugged and Ryder's apprehension receded. Taking his coat off, he handed it back to Hadlee, and apologized as the girls stowed the coats back inside the bed. "I've been so busy with the tunnel that I haven't kept up with things here very well."

"We need to go over what still has to be done," Kytan said. "Our time is getting short."

Ryder nodded, "You're right. We need a good review and planning session. I should be able to take some time off this evening, now that the blockage in the tunnel has been breached."

They descended the stairs and were almost at the bottom when the door opened.

Ateron and his pet strolled in.

Four hearts immediately beat faster. Ryder and Kytan dropped to their knees, Hadlee gave the king her best artic stare, and Taya lowered her eyes with a bow.

Ateron took up residence on a thickly padded and ornately carved gold bench. Cartu stood behind him like a sentinel.

"The moon has made two and a half cycles since Hadlee started learning her part. There is just that much time left until the Lunar Celebration. I would like a demonstration of her progress," Ateron said.

Ryder consulted the floor, hiding his guilty eyes. He hadn't done much work with Hadlee on her part in the past couple of weeks, leaving that to Kytan, who now shared his living quarters. Under the pretext of jewelry fittings, Kytan spent more time than he did with Hadlee. He hadn't even check on her progress in the past few days. Instead, he spent his time in the apartment team teaching the gospel with her, instructing everyone on climbing techniques and making the girls do the exercises he taught them to build strength in their upper bodies and arms.

He dipped his head to the king then looked up at Hadlee. "The king wants you to recite your lines. Please tell me you've been working on them." One corner of Hadlee's mouth lifted ever so slightly. Ryder breathed easier. "Do you know all of them?"

"No. At least not perfectly, but then if you want to spend more time here, it will be okay if I don't quite make it to the end. Won't it?"

Ryder's heart gave a particularly hard thump. *Does she really want me to spend more time here?* A dizzying spiral of hope drilled into his heart. It was instantly followed by a resounding mental kick. *I'm doing it again.*

Walking to the middle of the living room, Hadlee turned her back on Ateron and Cartu. She winked at her friends; took a deep breath and whirled around, her face set in a regal stare. Raising both hands slightly above her shoulders, she thundered, "Stop." Striding around the living room, she recited Ansuetra's lines. As she came to the last ones she began to pause, stumbling over the words. She stopped with a shrug and sat down.

Her performance was met by silence. Ateron stared at her pensively, while she blatantly ignored him. He shifted his cold eyes to Ryder and said, "You may tell Hadlee that I am pleased with her performance—up until she began to stumble over her lines. But, I am also very *disappointed* that she doesn't know the entire thing."

"Sire, I've missed some language lessons with Hadlee while I've been trying to clear the tunnel," Ryder said, contritely. "As soon as it's completely open—which hopefully will happen before the end of the day—I will be able to spend more time helping her learn the rest of her lines."

"Make sure you do. I want to see a perfect performance in one week's time." Ateron's cold black eyes pierced Ryder's. "Do not disappoint me again."

The conspirators breathed out relief when the door closed behind the king.

"That was much too close," said Taya, taking Kytan's hand. "It was all I could do not to look over my shoulder to see if you were all the way down the stairs."

"I violated my own rules, and we almost got caught." Ryder rose from his knees and promptly collapsed into a pile of cushions. "But, Pilot, for someone who says she can't act, you were great." He smiled warmly at her.

Hadlee curtsied. "You can thank my drama coach," she said dipping her head to Kytan. "He taught me all I know."

"You are a great pupil," Kytan said. "I am sure you will be ready to give a complete performance in a week's time."

Hadlee's countenance took on the ruthlessness of a saboteur. "I'm sure I will be ready to give the performance Ateron expects, but I still need some help with my version."

Ryder sat up. "What do you mean—*your version?*"

She waved away his question and said, cryptically, "I have a few of my own plans for the big celebration."

"Pilot, what are you up to? If you don't tell me, Kytan *will.*" Ryder threw his brother a threatening scowl.

Kytan sent Hadlee a pleading look.

She bristled and flung the words at Ryder with the force of a challenge. "If you must know, I plan to free all the slaves in Injanae the night of the celebration."

Ryder fell back into the deep pile of pillows and let out a shout of laughter. "That's brilliant. Nothing short of chaos will erupt when you make that announcement; giving us the perfect distraction we'll need to leave." His smile embraced her. "Make it just as you exit. That will give us the best chance. While the king, Cartu, and the guards are dealing with the impact of your decree, we can escape the palace and the city, unnoticed."

"I can't believe you like this idea," Kytan said, his tone incredulous. "It is very dangerous. This society largely depends on slave labor to function. Freeing the slaves could cause them to riot, and start a rebellion among the nobles and common people."

"I don't care if it starts a riot." Hadlee faced off with Kytan. "It is time slavery in Injanae stopped! Surely, after working in the copper mine as a slave, you don't approve of slavery, Kytan."

Kytan shot back, "No I don't, but if you free all the slaves the streets might be overrun with rioters and revelry, making it *more,* not *less,* difficult for us to leave."

Taya put her hands over her face, rocking back and forth. Ryder stopped interpreting their words for her, and held up his hand to the others. "What's the matter Taya?"

"Please, don't argue. We can't afford to be at odds with each other right now. Don't we have enough to do and worry over without trying to change this society too?"

Hadlee sat down next to her, laying a hand on her arm. "I'm sorry. I didn't mean to upset you. Forgive me. I just hate being Ateron's slave. If freeing the slaves will help us leave, isn't it worth doing?"

Taya didn't respond after Ryder finished translating, morosely examining her hands.

Kytan sat down on the other side of her, putting his arm lightly around her shoulders. "Forgive us. We aren't angry with each other, we are just considering options." He smiled at Hadlee, who instantly returned it.

"What do you say we think on this? Right now, if I am going to be able to get back here tonight, I better go to work." Ryder got up from the cushions; took Taya's hand and pulled her to her feet. "But before I do, I think we could all use a hug and a prayer."

Thirty-seven

Kytan's work on a delicate netting of silver, which would be attached between the empire-line bodice of Ansuetra's gown and the long fitted skirt that flared out dramatically at the bottom, kept him in the apartment after Ryder left. He needed the exact measurement of the bodice's edge. As he measured it, he discussed the netting's length, and finishing trim with Hadlee. The girls' company was so enjoyable he lingered, deciding to stay until lunch to help Hadlee with her lines.

Just before noon, Taya left with a heavy basket of laundry she needed sent down on the dumb waiter in the king's hall. Kytan usually helped with this chore, when he was there, but today he used Hadlee's lines as an excuse, letting Taya go by herself.

His dimples flared to life as soon as Taya went out the door. "I want to show you something," he said, producing a small leather pouch. Taking Hadlee's hand, he pulled her out onto the terrace. "I asked Ryder to tell me how a man asks a woman to marry him in the United States. He told me it is customary for the man to give the woman a ring as a token of their engagement to marry." He placed the pouch in her hand. "I want to know if this will do."

Hadlee extracted the ring from the pouch. *"Oh,* Kytan, it's gorgeous. It's the most beautiful ring I have ever seen."

Slipping it part way down her little finger, she examined the delicately worked gold ring. It was crowned with a large square diamond set on an angle, surrounded by several smaller ones of differing sizes and shapes.

"It's even more beautiful than the jewelry you're making for Ansuetra, and that's saying something."

Kytan dimpled with relief. "Good, as soon as we leave Injanae, I intend to ask her."

Hadlee was still admiring the ring when they heard the door to the apartment open, followed by the belfry chiming high noon.

Kytan's eyes flew to Hadlee's.

She jerked the ring off her finger. Pulled the pouch from under her arm and slipped the ring inside it.

Kytan stepped in front of her just before Taya joined them. "That was certainly a fast trip," he said.

"I didn't have to take the basket all the way to the dumb waiter. Zuph took it at the hall door." Taya sneezed and rubbed her eyes. "They must be working very hard in the tunnel. There is so much dust coming out of it today, I need a bath just from walking down the hall." She sneezed again and began dusting her face and arms.

"Why don't you let me dust your back off?" Hadlee offered.

Taya turned around.

Hadlee slipped the pouch from behind her back into Kytan's hand. He stuffed it back into the larger one he wore around his waist.

As Hadlee finished brushing off Taya's back, a long, low rumble reverberated through the stone floor of the terrace. The vibrations intensified. They were followed by a growing series of loud, resounding booms that sounded like a kettledrum finale in a battle symphony.

"Was that thunder?" Hadlee asked Kytan, after the final crescendo died away, scanning the wispy, white waves in the sky.

Kytan had gone rigid with the first moaning rumble beneath his feet, He knew that sound. He'd heard it too many times in the mine. Breaking through his paralysis, he bolted from the terrace.

"Cave-in!" The words flew over his shoulder—in Injanae.

"Ryder," Taya gasped, and rushed after Kytan.

Kytan bounded across the apartment, threw open the door and hurdled through it, nearly knocking Bayo down. Scrambling passed him, Kytan raced down the hall, vaulted through the hole in the wall, flew up the narrow staircase, and into the mouth of the tunnel.

Numo, Orat, and Ven materialized out of the foggy dust. They shoved passed him, shouting and bleeding from cuts to their faces and arms. The dust was so thick it stung Kytan's eyes and choked him. He pulled the bottom of his tunic up covering his nose and mouth, grabbed a torch and plunged into the tunnel.

"Who is in there?" A voice echoed through the tunnel at his back.

Kytan returned to the mouth of the tunnel. Cartu was standing just outside its door. "I have experience with cave-ins," he said boldly to the chancellor, gagging out the words through the dust clogging his throat. "Do you know if anyone else—besides the three guards I saw—was in there?"

"There were four guards in the tunnel with your friend. Po and Ryder have not come out, I take it," Cartu snapped, with obvious affront at Kytan's take-charge attitude.

"No," said Kytan, a chill crawling over him.

"If you have experience with cave-ins then the king will want to speak with you." Cartu drew himself up, asserting his authority. "Come with me."

"Excellency." Kytan bowed humbly. "Time is essential if we are going to get Po and Ryder out alive. There isn't enough of it to have a long discussion with the king. I can tell you what I need right here."

"What do you need?"

"Every man you can get—right now—including Ven, Numo, and Orat, along with the ones guarding Hadlee's doors. Bring rock-breaking tools, shovels, buckets of water, oil lamps—and more torches. The men will also need masks until the dust settles." Kytan paused, thinking hard. "Excellency, if Ryder and Po made it beyond the cave in, they won't have air for more than a few hours. Ask the king if we may go in through the balcony wall. There may be no more blockages between that wall and where Ryder and Po are trapped."

Cartu moved swiftly down the stairs.

Kytan faced the billowing dust cloud with squinted eyes and moved into its depths. He and Ryder had worked on a dozen cave-ins during their time in the mine. He knew the outlook wasn't good. Less than a tenth of the men caught in one survived. And even if they made it beyond the falling rocks, suffocation often killed them.

Praying silently, he picked his way through loose rubble until he came to the barrier that entombed his brother. He carefully inspected every inch of the blockade. By the time the men and tools arrived, he knew where to start breaking up the rocks. He barked out orders. Everyone went to work. No one questioned his authority.

It didn't surprise him when Pel brought word that Ateron wouldn't allow him to break through the balcony wall. "That would spoil the king's plans," Pel said.

The disgust in his voice told Kytan he knew the king's verdict could very well seal Ryder and Poe's fate. Shoulder to shoulder, faces set with resolve, they went to work.

The look on Kytan's face and Taya's exclamation kept Hadlee hard on Taya's heels, as she too darted through the apartment door.

Bayo, standing guard, stopped Hadlee cold, blocking her path. He was several inches shorter than she was, but very wide and muscular.

"Please," she said in Injanae, attempting to go around him.

He shook his shaggy head, grabbed her arms, pushed her back into the apartment, and shut the door firmly in her face.

She leaned her head against the door, pounding on it with both fists. With a howl of frustration, she backed away and began pacing the area in front of the door, straining for any sound beyond it.

When the belfry began chiming the half hour, she nearly jumped out of her skin. Switching directions, she continued to pace until Taya stumbled through the door. In a torrent of sobs, she fell into Hadlee's arms.

Panic constricted Hadlee's heart, tightening the grip of fear she was already fighting. She led Taya over to one of the large sofas, sat, and pulled Taya down beside her.

"Please, Taya, try to tell me what's happened." Taya kept crying and saying Ryder's name until Hadlee's fear exploded. "What's happened to Ryder? Why doesn't Kytan come and tell me?"

Her outburst stopped Taya's crying. Taya swallowed, wiped her eyes and stood. "Charades," she said firmly, walking over to the dining table.

"Yes," Hadlee said in Injanae, following her.

Taya surveyed the long table, went into her own small bedchamber, brought out two blankets and draped them over the table, creating a tunnel. Grabbing three large pillows, she pointed to herself. "Ryder," she said, moving into the dark makeshift tunnel.

Hadlee dropped to her hands and knees.

Taya went half way in, stopped, and rolled onto her back. Pounding on the underside of the table with her feet, she stacked the pillows between herself and the entrance to the tunnel.

Hadlee gasped. "No!" She jumped to her feet, and shook her head, making her ponytail whip back and forth. "No!" Goose bumps riddled her. She turned wide dilated eyes to Taya as she emerged from the tunnel. "Is he—is he—*dead?*"

"Ryder"—Taya shook her head and shrugged her shoulder—"Okay?"

Hadlee expelled the breath she was holding. At least he wasn't known to be dead. That meant there was still hope. Putting her hands together, she fell to her knees. Taya followed suit. The apartment resonated with their desperate pleadings.

The clock tower chimed one.

Taya got to her feet, pointing at the door.

Hadlee's ponytail bounced. "Yes go and see what you can find out."

Another hour passed.

Hadlee winced every time the belfry chimed another quarter hour. Unable to sit still, she paced, rushing to the door each time Taya came back from another information-seeking trip.

After two hours dragged by with no news, Hadlee was shaking with a fear she never thought she could feel for Ryder Garrison. *Am I truly afraid for him? Maybe, I'm just afraid for myself, because my chances of escaping Injanae will evaporate without him.* That thought was so disturbing; it turned her already unsettled stomach into a churning caldron. She clutched it and paced until Taya made her lie on the sofa and forced a cup of hot herb tea down her.

Thirty-eight

The rescue crew had worked their way through three feet of loose rocks when they uncovered the tip of a boot. It brought the work to an instant and silent halt.

Kytan inhaled courage and dug away dirt and rocks until the boot was fully exposed. He expelled the breath he was holding; *it isn't Ryder's.*

No one said a word until the grisly duty of pulling Po's crushed body from beneath the rocks was completed.

"We will find Ryder like this too," Sual said, breaking the silence.

His sentiments were echoed by many of the guards as they laid Po's remains on a stretcher.

"It might be better to just leave Ryder's body entombed in this tunnel-grave, instead of continuing to dig our way to him," Lul said, covering Po with a blanket.

The idea won an instant chorus of agreement.

Kytan refused to entertain the thought. One way or the other, he had to know. Besides, he reminded the guards, the king gave them no choice.

After another hour of breaking and moving large rocks even Kytan began to lose hope. They didn't seem to be any nearer to breeching the barrier.

He looked at the rock wall in front of him.

Defeat stared back at him.

Even if Ryder isn't under the rocks, it is very unlikely he will be alive by the time we reach him. Desperate for guidance, Kytan gave the men a short break and went to Hadlee's apartment.

He entered the apartment knowing he looked like he'd just emerged from the grave.

Taya leaped off the sofa, shrieking at the sight of him.

Hadlee sprang to her feet too, clutched her head and fell back onto the sofa.

Clouds of dirt billowed out around Kytan as he walked across the room and sat down next to Hadlee. He took hold of Taya's hand and pulled her down on his other side. Unconcerned by his filth and sweat, he took Hadlee's hand, still holding Taya's tightly in his other one.

Tasting the gritty dirt between his teeth, he informed the girls, "We haven't found Ryder yet, and I don't know when we will. Even if he made it to the other side of the cave-in, there isn't much time left before he will run out of air." Tugging on their hands, he pulled them to their knees on the soft alpaca rug. "I need you both to pray with me. I need to find a way to break through—right now."

Tears flowed down their faces as Kytan prayed. He pleaded for Ryder's life and desperately sought guidance. They stayed on their knees when he closed the prayer, each offering additional silent petitions.

The anxious minutes passed.

Kytan's head jerked up. He sucked in a sharp breath. Squeezing each girl's hand, he leaped to his feet. Shedding dirt on everything he passed, he raced back to the tunnel.

Yelling for the guards, he took the stairs two at time and raced through the tunnel knowing just where he should dig. It wasn't logical to start at the bottom, but a voice inside him was directing him. Even before the guards returned to help, he was digging away at the mountain of dirt and rock still standing between him and his brother.

"What are you doing?" Pel asked him as he frantically dug between two large boulders at the base of the blockage.

"Right now the most important thing is to get air to the other side. There can't be much more than six or seven feet to go," said Kytan. He stopped digging and looked up at Pel. "The boulders on either side of this area"—he gestured with his shovel—"and the one perched across the top of them will create a passage way. I can dig through the passage to the other side of the blockage. It is just filled with loose dirt and rocks. The area between the boulders is wide enough to pull Ryder through."

"How do you know you can go all the way through between these boulders? It is more likely you will hit another one before you get through."

"I won't. This is the way through. I can't explain it, but I am sure of it. Please, just help me!"

His air of certainty and urgency won Pel's cooperation. He too, along with the returning guards began to work on the area between the boulders.

Digging like a mole, Kytan wiggled into the widening space on his belly, shoving the dirt and rock out behind him as he went, letting the guards clear the debris away.

Thirty minutes later, he gave a yell of triumph when his shovel gouged into empty space.

Encouraged, the guards widened the passage between the two huge boulders that still contained a large quantity of rocks and dirt while Kytan clawed with his shovel until the breech was large enough to admit his broad shoulders.

The blackness beyond the cave-in was absolute. Kytan scuttled backwards, rasping out a request for an oil lamp.

Pel quickly put one into his hand.

Pushing the lamp in front of him, he wiggled back into the passageway, squeezed through the breach into the oppressive darkness beyond the cave-in, and lit the lamp.

Thirty-nine

The flame produced by the small lamp flickered ominously, a warning there was little air. The puddle of light it provided only illuminated a tiny area around Kytan's feet. Holding it low to the ground, he moved with careful steps while the guards shouted questions. Ignoring them, he began slowly moving the light from one side of the tunnel to the other, picking a path through the jagged rocks littering the floor.

"*Ryder!*" His fearful voice bounced off the walls, reverberated through the tunnel and faded away in a ghostly mutter.

Hope and fear pumped through his veins as he stumbled over the rocky floor to his brother, sprawled against the tunnel wall. Setting the lamp down beside Ryder's head, Kytan turned Ryder's face to him. Dirt and blood covered it. Placing a hand on Ryder's chest and his cheek close to Ryder's nose and mouth, Kytan felt the shallow rise and fall of Ryder's chest and the breath he inhaled and exhaled.

"He is alive," he shouted to the still questioning guards. "Send two men in here with a stretcher, now! The rest of you keep digging. We need to clear everything out from between the boulders."

Shur and Tark, less fearful of confined spaces than the others, squeezed through the opening.

Pel crawled into the passageway, shoving a heavy canvas stretcher through with two additional oil lamps.

Lighting the lamps, the guards hurried over to Kytan and helped him clear the ground around Ryder before carefully rolling him from his side to his back.

Kytan again put a hand on Ryder's chest. The heartbeat that pulsed beneath his palm was much steadier than his own. Ryder wasn't conscious, but he was alive.

After a silent prayer of thanks, he instructed Shur to lift Ryder's legs while Tark helped him lift Ryder's shoulders. Together they moved him onto the stretcher. By the time they got him there, they were winded from inhaling the bad, dust-laden air.

Leaning over to catch his breath, Kytan called through the passageway for water. A small clay jug was pushed through the opening. He poured the contents slowly over Ryder's dirt masked face, hoping to bring him around.

Ryder didn't respond.

"Hold on a little longer and we will have you out of here," Kytan said softly to his brother. "There are two women, on the brink of collapse, waiting to see you."

Dizziness was starting to overcome all three rescuers by the time they cleared a path for the stretcher and pulled Ryder to the mouth of the opening. Kytan told the two guards to go back through and get some air. He stayed with Ryder, keeping close to the opening, taking in slow, deep breaths, hoping the exposure to better air would bring Ryder around.

Another fifteen minutes dragged by before the entire passage was wide enough to accommodate Ryder's massive shoulders.

Tark crawled back through, helping Kytan push the stretcher as far as they could into the passage between the boulders. The guards on the other side took hold of the emerging poles and hauled Ryder out.

"Take him to Hadlee's apartment," Kytan said, wiggling out of the passageway.

Six hefty guards hoisted the stretcher, navigated the rubble-strewn tunnel, shuffled down the narrow stairs, through the hole in the wall, and out into the hallway.

Kytan went around them, and open Hadlee's door.

Taya and Hadlee screeched Ryder's name, reaching out to touch him. He was caked from head to heels in a thick layer of dirt, making his skin and hair virtually indistinguishable from his clothes. It made the muddy-red streaks that seeped through the dirt all the more vivid.

Taya placed an anxious hand on his chest. It rose and fell in a regular rhythm under her hand. She sighed with relief.

Hadlee pushed his dirty hair back from his face, with shaky fingers.

"Where do you want us to put him?" Pel asked, making her jump back with a start.

Taking charge, Taya swept the blankets from the long dining table and barked out orders to the two nearest guards. "Norr, Yawt, help me pull the table out from the wall." They immediately did her bidding. She turned to the stretcher-bearers and commanded, "Lay him on the table. He will need to be washed and given medical treatment."

The men dutifully laid the stretcher on the long table.

"Remove the poles," Taya said over her shoulder and went into her supply closet.

"What else do you wish us to do?" asked Pel, when Taya emerged with a large tray of medical supplies.

He, and all eighteen of his men had crowded into the apartment and stood gaping at Ryder.

"I will need a dozen large pots of water and two mattresses." She put her tray down. "And tell the king I am working on Ryder. I will let him know how he is after I examine him." With those directives, she shooed all the guards out the door. After it closed behind the guards, she turned to Kytan, "Tell Hadlee to go get her water pitcher and some towels."

Hadlee was climbing the stairs before Kytan finished speaking.

He turned back to Taya awaiting more instructions. Taya took hold of his hands, raw from digging, and covered in dozens of cuts and scrapes. She looked into his exhausted face, stood on her toes and kissed his grimy cheek.

"You are wonderful. Ryder owes you his life. I need to wash and examine him. You need to wash too. I will give you some medicine for your cuts. Why don't you go and take care of yourself while Hadlee and I take care of Ryder."

"I will, but first let me help. I won't feel easy until I know how he is."

The understanding hand Taya ran down his cheek came away covered in dirt. He kissed it anyway.

"Alright," she said, "help me get his boots off then you need to take your tunic off and wash everything from your waist up. We don't need your dirt getting in the way."

Hadlee came down the stairs, a little unsteady on her feet, loaded down with a full pitcher of water and several towels. As she reached the bottom, Pel and his men delivered the large clay pots of water and the two mattresses.

Taya directed the guards to push aside the floor pillows, and put the mattresses, one on top the other, in front of the fire pit. "That will be the best place to put Ryder after we treat him," she said to Kytan.

At her request, Anlow and Sual stayed in the apartment. As the others filed out the door, she began her examination by feeling, moving, and bending Ryder's arms and legs. "Nothing is broken," she said when she was done.

Kytan told the good news to Hadlee in a short pantomime that made Sual and Anlow laugh.

Hadlee nodded her understanding.

Taya brought the guards' attention back to her. "Anlow help Sual roll Ryder to his side and hold him." They did, and she and Kytan tugged the stretcher out from under him. "Now, let's get his clothes off. I need to check all the places he's bleeding. Then we need to wash him head to toe and treat his injuries," she said to Kytan, undoing the belt at Ryder's waist.

Kytan cleared his throat. "Taya, I don't think he would want you to take everything off."

Taya waved a dismissive hand. "I'm a doctor."

"I know, but Hadlee isn't. If he wakes up and finds you or Hadlee taking his pants off, he will have a fit." Kytan shook his head. "It will be better if I do it. I can tell you if he has any injuries, and you can tell me how to treat them."

She shrugged. "Alright, cover him and take off his pants. Then wash his legs and feet, treat his wounds with this ointment, and bandage his knees—they look awful." She handed Kytan a pot of herb ointment and several long strips of cloth for bandages.

Kytan draped one of the blankets from the tunnel charade over Ryder's hip, removed his pants and started washing his bloody knees.

Taya gestured to Hadlee, did a short pantomime of her own, and glared at the guards for their sputtering chuckles.

Again, Hadlee nodded her understanding and began to help her take Ryder's tunic off.

After a short struggle, the torn tunic was removed, exposing dozens of cuts, scrapes, and bruises. The worst one was a deep gash on Ryder's left side. It began to bleed heavily when the fabric of his tunic was pulled away from it.

Hadlee reached for a towel.

Taya took it from her and did another brief pantomime. Hadlee went to work washing Ryder's back and treating the minor cuts and scrapes with the ointment Taya gave her, while Taya washed the ugly gash. When she was satisfied it was clean, she pressed a towel against it.

After Hadlee finished washing and treating Ryder's back, Taya made a quick inspection of it, nodded her approval and addressed Sual, "I need you to press down on this towel and hold it in place against Ryder's side until I come back."

He put his hand over hers and pressed down as she pulled hers out.

She turned to Kytan. "Hadlee and I will go to her bedchamber while you take care of Ryder's private needs." She took hold of Hadlee's arm and pulled her up the steps. "Let me know if you find anything that needs my attention," she said over her shoulder as they went through the curtain.

Kytan called them back in a few minutes, telling Taya he had only found bruises and minor cuts.

"Good now let's put a blanket under him and roll him onto his back," Taya said. When that was done, she thanked the guards and dismissed them.

As soon as the door clicked shut, Hadlee breathed out relief. "Thank heavens they're finally gone." She turned to Kytan. "Ask Taya how serious Ryder's condition is."

Kytan put the question to Taya.

"I don't know yet," she said, her expression worried. "But I am afraid he has lost a lot of blood from this wound."

A careful check of the gash in Ryder's side revealed it was still bleeding sluggishly. She pressed the cloth back over it and said, "There are several things I need Hadlee to do, while I work on getting the bleeding from this gash to stop."

Kytan conveyed her instructions to Hadlee, telling her to wash Ryder's face, inspect his head for injuries, and then wash his hair.

Hadlee picked up a clean rag and gently washed Ryder's battered face. The skin on the left side of his face was scraped from his forehead to his jaw line. There was a small bloody cut across the bridge of his nose, another along his right cheekbone, and one more on his chin. Carefully, she washed each one, applying Taya's ointment.

When she was done, she dropped the cloth into a growing basket of dirty, blood soaked washcloths and towels, and said to Kytan, "Tell Taya I will examine his head and wash his hair now."

Kytan relayed the message and said, "Taya says before you do, we better move him up so his head is partially off the table. It will keep the water from soaking the table while you wash his hair." He reached for a large basin, and put it on the floor. "This should catch most of the water so we won't have as much mopping up to do."

Hadlee made a wry face. "That's what Taya wanted to do with me the first time I needed my hair washed."

"Why?"

"Because she didn't want to wash my hair while I was confined to bed with a sprained ankle. She was afraid the bed would be soaked, and she wanted to keep my foot elevated."

Kytan smiled. "So you know how this works."

"No, I didn't let Taya do it that way, but Ryder doesn't have a choice." She frowned. "Moving him up is going to be pretty hard. Maybe you should go get a couple of the guards."

"I think you and I can do it, if we just pull on the blanket underneath him."

Hadlee took hold of one of the blanket's corner next to Ryder's head.

Kytan told Taya what they were going to do and went around the head of the table. He gripped the other corner, looked up, and stiffened.

Forty

The king and Cartu stood just inside the apartment—gaping at Kytan.

Ateron walked across the room. "It seems we have come at a very opportune moment, Kytan." He pursed his lips. "Although I didn't understand your *lengthy* conversation with Hadlee, it was most . . . enlightening." His eyes shifted to Hadlee in a considering way. "Hadlee may feel equal to the job, but it would be better to have Cartu help you pull Ryder up, as he is a very large man, and Cartu is stronger than Hadlee."

Kytan's eyes shot to Hadlee. "Ryder is going to skin me alive when he wakes up, but there is no point in trying to deceive the king any longer. The chancellor is going to help me pull him up so you can get started."

"Have Hadlee hold his head while you move him," Taya said as Kytan and Cartu took hold of the blanket.

Hadlee placed her hands on either side of Ryder's head, lifting it while Kytan and Cartu pulled on the blanket, slowly moving him up. When most of his head was over the edge of the table, Hadlee told Kytan to stop. Rolling up a towel, she put it under Ryder's neck to support his head.

Ateron's attention shifted to Taya. "How is my slave doing? Are his injuries serious?"

"Most of them are minor, but there are a couple of things I am concerned about. He has a deep gash in his side. It is bleeding, and I don't know how much blood he has lost from it. He is also still unconscious, and that worries me. If he has a head injury, then things could be very serious. I think I should keep Ryder here for a few days. He will need to be closely watched, and it will be easier if I have Hadlee's help."

"Certainly, do what you feel is best. I want Ryder back on his feet as soon as possible." Ateron tilted his head. A cold smile graced his handsome face. "Kytan, you are proving to be a man of many talents. It is time I utilized them better. Report to my private judgment chamber tomorrow morning at . . . nine bells."

"Hateful, hateful man." Hadlee threw a dirty, wet towel at the closing door. She picked up her pitcher, ready to pour water over Ryder's hair.

Kytan reminded her to examine Ryder's head, and somberly went back to bandaging Ryder's knees.

She set the pitcher aside, rolled Ryder's head to one side, and carefully ran her fingers through his thick hair. It was matted with dirt that clung to her fingers and burrowed under her nails. Not finding anything on the right side of his head, she turned his head to the other side, repeating the process.

"Oh! He has a huge lump." She frowned, feeling the large goose egg on the back, left side of his head. Gently probing it made her fingers sticky. "And it's bleeding."

"Let's trade places so I can look at it," said Taya, still pressing on the towel she held against Ryder's side.

Hadlee quickly washed her hands and took over applying presser to the gash on Ryder's side while Taya examined his bleeding head.

"The cut is only a scratch, but he took a bad blow to the head. I am afraid there isn't much I can do. We will just have to—"

"Wait a minute!" Hadlee interrupted as Kytan interpreted. "I know how we can tell if he has a concussion."

Again, the girls traded places.

Hadlee stood at the top of Ryder's head, carefully pulled open both his eye lids with her thumbs and peered intently into the golden depths of his eyes. "His left pupil is definitely larger than the right one. That means he has a concussion, but I don't know how bad it is." Uncertainty clouded her face.

"The longer he's unconscious, the worse it is—I think. We'll need to watch for nausea and dizziness," she said, picking up her pitcher and pouring water over Ryder's hair.

Kytan passed along her diagnosis and concerns to Taya, as he finished bandaging Ryder's knees. The two conversed for a few moments. He blew out a breath, bent down as though he was afflicted with severe arthritis and retrieved his dirty tunic from the floor. "Taya wants me to go bathe and bring back clean clothes for Ryder," he said to Hadlee, and trudged out the door.

Hadlee refilled her pitcher and again poured the water over Ryder's hair, rinsing out more of the dirt. She repeated this several more times, before carefully massaging soap through his hair and into his scalp, thoroughly cleaning the wound. After rinsing and squeezing the water from his long hair, she wrapped it turban style in a dry towel. Rolling another clean dry towel, she replaced the one under his neck as the door again opened.

Kytan, clean and still dripping water from his long braid, came in, carrying clothes for Ryder. He put them down on a chair and inquired what more he could do. His exhausted tone brought concern to Taya's voice and eyes.

Hadlee added her own concern. "You have done enough. You look ready to collapse."

"That is what Taya said too. She wants me to sit down while you two finish, then I will help get him dressed." He pulled up a chair near Ryder's head, slouched into it and closed his eyes.

Hadlee plunged a clean washcloth into a basin of water, wrung it out and bathed Ryder's right arm. When she got to his hand, his fingers twitched; then closed around hers. She gasped, let go of the washrag and returned the increasing grip of his fingers. "I think he's coming to!"

Forty-one

Ryder could hear the murmur of voices, like a distant babbling stream, but distinguishable words eluded him. *If I could just open my eyes . . . ,* but as hard as he tried, they simply wouldn't open.

He quit trying, retreating into the feel of the soothing ripples of water running down his arm and into his hand. The sensation brought intense thirst. He desperately wanted to drink the water.

Trying to capture the precious liquid, his fingers closed around something wet. He brought it to his lips.

"Ryder, open your eyes. It's alright, you're safe."

He knew that voice.

She pulled their intertwined fingers from his lips, but didn't release his hand. He felt the fingers of her other hand lightly brush his brow. His mouth curved in a ghost of a smile. Tightening his clasp on her hand, he felt the brush of her ponytail tickle his shoulder and knew Hadlee was leaning over him.

"Thirsty," he croaked out.

Kytan and Taya's cheer crashed together like cymbals inside his head. He groaned.

A chair tipped over. Footsteps hurried away and returned. Hadlee's hand left his brow and slipped under his head, lifting and turning it. A cup was pressed to his lips. He drank three cups of water before Hadlee lowered his head back down to the table. Nothing had ever tasted so good.

He sighed, and forced his eyes open. "Am I alive?" he whispered hoarsely.

Hadlee's lips trembled. "Yes—thank heaven—you are very much alive. Although I'm afraid you're going wish you weren't for a couple of weeks."

A tear splashed down on Ryder's cheek. "Don't cry, Pilot," his voice rasped through his dust scraped throat. "I'm glad I'm among the living, even if I'm miserable for a while."

She sniffed back more tears, gave him a quivering smile and hugged the hand she still held.

His face broke into a painful, lopsided attempt at a smile. He tried to turn his head to look at Kytan and Taya as they expressed their feelings, and took turns hugging his other hand, but it was bundled up in something and trying to move it hurt too much.

"Tell me how I got out," he said to Kytan, closing his eyes.

"Not now," Taya said. "You need to be quiet while we finish washing you and treating your wounds."

His eyes flew open. He tilted his head down slightly and saw the blanket covering his hips. He slid his hand beneath it. His face reddened. "Who removed my pants?"

"Now just who do you think did? Don't worry; I protected your modesty and took care of the needed treatment." Kytan's dimples laughed at him.

Ryder glowered in return, pulled the blanket farther up his body and choked out, "From this point on, I'll take care of my own private needs, if that's alright with everyone—and even if it's not."

He tried to make himself relax as Hadlee gently washed and dressed the cuts and scrapes that were glaringly visible on his arms and chest, but full consciousness brought excruciating awareness of his injuries. Searing pain jackhammered through his head and danced like firebrands over him. Every rock-bludgeoned place on his body screamed.

"Taya, *please*, give me something for the pain."

"I will, after we know where all your injuries are. If I dull your pain now, I might miss something important. Be patient a little longer," she said, finally releasing the pressure on the towel pressed against his side. With painstaking care she removed the bloody towel.

He gazed down at the deep gash in his side.

"Good, the bleeding has finally stopped." Taya nodded, and patted a smelly ointment on the gash, making him inhale sharply. She put a thick pad over it, and with Hadlee's help, wound a long strip of gauze around his waist to hold the pad in place.

Wishing he were still unconscious, Ryder gritted his teeth during the hours it seemed to take for Taya and Hadlee to finish washing and treating the rest of his injuries.

When they were finally done, Taya reassured him that most of his injuries—however painful—were minor, ending with the need to watch him closely because of his concussion. "Now Kytan can help you put your pants on. Leave your tunic off so we can keep an eye on your side. Then we will put you in Hadlee's bed."

Ryder eyes leaped to Hadlee's face.

She blushed from her neck to the roots of her pale blond hair and quickly explained, "Since you will be staying here for a few days, we decided you need the comfort of the box springs more than I do."

He expressed his thanks, and the girls retired to Hadlee's room while Kytan helped him put his pants on.

"You are going to be quite a sight by tomorrow," Kytan said, shaking his head pitifully. Then amended, "Actually you are quite a sight now, but I bet you will turn black and blue all over before morning."

"If I do, you will have to protect me from Taya. She'll want to put that terrible herb paste all over me, and I'll die of the smell."

Kytan's dimples laughed for a moment, and died. He eyed Ryder doubtfully. "Do you think you can make it up the stairs, or should I get a couple of guards to help?"

"I'll be fine. Just lend me a hand." He grimaced as Kytan took his arm. "Tomorrow, without fail, I want to hear everything. Right now, I want Taya to make me unconscious again. My head is about to come off."

White lights sparked in front of his eyes, and a tornado of dizziness spun him around as Kytan helped him sit up. He pulled the turban from his head, groaned, and swung his feet over the edge of the table. The room went in and out of focus several times. He clutched his head, swaying backward.

"Do you really think you can do this?"

Kytan's concerned face swam before his eyes.

Before he could answer, Hadlee called from the bedroom, "Can we come back yet?"

"Yes. I am going to need your help to get him up the stairs." Kytan held on to Ryder as he continued to sway.

Hadlee hurried down the stairs, eased Ryder's arm across her shoulders then wrapped hers around his waist, carefully avoiding the wound in his side.

He inhaled an adrenaline surge.

Kytan took the same hold on his other side. Together they slid him off the table and onto his feet.

His knees buckled with his first step.

"Wow"—Hadlee staggered—"you weigh a ton."

"Sorry," he said through clenched jaws, battling the darkness that threatened to overcome him. His spinning head left him no choice but to lean heavily on them. They half-carried him up the short flight of stairs and put him diagonally onto the bed. It felt like heaven to his pain-riddled body.

After settling him onto his right side, which had sustained the least damage, Hadlee left to get more pillows for his comfort. Taya went to make her pain potion, and Kytan left to start cleaning up.

Hadlee returned and arranged the pillows to his satisfaction. "Are you hungry? You haven't eaten anything since breakfast. Would you like me to go get some bread for you?"

"I'm not hungry. My stomach's feeling kind of . . . queasy."

"*Oh?* I'd better look at your eyes again."

He turned his face up to her. She leaned over him, peering intently into his eyes. Her long ponytail brushed his chest. Her nearness ratcheted his heart rate up to the speed of a firing tommy gun. His head reeled.

Her face was so close, the temptation to lean up and kiss her was as powerful and excruciating as the throbbing in his head. *I can't imagine a better pain reliever,* he decided, unable to block the desire.

She drew back. "They still look very uneven, so we will need to wake you up a few times just to make sure you're alright."

"Will you sit with me until I go to sleep?"

"If you want," she said, and scooted the dressing table chair up to the bed.

He took her hand.

She returned his grasp.

He focused on her long slender fingers. "Before I lost consciousness, I couldn't stop thinking about . . . all of you. I wanted to stay alive to help you get out of here."

"We prayed very hard for you," she said, her voice wavering. "And tomorrow, if you're better, you can tell us what happened."

Taya came through the curtain with the pain and sleeping potion. "Let's get this in you. It will dull the pain and help you sleep. I made it strong, so it should work quickly."

Releasing Hadlee's hand, he took Taya's and kissed it. "What would I do without my angel of mercy?" he asked, and drank the bitter concoction.

"Today you had almost a legion of them, but mostly you can thank Kytan, he is the one who got you out, and you can hear all about it in the morning." Taya kissed his cheek.

Hadlee stood, brushing her hand across her eyes. "I'll get another towel to put under your head." Her chin quivered. "You won't sleep well on a wet pillow."

She went down the stairs, and Taya took her place. "You have no idea how bad this day has been for us. I know it has been terrible for you, but we have suffered too." She sniffed away the tears that threatened. "Not knowing if you were alive . . . or dead." She shivered and took a breath. "By the third hour, Hadlee was so upset she was shaking. I need to make her eat something. She hasn't been able to all day, and I know she is exhausted. Do you want anything?"

"No. I don't want to eat right now." The knowledge he'd again caused Hadlee distress, added to his pain, but it also fueled the flicker of hope her concerned eyes had ignited.

"I need to go examine Kytan. Digging you out won him scores of cuts and scrapes that I haven't had time to treat."

"Yes, go take care of my brother." He squeezed her hand. "He deserves your tender care."

She nodded and went through the curtain.

Hadlee reentered the bedchamber armed with two thick towels, and carefully lifted his head.

He cringed.

She winced. "Sorry."

Sharp, shards of pain ricocheted around in his skull as she positioned the towels. He rode the pain like an unbroken stallion, inhaling through his nose and exhaling through his mouth. In an effort to loosen the pain's grip, he focused on what Taya had said. He searched Hadlee's face, noticing the shadows under her eyes.

After she resettled his head, he again took possession of her hand. It trembled in his. He frowned with concern.

She forced a smile. "Taya is treating Kytan's hands. They are almost as bad as yours." She examined the hand that gripped hers, pressing her quivering lips together for a moment. "Is there anything else I can get you?"

"No, just sit with me."

She sat down on the edge of the chair. "Are the herbs starting to work? I think I'll ask Taya for something to make me unconscious too. This has been a horrible, horrible day."

"I'm sorry. Giving people horrible days seems to be one of my unfortunate character traits. I've certainly given you too many."

Her eyes flashed with—what he thought was—momentary agreement, but her ponytail swished side-to-side in denial. "That concussion must be addling your brain."

He winced. His brain was addled, but not by the concussion—by her. She'd been addling him from the moment he laid eyes on her, twelve years ago. He fell into her spectacular eyes, now full of concern for him and wondered how many men had fallen into their depths and lost themselves. They were more beautiful now than when he'd first encountered them, but they were different too. The innocence was gone, and in their depths he saw grief, pain, loss, and loneliness—all the horrors his actions had put there—horrors that should never have touched those exquisite eyes. That knowledge invoked pain so intense he couldn't hide it.

She patted his hand in a soothing gesture, "What happened today wasn't your fault. It wasn't anyone's fault—well, maybe Ateron's. You're alive, and in a few days you will be back to your take charge, dictatorial ways."

"So you think I'm a dictator, do you? I'm sorry about that too." He tightened his grip on her hand. "I guess I need more mending than just my hide. I'll work on it," he said, fighting his drooping eyelids.

Holding Hadlee's hand brought him exquisite comfort, something Taya's herbs couldn't do. He took in a long breath, holding tightly to that comfort, feeling the herbs begin to blur the edges of his pain, making his mind fuzzy. He quit fighting the herbs and embraced the fuzziness, letting go of everything, but the incomparable feel of Hadlee's gentle hand holding his.

When his eyelids fluttered close, Hadlee brushed an obstinate tendril of hair from his forehead. *His eyes really are amazing,* she admitted. *They would put a leprechaun's pot of gold to shame. They are pure twenty-four carat, and the way they can turn to liquid . . .* she abruptly slammed the brakes on that course of thought and refocused her mind.

Staring at his huge hand, covered with cuts and scrapes, still clinging to hers, she admitted what she'd said to him was unfair. *You really aren't a dictator. All of us look to you to get us out of here. I know everything you ask of us is meant to protect us and help us gain our freedom. Maybe it's just your size and overwhelming masculinity that makes everything you say seem like a command. Or maybe, the resentment I'm still fighting makes your directives seem dictatorial,* she silently confessed to him.

Fifteen minutes passed before his grip on her hand completely slackened.

"Rest and get better, you ridiculously over grown Boy Scout. We need you, I—"

The rest of the words stuck in her closed throat. Her face puckered. She stroked his badly scuffed hand, placed it carefully on the bed, pulled the blankets up over his shoulders, and brushed back the obstinate lock of hair that again drooped over the left side of his forehead.

Forty-two

In two-hour shifts, Taya and Hadlee took turns sitting with Ryder through the night. Even with the pain and sleeping medication, he was restless and fretful. When Taya came quietly through the curtain to take her second shift, she noticed he was much calmer.

Hadlee was holding his hand and brushing the fingers of her other hand lightly through his hair, murmuring softly to him. She beckoned to Taya, took her hand and placed it on Ryder's. Standing, she gave Taya the chair, and stretched. Then took Taya's other hand, put it on his hair and whispered, "Okay?"

Taya nodded, imitating Hadlee's bedside manner, but she noticed during that shift, and her next one, Ryder was more restless under her care than he was under Hadlee's.

Kytan was the only one who slept through the night. Taya slipped him the sleeping potion Hadlee refused to take, urging him to relax with some herb tea. Understanding his concern and unable to convince him to go back to the quarters he shared with Ryder, the girls gave in, letting him take up residence on the mattresses near the fire pit.

He woke to the racket of a pair of quarrelsome birds and the morning light seeping through the terrace door. Tossing aside his blanket, he bounded up the steps to the bedchamber and poked his head silently around the curtain.

Hadlee's head was cradled in her arms, resting on the edge of the bed. Ryder was curling a long strand of her platinum hair around his finger.

Kytan opened his mouth and paused, transfixed by the expression on his brother's face. His astonishment grew when Ryder leaned down, carefully placing a feather light kiss on top Hadlee's head.

Kytan sucked in a breath.

Ryder's eyes came up. He put his finger to his lips.

Kytan gave him a penetrating stare.

He shrugged and waved his hand, shooing Kytan away.

The escalating ruckus between the quarreling birds inevitably woke Hadlee too. She sat up with a start, meeting Ryder's eyes. A guilty flush crept up her cheeks.

He studied her with an increasing frown, noticing the shadows under her eyes were larger and darker, and her face looked drawn and pale.

She stared back at him with a constrained smiled. "How are you doing? Are you hungry? What can I get you?"

"Nothing. You look like you're ready to pass out. Kytan can bring me something to eat. You need to go to bed. I don't want to see you for at least eight hours," he said, worry making his voice gruffer than he intended.

"I'm alright, and I can see you're feeling better because your dictatorial manner is back intact." Her lips twitched. "You look terrible. Frankenstein has nothing on you!"

He laughed and then moaned, holding his hammering head, his body throbbing from countless scrapes and bruises. "At least I don't have to look at myself. I'm sorry you do, which is another good reason for you to go away and get some sleep."

"What, and have nightmares about monsters?" She put the back of her hand over her silent, screaming mouth, imitating Hollywood's best expression of terror.

Taya and Kytan came through the curtain to Ryder's groaning laughter, carrying heavy trays of food. The smell of freshly baked bread and fried fish wafted through the room.

Ryder's stomach rumbled.

"Kytan told me you were awake, and we decided the best medicine for all of us is to have breakfast together," Taya said.

Over breakfast, Ryder answered their questions about the cave-in. "After we opened the passage, I told the guards to stay in the braced part of the tunnel while I did a tour of inspection. I was about thirty yards in when the first rumbling tremor started."

Hadlee shivered. "We felt it too."

"I bolted for the braced area as the rumbling grew. I only covered about two-thirds of the distance before rocks began raining down in front of me. I pulled up as the rock shower intensified, turned and . . . frankly fled, into the depths of the tunnel."

"Thank heaven you did," said Taya. "Or you would be dead like Po."

Ryder groaned. "Po died in the cave-in?"

"He followed you in and didn't make it back into the braced part of the tunnel before the ceiling fell," said Kytan.

"I'm sorry he didn't listen to me." Ryder drew in a shaky breath, "I just barely made it beyond the falling ceiling myself. With rocks raining down on me, it got harder to make any progress. The floor turned into a minefield, tripping me up as I tried to keep moving.

"It is a miracle you could move at all, with rocks falling all around you," Hadlee said.

"A rock did finally bring me down." He rubbed the back of his head. "Thankfully, it was only a glancing blow, but it sent me to my knees."

"That explains your concussion," Taya said.

"And your knees," Kytan added. "The floor of the tunnel— where I found you—was covered with jagged rocks."

"Just after the rock hit my head, another one tore the torch from my hand, extinguishing it. I knew I had to keep moving, even though I couldn't see anything. I managed to get to my feet and stumble forward a few more steps, still hoping to get beyond the shower of stones before the ceiling completely collapsed."

Taya covered her face with her hands. "I can't believe you survived all that."

"Unfortunately that wasn't the worst of it. I'd only taken a few more steps when an explosion of—what must have been—falling boulders, behind me, rammed me into the ground. It was followed by a concussive burst of small stones that hit me from behind with so much force I skidded across the tunnel floor."

"Well, that explains your poor face," said Hadlee, her own flinching.

"Yeah, and the only thing I could think to do at that point was try and make it to the side of the tunnel, hoping it might offer me a small measure of protection. In the darkness, I had no idea how far away the wall was. I rolled over the rocks and hit the wall so hard, I almost blacked out."

"I think that saved your life," Kytan said. "From what I saw, you just barely escaped being clobbered by a few very large rocks."

"I did get clobbered by one." Ryder touched his bandaged side.

"Ah," whispered Taya.

"It seemed like forever, before the thundering and shaking of the tunnel died away. I kept myself pressed against the tunnel wall, listening to the thud of rocks still breaking from the ceiling."

"I can't even begin to imagine how terrifying it was to lay there in utter darkness, listening to rocks fall, wondering if the next one might kill you." Hadlee shuddered, and hugged herself.

"Actually by then, the rocks were the least of my worries. Breathing was my biggest problem. The air was so thick with dust that I inhaled it with every breath. It was suffocating. I tore a strip of cloth from the bottom of my tunic and used it as a mask to breathe through. Not that it helped much." Ryder swallowed painfully through his raw throat.

"I know how you felt, it took forever for the dust to settle," Kytan said, his throat just as raw. "I had to let the guards rotate in and out to keep them from passing out."

Hadlee touched Ryder's arm, asking hesitantly, "What did you think about, laying there in the darkness, knowing you were trapped?"

"At first I thought about trying to make it to the end of the tunnel. I was pretty sure I could break through the wall on the balcony, but every time I moved my head, the darkness invaded me."

"I am surprised you were even conscious," Taya said.

He swallowed painfully, looking at his badly bruised arms that had taken the most punishment in his efforts to protect his head. "I wanted to stay conscious, so I gave up the idea of making it to the balcony wall and did the only thing I . . . c-could," his voice cracked, "I prayed for my life . . . and for all of you. I prayed you could climb out without me. I didn't want my death to cost you your chance for freedom." He stopped, the lump in his throat silencing him.

The conspirators' hands became a jumble of fingers intertwined with Ryder's, and each other's, expressing feelings their own closed throats wouldn't allow.

Ryder glanced at Hadlee, knowing he couldn't tell her the most urgent desire in his heart just before the pain in his head, and suffocating dust, made him lose conciseness. *Forgive me Hadlee, please . . . forgive me,* he'd pleaded into the darkness. That desire still ached in his heart more painfully than all his injuries.

He cleared his throat and broke the silence. "I'd like to hear how you got me out," he said to Kytan.

Listening to Kytan expounded the details of what happened, and the parts everyone played, Ryder's appetite waned. Emotion over took him again and tears splashed down his battered face. His eyes touched each of the conspirators, trying to express his heart-felt gratitude.

He took in an unsteady breath. "Thank you for your prayers, I know they saved my life." His bludgeoned fingers grasped Kytan's arm. "Most of all I owe you my life, brother. Thank you for not giving up on me."

Guilt swept Kytan's handsome face. "Ryder, there is something I need to tell you before you decide I deserve your gratitude."

"What?" Ryder asked, noticing the same expression Kytan wore was mirrored by Hadlee and Taya.

Kytan raised his lowered eyes and met Ryder's.

Before he could speak, Hadlee's chin came up. "Our attention and concern was completely focused on taking care of your injures"—she swallowed—"so much so, we didn't hear the door open."

"Are you telling me someone overheard you and Kytan speaking English?"

"Not just someone," Kytan said. It was the king and"—he looked at Hadlee—"his favorite pet."

Ryder groaned and clutched his head, "Well, it can't be helped now. How did Ateron take it?"

"Kytan is supposed to go see the king in a little while," Taya said fearfully.

Kytan shrugged. "He wants to put my *talents* to better use."

"Make sure he knows it was my idea not to tell him about your ability to speak English. At the moment, I don't think he'll try to do me any harm. I don't want you to take the blame for this." Ryder held his brother's eyes. "Whatever happens, just remember to wear your slave-face."

Kytan nodded grimly.

"What in the world is a slave-face, and how will wearing it help?" asked Hadlee.

"A slave-face is a blank face and the only thing a slave really owns," Kytan said. "Ryder taught me to wear one when we were mine slaves. Wearing a slave-face has a great impact on how a slave is treated."

"Why," Hadlee asked.

"Because if your face shows any kind of emotion, your master will know how you feel. He can use that to intimidate you, but if you control yourself in look, attitude, and action, you can earn some respect. Slaves who learn to do that are often treated with less brutality and greater dignity," Kytan said.

"Remember it, brother." Ryder shared a knowing look with Kytan.

"Hadlee and I need to learn to wear slave-faces too," said Taya, gripping Kytan's hand.

Kytan gave hers a squeeze. "It won't be that bad. He still needs me, and now that he knows I have experience in tunneling I may end up working there—at least until Ryder gets better."

"Be very careful. That tunnel should never have been reopened. The roof is too unstable. Take your time clearing it, and brace every foot," Ryder said, grimly. "Don't let it cost anyone else their life."

"I will." Kytan gripped his extended hand, dimpled to reassure Taya, and went to face the king.

Forty-three

Ryder slept most of the day away due to the heavy doses of medication Taya gave him. Hadlee too, after a virtually sleepless night tending Ryder, went to bed in Taya's room, immediately falling into a heavy slumber. However, with no word from Kytan, Taya couldn't rest. Instead, she kept a watchful eye on Ryder.

When Kytan hadn't returned by late afternoon, she went in search of him. Learning he was directing the work in the tunnel, she plunged into its depths.

Kytan's voice drifted down the tunnel to her before she caught sight of his broad shoulders in the faint light of the torches. His back was to her as he instructed his crew.

Orat pointed over Kytan's shoulder at her.

Kytan glanced over his shoulder, turned back to the crew, and issued orders as he backed toward her. Without a word, he took her arm and led her back through the tunnel. She meekly walked through the dimly lit corridor at his side, waiting to speak to him until they were out of hearing range of the guards.

They stopped under the light of a torch, just inside the tunnel entrance. Taya looked up at him and gasped. Her hands reached up to cradle his face. Blood was crusted along a cut on his right cheekbone. Both sides of his face were bruised, with another one growing on his throat.

"Did Cartu—"

"I am alright." He drew her into his arms, leaned down and kissed her. Holding her close, he told her of the king's assault on his face, and Cartu's vicious contributions.

"Ateron was furious with me for not disclosing my ability to speak English, but I think I got off pretty lightly." His dimples twitched. "My face suffered, but my back, for the moment, is unmarked."

"Monsters," she said through her tears.

Kytan stroked the gleaming midnight hair that cascaded over her shaking shoulders. "Tell Ryder and Hadlee everything is okay. I am doing just what we thought, working in the tunnel during the day and on the jewelry at night. My punishment is not being allowed to leave the palace without Cartu's permission. When I do, a guard will be my companion." His hands cupped her face. "The worst part is I am not allowed in the apartment until Ateron permits it."

The tears she couldn't keep from running down her face brought additional pain to Kytan's bruised one. Encircling her in his arms, he lifted her from the ground and kissed her again, with gentle fervor.

Her arms tightened around his neck, clinging to him.

He held her against his heart and whispered into her ear, "It will be alright, my sweet angel, we will be out of here soon."

She nodded her head, but couldn't keep the doubt from her eyes. "I will bring medicine for your face," she said, struggling to control her voice.

"No." He set her down and took hold of her hands. "You need to go now and don't come back here again. I don't want anyone to see you with me. Cartu is already suspicious. His jealousy could be very dangerous to us."

"But—"

"No, you shouldn't have come, and you have already been here too long."

He let a gentle kiss soften his refusal, and allowed her to use the sleeve of her tunic to wipe as much of the dried blood from his face as she could, before he escorted her through the tunnel door.

She looked back over her shoulder as she descended the stairs, her emotions swinging wildly from one end of the spectrum to the other. She'd never been kissed before. It brought a blush to her cheeks and made her heart flutter wildly, but Kytan's injured face made her burn with anger.

He was still standing at the top of the stairs when she reached the bottom. She gazed up at him for a long moment, and blew him a kiss before she climbed through the hole in the wall and stepped back into the hallway.

Ryder pushed off his covers and looked down at his arms and chest. His bruises had blossomed into a spectacular display of color. He opened his mouth to call for his nurses—whose voices he could hear beyond the curtain—but the scraped left side of his face, stiff with the beginning of a scab, made it hard for him to move his jaw when he tried to speak.

Like an old, decrepit man, he sat up, groaned, put his feet on the floor, took hold of the bedside table, and stood. The room reeled for a moment then steadied. He shuffled to the closed curtain of the bedchamber.

As he reached it, he heard Hadlee say, "Not even Ryder could eat all this in a week."

He clutched the wall, pushed back the curtain and surveyed the banquet set out on the table. Through the right side of his mouth, he said, "Oh, yes I could."

In a two-language harmony, he was scolded as the girls rushed up the steps. The swaying of his body, as he clung to the wall, proclaimed his head was still spinning. Reaching him, they took hold of his arms, steadied him, and turned him back toward the bed.

"I'm hungry," he said looking over his shoulder.

"Good," said Taya. "Let's get you back in bed. Then we will bring you as much as you can eat."

As they led him across the room, he whined, "And I'm tired of being alone."

The girls laughed.

He blushed. "I sound just like a sick, crabby, little kid, don't I?"

"You do, but you have every right to feel that way." Hadlee pulled up his covers. "Now just sit tight, and we'll go get the food and come eat with you."

"And after we eat, I will give you another examination," Doctor Taya said, and followed Hadlee through the curtain.

Ryder adjusted his position in the bed, sitting up and leaning back against the headboard. "Hang on, the food will be here in a minute," he said to his growling stomach.

The girls returned with platters of food and settled in for a long, leisurely feast.

Plucking golden berries from their stems, Hadlee said, "Ryder ask Taya why all this food is here."

Swallowing a piece of fried flat bread, topped with cheese, and smoked pig, from a recent royal hunt—a delicacy never given to slaves—Ryder put the question to Taya.

"It seems you are quite a favorite with Ceeona," said Taya, gesturing toward the smoked pig. "When she found out you'd had an accident and were confined to bed, she started sending up food with the guards."

"Does she know how you got hurt and where you are?" asked Hadlee, after Ryder translated.

"No, Taya says the rumor Cartu told the guards to start is that I fell off the balcony stairs when one of them crumbled under my weight. I am supposedly in my own quarters, unable to see anyone right now."

Hadlee laughed. "So Ceeona is trying to fortify you with substantial quantities of food?"

"Apparently, and if I'd known Ceeona would pamper me this much, I would have arranged an accident for myself weeks ago. Oh, how I love a woman who can cook. Remind me to kiss Ceeona. I'd marry her if she was single. She certainly knows the way to my heart," Ryder said, carefully opening his mouth to inhale more smoked pig.

"Oh, so that old adage is true, is it?" Hadlee rolled her eyes. "If that's the case, I will never win any man's heart. I hate to cook and avoid it whenever possible."

"So you can't cook, huh? How will you ever find a husband?" Ryder teased.

"I didn't say I couldn't cook. I just said I didn't like to. There is a difference."

"It looks to me like no one will need to cook for a couple of weeks. Or maybe, in your case, Ryder, Hadlee's wrong, and the food *will* only last for a day or two." Taya grinned impishly at him.

He threw a golden berry at her. She picked it up and threw it back at him. They played a game of three-way catch, until he asked, "Has Kytan been here? I want to know what happened with Ateron."

Taya's face crumpled. She dropped her head and covered her face with her hands.

Ryder exchanged an alarmed look with Hadlee then gently pulled Taya's hands from her face. "What happened to Kytan?"

In short, angry clips, Ryder translated Taya's account for Hadlee of the king and Cartu's assault on Kytan. "While Kytan was kneeling at the king's feet—taking the blame for not telling Ateron about his ability to speak English—Ateron back handed his face, opening a long cut on Kytan's cheekbone from that ring he always wears. Then Cartu punched him on the other side of his face, knocking him over. He pinned Kytan to the floor with a boot pressed against his throat. Taya says the bruises on his throat tell her Cartu must have pressed down very hard. He held Kytan like that, gasping for breath, while Ateron outlined his punishment."

Hadlee jumped up and paced the space between the bed and the bathroom wall, clenching and unclenching her fists, as Ryder told her what Kytan's punishment was.

Her agitation, and Taya's tears, added to Ryder's own simmering anger. "I'll be back to work in a few days. Then Ateron will let Kytan come back and finish Ansuetra's finery. He also still needs one of us to translate and help with Ansuetra's lines." He took Taya's hand, reassuringly, "Don't worry too much, Taya, he'll be back."

"I know, but it doesn't make sense to keep him away from the apartment when it will put him behind schedule on Ansuetra's jewelry," Taya said, wiping her eyes.

"Yeah, but I think Ateron knows it is the worst thing he can do to Kytan, and that's why he's doing it."

Hadlee flounced down into her chair, "And what if this *punishment* is just the first step in a plan to separate us—permanently."

"Do you think that is what he means to do?" Taya continued to sniff back tears.

"I don't know, but by withholding the information that Kytan could speak to Hadlee, we've just confirmed the suspicions—I'm sure Ateron already had—that we are plotting an escape. He's a shrewd man, and it doesn't take a genius to see the bond between all of us or to figure out Hadlee and I want out of here."

A very unladylike snort erupted from Hadlee. "Even a moron could figure that out."

Ryder nodded agreement. "Ateron would be a fool not to believe we're working on a plan to escape. Since he needs our cooperation until after the celebration is over, he's going to do whatever it takes to keep us in line, and if that—in his mind—means keeping us apart, that's what he'll do."

Hadlee leaned forward in her chair, her voice shaking with barely suppressed fear. "If he keeps us apart, our chances of escaping will diminish to almost nothing."

"Let's not panic." Ryder held up a badly scrapped hand. "You two will still be together, and you will see either Kytan or me every day, just not together. I'll probably be the one you don't see, but that won't hurt us. Taya and Kytan aren't restricted to this apartment; they can't be and do their jobs. They will be able to contact me and relay things between us."

"Maybe I can make Ateron let us stay together." Hadlee brightened. "He can't afford to make me angry if he wants my cooperation." Her eyes narrowed. "I think he's starting to feel a little panicky about everything, which gives me the upper hand."

Ryder shot a warning look at her. "That may be true, and it might only make him more dangerous."

"Remember too, that everything is supposed to be ready two weeks before the celebration. That is when we will be in the greatest danger. Ateron won't need anyone but Hadlee then," Taya said.

"Oh yes he will, or I won't perform," Hadlee said fiercely.

"I think we should stick to what we know," Ryder said, trying to calm things down. "All we really know is Kytan isn't allowed to come here right now."

"But what if Ateron does separate us? Do you think he will let Kytan and me keep in contact with you if you are banned from here?" Taya asked Ryder.

Hadlee held Ryder's eyes, "We need to come up with a plan to be sure we can communicate with you if Ateron keeps you away from here."

Forty-four

Taya drew back the curtain as the city bells chimed nine times. She held it for Hadlee, who started down the steps carrying the last of the dinner dishes out of the bedchamber.

Ryder heard the door to the apartment open, and watched Hadlee stiffen as she reached the bottom of the steps.

Ateron and his pet strolled in.

Ryder caught a glimpse of the cold glance Hadlee threw the king, before she walked out of his view. He heard her set the dirty dishes down with a clatter, and begin to put them into the washbasin next to the fire pit.

"I have come to see how your patient is doing," the king said to Taya.

"He is awake, if you wish to see him," she said, hooking the curtain against the wall.

The king and his chancellor mounted the steps.

Ryder schooled his battered face, enduring Ateron's intense scrutiny.

"Have you been out of bed today?" he asked.

"Only for a few moments. My nurses made me get back in. Apparently, I got quite a good crack on the head, and I'm still pretty dizzy."

"His concussion will require several more days of bed rest, before he should be allowed on his feet, Sire. He also needs to be kept quiet and carefully watched for any complications, both from the concussion, and the gash in his side," Doctor Taya said.

The King pursed his lips. "I certainly don't want you to have any setbacks in your recovery, and I am sure Kytan won't either, since he is taking your place while you are indisposed. His days are going to be very long, doing both your job and his. I am afraid he won't have time to come and talk with Hadlee."

Ryder inclined his head, "Sire, I persuaded Kytan not to tell you he could speak my language."

"Indeed," Ateron said, softly. "Kytan convinced me the crime was his, I believed him . . . sure you had learned your lesson in loyalty. Apparently, it was insufficient. That will need to be remedied." He paused, and Ryder received the full benefit of his piranha eyes. "For now, we will postpone the discussion of punishment. I don't want anything to delay your return to your duties."

"I'm sure I'll be back to work in a few days."

"Yes, you will." Ateron stepped to the bed and pressed down on the mattress. "Tell me, where is Hadlee sleeping while you occupy her box springs?"

Ryder's hands clenched beneath the blankets, his bruised muscles tensed and burned with the effort it took to keep his fists from slamming into Ateron's face. The anger that coursed through him robbed him of the ability to summon a civil reply.

Taya came to his rescue. "She is sleeping in my bedchamber. I had additional mattresses brought up."

"I see." Ateron lifted a concerned brow. "I am sure you wouldn't want Hadlee to have a relapse of her back problems, while you occupy her bed, and frankly, I can't afford to have that happen." He motioned to his chancellor.

Cartu left the bedchamber and returned a minute later with Pel and Sual.

"They will take you"—Ateron waved at the guards—"to your own quarters. I have had Pel but an extra mattress on the floor for your comfort. Taya can come and keep an eye on you until you are well enough to go back to work."

Ryder nodded curtly, sat up, pushed the blankets off, and swung his feet over the side of the bed.

"Ryder, what's happening?" Hadlee rushed up the steps.

"I'm going to my quarters."

Fear and anger battled for control of her face.

"I'll be okay. Pel and Sual are going to help me get there, and Taya will keep an eye on me. Just remember what we talked about and everything will be alright."

"No it won't, *it won't*. You need to stay here so we can take care of you." She turned on Ateron. "He needs to stay—Ryder, tell him I want you to stay."

Ryder brushed his fingers across her hand. She caught them and held on. Her clasp vibrated fear, but her stance proclaimed defiance.

"Hadlee let it go." The use of her name turned her to him. His eyes smiled at her through his Frankenstein face. "This isn't the battle we need to fight."

Without another word she released his fingers, backed away, walked down the stairs, and disappeared through the terrace door.

Taya helped Ryder put his boots and tunic on. Pel and Sual pulled him to his feet.

Shockwaves of dizziness made him sway backwards. The guards steadied him. The pressure of their hands on his bruised arms made him grit his teeth. He took a step forward, then another, willing himself to stay upright. Aided by the guards, he made it down the stairs.

With Taya in the lead, to make sure everything was in order in his quarters and see to his needs, the little parade when through the apartment door.

The guards carefully deposited Ryder on his bed, and left.

Taya settled him in; then sat on the floor beside him, holding his hand. "Ateron is punishing us too, isn't he?"

"Yeah, he is definitely *enjoying* himself. But I promise you, he's not going to get the last laugh."

"The last laugh? What does that mean?"

"It means the day we stand on top of Farlana, free from Ateron and Cartu, we will be the ones laughing."

Taya put another pillow behind his head. "Do you think Ateron will allow Kytan to come back here tonight?"

"I hope so. I need to tell him about our plans to keep in touch if I'm not allowed back into the apartment. And I need you to tell Hadlee something for me. Tell her . . . to have faith." He repeated the English words again, and asked Taya to repeat them back until he was sure she knew them.

"I am worried about her, Ryder."

"So am I. I'm afraid the pressure of becoming Ansuetra and being confined to the apartment, are beginning to take a heavy toll on her. She needs to rest. I think she needs it as much as I do."

"At least in your case, I can help you rest." She offered him a strong, sleeping potion.

He put the cup down beside his mattress. "I want to be awake when Kytan comes in."

"Promise me you will take it."

"If he's not here by eleven bells, I'll take the herbs."

Tucking his hair behind his ears, she kissed his cheek. "Tell Kytan I miss him."

Forty-five

It was after eleven bells when Kytan walked into the quarters he and Ryder shared. Ryder's herbs sat next to his mattresses, untouched. Kytan found him sitting on the small balcony, peering out through the darkness at the shadowy outline of Farlana, towering in the west.

"What are *you* doing here?" Kytan asked, sitting down next to him. "I thought Taya wanted to keep you in the apartment for a few days."

"She did, but Ateron decided I shouldn't deprive Hadlee of her box springs any longer," Ryder said, his eyes locked on the dragon that never ceased to mock him.

"Ateron made you *leave?* I don't like it. First I am banned from the apartment, and now you have been sent away when you still need Taya and Hadlee's care."

"I'm not happy about it either, and I'm afraid I'm the one that's going to be permanently banned from the apartment." Ryder turned to him and groaned.

Kytan laughed. "I know. I look almost as bad as you do."

"I'm sorry you took the punishment for my decision. I should have known we would be found out." He laid a hand on Kytan's shoulder. "Forgive me."

"Tell me; just how many times did you take my punishment during first weeks I was in the mine? There is nothing to forgive. I am the one that needs to be forgiven. You warned us and I was careless."

"It doesn't matter now. The only thing that matters is finding ways to circumvent the consequences Ateron is sure to impose."

"Like you being banned from the apartment."

"That's what the girls are afraid Ateron means to do." Ryder outlined the plans they'd made for communicating if he was no longer permitted in the apartment, and added, "I'll find out how things stand in a day or two. I'm supposed to go see Ateron as soon as Taya says I'm well enough to be up."

"Speaking of that, what are you doing up?" Kytan stood, extending his hand. "Let's get you in bed. Then I want to hear about everything that has happened since I left the apartment this morning."

"I got up because now that I've spent a night in a decent bed, I'm spoiled. And those"—Ryder pointed to the straw mattresses on the floor—"are killing me. I had no idea how many bruises I had until I laid on that pitiful excuse for a bed."

Kytan pulled him to his feet, steadied him, and led him into the room. "You know, I used to think you were a fine specimen of a man." His dimples danced. "It is amazing what rocks can do."

"When we get out of here, I'll take you to see a movie called Frankenstein. Pilot says I look just like him. Oh, and Taya says to tell you she misses you."

Kytan's dimples faded. "Being away from Taya is the worse punishment of all. Going a whole day without seeing her—and not knowing how long it will be before I am allowed back in the apartment—is torture." He groaned with frustration. "Actually, I won't be truly happy until I get to see Taya every hour of every day."

"I know. You two are pathetic to watch." Ryder chuckled, grinning lopsidedly.

Kytan didn't return it. He settled Ryder onto the mattresses. "I think it is time I said the same thing to you about Hadlee that you said to me about Taya. Don't forget what I saw today, and I am not just talking about the kiss either, it was the look on your face too. I want to know your intentions toward Hadlee." He dropped onto the chair next to the mattresses, holding Ryder's eyes in a hard stare. "I love her the way you love Taya, and I will not allow you to hurt her."

Ryder broke Kytan's stare, closed his eyes, and massaged his forehead. "I need to tell you something—about Hadlee."

Kytan leaned forward, chilled by Ryder's brooding tone.

"I met Hadlee a long time ago, when we were just kids."

"So you have known each other for a long time?" Kytan asked, surprised.

Ryder's hand dropped away from his forehead. "No. We only met—briefly." He locked eyes with Kytan. "We met the day I . . . killed her mother."

Kytan choked, straightening in the hard chair. "What do you mean, *you killed her mother.*" The room suddenly felt airless as he stared at his brother in the flickering glow of a small oil lamp that made ugly masks of their battered faces.

Ryder sat up slowly, folding his legs Indian style. "I think I better start at the beginning." Then holding up a hand, he added, "Please just let me get through this before you say anything." Staring at the wall in front of him, he told Kytan everything, without excuse, or minimizing his responsibility.

"Hadlee has every right to hate me. I'm responsible for her mother's death and all the suffering she's gone through since."

Kytan tried to hide his distress behind a salve-face, but knew he'd failed when Ryder dropped his head and rubbed his neck. Desperately, Kytan searched his mind for words of comfort. "Ryder, it sounds like you have repented."

"I have, and I haven't." Ryder lifted his head and faced Kytan. "I've only begun to repent for the death of the baby and the consequences I brought into Hadlee's life. He rolled his bruised shoulders. "That's why I took off. I've never felt that kind of pain. I'm . . . tormented by it. And not just by what I did, but because I can't make restitution for any of it."

The agony in his voice was etched into his face. It told Kytan how deep and raw the pain still was. He put a consoling hand on his brother's shoulder. "Everything I know about you, tells me you are a good man, faithful in your covenants, honorable in your personal conduct. I am sure the Lord knows that too. I will pray that you and Hadlee can find peace and forgiveness between you, and from God." He paused. "Does Taya know this?"

"No, I haven't told her. She knows there's something wrong between Hadlee and me, but not what. I've been holding my breath since you met Hadlee. I thought she might decide to confide in you and Taya. I haven't told you because it's her right to tell you if she chooses. The only reason I'm telling you now is because of what you saw."

"Are you afraid if Taya know it will change her feelings for you? It won't. She loves you and always will, regardless of what happened between you and Hadlee in the past."

"I hope you're right. I would hate to lose her good opinion almost as much as I would hate to lose yours." Ryder again hung his head and rubbed his neck, "If I haven't already."

"It would take a great deal more than a mistake from your past to make me think less of you."

Ryder lay down, clasping his hands behind his neck. He was silent, and Kytan didn't break that silence.

Lost in his own thoughts, Kytan tried to understand what his brother was suffering and think of a way to help him. "Ryder," he finally said, "you have taught me about repentance and what the Atonement can do. Are you and Hadlee letting it heal you?"

"We are." Ryder outlined their efforts to repent and added, "I'm sure in time we will feel the Lord's, and Hadlee's family's, forgiveness. Even with that, I know I will never be completely whole until Hadlee forgives me—if she can."

"But that's not all you want—is it?" Kytan keen eyes probed his brother's.

Ryder looked away. "What I want . . . is to keep her safe, get her out of Injanae, and help her find peace. Nothing else matters."

"And we are going to make that happen. No matter what obstacles Ateron puts in our path."

"Yes, we are."

"You know, I think there is something I can do to help you."

Ryder raised a doubtful brow. "What?"

"You told me, when you or someone you love needs the help of heaven, you can fast for them. You and Hadlee need the help of heaven. I would like to fast for you and Hadlee."

Emotion further distorted Ryder's face. "I'll fast with you."

Kytan slid off the chair and onto his knees. "I think you better just stay where you are. I will offer the prayer."

It was evident to Ryder by the following night that Hadlee's fears were justified. When he pulled on the door handle of his quarters, he found it locked. His fears grew when the night passed without Kytan's return.

Two more days dragged by, and he couldn't even ask Taya where Kytan was, or how Hadlee was doing. Taya's daily visits to monitor his progress were always attended by a guard, making it impossible to have even a few private words, but her expressive eyes told him the situation was grim.

Locked in his quarters, all he could do was worry and think. *Was I wrong? Should we have made a fast break for it?* He scanned the western cliffs and up the east face of Farlana. *No. We need to be well prepared, if we're going to have any chance of climbing out of here, making it to the top of Farlana, and getting back to Lima. We need all the equipment and supplies on our list. Besides, the girls still need to work on their upper body strength for the climb out.*

The daunting responsibility of taking Hadlee and Taya up a sheer five hundred foot cliff preyed on his mind constantly. *Even Farlana won't be that hard—I hope.*

Equally daunting were the tasks of getting the conspirators out of the palace, out of the city, and far enough up the cliff face before they were discovered. He still felt the night of the Lunar Celebration would be their best opportunity.

Kytan agreed—on the night he found Ryder in their quarters—that letting Ansuetra free the slaves would be the most effective diversion for their escape, even if it did cause a riot, which might or might not help them. Still, that was cutting it very close. After that night, Ryder knew none of them would be safe.

He prayed long and hard over all their plans, grappling with the lack of a solid, reassuring answer.

After five days of confinement, he was as restless and irritable as the jaguar his gold eyes reflected. The longing to see Hadlee had grown into an unrelenting ache he just couldn't rid himself of, or keep from brooding over. Taya's pronouncement he could resume his duties on a very limited basis was a welcome relief.

He still looked like Frankenstein, but his head no longer ached, his equilibrium was back, and the gash in his side was closed. Even with his body covered in a colorful display of bruises, cuts and scrapes, that were still very painful, he felt he could at least direct the work in the tunnel, if not help.

The moment he was allowed to leave his quarters, he headed straight for Hadlee's apartment. He wanted to reassure her he was all right and reassure himself that she was too, before he met with the king and went back to work.

Etin stopped him at the hall door. "You are not allowed to go into Hadlee's apartment," he said, folding his heavy arms across his chest.

This edict wasn't unexpected, but disappointment rose like bile in Ryder's throat. It tasted so bitter he had to fight hard to keep his slave-face intact.

Hadlee's distress over his removal from the apartment haunted him. She'd been struggling with her emotions, emotions that surprised him. Her concern was an unexpected gift, and he wanted to express his thanks.

His longing to see her almost overpowered his judgment. He considered Etin's bulky frame, judging his strength. He felt like knocking Etin down, charging down the hall, and bursting through the apartment door.

He unclenched his fists. *Don't be ridiculous.* He blew out a breath. "Can I go into the tunnel?"

Etin nodded, and Ryder went through the door.

He reached the hole in the wall that led to the tunnel stairs, and paused, staring at Hadlee's door. Zuph was standing guard. Ryder's hesitation made Zuph's hand move to the hilt of his sword. Ryder turned away and stepped through the hole in the wall. He walked stiffly up the steps, and into the tunnel, listening to the echo of hammers hitting chisels and men's voices.

The work stopped abruptly when the guards saw him. Kytan came forward and lightly clapped his shoulder, giving him relieved dimples. The guards on tunnel duty smiled too.

He thanked them for their efforts in saving his life, and laughed good-naturedly with them over his distorted face and colorfully tattooed body. They in turn, recounted all the details of his rescue.

"When are you coming back to work?" asked Orat, the most jovial of the king's bodyguards.

"I'm on my way to see the king now, and I expect to be back to work right after that interview, but I don't know how much help I'll be for the next few days."

"I was told to see the king today too—when the guards take their lunch. I will tell them to do it now and come with you. If we are in for a bad time, we might as well face it together," Kytan said in English, giving Ryder a grin that displayed the full impishness of his dimples.

The right half of Ryder's mouth returned the grin.

Forty-six

Kytan entered Hadlee's apartment that evening for the first time in nearly a week, with his slave-face firmly in place, and Yawt at his heels.

Hadlee walked up to him, as though Yawt wasn't there, and hugged him. "Let's sit on the sofa," she said, taking his hand and reaching for Taya's as they walked by her.

With their hands firmly in her grasp, Hadlee propelled her friends over to one of the large overstuffed couches.

The girls sat on either side of Kytan, each holding one of his hands. Hadlee sat on the far side, away from Yawt, who stood stiffly inside the door of the apartment, his burly arms folded across his chest.

When Kytan turned to Taya, Hadlee jumped up and moved in front of them, effectively blocking the guard's view. She gestured for Yawt to sit on one of the hard chairs near the dining table.

He shook his head.

She walked over to him; touched him lightly on the arm and again gestured toward the chairs.

Kytan took advantage of the diversion that effectively held Yawt's attention, giving him a few precious moments of privacy with Taya. He let his eyes express the feelings he didn't dare utter.

Taya's fingers stroked his still healing face. The cut was now a scabby line, and the bruises were turning a defused yellowish-green.

He took the hand that caressed his face, brought it to his lips then quickly set it back on the sofa.

"Thank you," he said when Hadlee rejoined them, grateful he could speak freely with Hadlee as long as he wore his slave-face and kept his voice neutral. But he immediately had to adjust his slave-face when the first thing Hadlee asked about was Ryder.

He shot a glance at Yawt. "My brother is no longer in our quarters. He is confined to the guardhouse when he is not working, forbidden to have contact with any of us. It is his punishment for not disclosing my ability to speak English. I am now your interpreter and teacher."

The blank expression on Hadlee's face dissolved into distress. "Oh no."

Kytan's hands tightened on the girls. "Not only that, but everywhere I go, even in the palace, I have a shadow with me." He gave Yawt another sidelong glance. "I don't know how I will be able to finish making the pitons and carabineers with a guard watching my every move. Up until now, the guards didn't take much notice of me, and I could go wherever I wanted without question." He shook his head. "Not anymore."

"And how are we going to contact Ryder while he's a prisoner in the guardhouse? It's just what we were afraid would happen, but we didn't plan for this particular contingency. We didn't think he would be completely cut off from all of us." Hadlee slumped against the back of the sofa.

"I think the best hope we have for making contact with Ryder, is for me to finish making the jewelry. The King has ordered me to help in the tunnel as soon as it is done."

"But the last time you were here, you told me the jewelry wouldn't be done for a few more weeks." Hadlee straightened. "We can't wait that long." She stared into Kytan's eyes. "I think it's time I tried my hand at poker."

"What is poker?"

"A game of chance and bluff. I want you to tell Ateron that until Ryder is allowed back, I'm not going to work on Ansuetra's lines."

"No, Hadlee. That is too dangerous a game to play with the king in such an ugly mood."

"Well my mood is uglier than Ateron's. And I don't think he will risk making me any angrier than I am now—not at this late date. He can't afford to. So you just tell him I won't work until Ryder is allowed back, and we'll wait and see."

Kytan refused to do what Hadlee asked, and when she again provided a diversion allowing him to tell Taya what she proposed to do, he tried to enlist Taya's help to change her mind.

Taya grinned wickedly. "I think Hadlee should try her *poker*. We must do something to make Ateron allow Ryder to come back, and since it will take too long for you to finish the jewelry, I think what Hadlee wants to do is worth a try. We are running out of time, and we need Ryder with us. There is still so much we have to decide about our escape, and we need him here to do it."

Daily Kytan tried to convince the girls of the danger. Stubbornly they continued to disagree, and Hadlee—backed by Taya—resisted all his efforts to get her to practice.

Her rebellion was reported to Ateron by Kytan's ever-present guards.

Three days passed before the king came. He stalked into the apartment, snapped his fingers at Cartu, who slammed the door in Lul's startled face and strode purposefully across the room. He grabbed Taya roughly by the arm, threw her to the floor and raised a rapa.

She rolled, turning her back to him, curled herself into a ball, using her arms to protect her face and head.

Cartu looked to the king for the signal to strike her.

"*No!*" Hadlee shrieked the word in Injanae, sprinting across the room. Falling on her knees in front of Taya, she shielded her from Cartu.

The chancellor's fingers dug into her arm. He jerked her off Taya and threw her backwards. The back of her head bounced off the stone floor as Ateron snapped his fingers.

The sound of the rapa harmlessly whipping the floor was drown out by Taya's gasping cry, when one stray strand tore through the shoulder of her tunic. Her body convulsed with the impact of the lash that flicked her blood onto Hadlee's arm and face.

On a frantic sob, Hadlee staggered to her feet. She dashed across the room, and skidded to her knees in front of Ateron, prostrating herself on the floor at his feet.

A delicious feeling of conquest coursed through Ateron. Hadlee's submissive posture brought a gloating twist to his lips. Her forehead was pressed to the floor, and her shaking fingers grasped the sides of his finely tooled sandals, in groveling supplication.

I have endured your hostile eyes and haughty disdain for too many weeks. With pleasure, he listened to the sound of her sobbing pleads and patiently allowed them to go on for some time.

He exchanged a triumphant sneer with Cartu, then regally bent down, cupped Hadlee's chin in his hand, lifted her tear stained face, and gently caressed her cheek with his fingers, wiping away Taya's blood.

Hadlee's large eyes were swirling wells of fear. Her uncontrollable trembling deepened the gloating triumph beating in Ateron's heart. Holding her eyes, he let his piranha ones devour her; then forcefully proclaimed his victory, tangling his hand in her pale hair.

Long after Hadlee treated the ugly gash on Taya's left shoulder blade, they sat together holding on to each other unable to control their tremors. Hadlee's guilt poured out in inconsolable tears and bitter self-loathing.

Taya tried in vain to comfort her, insisting what happened was just as much her fault. But Hadlee felt worse than she did when she saw Ryder's back.

Kytan had warned her. Even Ryder had warned her, but she hadn't listened. She knew it was *her* stubborn insistence that caused Taya's injury. And Ateron—without so much as a word—proved to her, she was entirely at his mercy.

Touching her shoulder, Taya said, "No, Kytan."

Hadlee repeated it. Agreeing not to tell Kytan what had happened.

When Kytan came back from his shop that evening he found Hadlee rehearsing her lines.

"I decided you were right. The king hasn't changed his mind and making him angry won't help us."

"I am glad you have changed your mind." Kytan displayed relieved dimples. "Let's work on your speech to the nobles."

Hadlee rose from her bed as the tower clock chimed midnight. Weighted down by fear and guilt, she crept out onto the terrace. It was a place she spent too many nights pacing, feeling forsaken, fighting her fears, and struggling with her emotions. Since the night Ryder left the apartment—nearly three weeks ago—she'd been plagued with a growing sense of doubt and feelings of despair.

Scanning the dark face of the sky, she confessed to the stars, "I actually miss that overgrown Boy Scout." It was an unwanted, disturbing discovery that further robbed her of sleep, and her peace of mind.

The following morning, she masked her increasing fatigue, turning away to suppress a yawn, when Kytan and Ateron entered the apartment right on schedule. Ateron came daily now to listen to her recite her lines. He criticized and instructed, on what he considered the proper gestures and mannerism Ansuetra would use, giving directions on the correct delivery of each line. His directions always included touching her.

Exchanging a meaningful glance with Taya, Hadlee put on her slave-face and faced Ateron while Taya drew Kytan away. As much as she abhorred Ateron's daily visits, they had accomplished one thing. She could now wear a slave-face, almost to perfection, and she needed to for Kytan's sake.

Taya agreed that she couldn't afford to let Kytan see how much Ateron's touch disgusted her. He wasn't handling it well. Every time Ateron touched her, it got harder for Taya to keep Kytan from doing something that would get him killed.

Hadlee took a deep breath, forced her muscles to relax and tried to hold on to the message Taya had brought from Ryder "to have faith" as Ateron decided where she should start her rehearsal.

Taya watched Hadlee inadvertently flinch as Ateron took her arm with growing alarm. It was obvious to her that Ateron's constant visits were pushing Hadlee's nerves to the breaking point. *She is not sleeping, and I can hardly get her to eat.*

"There is no more sparkle in her eyes," she whispered to Kytan as they listened to her recite the nobles' speech to

Ateron. "Now all she does is practice her lines, do our strengthening exercises, and sew."

Kytan shot a glance at Ateron. His attention was fully fixed on Hadlee. He whispered back, "Has she finished sewing the silver netting onto Ansuetra's gown?"

"Not yet. She only works on that during the day, when the guards poke their heads into the apartment. As soon as the night guards are in place, she works on the leather gloves we need for the climb out. Most of the time, dawn has broken before she will go to bed." Taya groaned frustration. "I can't continue to watch her deteriorate and do nothing."

"What she needs is rest."

"Yes she does."

As soon as Ateron left, Taya asked Kytan to help her convince Hadlee to take a sleeping potion. Taya took her hand as Kytan interpreted her words. "You have not slept for many nights. Taya wants you to take a sleeping potion. She is sure if you don't get some rest, you will become ill."

Hadlee hugged Taya, but shook her head. "I will just have nightmares about Ateron's constant intrusions. Even worse, I might wake up to find him standing over me."

Taya brooded over Hadlee's refusal, and after she found Hadlee pacing the terrace in the wee hours of the following morning, concern led her to take matters into her own hands.

That evening, after Kytan left for the night, she handed Hadlee a cup of the refreshing herb tea Hadlee usually requested when she was planning to work into the late night hours.

"Thanks," Hadlee said, and sat down on the sofa, sipping the tea. "Maybe this will revive me enough so I can get the last pair of climbing gloves finished tonight."

Taya curled up in a chair near her, sipping her own cup of tea. "Maybe," she said, watching Hadlee drink the tea that contained a strong, tasteless, sleeping potion.

She took the cup from Hadlee when she finished the tea, studying her as she stood up. Hadlee yawned and swayed slightly. A puzzled expression clouded her eyes. She shook her head as though trying to clear it.

Taya gave an exaggerated yawn, and stood too. "Sleepy," she said, then asked, "You too?"

Hadlee blinked at her; nodded and shuffled to the steps to her bedchamber.

"Goodnight," Taya said, as Hadlee staggered up the stairs.

The sleeping potion worked so well, Hadlee slept for twelve solid hours. She came down the stairs from her bedchamber late the next morning looking better—in Taya's opinion—than she had for the past few weeks, just as Kytan entered the apartment, accompanied by Shur, his guard for the day.

In a well-rehearsed routine, Hadlee loaded a plate with the fruit Taya laid out on the table and offered it to Shur, giving Taya the opportunity to pull Kytan aside. Unrepentant, she confessed to Kytan, what she'd done.

"You must tell her," she whispered to him, and went to pull a loaf of bread from the oven in the fire pit. She glanced over her shoulder as she wrapped the hot bread in a towel, saw Hadlee's eyes widen, and knew Kytan was telling Hadlee what she'd done.

When Taya returned to the table with the hot bread, Hadlee slid an arm around her and whispered in Injanae, "Thank you."

Taya searched Hadlee's eyes. They were clear and bright, and shining with something Taya couldn't identify, but had never seen in them before.

Forty-seven

Massaging his neck after a long work shift, Ryder, surrounded by his crew—that always became his guards as soon as the workday ended—marched along the short hallway that connected the guardhouse to the palace. This appendage to the palace stood against the cliff face on the south side and had been set aside for the private use of Ateron's bodyguards.

The tired guards straggled through the door and fell into the numerous sofas and floor pillows scattered around the large common room, demanding to be fed.

Their personal cook, and his assistants, hurried to set out platters of fish, pork, potatoes, fruit, bread, and cheese on a huge serving table.

Ryder silently sat on a hard chair at the slave's isolated table and waited for his turn to eat. As a prisoner and slave, he wasn't allowed to fill his plate until after all the guards were eating.

The cook announced that everything was ready.

The guards jumped up to fill their plates; then took seats at the tables that sat around a large fire pit and dug into their food.

Pel was the last to fill his plate. He smiled faintly and nodded at Ryder as he sat down.

Ryder rose and quickly loaded a plate to overflowing. He continued eating for some time after the guards pushed aside their plates in favor of drinking the generous rations of wine Ateron always sent to accompany the evening meal.

Ven reached for the wine bottle.

Pel snatched it away. "Six cups is enough, Ven. If you don't stop, you will be unprepared for the morning drills."

Ven scowled and banged his cup down on the table.

Pel's eyes went hard and cold with a threat that made Ven immediately apologize.

Ryder hid a smile and kept eating. Since becoming a resident of the guardhouse, he'd paid careful attention to everything that went on there, even giving up sleep to learn the guards' early morning routine, and their late night habits. He discovered that every morning, before the work day started, they practiced their fighting skills in a large empty part of the guardhouse set aside for that purpose, or in the courtyard when the weather was good.

He studied the guards' fighting drills with intense interest. He also carefully watched the coming and going of, not only the guards, but their servants, slaves, and friends. It soon became apparent to him that the guards liked to entertain, and it was often late before they retired to their individual quarters, which were part of the original cave dwellings the people of Injanae first inhabited.

The caves had been enlarged over the centuries until they were now small apartments. They occupied two levels, accessed by open walkways and stairs that ran along the face of the cliff.

Ryder wasn't given one of these comfortable apartments. His bedchamber was nothing more than a hole in the cliff face. It was located at the southern end of the guardhouse, and sat twenty feet above the floor, accessed by a ladder that was removed at night.

His only privacy was to sit in the back of the eight by eight foot space, because there was no door. Even without a door, it was still such an airless little tomb that for the first week of his incarceration, he positioned his mattress, and head, at the edge of the cell's lip, just so he could breathe. While he was lying there—looking up at the cliff face and scanning the ceiling—worrying over the unstable roof of the tunnel, inspiration dawned.

After clearing a passage through the cave-in blockage, the tunnel was found to be unobstructed all the way to the balcony wall. That discovery should have enabled the work of bracing the ceiling to progress rapidly, but two more minor cave-ins, which resulted in cuts and bruises for many of the guards, convinced everyone the tunnel was a deathtrap, and the work of bracing it progressed at a careful pace.

Ryder was determined to keep the tunnel from taking another life, and it had to be as safe as he could make it for Hadlee. That objective, shared by Ateron, gave him the perfect opportunity to set his inspiration into motion.

He started his plan by pulling his mattress back inside his sleeping hole, so he couldn't be seen by the single guard that stood night duty—suffering the claustrophobia of his small cell, but establishing that norm. Then, he requested Ateron make the guards work double shifts on a particularly difficult section of the ceiling, hoping the punishing work shifts would take their toll.

Finished with his meal, Ryder rose from the table. He stowed his plate in the washtub, climbed the ladder into his tomb to the accompaniment of the guards' boisterous chatter, and scratched another line into the wall of his cell.

Twenty days. It feels more like twenty years. He groaned. *I'm going to go mad, or do something rash, if I can't escape this prison—and soon.* His longing for his friends—and a tall, blond, blue-eyed one in particular—was getting worse with each passing day. *How many more days will it take?*

Discouraged, he dropped the rock on the floor of his cell beneath his crude calendar and rolled his shoulders, feeling the accumulated exhaustion of the double work shifts he'd been doing for the past ten days. With a sigh, he stretched out on his thin mattress, letting his feet dangle over the edge.

He resisted sleep; listening to the familiar sounds of the cook and his crew clean up the evening meal before they left for their own tiny cells located on the third floor of the palace. After they left, he listened to the guards grumble to Pel about the long hours of slave labor forced on them due to the tunnel's unstable ceiling. Pel stoically told his men the harder they worked, the sooner they would be done with the unpleasant task. He then went over the next day's duty roster.

Thirty minutes later, an uncharacteristic quiet rewarded Ryder's vigil. Stillness grew in the room below him. He sat up, scooted to the edge of his mattress, and peeked out over the lip of his cell, inspecting the room.

Only Amin, the guard that had replaced Po as one of Ateron's bodyguards, sat at a table near the door, pulling night duty. The dying flames in the fire pit revealed the look of weary boredom his face held as he rolled a set of dice. The gentle clatter of the dice was the only sound that disturbed the silence.

Ryder drew back, and flopped down on his mattress. *Finally!* He smiled his victory at the rocky ceiling, closed his eyes, and slept.

Forty-eight

Ryder's eyes opened on the first note of the city belfry heralding midnight. He poked his head cautiously out the entrance of his cubbyhole, surveying the silent room below him in the soft light of the torches. The stairs to the guards' apartments were deserted, and every apartment door was closed. Amin's head rested in his arms on the table, the dice lay in his open palm.

A soft humming sound drifted up to Ryder's ears. He grinned and secured footing on a small ridge of rock, sticking out of the wall next to his tomb. Reaching for a narrow fissure with his fingers, he began to climb with the agility of a monkey. The dim light from the torches in the room below him didn't illuminate the wall well enough to aid him as he climbed, forcing him to feel rather than see his next move.

It took ten grueling minutes to reach the shadows above the fire pit in the corner of the high ceiling. The smoldering fire sent wisps of smoke curling around him. Taking shallow breaths to keep from coughing, he eased his shoulders through the warm smoke vent, pulled himself up under the clay hood that shielded the vent from rain, and slid out onto the roof of the guardhouse.

Hugging the cliff wall, he scurried across the roof to the edge of the palace wall, near the stairs to the rooftop garden.

A night guard stood watch at the bottom of the stairs. He faced away from the deeply shadowed corner where the cliff face met the palace wall. His job was to keep intruders from using the stairs to access the royal apartments via the rooftop garden. It was a necessary precaution, because

Ateron decided not to pull the removable part of the stairs up until after the Lunar Celebration was over.

Ryder knew there would be another guard in the rooftop garden with the same directive.

Utilizing the palace stones and the rough cliff wall, Ryder's experienced fingers located shallow crevices and hidden fissures, while his toes found small jutting spurs of rock. The joy of climbing banished the fatigue of the long day. He scaled the wall with the skill of a sunqara to the rooftop garden and peaked over the wall.

The rooftop guard sat at the entrance to the stairs with his head leaning against the railing. Ryder slithered silently over the top of the wall and crouched next to it, looking and listening for any sound or movement from the guard.

The guard didn't move, or even seem to breathe.

Noiselessly, Ryder's soft leather boots padded across the garden to a wooden roofing beam suspended ten feet above the garden floor. Grasping its edge, he pulled himself up and over the rim of the steep center roof.

Hugging the shadows of the cliff face, he moved with the stealth of a cat burglar against a waning moon; climbing up and across the broad center bridge of the roof to the north side of the palace. After carefully sliding down the other side, he lowered himself down half a story, onto the roof of Hadlee's hall.

Belly crawling, he moved toward the edge of the roof overhanging Hadlee's terrace, watching the night guards patrol the palace grounds far below him. When they passed from his sight, he gripped the lip of the roof, quickly letting himself down over its edge, and dropped lightly onto the terrace floor. Silently, he opened the terrace door.

In the dying light of a smoldering torch, he caught a glimpse of a shadow moving toward the apartment door. He sprang across the room, catching the shadowy figure before she reached the door.

She gave a startled yelp.

His hand covered her mouth. He pulled her against him, holding her still, and whispered urgently, "It's alright, it's just me. Where do you think you're going?" he asked, uncovering her mouth.

"Ryder," Hadlee clutched the front of his tunic. "How did you get here?"

"Let's go out on the terrace, the last thing we need is to be surprised by anyone coming through that door. Then you better tell me what you're up to."

When they were settled on a bench at the end of the terrace, he demanded again—appreciating the close fitting pants and bomber jacket she wore. "Now where were you going?"

She ignored his question. "You didn't come through the door, so you must have come by way of the terrace. You came over the roof and dropped onto the terrace, didn't you? Can you go back that way?"

"Yes, I came by way of the roof, and yes, I'll go back that way. Now where were you going?"

"I'll tell you when I'm on the roof."

He opened his mouth to refuse.

"Please, Ryder, get me out of this prison, just for a little while."

It wasn't a good idea. Still, he wavered, knowing—too well—what it felt like to be in prison and found it impossible to say no when she took his hand, looking pleadingly into his eyes.

"Alright, I'll go up and look around. The night watch patrols the palace grounds. If we time it right, we can make it to the roof in between their rounds."

His standing jump easily allowed his hands to secure a hold on the top of the fifteen-foot wall. Chinning himself up, he peeked over it, watching the night patrol pass. Then in one fluid motion, he pulled himself up, straddled the wall, and gripped it with his knees. Leaning his body back down over it, he stretched his arms toward her.

"Reach up and take hold of my wrists." Her hands grasped his wrists as his closed over hers. "When I lift you, put your feet against the wall so you don't get scraped up. Ready?"

"Yes."

He drew her up, almost to the top of the wall. She gasped when he let go with one hand. His arm encircled her waist, and he drew her up the rest of the way. Seating her on the wall, he held onto her until he was sure she was securely balanced.

"Hold on to my belt and follow me," he whispered into her ear.

Staying low, they moved as fast as they could along the top of the wall, stepped carefully over the flowering trellis vine—spectacular now with its large white blossoms open and glowing in the night—to the edge of the roof, two feet above the wall of the terrace. They crouched in the shadow of the roof's overhang, watching the guards again pass by beneath Hadlee's apartment. As soon as they were gone, Ryder boosted himself onto the roof and lifted Hadlee up beside him. They quickly climbed the sloping tile, melted into the shadows of the high center roof, and sat down with their backs against the cliff face.

"You've lost your Frankenstein resemblance," Hadlee said, then asked, "Are you alright?"

"I'm fine. My side and head are all better."

She nodded and leaned her head back against the cliff, gazing into the vast expanse of the sky.

They lapsed into an easy silence, letting the night envelop them. The nearly cloudless night was cold, but inviting, kissed by a crescent moon and pulsating with the sound of the falls coursing down the cliff to the pool. Their view of the falls was blocked by the high center roof, but the sound was loud and constant in the quiet of the night. Beyond the walls of Telquset, the darkly veiled valley presented a panorama that beckoned them and lifted their eyes up from the forest of Lanka's ghostly trees to the star spangled heavens above them.

Ryder stole a look at Hadlee, drinking in her joyful expression by the soft light of the moon hanging in the western sky, watching her taste the delicious, if momentary, flavor of freedom. Breathing in the cold air, he listened to her sigh. In it, he heard and shared her worry about the extent of the larger prison they had to escape to be truly free.

He pointed across the valley to the mountain the moon illuminated. "That's Farlana, the mountain we have to climb to get back to Lima."

"I remember how strange I thought it looked when I was floating down. It's really amazing how dragon like it is," she said, drawing up her knees.

"That's what brought me to Peru."

"Really, you came to Peru to see Farlana because it's shaped like a dragon?"

A wry grin twisted his lips. "Actually, I came to slay it."

"Oh and how do you slay a dragon made of rock?"

"You climb it." He pointed to the north and described his challenging climb.

"Wow." Her fingers twisted her braid. "Please don't tell me we have to go back that way."

"No, we can't follow that route back. I'm hoping I'll remember—once we're out of the valley—how I climbed down this side of Farlana. Even if I don't, I'm sure we will find an easier route than straight up his throat," he said, scanning the perilous east face of the dragon.

"I hope so, because we're all going to have to slay that dragon to get home." She paused. "Are we going to get home, Ryder? It's been hard to believe lately."

"I know; but don't give up hope, Pilot. With heaven's help, we'll make it. Now tell me, where you were about to go when I . . . dropped in."

"Very funny," she said dryly. "I was going to try and get to Kytan's quarters. I wanted to know if I could get by the guards. Pel changed things just after you were banned from the apartment. Now both guards are inside the hall at night. I wanted to see if they still fell asleep, like you told me they did, before the change."

"And just how did you plan to go through the door at the end of the hall? Even if the guards were asleep, the hall door would be locked. You would have to take the key off one of them." He shook his head. "I can't believe Taya would let you try something like this. It's not like her."

A giggle gurgled up Hadlee's throat. "I turned the tables on her tonight. She's been slipping a sleeping potion in my herb tea for the past few nights, because I haven't been sleeping very well." Ryder's brows came together and she quickly added, "I'm alright. Anyway, tonight when she brought the herb tea, I asked for some bread too. When she went to get the bread, I switched mugs with her. The sleeping potion put her out like a light."

"Who taught you to be so sneaky?"

"My cousin Sky—he's a master of sneakiness." She pressed her lips together, but a soft, sputtered laugh escaped anyway. "Watching Taya fall asleep so fast gave me an idea about how we could smuggle Kytan in for a meeting without our guards knowing about it."

"You want Taya to slip the guards a mickey."

"Uh-huh. We desperately need another planning session to finalize our escape plan from the palace, without the listening ears of our guards. I thought as long as Taya was sleeping so soundly, I would try my luck and see if I could get passed the goons. If they caught me, what could they do but escort me back to the apartment, and if I did get out—and could make it to Kytan's quarters—I could tell him about my plan. He's going to start working in the tunnel tomorrow, now that the jewelry is finished. And I was hoping, with both of you working there, he would be able to start passing messages to you." She grinned roguishly. "Obviously, he won't need to. Now you can simply join our meeting."

"It's a great idea. I need to know how things stand with our preparations, and we need to come up with a concrete plan to get out of the palace once you free the slaves."

"Kytan's probably right about the riot that decree will cause," she said, frowning. "But I can't stand the idea of leaving here without at least trying to free the slaves."

"I agree! So we need a plan that minimizes its interference and maximizes its benefits for our escape. We also have to figure out where we can requisition some fast transportation out of Telquset."

"Yes, we haven't talked about any of that yet."

The moon burst through a passing cloud, shinning on Hadlee's upturned face. Ryder held in a sigh, intensely aware of her nearness and lost his train of thought. "I can't tell you how much I've missed . . . all of you," he stammered, editing what he really wanted to say.

"We've missed you too."

Her words touched him like a caress. Before he lost himself in the futile hope that the "we missed you" really meant she missed him, he forced his mind back to business. "Let's see, I think we should plan to meet five nights from now, on the night of the new moon. I shouldn't do the roof top shuffle too often, or my odds of my being caught will skyrocket, so the darker it is, the better it will be for me."

"Okay, five nights from now, at midnight." Again, she leaned her head back against the cliff and resumed her search of the sky. "You have no idea how wonderful it feels to be out of my prison and under a starlit sky." She tisked out a breath, "Well, of course you do."

"Yeah, I do."

"More than anywhere else, the sky is my home."

Ryder leaned his head back against the cliff too, his gaze fixed on Farlana. "You feel about the sky the way I feel about the mountains. They're a sort of sanctuary for me."

"A sanctuary . . . yes, that's what the sky is for me. I always feel that way when I'm above the clouds—you know, closer to heaven. It is a place I can see things from the right perspective and hear heaven's voice more clearly."

"Above the clouds," Ryder said slowly, feeling the words. "I've often pondered on the fact that many of the prophets of old were told to seek high places, or were carried away to high mountains. It set them far enough above the earth—and the clouds—so nothing was between them and heaven, between them and the Almighty."

"Exactly."

They basked in the silent comfort of a new empathy. Letting the minutes pass, they enjoyed the dancing, distorted images of the night, accompanied by the constant rhythm of the falls, and the music of the nocturnal creatures that floated on the brisk night air.

Ryder found himself alternately lost in the joy of feeling a new affinity with Hadlee and fighting the impossible emotions he just couldn't seem to control any longer. Sitting next to her, intensely aware of her shoulder touching his arm, he tilted his head toward her, inhaling the soft, spicy scent of her hair, and the herbal soap that always lingered in his senses after he left her.

She broke their companionable silence. "Ryder, I need to tell you something."

Forty-nine

Ryder's heart lurched with the grave tone of her voice. "Is there something wrong that I don't know about?"

"No." She turned to him. "I want to tell you about a dream I had."

"A dream?"

"It was more than a dream. It was an answer to my prayers, and it wasn't just meant for me. It was meant for you too." Her mouth curved up.

His heart did a summersault.

Her eyes closed, and she drew in the crisp fragrance of the night. "Mama and I were in the kitchen of our house in Provo, laughing and talking. She looked just like she did when I was ten, but I was as I am now. It was Thanksgiving— a turkey was cooling on top of the stove. Dad came in to ask how much longer it would be before we ate because the smell of the turkey was making his stomach rumble."

She chuckled.

He memorized the tone of her laugh, not able to think of a more beautiful sound.

"We gave him a roll just out of the oven. He asked Mama if there was time to steal me away before we ate. She shooed us out of the kitchen, and we settled into the old sofa in dad's office." Her voice softened, "He put his arms around me"—she crossed her arms, hugging herself—"and told me he was sorry he had to send me to live with my aunt. He asked me to forgive him," she said with amazement.

Clasping his hands, Ryder lassoed a knee and hugged it, firmly restraining the nagging desire in his arms.

"Dad said he made the decision because he had Leukemia."

Ryder sucked in a startled breath and felt an unbearable weight lift from his soul. "So that was it. Pilot, I'm so sorry, and at the same time, I'm grateful to know there was a good reason."

"So am I. He could barely take care of himself, let alone me. All those letters I wrote him tore him apart, but he couldn't keep me. He was in the hospital off and on for a few years taking experimental treatments that made him very sick. That's why his visits were so erratic and infrequent. He went into remission just after I turned seventeen. By then, I'd been living with my aunt for so long he thought it was better just to leave it that way. He didn't know how long his remission would last."

"Why didn't he tell you he had Leukemia when you got older?"

"Because he thought it would be too hard for me to watch him die—after watching Mama die. And he wanted me to be firmly established as a member of my aunt's family before the Leukemia took his life." Tears glistened on her eyelashes.

Ryder's lassoed arms, cinched in his knee until his muscles bulged. "He was such a kind, gentle soul. I can't even imagine how hard that was for him."

"It . . . was," she whispered.

The soggy tone of her whispered reply, wrenched his heart. A dark shadow, cast by clouds drifting across the moon hid the sight of her grief from him, but he felt it.

"He told me he decided if I was going to become a part of my new family, he needed to make as clean a break as he could stand. That's why he was so distant and never talked with me about Mama—or the baby."

"He knew about the baby?"

Her hand brushed her damp cheek, "Yes, but not until about a month after Mama died. He found out when a doctor's bill came. He didn't know I knew and decided it would be best not to tell me—or you."

She held his eyes.

Tight-jawed he rode the bucking bronco of his feelings, and fought the fierce ache that burned in his arms, suffering through an agony of longing as another moon-glow tear escape her lashes and slid down her face.

"He didn't want either one of us to suffer any more than we were." Her lips quivered. "He told me he didn't blame me for the accident." She turned away, her shoulders shaking.

The steel-corded lasso he held on his knee broke as the bronco threw him. He reached for her hand and was surprised when she allowed him to take it. He brought their joined hands to rest on the roof between them.

"Then Mama came in." She sniffed, staring out across the valley at Farlana. "My parents sandwiched me between them on the sofa, hugged me, told me they loved me, and didn't blame me for anything. They said they're proud of me and just want me to let go of my guilt and be happy."

Twisting toward him with a wet, radiant face, her free hand reached for his. His heart felt as though it would explode from his chest as she held his hands.

"Our doorbell rang."

A tremor ran from her hands to his. Hers tightened, squeezing his intently.

"Mama opened the door—to you."

Silver-blue eyes locked with molten-gold ones.

"She put her arms around you, hugged you, and kissed your cheek. Dad hugged you too. Mama said they were sent to tell us we've been forgiven, and we need to let the past go."

The sob escaped him without warning.

She took her hands from his and wiped his streaming cheeks then laid her hands on the sides of his face, her eyes shimmering with wonder. "We've been forgiven, Ryder. When I woke up, I felt so peaceful. I've never felt that way before. When I prayed about it, I knew it was true. The Lord has forgiven us—so has my family. It's the most wonderful feeling I've ever experienced."

Her face glowed with a serenity he'd never seen before. He drank it in with an insatiable thirst.

"I want you to feel it too," she whispered.

He shook with the force of his feelings when her arms hesitantly slid around him. Years of guilt and pain flowed out of his soul, replaced by a peace that filled him up. Without hesitation, he returned her embrace.

Wrapping her in his arms brought them exquisite relief. He hugged her to him and pushed the words out through his closed throat, "There aren't any words that can adequately express how I feel and what this means to me. I know what you have told me is true—*I feel it.* We *have* been forgiven. Thank you for telling me."

Laying his cheek against her hair, he held her, and she held him. It was the most sublime feeling he'd ever known. He tried, but couldn't decide, if the joy he felt was purely the result of being forgiven, or because Hadlee was in his arms, and her heart was beating against his. The only thing he knew for sure was he wanted the feeling, and this moment, to go on forever.

The belfry chimed one-thirty.

He savored the joy and tranquility she infused him with for a moment longer; reluctantly released her and came to his knees. They offered a prayer of gratitude for her wonderful dream and the peace that filled them.

Ryder rubbed his hand over his face. "I need to get back to my jailors. I wouldn't want them to discover I'm missing."

"No, that would ruin our plans." She sniffed and wiped her eyes. "I'll see Kytan in the morning and tell him about our plan. That way you two won't have to find a way to talk privately when he starts working in the tunnel tomorrow."

"Good. Kytan and I can't afford to make our guards suspicious about anything we do or say. "

"I can't tell you how much I admire Kytan. He has absolute faith we're going to escape. He's even found ways to have short prayers with us under the scrutiny of a guard."

"You know"—Ryder confessed with a smile—"the first time I read the Book of Mormon, I wanted to be a Stripling Warrior, and I've always wanted to meet one. When I met Kytan, I knew I had. You will never meet a better man."

"That's what he says about you."

The pain of many years flickered in his eyes. "Pilot, we both know that's not true."

Her eyes bore into his. "I don't know any such thing. I believe the rebellious, tortured boy that hit my mother with a car—died the day she did. You paid a terrible price for that day. Everything you've suffered, and all I've put you through—even what you've endured in Injanae—along with all you have accomplished in your life since the accident, tells me, you *are* as good a man as Kytan."

He searched her face. His heart throbbing painfully, afraid to believe what she said was truly what she felt—and what he hoped it meant.

She laid her hand on his, "You've learned through repentance to live with your deep scars, and you have taught me how to do it too. The sickness I carried so long in my soul would never have started to heal without meeting you again. As terrible as facing my own responsibility for Mama's death has been, without you, I never would have done it."

The night went still all around them, as though all creation held its breath, just as he was doing.

The silver gleam of the crescent moon hung in her eyes. She gazed gravely into his. "What I'm trying to say is . . . I forgive you too—for everything."

Her words were the balm he'd longed for, hoped for, and prayed for, the only thing that could fully heal his scorched soul. He felt the dragon's dying breath fade away and was completely undone.

A baptism of peace bathed his face. He labored for control and finally mastered his voice. "For twelve long years . . . my heart has yearned to hear those words from you. I know I can't restore what I've taken from you. It's a weight my soul will always carry, but your forgiveness will make that burden bearable, now. Thank you, Pilot."

He felt the depth of her forgiveness in the gentleness of her fingers, as they wiped the tears from his cheeks.

"I'm sorry too. Sorry it took me so long to say those words, and to feel them. I should have done it a long time ago, but I hid my own guilt by blaming you. I know, now, you were just a boy who made a wrong choice trying to escape intolerable cruelty, with no intention of hurting my family, or me. Certainly not the way I intentionally hurt you. I hope you can forgive me for what my anger and hate cost you."

"I don't blame you for anything that's happened to me. Meeting you again has been the greatest blessing of my life. I will be forever grateful for your forgiveness."

Her smile was tremulous, untainted by animosity, shame, guilt or resentment. It was the first completely genuine smile she'd ever offered him. He fell into its luster, clinging to its warmth, his mind snapping off picture after picture, to keep and treasure as the most precious gift he'd ever been given.

She extended her hand, "Friends?"

The word rose up against him—a mountain in his path—cutting off all other possibilities, putting him irrevocably in his place.

The grinning jaws of Farlana mocked him.

He gripped her hand, feeling the dragon's jagged teeth tear into his heart, and echoed the painful word, "Friends."

Hadlee sat on the terrace watching the sky, long after Ryder left to return to his prison in the guardhouse, absorbed in both the wonder of being forgiven, and forgiving.

The blackness of the night faded slowly, turning into pale silver, mirroring the growing lightness she felt in her soul—now that she'd forgiven Ryder. *The contrast between the darkness my heart harbored for so long, and the light I feel inside now is—astonishing.*

The simple gesture of offering her hand to Ryder in friendship filled her with quiet serenity. Then suddenly, with acute sadness, she realized that the tranquility she felt had always been available to her. *But it was untouchable until I could forgive—with all my heart.*

Her brows contracted as her gaze shifted from the sky to the large white flowers on the trellis, their faces now closed against the breaking dawn. *I have been like these flowers. For too many years, my heart was closed against the truth, shutting out the light of forgiveness.*

She pushed away the pain and sadness of the years she had wallowed in darkness and hate, resolving to cultivate the forgiving heart that now beat within her. Peace returned just as rays of sunlight burst over the eastern mountains bringing with them something she thought she had lost. *Hope!*

That feeling had slowly died over the past few weeks.

Is Ryder's ability to escape his prison the reason I feel this surge of hope? She consulted the bright beacons streaming across the sky. *Yes, but it is more than that too.*

Clarity dropped her to her knees. "Forgive me for feeling so forsaken. I know—now—I've never been alone."

That certainty found a home in her heart, and she gratefully acknowledged the true source of her hope. "Ryder's remarkable strengths and skills will certainly help us, but I know it will be by thy hand that we escape Injanae." Tears of longing filled her eyes. "Please, Father, extend thy hand and help us—get home.

Turn the page for a preview of what coming in
FOR ALL TIME ~ Part 2 ~ Beneath the Moon.

Although Ryder and Hadlee have finally found peace concerning the death of Hadlee's mother, and the door to a fragile friendship has opened, inescapable consequences remain. For Ryder the final consequence—he is powerless to change—is the torment of loving Hadlee. He knows she will never give him her heart, and he must never reveal his.

As Ryder struggles to conceal his love for Hadlee, an unexpected experience restores the memory of how he came into Injanae. Before the conspirators can complete the new preparations that dangerous escape will require, the king sets in motion the last deadly twist in his plan to keep the conspirators enslaved, and force Hadlee to become Ansuetra—Goddess of the Moon—on the night of the Lunar Celebration.

Using Hadlee as Ansuetra is Ateron's key to reclaiming the power of the high priest from Darvoe, abolishing the nobles' council, and finally enthroning himself as the only power in Injanae. But he hasn't counted on the strength, faith, and ingenuity of the conspirators. In a desperate bid to escape Injanae, they unleash their own plans.

Do you **hate** to wait a year for the next book in a trilogy? You won't have to with **FOR ALL TIME**. For information about the release dates for—

Part 2 ~ BENEATH THE MOON

&

Part 3 ~ THROUGH THE MIST

Go to—**fablespinnerbooks.blogspot.com**

To listen to the song **"Only You"**, go to YouTube:
http://www.youtube.com/watch?v=IHd4M11YCQQ
http://www.youtube.com/watch?v=GmN8QnMVWQo

www.ingramcontent.com/pod-product-compliance
Lightning Source LLC
Chambersburg PA
CBHW022144170626
46807CB00005B/2064